DIANE DUANE

OMNITOPIA DAWN

DAW BOOKS, INC.

DONALD A. WOLLHEIM, FOUNDER

375 Hudson Street, New York, NY 10014

ELIZABETH R. WOLLHEIM
SHEILA E. GILBERT
PUBLISHERS

http://www.dawbooks.com

First Paperback Printing, August 2011
1 2 3 4 5 6 7 8 9 10

For Erin Roberts
and all his erstwhile associates
at Electronic Arts / Origin
who showed me the ropes way back when

PROLOGUE

RIK MALIANI STEPPED OUT OF NOTHINGNESS into the narrow cobbled confines of Troker's Lane, overhung on each side by ancient half-timbered houses . . . and as his second step went *squish,* he realized he'd just put his left foot down right in the middle of a turd.

He stood there for a moment looking down at his booted foot and the unsavory dinner-plate-sized object he'd stepped into. It was blue. Rik stood on one foot, lifted the other one up and looked over his cloaked shoulder at the sole of it, sniffed. He immediately caught the unmistakable acrid whiff of griffin poop. Rik shook his head and smiled, impressed for about the hundredth time this week. *Technology,* he thought. *Don't you love it when it works!*

He went over to the curbstone in front of the nearest shuttered house and used it to scrape the griffin crap off, or at least as much of it as he could see in this light. Above Rik, between the raggedy-edged, mossy tiles of the hanging roofs, only a strip of indigo blue showed, for it was coming on toward evening in the City. The usual town smells floated through the air: roasting meat, rotting garbage, frying fish, woodsmoke, perfume, the multispecies sweat that the perfume couldn't cover . . . and, of course, ordure. The droppings of various animals, fabulous and otherwise, were something you just couldn't help but notice here, especially once you had the right hardware. In the face of numerous complaints about the problem, and the ever increasing traffic, the City had redoubled its claims that it was going to do

something about the problem soon. But as for the magi-
cians that the City kept hiring to do the job . . .

As he scraped the last of the stuff off his boot, Rik
glanced up and around at the oriel windows of the old
inward-leaning buildings, just to make sure that somebody
wasn't about to enrich his game experience—and the crap
quotient of the laneway—by emptying a chamber pot over
his head. The word on the City newsfeeds had it that the
present administration just couldn't keep wizards on the
payroll long enough right now. But maybe this was understandable, since no magician worth his or her spells would
waste time on a sanitation job when wizardry could be much
better employed—and better paid—on one or another of
the big campaigns that was running now. A huge and bloody
war had just broken out in the TwoMoons Macrocosm (now
that the necessary threshold number of Moonies had finally
responded to their invitations). Over in Pandora they'd just
had a coup, and the deposed queen in question was busy
recruiting an army as fast as she could. Dasheth Prime and
LongAgo Three were also in the middle of rebellions or battles between major game guilds. And those were merely the
"conflicted" game worlds Rik could think of off the top of
his head: there might be ten or twenty others, Macrocosms
he hadn't been following, that were either actively rumbling
or getting ready to. With business so brisk and prospects so
positive for a smart war wizard or combat mage, odds were
even that Omnitopia City was going to have to find other
ways to handle its garbage management besides magical
ones. And since no one with a brain would willingly spend
valuable game time picking up street crap by hand, Rik felt
sure that until out-universe matters calmed down a little, the
ordure was going to stay right where it was.

But none of these matters were really issues for Rik
right now. And anyway, at the moment he wasn't Rik; he
was Arnulf the Manyfaced, a paramage member of the
Human League organization MediMages Without Frontiers, and he was on his way to Meruvelt to spend a little
bit of hard-earned game gold on some new magian equipment in that Macrocosm, and to socialize with some folks
he knew who also played and fought and healed there.

With his boot now cleaned to his satisfaction, Arnulf turned and strolled upward along the lane toward the light of the nearest cresset, which was stuck into a wattle-and-daub wall some twenty yards or so farther along. Up there, at the corner where Troker's Lane crossed the only slightly broader Shade Street, Arnulf paused and leaned against the wall for a moment, enjoying the feedback from the new RealFeel synesthetic sensory input system he'd finally been able to afford. His wife Angela had protested a little at first about how much money he'd spent on it, but he'd taken some time to explain to her—not entirely untruthfully—how having it would actually make it quicker and easier for him to play the game effectively. When she understood the difference it would make, Angela had rolled her eyes at Rik, not particularly fooled by the spin he was putting on it. But she'd also stopped complaining.

Rik considered himself lucky that Angela genuinely didn't seem to mind all the time he spent in Omnitopia. It probably helped a lot that he brought home a little money from the game every month via his crafting of custom tools and accessories for other players who were interested in the medical side of magery. He thought Angela realized, too, that in Omnitopia he was able to do the socializing that the double shifts he frequently worked for the country's second-biggest parcel carrier didn't leave him any other time for. *I really do have it better than a lot of people,* Arnulf thought, running a hand down the knotted, splintery surface of the half-timbering at the corner of the buildings that fronted on Shade Street. It was going to be a long time before he was bored by the fact that he could now actually feel the wood, smell the scents programmed into the air, even taste the virtual food. Though admittedly sometimes the tastes were a little weird, as that feature was very new and the game warned you when you added on the Extra Helping module that "your flavors may vary." Rik didn't understand the mechanism that allowed him to receive touch and taste and smell information via his optic nerves—but, frankly, he didn't care. Omnitopia had been like another home to him for years. Now that he had the new hardware interface broken in, Omnitopia felt physically

real as well as just looking that way—and as long as there
were no long-term effects from the software spoofing his
brain by way of his eyes, that was fine by him.

Arnulf glanced up and down Shade Street. It was empty,
a little unusual for this time of day; but then it *was* getting on
toward dinnertime in Omnitopia City, and a lot of transit-
ing gamers in this part of town, historically more residential
than commercial, would be heading for the pubs and tav-
erns and cookshops, preparing to do a little business, make
a little trouble, or just sit down and have a good time with
their fellow Omnitopians. Arnulf considered the possibility
of going down to Uncle George's Flat Patty Place at the far
end of Shade Street, or maybe Prince Dave Bongo's over in
Halflight, on the off chance that he might meet somebody
there who would send a little more business his way. Uncle
George's in particular was well known as a place where
medimages, midwives, herb doctors, and others interested in
Arnulf's trade hung out before heading outworld. *But no,* he
thought then. *I want to get my hands on that new magia kit.
And those league robes with the new sigils for the campaign
next month—I've been talking about them for days. If I don't
bring them home today, Angela's going to start giving me grief
for being indecisive, or wasting time . . .*

Arnulf let out an amused breath and continued on
down Troker's Lane, now widening into Hook Street as
it headed toward the center of town. This landscape was
one into which Angela had never set foot: his wife was no
gamer. But this had never been an issue between them, and
she was happy enough to let him indulge his otherworldly
life . . . while still very much functioning as the knot in Rik's
balloon. He was always full of fantasies, but she was full of
more than enough practicality to balance him; she probably worked more double shifts than he did so that the two
of them could keep food on the table for their three kids,
and for the dog and cat and the bird and the hamsters and
whatever other livestock might turn up in the company of
their insatiably pet-loving children. Sure, sometimes Angela would come into the little spare room that functioned
as their game room while Rik was online, and she'd give
him that look from under her eyebrows that seemed to

say, *you* do *know what I'm doing for you, don't you?* But
that was all she did, and all she needed to do. The knowledge that he needed to do right by Angela in return for her
understanding kept Rik grounded. And it kept him aware
that, even here, he needed to have the family's interests at
heart—at least some of the time. He *was* also allowed to
enjoy himself.

So he turned his attention back to doing that, making his
way past the lantern-hung shops and stalls of Little Cheap-
ing Street and continuing on through the pens and cages
of the beast-market of Welladay Square, now shut down
for the day, toward the town center. Omnitopia City had
grown rather peculiarly, in fits and starts, and in this part
of town, one of the oldest, the peculiarities were obvious.
Probably why I like it so much . . . As Arnulf walked on, the
architecture of the houses and shops around him shifted
abruptly from muck-plastered Pythonesque Retro Feudal
to sandstone-arcaded Mitteleuropean to prefab neo-Tudor
to bleak Sixties revisionist to suburban stuccoed strip mall.
Buildings in styles that in the real world had existed separated by thousands of years and thousands of miles—if
they'd actually existed at all—had sprung up here in little
groups and ghettos, as if huddling close for company, or else
they hunched down or speared up singly and with apparent
unconcern right next door to one another. This haphazard
but enthusiastic arrangement went right back to the time
before the City had grown itself an actual government. The
earliest gamers exploiting the site, finding no controls yet in
place, had thrown the buildings up to their own tastes, with
great speed and utter lack of concern about the general
look and feel of any given neighborhood. As a result, this
part of the city looked like the creation of someone who
had visited Disneyland while on crack and then the Mall
of America while on acid, and afterward had attempted to
synchronize their styles.

But to Arnulf's mind, this architectural form of ADD just
added to the neighborhood's charm. It physically reminded
you that once upon a time, this place had been nothing but
a small rough rocky island off the coast of Himardell, itself
probably the least interesting minor continent in all of old

Telekil. It had been the sort of place no one bothered jour-
neying to, a useless scrap of territory that no Elf or Man or
even Gnarth could have been bothered to get into a fight
over, because there was nothing *to* fight over. Elich Island
had been nothing but a houseless rock in the sea, straggly
around the edges with seaweed, streaked with bird droppings, and worthy of no attention whatsoever.

But then everything had changed.

As Arnulf walked, the streets got broader, and people
began to pass him. Every kind of person, every kind of
character you could imagine, and a lot that you couldn't,
became more and more frequent as you approached the
town center: Dwarrows wearing three-piece suits and carrying Armani ax-cases; strolling, elegant Elves burdened
with swords and spears and shopping bags; Men in every
kind of human dress; holidaying Gnarths in Hawaiian
shirts and fanny packs, pointing cameras at everything and
ignoring the uneasy sidelong glances of the humans and
other species; pack unicorns, hedge-dragons, and basilisks
in mirrorshades; half-beasts and werebeasts and hunting
cats and wolven—creatures familiar and creatures unimag-
inably strange, all making their way purposefully toward
or away from the center of the City, like blood entering
or leaving a hidden heart. Finding the buzz contagious, Arnulf quickened his pace as he crossed the boundary into
Third Quarter. Here the street in front of him opened out
even further, the cobbles gave way to fine set stone, and the
houses on either side started to look more like Italianate
palazzos than anything else, with ornate gilded ironwork
and stained glass windows. Here and there an old blunt
fieldstone tower or other feature of someone's stubbornly
unredeveloped unreal estate still broke through the surrounding glossy veneer of wealth and success, suggesting
that it was still location, location, location that really mattered, not the fancy trappings of the nouveau riche. And
indeed, if you had managed to pick up a piece of property
in this part of Elich Island when the city was building, then
you could truly be said to be successful. Especially just
here, right by the most famous reminder of the Change.

Arnulf came out at the bottom of Quarterlight Street

into the Plaza of Exploration, its smooth-paved expanse brightly lit by torches and magelight-powered spots. There it was, at the center of it all, surrounded by a many-spouted ornamental fountain with stray dogs drinking out of it, and a hungover waterdragon lying on its back under one of the spouts: the great bronze statue of Lahirien the Excessively Far-Traveled. As he crossed toward it, Arnulf wondered how much of the story about her, or the player who ran her, was true. *Is she just some kind of marketing ploy, something the game designers made up?* Yet at the same time, even back then, there had been gamers so obsessive that they'd spent all their time using their avatars to visit every single part of Telekil that could be visited by a gamer. Even now, there were lots of people more interested in exploring a given world than in playing in it. It wasn't a mind-set Arnulf understood—himself—he was all for the prewar intrigue, the battle, and the après-fight camaraderie. But it made sense that it would have been one of those more abstract-minded players who, by sheer doggedness, would have eventually discovered the island's secret.

And if she is real, did they ever give her a bonus for that, I wonder? Arnulf thought as he paused for a moment, halfway across the plaza, to gaze up at the statue. It portrayed a slender young woman, her long hair tied back, her cloak streaming away from her shoulders in the prevailing westerly wind, as she gazed thoughtfully out over what in those days would have been an extremely inhospitable strait of the Himardell Sea. Behind her on the great bronze pedestal were replicas of both the coracle in which she had sailed here, and of a rather seasick-looking cow—a reminder of the time when Elich Island's only useful resources had been its tiny scrap of summer grazing and enough seaweed to keep a shore-based farmer's cow alive through the winter. Once such resources had been precious in this barren, overlooked part of Telekil. *But that was a long time ago,* Arnulf thought. *And who even thinks that much about Telekil anymore?* All around the pedestal of the statue ran an inscription that now graced many a commemorative menhir across the hundred and twenty-one Macrocosms, the words set into the stone in letters of water-greened bronze:

TO THE EVERLASTING GLORY OF
LAHIRIEN THE EXCESSIVELY FAR-TRAVELED,
KNOWN IN THE SO-CALLED REAL WORLD AS
MALLORY LYNN REAVES

And under that, in smaller letters, the wise words of the great Discoverer of the Way to the Outworlds:

"I JUST COULDN'T STOP WONDERING
WHY THE COW WAS SO FREAKED"

Like many other passersby, Arnulf waved a hand in salute to the statue and then went on through the plaza, all surrounded by its high and stately houses, built and rebuilt many times now by those wealthy gamers who'd been smart enough to realize quickly just what it was Lahirien had found. Out the other side of the plaza Arnulf went down Left Ring Street, making his way into the much larger Court of the Wanderers. At the court's edge, Arnulf stopped. Here the buildings surrounding the court had been kept back a decorous distance from the street. But that only made sense, for from the many streets and avenues that poured into the great circle, a constant stream of players was coming and going. Here the buzz wasn't just something you felt, but something you could hear. And here in the middle of it all, massive, ancient, and softly humming with the power of ages, stood the Ring of Elich.

It looked like Stonehenge on steroids. A massive circle of trilithons and pillar-stones a quarter mile wide now surrounded the site of the original, time-weathered circle, whose stones had long since been moved outward and incorporated into the expanded Ring to accommodate the huge traffic of travelers from all over Telekil, the old game world. This was Omnitopia's engine: the magical transit circle that let players with enough gold, or enough other qualifications, out into the Macrocosms of Greater Omnitopia. The discovery of this gigantic game within a game, four years ago, had turned the massively multiplayer online gaming world on its ear. No one had ever dreamed that such a number of gaming worlds, of such complexity and magnitude, could or would ever be staged inside the same platform—or that they would all be made available for no more than what you were already paying to get into the original. For hard-core gamers like Arnulf, the day the old "Otherworlds Campaigns" game had suddenly turned into Omnitopia had been like Christmas and all your birthdays and your wedding day rolled into one. *Except that it costs a lot less than your wedding day.*

The blue crackle of transit fire leaped from stone pillar to stone post of the Ring of Elich, connecting the lintels at the top of the circle. Players stepped through the doorways, verified themselves with the game systems, and vanished. From other portals around the ring, other gateways, players appeared from worlds far off in the Omnitopian Pattern of universes, or worlds very close. Here came a ten-man cadre of a warrior guild returning from some battle, possibly even the one in Pandora that Arnulf had been considering. They were carrying two downed colleagues, and behind them came the guild's paymaster, staggering under sacks of loot, while behind him came a dragon on a lead, panniers over its huge back, carrying even more. Over there, a laughing group of human "crossbreed" adventurers, dressed like Elves in dagged tunics and bright hose, with bows slung over their shoulders, vanished into a gateway that lay briefly open on the green fields of Whereaway. Each time a group transited, the vista behind them flickered to show where they were going, or where they were coming from. World after world, Macrocosms, Microcosms, foreboding landscapes and benign ones, mountains and meadows, vast oceans, other planets—they were all there. Other gates revealed race courses full of careening vehicles with exhausts afire, or grim looking concrete labyrinths full of people and creatures shooting at each other. The vistas flickered in and out sometimes too quickly to get a grasp of what they were. The Ring of Elich was the second-by-second proof by which Omnitopia lived up to its name. *Any* kind of game you could think of was here somewhere, either as a Macrocosm built by the game company's in-house staff, or as Microcosms built by favored gamers. Endless possibilities, endless challenges were here—and at least part of the buzz in the Ring right now was because the whole Omnitopia scenario was about to widen out again in three days' time, on Midsummer's Eve, when the walls between the worlds traditionally got thin.

Arnulf stood there a moment longer, drinking it all in. *Just three days until the rollout,* he thought. *Another shift in the paradigm. What are they going to pull on us this time? What's going to happen here? I can't wait to find out!* The hair actually stood up on the back of his neck at the thought.

But then he took a deep breath. Outside, in the real world, time was flying: Angela was going to have words with him if he took too long about this. *Okay,* Arnulf thought. *First, out to Langley B. That's going to take about half my transport gold for today. Head to the artificer's there, pick up that new magian kit. Then back here and do the gating to Meruvelt. Get those robes, then meet up with Tom and see if his people are really serious about doing that run into Pandora . . . they didn't seem to have their minds made up the last time. Stop in the tavern with them, shoot the breeze for a while, then head back home. Angela did say she wanted me to mow the lawn tonight—*

"Excuse me?"

Arnulf turned around and found himself looking at a gawky young human male, dark-haired and pale, dressed in Omnitopian beginner's standard issue: the brown cloak, bleached linen tunic, cotton hose, and brown leather boots of a low-credit kern. He was almost the archetypal Clueless Noob—almost certainly some kid in here for the first time, caught up by the worldwide hype about the expansion rollout. "Well met, comrade," Arnulf said putting out a hand. "What's the score?"

The noob was so new that he didn't even know yet to clasp Arnulf's arm in return of the greeting. "Uh, yeah," the noob said, "everything's going pretty good. I think." He looked past Arnulf, staring at the Ring. "Except, uh, I'm not real sure where to go from here . . ."

Rik/Arnulf kept the smile off his face. *I must have been like this once,* he thought. *But then who wasn't? I can never understand the schmucks who like making fun of these poor guys . . .* "It's okay," Arnulf said. "Everything's a little overwhelming your first few times. You heading outworld?"

"Oh, yeah, just got my first transit bonus."

Rik nodded. He'd heard on the feeds that this had been happening a lot in the run-up to the rollout; noobs were being given outworld transit allotments as soon as they signed up—maybe a little too early, in Rik's opinion. But the people running the game probably wanted as many new gamers as possible to get out there, see the other worlds, and get their friends excited about it too. "Where were you thinking of going?"

"Well, I heard about this place called Pandora— "

Rik looked the noob over while trying not to be too obvious about it. Kerns couldn't afford a concealed-carry license, so it was immediately obvious that this one didn't have a weapon, not even a knife. He probably didn't even know he needed one. *Or he thinks they're cheaper somewhere else, or—oh, heck, who knows what he thinks? But you can't let somebody like this just charge in there.* Though Rik knew there were gamers who would, amused by the prospect of having sent a clueless noob into a war zone unprepared. *Serve them right,* such people would say afterward. *They should've read the docs first, they should've done their homework, blah blah blah.*

Rik/Arnulf shook his head. "I'll tell you the truth," he said. "Unless you're a really high-level gamer hiding in a noob suit—and don't get me wrong, I know it can be fun to do that, I've done it myself on occasion—then I really don't recommend you go into Pandora right now. Things are kind of busted loose. There are mercenary bands all over the landscape, and they'll grab you and chain you up with a caffle of other slaves and sell you off to turn somebody's grist mill or haul some big heavy war machine all over the landscape till they've whipped your avatar to death. Not the best way to get the feeling of the game, huh?"

The clueless newbie shook his head vigorously. "So I'll tell you what," Rik said. "If you go over there—" He pointed off to one side of the Ring. "See that little booth off to the right of the Ring, by where Dancer's Street comes into the circle? Not that one—a little more to the right. Yeah, the pavilion with the red silk walls. You go over there, tell the Magister behind the counter that you're new in town and you'd like an in-and-out transport to Pastorale. It's a really nice Macrocosm, a good place to walk around, trade for a while, get the feeling of your new skin, meet some other people. There'll be a lot of other n—" Arnulf stopped himself. No point in rubbing the poor noob's nose in it. "—A lot of players just getting used to the scenario. And there are plenty of really friendly game-generated characters there who'll help you get the ropes sorted out. Go get yourself some nice souvenirs, help out some bunny rabbit in distress, pick up a flower fairy or two, make a couple of friends, and get out of there with a little extra credit. How does that sound?"

The noob nodded enthusiastically again, smiling. "Uh, thanks, thanks a lot! It's all so—"

"I know," Arnulf said. "It's really, really big. You have no idea! But you want to survive long enough to learn to enjoy it."

"Yeah. Yeah, I will. Listen, thanks—"

The guy waved at him and actually ran off toward the Magister's Pavilion. For a moment, Arnulf just watched him go, amused. But he remembered how excited, how completely blown away he'd been the first time he saw the Ring and realized what it meant to his future gameplay. *Hope he does survive,* Arnulf thought as the noob vanished into the Pavilion. *So: there's my good deed for the day. Time to get moving, though.*

He headed across the circle toward the Ring. The actual transit was a simple matter. As you got close, the Ring protocols checked your game status and points balance, looked to see if you had enough gold, valuta, or other game credit to pay for the transit, and then noted whatever destination settings you'd laid in at the beginning of this session. All you had to do was find a portal that wasn't occupied with an incoming transit—those were easy to identify, as they grayed themselves out with swirling, iridescent fog—salute the Ring, and step through.

Arnulf got in the shortest line in front of one of the portals on this side of the Ring—though it was hardly even a line, just a group of ten people. There were about ten people in it, all dressed like contemporary Arctic explorers in parkas and furs. Some of them were hauling "hybrid" sledges on wheels, the runners clipped up at the moment; others were trying to control two leashed sets of excitedly barking huskies, and mostly succeeding. In front of them, as they raised their hands more or less as a group to salute the Ring, the massive portal went from starry darkness to a ferocious obscurity of blowing snow—whiteout conditions that made it impossible to tell what 'cosm they might have been heading for. At the sight of it, the dogs barked with joy and plunged through. The players went after them in haste, vanishing into the screaming whiteness, then the portal went dark and starry again.

Arnulf Manyfaced stepped up to the doorway, spending only a moment gazing into the endless depths. Then he raised a hand, saluted the Ring, and stepped through—

—And found that there was something very wrong. It was completely dark all around him, and the hill-town vista surrounding the City of Artificers on Langley B was nowhere to be seen.

What the heck?

Cautiously, Rik turned in a slow circle, wondering whether he'd run into some kind of game glitch associated with the upcoming Great Rollout. But then he caught the faint glow off to one side. Blinking a little in the darkness, he turned toward it.

All around him, and all around the source of the glow, that utter, bottomless blackness remained. But the vague warm light hanging in the sky slowly got brighter and brighter, like a very localized dawn. Suddenly Rik realized that the glow was coming together, coalescing into letters, then finally into words. And in shocking pink and blue, the words said:

THIS SPACE
FOR RENT

Rik's eyes went wide, and the breath went right out of him as he realized what he was looking at. Standing there, looking through Arnulf's eyes, it took some moments before he could even summon enough reaction to activate the "player services" control in the game software and bring up his account info. A little graphics window popped open in the darkness next to him, glowing with basic information: his lifetime score history, acquisitions, game gold balance, overt karma, professional in-game associations. And there, by the cross-and-wand logo of MediMages Without Frontiers, he saw something he had never expected to see, never even considered possible: a symbol that looked like a golden apple.

Oh . . my . . . God!

In the master info panel, the little envelope logo for his in-game messaging inbox was flashing. "Go to mail," Rik whispered.

The window cleared, showed him the messaging pane. One new message, from Omnitopia Microcosm Management to R. Maliani.

"Open message," Rik said.

Dear Rik,

Congratulations and welcome! Your game status average and other criteria have qualified you for entry to Omnitopia's Microcosm Development Program. Attached to this message you will find introductory materials and links that will allow you access to . . .

He had to stop and get control of his breathing: he was actually starting to hyperventilate. *Oh. My.* God!

"Game on hold," Rik said hurriedly. The big pause symbol superimposed itself over his control window and began flashing on and off. He stared up at the glowing words hanging in the empty sky. They didn't go away.

"Save position and exit game!" Rik said.

"Game position saved: exit recorded at seventeen fourteen local time," said the dulcet Omnitopia control voice. "Thank you, and come back soon to Omnitopia!"

Between one blink and the next, the darkness vanished. He was lying on the couch in the game room, with the Real-Feel goggles and headset screening the rest of the room from view. He pulled them off, still breathing hard. Acoustic ceiling, coffee-colored walls, bookshelves, slightly tatty rug, everything was perfectly normal. *Except for what just happened. Not normal, not at* all. *Maybe we're finished with normal as we've known it . . .*

He leaped up from the couch, yanked the game room door open, and ran down the upstairs hall. "Angela? *Angela!*"

No answer. Rik reached the stairs in the middle of the hallway, grabbed the banister, swung himself around on it, and went down the stairs as fast as he could. At the bottom of the stairs, eight-year-old Mike, about to head up to his and Davey's room, had stopped and was staring wide-eyed at his dad. "Mike, where's Mommy?"

"Out back, Daddy—"

Rik plunged past his son and ran around the corner and down the hall that led to the kitchen and the back door. "Angela?"

She had been sitting out on their little concrete patio reading a book. Now, though, almost certainly having heard him shouting upstairs, she was on her feet, heading toward the back door. He caught her halfway in a bear hug, swinging her around and around.

She stared at him. "Rik, what is it, what's the matter?"

"Absolutely nothing!" he shouted. "Everything's great!"

After a moment or two Angela dug her feet in and stopped him from twirling her around. "What?" she said. "What is it? Did we win the lottery or something?"

"Better than that!"

She gave him a strange look. "What? What could be better?"

"I just got a message from Omnitopia. They've elected me to the Microcosm program! I'm going to have my own Microcosm!"

She blinked at him. "And this is good?"

He swallowed, trying to calm himself. "Honey," he said, "how many people play Omnitopia?"

Angela shook her head. "I don't know. You've told me once or twice, but I have to admit I probably wasn't listening. Fifty million or something like that?"

"Two *hundred* million," he said. "That company makes about a million bucks a minute—"

"At least one of them off you," Angela said, giving him an amused look.

"Nothing like that much. But don't you get what this means? They want me to come build a world for them that'll run *inside* Omnitopia! And every single time somebody comes to play in it—*we get money!*" He hugged her hard. "They call it 'one percent of Infinity.' If this works out—we could make . . ."

She looked at him with suspicion, though it was tinged with interest. "How much?"

There she was, Mrs. Practicality again: but right now Rik didn't mind. "I don't know. It depends. But it could be a lot! There are some Microcosm builders who've made a million bucks in their first year!"

Her eyes went wide. Then the caution showed again. "Okay. And how many?"

"Not a whole lot. Okay, a handful! But you don't have to become a millionaire from it for it to make a big difference! It could mean a few thousand extra bucks a month for us, and for quite a while. A few less of those double shifts for you and me. Maybe even that new kitchen you've been wanting . . ."

"Wow," Angela said softly. "You really think it could make that much of a difference?"

"It could. It could. If I'm smart about what I do. If . . ."

And there the knot in the balloon tightened down hard, without Angela saying a word. "If I can figure out what to do," Rik said. "I've never thought about this before! I never thought this had the slightest chance of happening to me! Somebody's handed me the world on a plate, I can build my own universe, and I have *absolutely no idea what to do!*"

And Rik broke out in a cold sweat of sheer terror. But after only a moment or so he had to find room for some surprise as well, for Angela was simply standing there and smiling at him. It was an unusual sort of smile, one he didn't see often enough to suit him, but which delighted him when it turned up: absolute pride.

"You will," Angela said. "You'll figure it out. And you've

finally succeeded in convincing me that the people who run that game are worth something. Because it looks like they've realized that *you* are."

She took him by the arm. "Come on," Angela said. "That other bottle of Cold Duck in the fridge from my birthday party? Let's go pop it and celebrate."

His pulse still hammering in his ears, Rik let Angela lead him back into the kitchen. Everything was going to change, if he could just get this right, and the change would be far bigger for him, for the whole Maliani family, than anything that was merely going to happen inside Omnitopia in three days' time.

If I can just get this right, Rik thought as he sat down, dazed, at the dining room table. *If I can just keep from screwing it up!*

The bottle went *pop!* Rik barely heard it. A few moments later, Angela pushed a supermarket champagne glass into his hand. "To Omnitopia!" she said.

Rik nodded. "Omnitopia," he said. "And Dev Logan!"

They clinked their glasses together and drank.

And jeez, Rik thought, *do I wish I had him here right now, so I could say to him: okay, smart guy, what the heck do I do now?*

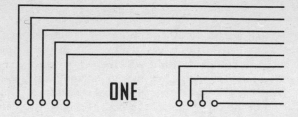

ONE

THE EIGHTH RICHEST MAN IN THE WORLD LAY VERY STILL, not really sure he wanted to open his eyes.

Did the alarm go off? I didn't hear the alarm go off. Did I forget to set it? Impossible. Today, of all days, that wasn't going to happen. I must have just been really tired . . .

From his side of the bed, in a whisper, the broadband radio box was saying, ". . . indicating that Typhoon Lupit has weakened to category two and may have shifted track enough to miss the Philippines. Russia today deploys the first of its new Sergey Gorshkov class frigates, a move that State Department sources says carries significant implications of a change of Russian defense strategy and power projection in the Middle East. And the state of Arizona gets back the capitol building it sold off in the depths of the Great Recession with help from a prominent citizen who describes his move as 'all just part of the game.' It's Friday, June 19, 2015, and this is *Morning Edition* from NPR . . ."

Dev opened one eye, turned his head. On the far side of the bed, snoring gently as usual, was Mirabel. She lay on her side, the pillow all bunched up under her, one hand under her chin in that little-girl way she had, the way that always made Dev wonder why she didn't sleep in some more comfortable position.

Dev quietly rolled over in her direction and experimentally opened the other eye. He'd left the bedroom blinds across the room open when he'd come to bed, intending to have the morning light wake him, ideally before the alarm went off. But it was still too early for that. The only light visible was the very faint blue glow from the mood-light submerged in the water feature out in the garden. The sky was still dark. *And I got exactly how much sleep?* Dev wondered, rubbing his eyes and moaning softly to himself. *Today when I need it most. Oh, never mind . . .*

On the other side of the bed, Mirabel stirred and muttered a little in her sleep. Dev leaned back against his pillow for just a moment more, looking at her with an affection so deeply ingrained that after ten years it seemed like it had been there forever. The blonde hair, straggling across the pillow, heading for the endless tangle of knots which she would later curse as she teased them out one by one; that pretty little round face with the buttony nose—eyes seeming almost purposely squeezed shut, as if with an effort. Dev could remember the party where Phil—ages ago it seemed, when their company had first hit its stride—had said to him, and not entirely in jest, "Miri's not the usual kind of wife for somebody on the Forbes Five Hundred list. You're supposed to have some kind of trophy babe." Dev had found himself staring at Phil as if he'd just fallen into that party from some other planet. The casually dropped line had told Dev more, maybe, than he was willing to know about Phil at that point. *Not that I wasn't already having my suspicions . . .*

Dev grimaced to himself. This peaceful and unfortunately brief interlude was not one to be cluttered up with such thoughts, which wormed their way into too many of his daylight seconds as it was. Dev spent a few moments more just looking at Mirabel, watching her breathe. Then he pushed the covers back, yawning, and got up as quietly as he could, intent on not disturbing her. Carefully Dev pulled the covers back into place, waved the broadband radio off, paused to hunt for the briefs he'd dumped on the floor last night, pulled them on, and then softly headed over to the window.

Down in the courtyard, two stories below, nothing moved except the ripple of water from the cascade that ran down into the central rock pool, glittering in the glow of the blue accent light at the pool's bottom. Dev yawned again, stretched again, and turned away from the window. The master bedroom was relatively small because Mirabel liked it that way. Outside it, though, the size and openness of the master suite's private lounge area more than made up for the relative coziness of the bedroom. The picture window that ran the full length of the room was smart glass, frosted over and grayed down at this time of day. "Clear up," Dev said to the room's control system. The glass cleared, revealing its view down into the central compound. Flagstone paths worked their way among patches of lawn and ornamental shrubbery; in the dimness, a single household cat, one of the gray tabbies, strolled about its business.

"Lights on low," Dev said. They cycled up. He picked up his plaid flannel bathrobe from over the back of a nearby easy chair, swung it around his shoulders, and slipped into it, briefly brushing at one sleeve: it was getting frayed. He could just hear Mirabel now: *Look at the state of you. Eighth richest man in the world, but you can't be trusted to buy clothes that don't look like they came from Sears. In fact half the time they* do *come from Sears! You're going to make me look bad in front of all the other billionaires' wives.*

Dev smiled slightly as he made his way across the private lounge, closing its far door behind him as he headed into the larger adjacent part of their suite, the breakfast bar and common room. The word "bar" probably wasn't a properly descriptive name for something that took up a whole side of the room: a mini-kitchen with fridge and stove and dishwasher, and most importantly for a caffeine freak, the coffee island. Atop the black marble of its surface, the coffeemaker—which knew Dev's rising habits and had as usual been primed by the household staff yesterday evening—now had a steaming glass pot of Ugandan Gold waiting for him. Dev reached up into the cupboard, rummaged around for a mug, and came down with a big white stoneware one. As he poured his coffee into it, Dev's eye fell on the message emblazoned on one side: ARE YOU READY TO THROW THE SWITCH?

He laughed just once, under his breath, and went to the fridge to get some milk. *Not even slightly,* he thought. *Another month's debugging time would be a gift from heaven. But all we've got now are three days. And we'd bloody well just better be ready . . .*

He came back with the milk carton and topped up the coffee cup. *But you're never ready,* he could just hear Mirabel saying. *If my dad hadn't pushed you into the church, you'd still be standing outside making notes and saying "There's just one more thing I want to fix," and I'd still be standing at the altar . . .*

Dev sat down in one of chairs behind the coffee island, cradling the cup and staring out across the interior compound. Here and there a light had already come on in the staff quarters on the other side: house security had doubtless sensed him turning on the lights, which they knew meant that pretty soon now Dev would be wanting the morning report—and that today he'd probably be wanting it more urgently than usual. He glanced at his watch. *Sixty-six hours until we throw the switch.* People who would normally have been on day shift were working strange hours at the moment, because they knew that Dev would be too. *Bet it's Milla bringing the report this morning, rather than one of her minions.* But that would be in her style. As head of his corporate affairs management staff, Milla liked Dev to know that when something important was about to happen, she was right on top of it. And there was nothing more important in Omnitopia today and for the next three days than throwing that nonexistent but profoundly important switch, and keeping an eye on anything that could affect its throwing.

Dev sighed, got up from the breakfast bar and went to the dressing room door at the far side of the common room, where there was a set of gray sweats hanging on the hook behind the door. He pulled them on and went back to the breakfast bar, drank the rest of his coffee in a gulp, and rummaged in the bread drawer under the counter for a couple of croissants. By the time he'd found a plate and a mug for some tea, the bell near the door at the far side of the common room was sounding its soft chime.

He went to the door and opened it. Milla Andreas was standing there dressed in jeans and a white shirt, looking weary but cheerful: a slender young woman with short shaggy blonde hair, dramatically streaked. She held a sheaf of folders and her laptop in her arms. "Are you ready for me?" she said.

"Absolutely. Come on in."

They headed back to the breakfast bar: Dev handed Milla her tea. "How was your evening?"

She nodded, putting down her laptop and opening it up. "Fine, Mr. Logan."

He didn't even bother sighing any more. Dev wasn't formal with his staff, but some of them took their work seriously enough that they refused to unbend, and Milla was one of the more surprising ones in this regard. "Anything interesting going on in the real world?" Dev said.

She raised her eyebrows at him. "You haven't even been online yet?"

Dev shook his head. "Such a late night last night," he said, rubbing his eyes.

"Well, briefly, no," Milla said. "Those forest fires in northern China, they're getting them under control. The usual pre-pre-election craziness here, those two Minnesota caucus groups taking potshots at each other over the 2016 primaries . . ."

"They figure out which of them is the legal one yet?"

Milla shrugged. "They're suing each other. May take a few weeks. A train strike in Italy, the EU is sanctioning those African rebels, the Australian labor unions are rattling their sabers again." Milla shrugged. "Nothing that affects us directly except the capitol building thing. That's getting a lot of play." She smiled, a wry look. "A lot of press opinion saying the place is so ugly that if you really wanted to do something nice for the state, you should've just knocked the thing down and built them a new one."

"Everybody's a critic," Dev said, holding out a hand for the files. He put them down on the breakfast bar and started flipping through them one by one. "First thing—"

"The bug list," said Milla, and handed it to him.

Dev took it with some trepidation, picking up a pen as he did so. Rolling out a new part of an old game was never a simple business. There were always bugs galore, places where the two game structures refused to interleave together correctly no matter how carefully you planned the shuffle. Add to this that it wasn't just the Macrocosms, the Omnitopian worlds and scenarios designed by the in-house staff, that had to interleave with the new server and game structures, but also the Microcosms built by Omnitopia-approved gamers on the basic platform, but with player-designed tweaks and twiddles. And then there was the master server structure itself, nearly sixty-four yottabytes of the newest bleeding-edge hyperblast memory. Yes, the huge heap of memory had been custom-built and configured by IBM/Intel and Siemens for Omnitopia's new megaserver configuration. Yes, the memory arrays and server implementations had been tested as thoroughly as anyone could figure out how. But the wise hardware jockey didn't trust such testing any more than the wise software engineer did. It was only when the hardware and software met at last in full-speed use, where the virtual rubber finally met the virtual road, that the real problems would reveal themselves.

But the list didn't look any worse than it had yesterday, to Dev's surprise. Some items had fallen off, some had been added: the software troubleshooting teams on campus here in Tempe, nearly a thousand people all told, were working at full stretch to reduce this list to nothing. Nonetheless, he glared at number three on the list, tapping it idly with his pen.

"A thought about that one, Mr. Logan?" Milla said.

Dev snorted. "That I wish it'd just go away by itself! Or that somebody would find out what's causing it . . ."

"I'm sure they will."

I wish I was that sure, Dev thought. *Oh, well.* He made notes next to a couple of other items on the list, then handed it back to Milla. "I'll make the usual rounds this morning, but I want some extra time with the intervention groups in Object Village. Tell them to have the trouble-team leaders meet me up there around eleven."

Milla nodded, made a note. "The ten o'clock meeting," Dev said, "with the Magnificent Seven . . ."

"Five out of seven are here already," Milla said. "Natasha got stuck at O'Hare last night—they canceled her flight. I sent the New York jet for her and she'll be landing at Sky Harbor in about forty-five minutes. Jim is driving in from Taos. His car's GPS says he's on I-10 just west of Tonopah. Should be here around nine."

Dev got up to pour himself some more coffee. "Why can I *not* get that man to fly?" he muttered.

"He just loves those wide open spaces," Milla said. "And hates airport security."

"He wouldn't get such a bad case of it if he'd just use one of the company planes!" Dev said, stirring the coffee. "And yes, I know he hates those too. Stubborn cuss. He's not planning to go anywhere for the next three days, is he?"

"No, Mr. Logan. He called the concierge at Castle Scrooge last night and told them to prep his suite for at least a week's stay."

"He bringing Daniela?"

"No, she and the kids are staying home, he said. The littlest one's graduating from kindergarten today."

"They grow up so fast," Dev said, smiling a little at the image of tiny redheaded Jackie in a mortarboard. "Make sure that Uncle Dev sends her something nice. She's big on rocking horses, isn't she?"

"Yes. It's all right, though. Frank took care of that for you yesterday." Frank was his PA.

"Okay," Dev said. "What else? Any significant overnight press for the rollout?"

"Here are the press clippings from the last twelve hours," Milla said, opening the bottommost file and pushing it across to him. It was full of laser-printed sheets from Web pages and Xeroxes from newspapers. Dev scanned through them quickly while Milla drank a little of her tea. "Nice articles in *Asahi Shimbun* and the South China *Morning Post*," she said. "*Mainichi Daily News*, too."

Dev turned over some pages, peered at one. "The *New Straits Times* article looks a little skeptical . . ."

"But not overtly negative." Milla bit into one of the croissants, took another sip of tea. "A lot of them—the Mumbai *Senachar*, Khaleej *Times*—just reprinted our own canned stuff."

"Yeah, well," Dev said, paging through the rest of the printouts, "not all of them. And I tell you, if I see the phrase 'former hacker wunderkind' again today, I'm going to barf."

Milla picked up one printout, glanced down it. "This one says 'erstwhile' . . ."

Dev gave her a dry look. Milla shrugged. "Once upon a time," she said, " 'hacker' just meant somebody who hacked away at a program until it worked."

"Doesn't mean that anymore," Dev muttered. "And I never like the implications when they use it. Well, never mind." He glanced over the files. "How are the markets?"

"Asia and Europe are buoyant," Milla said. "The Dow finished up last night. We topped out at nine ninety."

"Psychological barrier there," Dev said, closing the last file and pushing it back. "I really want to see us break a thousand during the launch. What are the odds?"

"Better ask Mr. Margoulies about that," said Milla. "I wouldn't venture an opinion."

"But you'd bet."

Milla flashed a grin at him, got up, and picked up the files. "Everybody here bets," she said. "And tries not to get caught. Should I incriminate myself?"

Dev laughed and got up too. "Not on my behalf. What about on-campus business? Any problems last night?"

"Nothing unexpected. Security's noted that there've been a few more attempts than usual to get into the campus after shutdown. They're putting it down to a combination of people getting excited about the rollout, and post exam excitement."

Dev chuckled softly. Omnitopia shared the city of Tempe with the biggest campus of Arizona State University, and graduation day was only a few days after Throw the Switch day. Understandably, the seniors were starting to get frisky. "Kids looking for somewhere to get plastered in private," he said.

Milla nodded, her expression suggesting that she was above that kind of thing, though her senior year wouldn't have been that far behind her—she was one of Omnitopia's youngest executive hires, a masters' degree holder at nineteen. "Okay," Dev said. "Everything seems to be running as expected for the moment. Thanks, Milla. Tell the staff over at ops that I'll be along in about half an hour."

"Yes, Mr. Logan. Good morning."

Milla headed for the door, closed it behind her. Dev stood there for a moment looking toward the courtyard windows, and the slowly growing light of dawn beyond them. Then he turned and headed back toward the bedroom side of the suite.

When he looked in the door, he found that Mirabel

was lying on her back with her arms crossed over her eyes. "What time is it?" said the muffled voice from under the arms.

"Just after six."

"It's not fair," Mirabel said. "You didn't get to bed until three."

"I'll sleep in October."

It was a traditional answer in their household to anyone who complained about short sleeping hours. Mirabel snorted at him, unfolded her arms. "October never comes. Or never the right one."

"It's not going to come in the next three days, that's for sure." Dev sat down on the bed beside her. "What's your schedule like today?"

She stretched, plopped her head back against the pillow. "Oh, God, let me think . . ."

Dev glanced at the bedside table. "Where's your PDA? Won't it be in there?"

"Always you with your machines," Mirabel said, and yawned. "Let me use my brain a moment, okay?" She stared at the ceiling. "I need to go into town first . . ." Between the two of them this meant Phoenix; downtown Tempe, closer and smaller, was "the village." "Got to meet with the board for the homeless charity about the new shelter."

"They finally get their planning permission?"

"Nearly," Mirabel said, rubbing her eyes. "One or two snags to iron out."

"Money snags?"

"No, it's something about the plumbing. The attachment to the city sewerage. Don't ask me for the details; Cara has those." Cara was Mirabel's PA. "Eleven o'clock, I think. I'll take the baby to preschool before I go."

"Okay," Dev said. "What then?"

Mirabel sat up in the bed and hugged her knees. "Uh, I think Cara said yesterday that the dress for the University Ball is ready. That'll mean I need to go for the fitting this afternoon. After that . . ." She pushed the covers away, got up. "Maybe I'll take Lola down to Coldstone Creamery in the village. She kept asking for an ice cream yesterday. 'I was good today, Mommy . . .'"

Dev grinned at the loving and perfect imitation of their daughter's voice. "Was she?"

"She drew a great picture of your bike," Mirabel said, going to the in-bedroom casual closet and pulling her white silk bathrobe off a hanger.

"Somebody's angling for one of her own . . ." Dev said. His big heavy black Dutch city bike was a source of much amusement among his staff, most of whom couldn't understand why he didn't ride one of the ubiquitous Omnitopia golf carts around campus, or at least a bike with a little more class to it. But Dev had his reasons.

"Don't think she wants her own just yet," Mirabel said. "She wants a ride on Daddy's. Did the new baby seat come? No way you're sticking her in the old one. She's too big now."

"I'll ask Frank if it's in," Dev said.

"You coming home for dinner?"

"I have no idea."

Mirabel sighed and went into the little private bathroom. "I'm gonna call security and tell them that if they can't show me video of you eating something decent by six o'clock, I'm gonna hunt you down and stuff a sandwich down your face. Don't care what meeting you're in, either."

"Threats, idle threats."

"Not so idle. . . . " She stuck her head out the door. "Oh, when you go downstairs, would you leave a note for Maurice? We need more toothpaste." Maurice was the concierge for their private quarters; he would be coming on duty in a couple of hours.

"Gotcha." He grabbed her before she could head back into the bathroom and kissed her. "Call me."

"Will do. Want to see if the baby's up yet?"

"Next thing on the list."

Dev headed out to the common room again and across it to his own bathroom and dressing room, where he plunged into the stacks of jeans and racks of polos nearest the door, grabbing one of each more or less at random. As he headed into the bathroom, his brain was already churning with what Milla had told him, tinkering with the priorities of what to handle first this morning, calls he had to make or have made, people he needed to remind that there was just one more thing that needed fixing.

The shower took place at its usual unconscious speed. Fifteen minutes later, scrubbed, shaved, and dressed, Dev was heading out of their suite and down the long antiques-lined corridor beyond the front door, wishing as he sometimes did that Mirabel's schedule didn't have to be quite so active, though this was a quieter day than some. Mirabel was all too aware that it was PR-smart for the wife of the world's eighth richest man to be seen doing something to offset the fact that she didn't need a day job.

Nonetheless, Dev knew that the PR issue would never have been what mattered most to her. She'd been the one, when they first started to get wealthy, who had insisted that with all the money they were getting, it was imperative to give a lot of it away. "What are we supposed to do?" Mirabel had said. "Just make a big heap and sit on it, and whoever's heap is highest wins?" She had snorted in derision at one more of a spectrum of behaviors she routinely referred to as "billionaire gonad games." "Other people helped us when we didn't have bucks. Now let's pass it on." And she worked at least as hard at this as she'd worked at her old day job. *But the point of being unconscionably rich was supposed to be that I didn't want her to need to work.*

As he approached the heavy mahogany security doors at the end of the corridor, Dev made a face. This issue was something that he just had to live with whether he liked it or not. He went up to the left-hand door and laid his hand on the spot in the wood under which the biometrics scanners were located.

The door swung softly open. Lights were on inside. Dev slipped in and waited for the door to close behind him. Before him lay a big common room space like the one he'd just left, but this one was decorated in bright buttercup yellows and blazing pinks, spattered with giant flower and butterfly art on the walls and windows, and scattered with soft child-scaled furniture. The room was empty at the moment except for the usual scatter of toys and stuffed animals with goofy or startled expressions.

Dev headed over toward the left side of the common

room, where another heavy door gave access to the private rooms, offices, and kitchen, and to the bedroom and bathroom suite that the staff called the LolaCave. Once through the door, he hung a left to the first office.

Sitting in the big comfortable office space at a computer desk was Poppy, a tall, big-boned, handsome woman who had been Mirabel's doula when she was pregnant with Lola. "Hey, Mrs. Pops," Dev said. "Good morning!"

"Morning, Dev," Poppy said, not looking up from her typing for a moment. She finished, then smiled her sunny gap-toothed smile at him. "Like father, like daughter, I see."

"Meaning she's up already?"

"About half an hour ago. I swear, you two are wired up somehow."

"She available?"

"Out of the tub, if that's what you mean. Marla's getting her dressed."

"Great." He headed down the hall to Lola's bedroom.

The space was much like her mom's and dad's, if smaller, more intimate, and much more brightly colored. As he opened the door, he caught a glimpse of Lola sitting on a mushroom-shaped hassock near her bed, kicking her feet and singing something tuneless but cheerful, while Marla, a petite African American lady, tried to work with the kicking while fastening the Velcro straps on Lola's shoes. Lola was wearing little blue corduroy overalls and a white T-shirt under it, looking very pert for this time of day.

At the sound of the door, Lola's head turned and her eyes fastened on Dev's like a scanning radar. "Daddy!" she shrieked and broke away from Marla, just as the latter held her hands up in the air with a pit crewman's "done" gesture, the second shoe finished just in time.

Lola charged across the room at Dev. He scooped her up and swung her around. "Morning, Lolo!"

"It's breakfast time!" Lola hollered in his ear. "I get an orange!"

"Absolutely you do," Dev said. "Whatever Lola wants, Lola gets!" He grinned past the headful of dark curls at Marla. "Morning, Mar. She behaving herself?"

"She's very good today," Marla said, getting up and dusting herself off. "She keeps telling me that."

"And I was good yesterday!" Lola said in Dev's ear, not quite loudly enough to puncture his eardrum.

"Oh?" He held her away, trying hard to look skeptical and certain that he was failing. "And why would that be?"

"So you'll take me on your bike! I want to go on your bike with you, Daddy!"

"Oh, I don't know," he said, carrying her toward her breakfast room and sitting her down on one of the seats by the low table there, where an orange, a boiled egg, and a piece of brown toast were waiting. "Everybody wants to go on my bike, Lola, there's a big list of people who want to ride it. Uncle Jim and Uncle Tau, and Aunt Doris and Aunt Cleolinda . . ."

"Is Uncle Jim here?" Lola shrieked. "Where's Uncle Jim?"

"He's not here yet, honey. He's driving here. He'll be here at lunchtime."

"I wanna see Uncle Jim!"

"If you're good," Dev said, "maybe you will. I'll ask him if he has time." He looked at Marla. "Is she on the usual Tuesday schedule today?"

Marla nodded, bringing Lola her plastic-handled little-girl silverware and putting the knife and spoon down by the plate and bowl on the table. "Play school over at Kid City from ten to twelve. Then lunch back here."

"That's fine. Mirabel says she'll take her over to school."

"Perfect."

Dev sat down on another of the low chairs and watched Lola rip up her toast, ingest it with single-minded speed, and then start working on her egg while delivering a matter-of-fact description of her previous day. "And Mattie said he was going to bite me, and I said if he did I'd bite him, and then he cried. And I was sad. And then I drew the bike. It was black! And Mattie stole the crayon! And I chased him until Mrs. Nowata said I was making him hipe—hyper—"

"Hyperactive?" Dev said, glancing over at Marla. "Who's Mattie?"

"Her crush for this week," Marla said, amused, starting to peel Lola's orange. "He's the son of a lady who works in human resources, I think. Sweet kid, but a little fragile sometimes. They're always hugging each other, though, those two."

"Crushes at four?" Dev said, shaking his head and looking in wonder at his daughter. "I would have thought not until six at least."

Marla shrugged. "Everything seems to happen faster than it used to," she said. "She's okay."

"I will do the orange!" Lola announced, in a tone that brooked no refusal.

Marla chuckled and handed over the orange. "What an autocrat."

"Just like her daddy," Dev said, getting up.

"Oh, sure," said Marla, in affectionate skepticism. "How're you holding up, Dev? Three days now, is it?"

"Almost three," he said. "One minute past midnight on June twenty-first, the night the walls between the worlds are thin."

"Well, you hang in there and don't let the stress thin *you* out," Marla said as Dev knelt down by the chair where Lola sat.

"Have to go to work now, punkin," Dev said. "Gimme a hug."

Lola turned her attention from the orange, now half raggedly peeled, and gave him a most piteous and calculating look out of those big brown eyes. "You're going to ride the bike," she said.

"Yes, I am," Dev said.

Lola heaved a sigh and went back to peeling the orange. "I am being *very good,*" she said.

Dev stood up, grinning at Marla. "You have a good day."

"You too, Daddy Dev."

Dev headed out, once again filled with relief that his daughter had such super people around her as Marla, Poppy, and Crazy Bob (whose nickname was apparently the result of the second of his two Ph.Ds, the one in Greek philosophy). The three of them were more like PAs for Lola than nannies, and were always on call, in shifts, ready to cover those times when neither Dev or Mirabel were able to be with her for much of the day. And Lola, thank

God, loved her life. She was a sunny child, independent for her age, fascinated by the (admittedly interesting) world around her, happy at the Omnitopia preschool, and completely oblivious to who her dad was, or why it should particularly matter. This blessed state wouldn't last forever, of course. Sooner or later, Lola would have to go out into the great world, with all the dangers that entailed; she couldn't stay in the Omnitopia play groups and crèche forever. But right now Dev was aware that he was party to a golden time in her life—and certainly in his—when every day he could break off work when he liked and come home to play with his daughter.

However, his next chance to do that was at least eight hours away. Right now he had to get to his main place of work and start putting out brushfires, some of which would have been kindled hundreds or even thousands of miles away, and some of which might turn out to be inextinguishable. *But you'll never know if you don't get busy.* Dev headed back to the elevator in the corridor and went downstairs.

There in the main-floor elevator lobby, standing against the polished marble wall by the guard's desk, was a big shiny black city bike with saddle baskets, old-fashioned bull's-horn handlebars, streamers coming out of the handlebar grips, and a big shiny brass bell. The uniformed guard at the desk looked up and said, "Anything you need, Mr. Dev?"

"Yeah, thanks for reminding me!" Dev said, went to the desk, grabbing a sticky pad and a pen. He scribbled on the pad. "Give that to Maurice when he comes in, okay?"

"No problem, Mr. D."

"Thanks, Rob," he said, and went to the bike, raising the kickstand. The glass doors of the downstairs lobby slid open for him. He walked the bike out, pushed it down the flagstone walkway, mounted up, and rode off across the little bridge that arched over the moat around the stucco-and-tile edifice that Omnitopia's employees referred to as Castle Dev. Quietly, under the indigo twilight of an Arizona summer dawn, the CEO of the world's fourteenth largest company pedaled off along the main drag of his main corporate campus, humming to himself as the third most important business day of his life began.

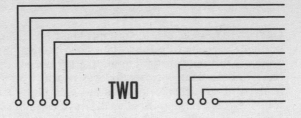

TWO

WHEN DELIA HARRINGTON PICKED UP HER RENTAL CAR at Sky Harbor and headed out of the airport in the direction of the Red Mountain Freeway toward Tempe, her nerves were already on edge. The weather forecast for the Phoenix area this morning had been for clear, hot, sunny weather. But half an hour out from Sky Harbor, clouds had suddenly appeared and the plane had begun to shake. If there was one thing Delia couldn't cope with, it was turbulence.

At least in the physical sense, she thought as she got onto the on-ramp for I-10. *There's going to be enough emotional turbulence before this is over. Ideally, not mine.* But turbulence in the air was another matter. "Oh, I'm sorry about this," the flight attendant had said when Delia had asked her about it. "It's just the monsoon. Though it's kind of early this year. Climate change, I guess."

Delia hadn't thought that the words "Phoenix" and "monsoon" belonged in the same sentence. Yet, as she now discovered, every summer the people here endured a period during which in the morning or evening there would be a sudden peak in the humidity, immediately followed by a thunderstorm, which then cleared itself away and left the skies cleansed and the temperature a little lower. On the ground, Delia might have found such a thing pleasant. In the air, though, as the clouds curdled dark around the Airbus and the plane began to rattle around her like a cocktail shaker, it was another matter entirely. Delia had clung white-knuckled to her seat for the next interminable twenty minutes, gritting her teeth and trying desperately to concentrate on what she'd come all this way to do.

It was, on the face of it, one of those assignments of a lifetime—the kind of thing that, if you got it right, would follow you through your career. But getting it right was the hard part. *Especially since I'm still not entirely sure why they picked me. Time* magazine had hundreds of "stringer" writers that its editorial staff could call upon for articles, and a pool of twenty or thirty who tended to pull down the plum assignments. Sometimes a given writer got an assignment by dint of his gift with the written word, sometimes because of her seniority, sometimes because of a specific sensibility or slant that he or she might be expected to bring to a subject. But in Delia's case—at least to her way of thinking, and throwing out any possible self-delusion on the subject—she had no idea how many of these factors might be operating. All she knew was that, a month and a half ago, she'd been asked to submit a list of questions she would like to ask and subjects she would like to investigate with the founder, president, and CEO of Omnitopia Inc.—if she ever got the chance.

She remembered staring at her monitor when that e-mail arrived, and reading it three or four times through, absolutely unbelieving. *This was meant for somebody else,* was the thought that kept coming into her head. *I mean, it's not like I wouldn't love to do it, but—* Yet there it was, and staring at it didn't make it go away. Finally Delia printed it out, took it home, and spent the next twenty hours in a fugue of desperate typing—partly because she was afraid she might lose the assignment if she took too long submitting the response. All that terrified, caffeine-stoked night, she'd sat hunched over the little kitchen table in her apartment in the New York suburbs, trying to come up with a list that would include not only questions she really wanted to ask but questions she thought her editor would really want someone to ask. As dawn had come up, she had found herself nodding off over her laptop, staring at words that hardly seemed to make sense anymore, absolutely certain that this was the best she could do and that she'd blown it.

Nonetheless, Delia had turned in the response, more an

article in itself than a list. If there was anything that interested her about Omnitopia, it was the desire to get past all the authorized biography stuff, past the sanitized corporate hype and the squeaky-clean good-boy image that always seemed to come up whenever you mentioned Dev Logan. There had to be more going on in the background, something more than just luck and hard work, more than a cadre of slavishly loyal coworkers and a pile of unsuspected business savvy. There had to be some shadows, some stuff that nobody was supposed to see. The chance to peer around that closely guarded business, get past the lavish employee perks and the manicured lawns and see if everybody was all *that* happy to be working for the billionaire golden boy of multiplayer online roleplaying games—*that* would be worth something. No company, no corporate entity, and especially no corporate figurehead of such massive wealth and power, could possibly be perfectly clean.

Delia had mailed her wish list away, and (after crashing for a few hours and turning up unrepentantly late for work) had resumed her research for the article on the vigilante approach to illegal immigration control that had most recently been occupying her time. And nothing further had happened until a week after the all-nighter, when just before lunch she got an unexpected phone call from somebody down in corporate travel, saying, "So can you fly on the nineteenth?"

"Fly where?" Delia said, completely stumped.

The e-mail confirming that *Time*'s senior commissioning editor was sending her to Omnitopia arrived in her inbox while she was still trying to figure out who the travel lady was really trying to reach. The remainder of the morning went by in a haze of amazement, delight, and a strange kind of angry satisfaction. *Somebody upstairs agrees with me,* Delia thought. *Somebody upstairs thinks that there's something worth finding out.*

Time to start digging.

She had spent the following week in a flat-out research blitz, reading absolutely everything she could find that had been written about the Dev Logan—the biographies, authorized and not, all the newspaper articles in any major paper for the last three years, and the output—that was the kindest word for it—of countless industry magazines, website columnists, and bloggers. By the time Delia was finished, she was probably one of the planet's best-read experts on Omnitopia's boss. And Delia noted—partly because it bemused her somewhat—that the more she found out about Logan, and the more positive it all made him look, the less she liked him.

That's a reaction I'm going to have to control, she thought, *or it's going to ruin this thing.* But she felt confident she'd be able to manage. In her time she had interviewed Russian Mafia chieftains, homegrown murderers, white-collar fraudsters, suspicious and angry politicians, and had in all cases managed to leave them with the sense that they were dealing with someone who would tell their stories fairly and accurately. Sometimes that had even been true.

But in none of those cases, she thought now, gripping the rental's wheel as tightly as she'd been gripping her seat's armrests, *had I just come off a flight like* that!

A blue Dodge pickup changed lanes in front of her unexpectedly, veering in front of her. Delia braked skillfully, leaned on the horn, shouted "Idiot!" then checked the lanes around her, signaled, changed lanes herself, and blew past the Dodge. *Come on, come on,* she thought then, forcing herself to breathe more slowly, *calm down. This is the worst time for this! You have got to get a grip. You'll be there in twenty minutes. Breathe.*

She breathed. She drove. The sky, which had been turbulent with clouds only half an hour ago while she was still picking up her luggage, was now almost completely empty of them, and the blue of the sky was turning hard and clear, while all around her a butterscotchy morning light spread itself over what landscape was visible past the beige gravel, sand art, and cactus plantings of the freeway.

That freeway actually went right past the Omnitopia campus, though there was no direct access. So the flatness of the Phoenix-area landscape being what it was, Delia caught sight of a few of the fabled "dreaming spires" from a few miles away. The phrase was a joke, she knew. The place was built mostly in the primarily horizontal Southwestern stucco-and-tile idiom, and no building on the campus was more than six stories high, that being part of the company's gentlemen's agreement with the city of Tempe when they first mooted the huge development. *Though no one would've been surprised if the city'd agreed to let them build the Empire State Building all over again, knowing what kind of money this company was going to bring into town.*

It had indeed been a sweetheart deal by anyone's reckoning. Tempe had been only one of eight cities to begin campaigning for Omnitopia's business when the company announced its intention to purpose-build a hundred acre main facility somewhere in the Southwest. Most of the other cities—Taos, Tucson, Albuquerque, Santa Fe, Pueblo, Amarillo, and Los Cruces—had, on the face of it, better sites or general offerings than Tempe, so there had been a lot of muttering among them when Tempe had carried off the prize by offering Omnitopia 150 acres of hitherto useless land north of the Rio Salado Parkway and south of the river's mostly dry wash basin, west of the flood barrier between the basin and Tempe Lake. After the fact, all kinds of sour-grapes speculations were flung about by the losers—some of them smacking seriously of conspiracy theory, like the suggestion that Arizona State University had made Omnitopia some kind of secret deal to let the company rent the ASU science servers when they were done with a clandestine military project that was coming to an end: or that a past president or new presidential candidate from the area had privately bent Dev Logan's ear and influenced the choice with promises of high-end political appointments to come. Other rumors were more straightforwardly whacko, such as the whisper that the Tempe site had better feng shui than the others—this involving some indecipherable gobbledygook about the site being perfectly positioned between air, water, earth, and fire in the forms of Sky Harbor (or the air rights for the contiguous dry wash area), Tempe Lake, Hayden Butte, and Sun Devil Stadium.

In any case, the deal had been done. The City of Tempe had gone away happily counting its very large pile of newly acquired dollars, and only two years after the groundbreak-

ing for the uplift piers, the completed roofs and towers of
Omnitopia City had risen on the riverbank and over the
dry riverbed—bringing something like six thousand jobs to
the Tempe area even after the construction was done, not
to mention millions of extra dollars per year in tax income,
and all the other money that all those new and fairly well-
paid employees pumped into the local economy.

Now Delia swung around the eastward curve of the freeway, past the admittedly beautiful "built butte" of carved
and cast sandstone landscaping that concealed the piers
holding Omnitopia's base platform high above the dry
wash, and had to shake her head in grudging admiration.
The pictures—and even the full-size virtual version of Omnitopia that existed as a Macrocosm inside the roleplaying
game for the reference and convenience of both visitors
and employees—did not do the reality justice. The many
low buildings, here and there with a modest tile-roofed
tower rising out of the trees to challenge the surrounding
skyline of Tempe, had a look about them both civic and
rustic, but rustic in an easygoing, modern way, very much
at ease with itself, and individualistic, but casually so. The
hot yellow Arizona day and the hard blue sky somehow got
drawn down and tangled into that handsomely contrived
landscape by the glitter of the sun off fronds and leaves in
the groves of subtropical plantings, so that light seemed to
be concealed in the landscape, revealed, concealed again.
The whole effect was absolutely the opposite of corporate:
a parklike kind of place in which people would probably
like to live. *And probably wouldn't mind staying around
to work extra hours,* Delia thought. *Just goes to show you
that the best money can buy the best design. Especially if the
bean counters think it'll benefit the bottom line.*

Buried in the heart of the campus, mostly concealed by
a small forest of imported eucalyptus and other desert-
friendly trees, was the chateau-peaked main tower of the
so-called Castle Dev, the combined residence and main
office of Omnitopia's "First Player." Delia caught just a
glimpse of it while changing lanes. *Maybe that's part of what
bothers me,* Delia thought as the campus poured past on
her right and finally dropped away behind. *All this oh so*

*correct fake populism, this more-ordinary-than-thou stuff,
when the guy comes from middling-big money in the first
place. It smacks of somebody protesting too much.* She let
out a breath as she headed down the off-ramp that would
feed into South Mill Avenue. It would take another ten
minutes' backtracking through the middle of Tempe to
bring her to the Omnitopia main entrance.

She was expecting some vast acreage of sunbaked parking lot spread out behind one set of guarded gates and in
front of another. But instead Delia found herself driving
into a large circular space like a cul-de-sac, paved in red-
brown flagstones. Surrounding three-quarters of the circle,
high raised banks of white and colored gravels decorated
in Pima and Maricopa motifs—sun wheels, wise lizards,
Kokopelli cane dancers and flute dancers—flanked a wide
half-circular flight of golden sandstone stairs leading up to
an area like an entry into a public park, but gateless and
open. Water from a small square pool at the top of the
stairs ran down a carved channel in the middle of the stairs,
splashing from step to step into a pool at the bottom. To
either side, wide accessibility ramps led up from the circle
through the banks on either side toward each of two low
tile-roofed stucco buildings and past the buildings, through
the open space between them, everything changed. Outside the space, except for that glinting runnel of water
pouring down the stairs, everything was bright, dry, arid.
Inside, past the two buildings, everything was cool shade
and bright splashes of floral color, small paths winding their
way under the green canopy through a landscape of low,
humanely-scaled, congenial-looking buildings. Delia pulled
the car up at the edge of the circle, stopped, and just sat
there a moment looking up the stairs, over the border into
Omnitopia. *It's like being parked in Kansas and looking
into Oz.*

Someone tapped on her driver's side window. Delia
turned quickly and found herself looking at a smiling
young brunette woman in a blue linen uniform with the
Omnitopia omega logo embroidered on one sleeve. Delia
touched the window control, rolled it down. "Uh, sorry, I
didn't know where to park—"

"Oh, no, Miss Harrington," the young woman said. "It's not a problem, we've been expecting you. If you'll just drive around there—" She pointed at one of the ramps off to Delia's right. "Follow the ramp down under the overhang, then hang a right into the guest parking area. Here—" She handed Delia two plastic guest ID badges, one on a neck lanyard. "Park anywhere you like in the 'A' area and leave the second card on your dashboard. Somebody'll be down for you in a few moments."

"Sure," Delia said. "Thanks."

The ramp that led through the sand-painted bank branched off just past it, one side leading up into the pathways of the main campus, the other diving underground through an entrance partly curtained by hanging plants. Delia slowed as she headed downward, expecting a few moments of blindness in the usual sudden parking-structure darkness, but much to her surprise, there wasn't any. The whole inside of the underground parking area space was lit, maybe not dazzlingly, but by what appeared to be natural sunlight filtered through clouds. Delia turned as she'd been told, found many empty parking spaces all emblazoned with "A"s, and parked in one of them. She then got out of the car to stare, fascinated, at the ceiling. It was completely paneled with squares of some material that glowed with a soft cool light.

From the far side of the parking structure, the sound of a small electric motor approached. Delia looked that way and saw one of the famous pink Omnitopia golf carts coming toward her with a slim young African American man in a polo shirt and chinos driving it. He pulled up next to her. "Miss Harrington?"

She smiled at him and slung the ID card on its lanyard around her neck. "That's right."

The young man stepped out of the cart to shake her hand. "I'm Joss McCann: I'm with the publicity department here."

That brought Delia's eyebrows up. He wasn't just "with" Omnitopia publicity here: he was the head of it, and the number two man in Omnitopia PR worldwide. She was astonished how young he was, and then realized that she was probably radiating that astonishment. "I'm sorry," she said. "I wasn't expecting you to be my ride!"

Joss flashed a dazzling grin at her that said, *And that's not all you weren't expecting, but I'm not saying a word.* He glanced at her rental car. "Don't forget your briefcase," he said.

"No, of course not...." She reached into the backseat after it, shut the car, locked it. Delia settled herself in the passenger seat of the golf cart, glancing around the parking lot. "Is today a day off for people here or something?"

Joss looked at her with slight surprise. "Why?"

"The parking lot's kind of empty."

"Oh! No, not a holiday," Joss said, starting the motor up again. "We've got a lot more room down here than we need. Most of our staff use park-n-ride facilities based off campus. There are shuttles that run all over town from the topside level."

He drove down toward the far end of the structure. Delia peered upward as they went. Joss glanced at her. "The ceiling?"

Delia laughed. "Yeah."

Joss nodded. "Solid 'cold light' like that has been a trope in science fiction and fantasy roleplaying games for years and years. When Dev found out that somebody'd finally figured out direct-glow electroceramic, he had to have it." He glanced up at the last of the roof as they drove up the ramp. "The boss is such a geek."

Delia blinked at that. This was not the kind of opinion she normally heard from upper management about upper-most management.

"But it's energy-saving too," Joss said as they drove up toward the sunlight. "So the bottom-line types like it. And it's supposed to never burn out, so the physical plant people *really* like it."

They came up into the sun near one of the two gate buildings, but only for a second; the next moment they were under the canopy of the trees. "So much for techno-geekery," Joss said. "Was your flight all right? Hear there was some pretty bad turbulence this morning."

"Uh, yeah, there was," Delia said. "I guess other people off my flight have come in?"

"Might have," Joss said, "but I heard about it from one of the board members this morning. They've all come in for the rollout. Your timing's perfect: we don't normally get all of the Magnificent Seven on campus more than a few times a year."

They were driving down a wide path that curved between plants and raised beds that partly concealed the buildings behind them: the path was full of people strolling, driving golf carts, riding bikes painted in the same shade of pink. "Forgive me," Delia said, "but I have to ask. Are all the employees here really this casual about the board of directors?"

"It varies," Joss said. "Some people like to be more formal. I know there's been a lot of press speculation that we're all just stock-option-brainwashed wage slaves who've drunk the happy happy corporate Kool-Aid." He shrugged, flashed that grin at her again. "I think you may find a little more variation in the sample when you're on the fifty-cent tour today. Are we well paid? Yeah, better than a lot of people at similar companies. If there are any similar companies."

"Which of course you're paid to tell me there aren't."

Joss gave her a wry look. "Of course. But, who knows, you might come to some similar conclusion yourself before you're done. Are we brainwashed? I don't think so. Trouble is, people who're brainwashed into thinking they're happy and people who're having a lot of fun doing fulfilling work for a decent wage tend to exhibit some of the same symptoms. Add the side effect that the second kind of people trigger in folks doing work they hate for crap wages, and the clinical picture gets kind of confused." Joss angled to the left when the path they were driving down branched. "But you'll get a fair chance today to check the corporate coolers for unnatural-colored fruit drinks. One of my horde of slavering minions will take you around the buildings, get you oriented. That'll take an hour or so. Make sure you make the minion stop and get you something cold halfway through: it's gonna be a hot one today. Then you've got a meeting with Ron Ruis, who's our chief worldbuilder, and Tau Vitoria, who's chief server engineer, the king of our hardware guys." Joss chuckled. "Watch out for him, he's a hand-kisser."

"What?"

"Tau's very European," Joss said, rolling his eyes in amusement. "He's a minor member of some deposed Slavic royal family or something, I forget which one. Tau's all manners and languages, but don't be fooled. It's just a blind to keep you from noticing that he's the kind of guy who'd still be wearing pocket protectors if his staff hadn't broken him of it."

"I should be taking notes," Delia said. It was meant, if anything, as misdirection: her memory was her one of her chief assets, one that made her more effective at what she did than some writers who were far more glossy prose stylists.

"Ask his staff for the latest gossip," Joss said. "Or rather, try to stop them from telling you." He took another branch of the path, where it ducked through a tunnel of green-ery formed by a pergola smothered with vines and the beginnings of bunches of grapes. On the other side was a small parking lot paved in the same sandstone flagging as the paths, with a semicircular three-story stuccoed build-ing embracing it. There were three or four golf carts and a scatter of bikes in front of it, both in a rack by the front doors and abandoned on the lawn around the parking area. Under a small patch of palm trees on one side on the lawn, a couple of employees were sitting on the grass, one ham-mering away on a laptop, another leaning against a tree and reading. To Delia's eye, they looked like they were just barely out of college.

Joss killed the golf cart's engine. Delia picked up her briefcase and followed him toward the doors, glancing at the young man and woman under the palm trees, and at the people going in and out of the doors ahead of them. "I guess I shouldn't be surprised at how young the workforce is here," she said. "A big tech company, after all . . ."

"Young, yes," Joss said as they went in, "but we're also the state's biggest employer of seniors. Possibly the biggest one in the Southwest, though I'd need to check the stats."

That surprised her. "Really? How many?"

"At least eight hundred people fifty-five or over," Joss said. "I think about five hundred people over sixty-five. It makes sense down here, after all! There are all these educated retirees who enjoy working from home on 'relaxed hours' or some other kind of flextime. A huge untapped resource."

It was of course the kind of thing that you would expect a PR person to be telling you about. Delia made a mental note to look into this another time, specifically with an eye to finding out what kind of wage these putative retirees were earning. "Anyway," Joss said, as they headed in through the building's lobby and up a broad flight of stairs in its center, "after you see Tau, Dev should be ready for you—assuming something bizarre hasn't happened to his schedule between now and three hours from now." They came up to the second floor, where a large central corridor followed the main curve of the building, and small informal open work areas budded off on both sides. The whole feel of the place was bright, open, airy. Delia looked up and was surprised to see what appeared to be completely unobstructed blue sky.

Joss chuckled. "Our famous glass ceiling," he said. "It's polarized—you get that it's-not-there effect until the sun hits it. Welcome to the Flackery! This is where we handle PR for the worldwide operation, so if things look a little crazy right now, it's all about the rollout . . ."

They walked down the corridor to the right. "Maybe it's just me," Delia said, "but if this is the building when things are crazy, then at a calm time it must seem positively comatose."

Joss looked up and down the corridor. "Nooo," he said, "too many people on Rollerblades for 'comatose.' Come back next month." They walked past a big kidney-shaped table with numerous large flat-screen monitors on it. Working in front of one of them, or perhaps playing, was a man in his forties, intent on a number of figures running around in some grassy landscape. They appeared, from the quick glimpse Delia got as they passed, to be playing tennis.

"He's in Namath," Joss said, after a glance. "It's a Macrocosm where all combat is in the form of Earth sports. Once a year each of the Sports Nations there holds a competition to determine who's going to rule each nation for the next game season." He shook his head. "I stay out of there. That 'cosm is *nuts*. Talk about your unbridled savagery and internecine warfare."

Delia had to laugh at that, considering the continent-wide conflict that she understood was commonplace in most of the other 'cosms. Joss chuckled too. "Have you been into the game yet?"

"Once or twice," Delia said. She had gone in on a staff Omnitopia account that the PR office had given her. But certain that the account was being monitored, and wanting to do a little sleuthing without being watched, she had also slipped in using a standard account bought online with an over-the-counter credit card voucher that belonged to a spare identity she kept for purposes of anonymous research.

"But you haven't really gotten into anyplace specific long enough to want to spend time there."

"Well," Delia said, "I haven't found where I'm really comfortable yet. I don't know if I'm wild about the idea of casting myself as some kind of wizard or warrior."

"No need to," Joss said. "The system's set up so that you can find out which 'cosm you prefer and choose a role from inside it. No one has to still be playing Otherworlds Campaigns if they don't want to. That's just a staging area for the other games now. Though we do get some players," and he grinned, "who stay in the old central game world, in Telekil, and never go outside of it."

That surprised Delia. "Don't you find that a little frustrating?"

Joss shook his head. "To each their own," he said as they walked past more and more office pods filled with people sitting in front of screens, standing in front of them, or walking around with headsets on, some of which covered their eyes as well as their ears. "But that's the whole idea of Omnitopia: that there should be something for everybody. If you can't find what you like, then just play long enough—or well enough—and you may get a chance to build it yourself."

That, of course, was the heart of the attraction that Delia suspected was the true cause for Omnitopia's wild expansion over the last few years. There was nothing like the hope of money, big money, to concentrate people's minds. "How many people are doing that now?"

They came into a large semicircular work pod at the end of the building. Its floor-to-ceiling windows overlooked a garden area, and through the trees and shrubs the occasional pink-biked cyclist could be seen passing by. In the middle of this space was a big semicircular desk with a phone, three flat monitors, a couple of comfortable chairs pulled up to the desk, and a statue of a lady in flowing Roman garments blowing a trumpet. A high, curved hardwood credenza stood against the wall. Joss opened a door in it, reached in, and came out with another plastic card. "How many?" Joss said, going to a cupboard in the credenza and opening it. "I haven't seen numbers for this week, but last week it was—" He frowned, trying to remember. "Eight thousand? Something like that."

Delia blinked at that. "Eight *thousand* other universes inside Omnitopia?"

"Well, I know it sounds like a lot," Joss said, closing the credenza's door, "but they're not as complex or as resource-hungry as the Macrocosms. I mean, each of the Macros has had hundreds of people working on it, and in it, for years. In those, you're talking about virtual landscapes that in some cases are nearly as big as the Earth's. The Micros are a lot smaller, simply because MicroLevelers can't spend anything like our kind of man-hours on them."

He walked back to his desk and picked up the phone, hit a button on its dial pad. "Robbie? Yeah. Miss Harrington is here. Would you come on down and take over for me? Thanks." He hung up the phone, then rummaged under his desk for a moment and came up with a sticky pad. He scribbled on it for a moment, then straightened and came around the desk again, fiddling with that second plastic card.

"Here," Joss said, peeling something off it: a curl of plastic. "Can I borrow your thumb for a moment?"

"My thumb?"

"Your right one."

Bemused, Delia held it out. Joss pressed the card against her thumb, then handed it to her. On the spot where Joss had peeled the plastic away, Delia now saw her thumbprint slowly fade in, developing in dark blue against the light blue of the Omnitopia omega and her printed name on the card. "This is your 'enter all areas' pass," Joss said. "After you're finished with your talk with Dev today, this is your key to the campus. Wave it in front of door readers to go into any public-access area of any building and some of the private-access areas like cafeterias. Show it to any staff member you want to talk to in order to establish your bona fides. Use it to step into any Omnitopian Macrocosm or open-access Microcosm, using whatever input-output method you like—keyboard, VR room, RealFeel setup. The staff will help you with I/O and anything else you need; all you have to do is ask. Don't worry about returning the pass. It'll expire either at midnight or as soon as you drive off campus, whichever comes first. Each day, when you come back, you'll get a new one until I'm told your work here is done."

Delia stared at the card, astonished. It had never occurred to her that she might be simply handed, on a plate, the kind of access to Omnitopia that this card entailed. *This story could*—I *could* . . . She shut that whole line of thought down for the moment. It was too soon to work out exactly what she *could* do. But the possibilities were staggering . . .

A beefy, sandy-haired man about six feet tall, dressed in a polo shirt and chinos, came into the room. "This is Robbie Wauhea," Joss said as the man smiled at Delia and shook her hand. "He works with me on North American publicity for Omnitopia in general, but he's also handling rollout-specific PR. He can answer all your questions about what's going to happen in the next three days."

"Pleased," Delia said.

"So, if you'll excuse me," Joss said, "I have a couple of appointments myself this morning. But in the meantime—"

He picked up from his desk the sticky pad he'd just been scribbling on, pulled off the topmost note and handed it to Delia. It was omega-branded faintly in blue, and over the omega was a seven-digit number, like a phone number in reverse. "That's the ID number of my own Microcosm," Joss said. "Once you get into Omnitopia proper, stop in and have a look around. It's a small thing, but mine own."

Delia nodded at him. "Thanks." And then something occurred to her as she put the note away. "You make a little extra off this?" she said. "Your percentage of 'one percent of infinity'?"

The look Joss gave her was cordial, and very managed. "Any proceeds," he said, "go to a nominated charity, the same as all the other proceeds from employee-run 'cosms. I favor the Innocence Project, myself."

"Touché," Delia said.

Joss nodded to her, visibly more as farewell than reaction. "Enjoy your visit!"

"I'm sure I will. Thanks again for coming down to get me."

"Would you like to head on down this way, Miss Harrington?" Robbie said. "I'll take you upstairs to our nerve center and you can sit down and start asking me questions."

"That would be super," Delia said. But in her pocket, where she'd slipped it, she could practically feel the second card burning a hole in her slacks, eager to be used. *Carte blanche to Omnitopia,* she thought. *And to the story of a lifetime, if I can just figure out how to make the most of this—and find out where some of the bodies are buried.*

Behind her, Delia was sure she could feel thoughtful eyes watching her go. She concentrated on giving no sign that she noticed, and, laughing and smiling, she went up a nearby flight of stairs with Robbie Wauhea, listening carefully to every word . . .

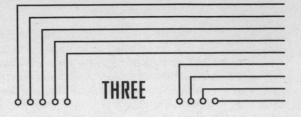

THREE

RIK MALIANI STOOD IN THE DARKNESS of his Microcosm in Omnitopia and gazed up at the glowing "neon" sign still hanging there unsupported in the virtual air.

His Microcosm in Omnitopia. The phrase wasn't through giving him the chills yet. Rik had spent almost all of last night reading through the orientation pack that had come in an e-mail from Microcosm Management. Throughout it, through the dry details of security protocols and pro tem templates and the complications of the royalty agreement—*especially* the royalty agreement, which included contingency plans involving numbers with more zeroes than Rik had ever seen or hoped to see in *his* checking account—he'd had to keep reminding himself, *You're not dreaming! This is real!* But the belief kept wearing off. He wound up taking the laptop to bed with him, and he lay there reading on it until Angela put the pillow over her head to shut out the light of the bedside lamp. Living up to her name, she hadn't even told Rik to cut it out and go to sleep, which was just as well, because he couldn't. Finally he'd turned out the light and just lay there reading by the screen's light until he at last fell asleep with the laptop still running.

In the early morning light leaking in through the bedroom's venetian blinds, Rik woke with a start to find himself in exactly the same position, but looking at a black screen: the laptop's batteries had run down. Angela was already up. Fortunately, he didn't have to get up yet. Last month the courier company had moved him onto a variant of what Rik's colleagues on the loading dock called The Unweekend Schedule—in Rik's case, Thursday through Monday at work, Tuesday and Wednesday off. Today being Wednesday, he could lie in for a little while, get up, take some time over his coffee, read more of the docs that Omnitopia had sent him.

Out in the hallway, Angela put her head in the bedroom door. He made a little "hi there" finger-wave at her. "I never mowed the lawn yesterday," Rik said.

"That you're even thinking about that right now tells me I have married a prince among men," Angela said. "It'll keep. You ought to have a little time to play with your new toy."

"*I* have married a queen among women," Rik said.

"So true," said Angela, and vanished.

Rik got up, showered, dressed, had his coffee, and the first thing he then did, in the relative cool of the morning—since the weather people had been predicting an early-summer heat wave for the Lehigh Valley this week—was go out and mow the lawn. There wasn't much of it: their little duplex's front lawn, and the strips of back lawn on either side of their patio and alongside the garage, involved half an hour's mowing at best. Still, having the job done left Rik in a domestic "state of grace" where he could afterward shut himself into the game room for an hour or so without feeling too guilty about it.

One of the links that had come to him along with the electronic in-game message from the Microcosm people, and the e-mail copies of the material, was an address for what the docs called his "MicroMentor." Logged into his Omnitopia account again, Rik once more glanced through the material. *Your Mentor,* it said, *is a picked Omnitopia employee who's committed to helping you understand the basics of setting up your Microcosm. Please see the attachment for information on your Mentor's name, location, and available hours*—

Rik was sitting in the little virtual private eye's office that was his in-game prep space—a beat-up desk and a couple of old chairs, dusty blinds looking down through fly-speckled windows onto a 1950s street in Los Angeles, and a glass-paneled door that had his name painted backward on the glass. Hanging in the air near the desk was his Omnitopia messaging panel, and now Rik scanned down it to see who this mentor might be. *Jean-Marie Mellie, Shawinigan, QU*— They were in the same time zone, anyway—that was convenient. And next to the lady's username, the little green dot was flashing: that meant she was online somewhere in Omnitopia. *But a female mentor? What's Angela going to think about this?*

That was when the virtual antique phone in Rik's pregame space started ringing, the signal that someone inside the game was trying to reach him. *It's probably Tom. Pissed off that I blew him off last night. Boy, wait till he hears ...* He didn't bother checking the messaging panel for ID, just picked up the phone. "Hello?"

"Hi there," said a male voice. "Is that Rik Maliani?"

"Uh, yeah." Rik sat there trying to think who the voice belonged to.

"Rik, sorry, I just saw you were online and thought I'd page you. This is Jean Mellie; I work for Omnitopia. I've been assigned to mentor you. Tell me if this is a bad time and I'll call back later. I know you must be pretty busy right now."

"Uh, no!" Rik said. "Jean, sorry, I thought—"

"I was a girl?" Jean laughed. "Happens all the time. Don't sweat it. Listen, it's good to talk to you. How're you holding up?"

"All right, I think," Rik said. "Kind of amazed."

"Makes sense." There was a pause. "Rik, I have some of your profile info, and I see you're set up for telepresence via RealFeel. So am I. You want to meet in your new space, and I'll talk you through some of the basic stuff? If you've got time right now."

"Sure. Give me a minute."

It took no more than that for Rik to shut down his office and exit into Omnitopia, this time not bothering with his normal route through Telekil, but stepping straight into that neon-lit darkness once more. A few breaths later, he heard a sound he hadn't heard here before: a doorbell. It was so prosaic that Rik laughed out loud. "Come in!"

A second later, another figure, lit by some sourceless illumination, was walking toward Rik through the darkness from underneath the "sign." It was a tall man, maybe six inches taller than Rik: big, burly, and dark-complected, with shaggy dark hair and a long face. He was wearing a hooded navy blue Omnitopia sweatshirt and jeans. As he approached, he held out a hand to Rik. "I'm Jean. Thanks for having me over!"

"Hey," Rik said, "it's your universe!"

Jean shook his head. "Our universe, maybe," he said, "but your world. Though it may not look like much at the moment." He turned to gaze up at the THIS SPACE FOR RENT sign, then back at Rik again. "So. First things first. Are you in shock?"

Rik burst out laughing. "Absolutely!"

Jean smiled a wry smile. "At least you're admitting it! Which is good. Being conscious that you're off-balance right now will keep you from making decisions about your space that you might not really want to be making yet. You have any questions you want to ask me right away before we get down to the details?"

"Uh, yeah." Rik gulped. "What happens if I screw it up?"

Jean nodded, but didn't smile. "You mean, are we going to take this space away from you if it's not an immediate success? No. The only reason we ever confiscate is if we catch somebody doing something that violates game terms and conditions after the player's got their approval to go live-and-open. Yeah, there are some real idiots out there, and crooks, and people who think we've given them a blank check to do what they like. But they don't last." He frowned. "Maybe you caught some news stories a couple months ago about the Playground scandal?"

Rik nodded. A little while ago every news source he could think of had been full of the story of some Microcosm builder who'd converted part of his 'cosm into a secret haven for pedophiles and those who, for whatever sick and twisted reason, enjoyed catering to them. It didn't seem to matter much to some of the news outlets that it was watchful Omnitopia security staff who had gotten wind of the nasty little pest-hole, shut it down, and called in the police in several countries to deal with the perpetrators. Angela in particular had been horrified, and had given Rik some trouble about "the kind of place where he was hanging out," not completely understanding that the 'cosm in question was one Rik had never even heard of, worlds away from the places he played. "Ugly situation," Rik said.

"It was. We have flying squads of people in the game who do nothing but hunt places like that down so we can eradicate them. Anyway, sure, you do get some 'cosm owners who discover that their worlds are too much work, or they just get bored with them and abandon them. But they're rare. A lot more Levelers find that their original plans weren't as workable as they thought, and they close them down to rethink or retool. Some of those relaunches are the most popular and successful Microcosms we have. You know about Mallomar?" Rik nodded: the newsfeeds had described it as "Candyland for grown-ups," the kind of place Rik felt it was probably smart for him to stay out of, as control of his weight since he got married was a hard-won thing at the best of times. "Mallomar was a *fourth* relaunch. So don't freak. There are a lot of us here to help you, and a lot of shoulders to cry on if things don't work out right the first time . . . or the second, or the third. This is a game, remember: ideally, it's supposed to be fun for you. And anyway, it's in our best interest for you to succeed, because if you make money, Omnitopia makes money."

Rik nodded.

"Okay," Jean said. "Here's how it works." Then he stopped, glancing around. "By the way," he said, "do you mind if I load in a template for the moment, while we're talking? So we don't have to stand around."

"Huh? Sure!"

"Just wanted to ask," said Jean. "This is *your* world. It's not nice to start moving the furniture around without asking permission."

A blink later, the two of them were standing in a lush tropical landscape—a high-canopied rain forest festooned with long loopy vines and many bright-colored, exotic-looking flowers. There were some odd things about it, though. Near the base of a gigantic, many-rooted tree, was a picnic table with a big blue sidesaddle sun umbrella hanging over it. There was also the creature hanging upside down from one of the branches of the huge tree. It had pointed leathery wings, clawed feet, and little round black sharklike eyes, which it fixed on Rik and Jean.

"That looks like a pterodactyl," Rik said

"It is a pterodactyl," said Jean. "Kind of. Don't look at Polly like that! He's not going to do anything. This is a conference scenario. Nothing's going to try involving you in some kind of gameplay."

"That's good," Rik said. He had annoying memories of one of the "Lost World" scenarios over in the Public Domain Macrocosm—the pterodactyls over there had been demonically assertive. "Come on," Jean said, "sit down, take it easy."

Rik sat down at the picnic table and relaxed there for a moment, just enjoying the lush and elaborate detail of the space around them. "You made this?"

"Some of it. It's a tweaked template." Jean leaned back, looking up past the vines and the trees to where sunlight flashed through the occasionally parting leaves as they moved. "A friend of mine did a rain forest. He lent me some of the terrain, and I started decorating it—hung a lot of my girlfriend's orchids all over it; she breeds them. But then it started to feel a little too domesticated, so I installed a lot of dinosaurs. Very nonstandard ones."

"I believe you," Rik said, as the pterodactyl stretched its wings out, yawned, and snapped its beak shut.

"So tell me," Jean said. "You have any idea at all what kind of game world you'd like to build?"

Rik blushed. "Absolutely none," he said.

Jean shook his head. "Don't worry about it," he said. "Lots of our new MicroLevelers don't. Even people who apply to level up and have all kinds of ideas sometimes lose them all of a sudden when they get elected. But you didn't actually apply for the program, did you?"

"No. I go to a lot of Microcosms, though."

Jean nodded. "I saw that in your record. How come?"

Rik had to think about that for a moment. "I don't know. They're just—more quirky. Maybe a little less, I don't know, *polished* than the Macrocosms. Funnier, sometimes. In fact, funnier a lot of the time." He laughed. "A long time ago I stumbled into Million Monkeys and had a lot of fun there. And I started to get, I don't know, impressed. It never occurred to me that Omnitopia would let people do *text* games in here."

Jean nodded. "Yeah, I like going there myself. I bet Shakespeare would like it too, once he got over the idea that people were writing turn-based collaborative fanfic in his universe. Hey, want a beer?"

"Sure."

"Brand?"

"Uh, Miller's fine."

Jean plucked a can of virtual Miller out of the air, handed it to Rik. Rik popped it open: Jean reached out again and produced a bottle with a label that Rik had never seen before. "Belgian," he said. "Fruit beer. Some guys in the Real-Feel sensorium design group are trying to get the taste nailed down right. I can't tell you how tired I'm getting of raspberry booze." He took a long drink, looked thoughtful. "Well, maybe not that tired. Anyway," Jean said, "here's how it goes. First thing: there are a lot of templates like this one available." He waved a hand at the rain forest around them. "There is absolutely nothing wrong with basing your first 'cosm on a template, especially since most of our templates are based on our most successful Macrocosms. What you *cannot* do is run an exact copy of a Macro. You have to vary it, in form, storyline, play style, or function, by at least ten percent. There are a lot of ways to do that math: we'll help you understand what they are, so don't make yourself crazy about it at the moment. But as regards templates, don't forget this: the more different your Microcosm is from the template you based it on, the more money you make. The percentage of your profit goes up as the divergence from the original goes up. So the more of yourself you build into your world, the more you'll take home if it takes off. *Capisce?*"

"Uh, yeah."

"Great. Now, once you're ready to start modifying your template, that's when things start to get a little complex." Jean gestured at the air.

Things around them suddenly went dark, except for bright wirelike outlines of light that described where everything—table, trees, flowers, upside-down pterodactyl—had been. "What you're seeing here," Jean said, "is a visual expression of the framework that the virtual textures and other sensory information are hung on. The framework, and the textures, and all the descriptions of the virtual space itself—stuff that determines how fast time goes by in here as compared to the real world and the other games in the Omnitopia structure—all of these are written in a subset of a programming language called ARGOT."

"Oh, God," Rik said, staring at his beer. What had a moment ago been an apparently perfectly normal can of beer, with a little foam on the top that had popped out when Rik pulled the tab, was now a delicate cylindrical wireframe in blue, silver, and gold. He sloshed it experimentally in the air, and could see, inside the shape of the can, a wireframe representation of sloshing liquid, complete right down to the little wireframe bubbles rising inside it. "Oh, no . . ."

"What's the matter?"

"I'm no good at math," Rik said. "Or languages. It's why I skipped college."

He was blushing, and ashamed to be doing so. "Rik," Jean said, "this isn't that kind of language, and unless you want to, you don't have to touch any math harder than long division. Not even that, actually." He took a drink of his own wireframe beer. "Huh," he said. "Weird. The flavor changes slightly when the texture's turned off. Your beer taste any different to you now?"

"Uh—" Rik had to look at the can and make sure of where the poptop was supposed to be. He took a drink, spent a moment tasting what he was drinking. "No," he said, "tastes the same as before."

"Okay," Jean said, putting his bottle down on the wireframe table. "Let me make a note . . ." He pulled a pen apparently out of the empty air and scribbled for a moment, apparently on the table itself. "You ask me, the beta team in Belgium's spending too much time drinking the real thing for comparison's sake, and not enough time programming the virtual stuff ... Anyway." He put down the pen of light he'd been writing with. "About the programming language. All the Microcosm templates are based on a very cut-down version of ARGOT called WannaB. It reads like English, and you work with it in paragraph-sized chunks called 'modules.' They describe everything—shapes, textures, mass and time relationships, the works. They're held together with special commands we call 'connectors,' because they're kind of like the connectors in a set of TinkerToys. It sounds, complicated right now, but I promise you that if you get interested enough to start working with them directly, you'll be able to pick up the details really fast. If you can speak English, you can work in WannaB. But don't worry about that right now, okay? Right now you should be working on the most basic concepts of what you want to build here. That boils down to just a few questions. What kind of game? What kind of time frame? How many players? What payoff at the end? And what kind of environment?"

"A lot of questions," Rik said. He suddenly felt helpless, even more confused than he'd been earlier.

"I know," Jean said. "You should have seen me the first week. I went to bed for three days and refused to get up."

Rik looked surprised. "I thought you worked for Omnitopia!"

"I wasn't working for them then," said Jean. "I was working at McDonald's. They fired me." He smiled.

"Wow," Rik said, and examined his beer can again.

"Whoops, sorry," Jean said. Suddenly the normal landscape—if that was the word for it—came back. Rik had a long drink of his beer, and then noticed that a shadow had fallen over him. He glanced up and saw that the pterodactyl was eyeing his beer can.

"He eats them," Jean said. "All the dinos here do. It keeps the place clean ... So Rik, just be clear about this: you don't have to program your 'cosm from scratch. You can go completely modular. There are thousands of free basic modules available: you plug them into your basic design, altering specific kinds of terrain, or textures or shapes or timeflow or other characteristics of your space and behaviors of your characters. Or you can use game gold to buy modules from other players. There are forums and groups where players pool their talents to produce co-op modules, and then pay each other off in the various kinds of game value, or else thrash out sub-royalty agreements with each other. If you like, you can even commission other MicroLevelers to produce modules for you, though that can get expensive."

Jean finished his beer, threw the bottle in the air. The pterodactyl dropped off the limb from which it had been hanging, swooped down, and grabbed the bottle in mid-air, then flew off with it, crunching loudly. "So think about what you want to see here. There's a checklist in the info pack that came to you in the e-mail. What landscapes do you love most—or hate most? Where would you really love to live—or never want to? What kind of game do you like playing the most? Do you ever get the urge to rewrite history—and if so, which part?"

"Alternate histories," Rik said softly.

"A very popular theme," Jean said. "There are hundreds and hundreds of Microcosms built along those lines. Doesn't have to be a huge swath of history, either. Ask yourself a single 'what if?' question and build from that. We have medieval scenarios with tanks and machine guns. Roman Empires based in North America. A golden age of Spanish exploration that went sideways and established the kingdom of New Spain in California after Europe was destroyed by a series of massive earthquakes. Vikings in Manhattan, rain forests in Antarctica after the Earth's poles flip."

Rik sat there for a moment thinking about some of the classic tales he'd read when he was a kid, in ancient tattered pulp novels that his dad had given him. "The Hollow Earth," he said.

"Got a few of those already," said Jean. "Not that the theme's overdone. Two of the present ones are comic-book based, licensed in Omnitopia by permission of the copyright owners. One's based on Verne. But if you can bring something new and interesting to the concept, there's always room for more. Always assuming you can get people to come and play in it."

That was the part that had been freaking Rik out. "Marketing," he moaned. "I don't know if I'm cut out for this."

"I knew *I* wasn't," Jean said, "and look at me now. I got into designing custom weather. Now I license it to other Levelers." He glanced around him at the rain forest. Overhead, the sky was darkening. He smiled. "Rainstorm coming through," he said. "Watch this."

"Uh—" Rik looked up at the clouds. "Shouldn't we move?"

Jean waved at him to sit still. "Wait."

The trees above them stirred: a rush of wind that sounded like the whole rain forest taking a deep breath went through them. Then the rain came down—not gradually, but all of a sudden, all at once, like a solid thing. It soaked everything but Rik and Jean, even though they weren't under the umbrella. Thunder roared overhead, lightning cracked the leaf-fragmented sky above the trees from side to side, strobe-freezing every falling raindrop into a streak of liquid fire, then vanishing again. But miraculously Rik and Jean remained unaffected. The rain hammered on a dome shape that hovered over each of them like an invisible umbrella, and Jean leaned back, looking up into the rain with great satisfaction. "Terrain is easy," he said. "Water is hard—so to speak. I was always a screen-porch sitter. Love to watch it rain. Hate to get wet. Now I never have to. I've built myself a screen porch the size of a world."

"With recycling pterodactyls," Rik said.

Jean grinned. "Recycling is important. And we all have to eat."

The rain passed. Under the shadows of the trees, Jean's pterodactyl came flapping heavily back, soared upward over their heads, seized the branch above them in its talons, and swung around to hang upside down again. "Rik, I'd stay," Jean said, "but I have about twelve other people I have to be helping out today. So let me get going. I've passed you the linkname of the O-space where you can go browse some different templates, since I doubt you want to have Polly-Wanna-Beer-Can here hanging over your shoulder all day. You've got my username and my e-mail address: message me when I'm in-world, or mail me if you have any questions, and I'll get to you just as soon as I can. Usually within an hour or so, if I'm on shift." He grinned again. "Sometimes quicker, if I'm not. My girlfriend says I have no life."

Rik wondered if Angela was about to start saying that about him. *But maybe she won't mind so much when the first check arrives.* "One question before you go?" he said.

"Sure."

Rik shook his head. "I keep asking myself, why me?"

Jean looked thoughtful. "That part of your records isn't open to me," he said. "But I can make an educated guess. Probably a combination of two factors: your 'cosm visitation habits, and your general karma in the game. Somebody up in the supervisory structures caught sight of you during some random audit, liked the way you carry yourself in the game, and said to somebody else, 'That's the kind of person we want as a MicroLeveler. Let's see if he's game.' And so you got knighted." Jean smiled.

Rik thought about that. "I wonder. I met kind of a Clueless Noob type just before I went through the Ring . . ."

"He could possibly have been a 'hall monitor,'" Jean said. "There are a lot of them out there, awarding people points for good behavior. But it could also have simply been an automated Random Acts of Kindness update to your karma. The game's structure is very semantically sensitive. You might have gotten just that extra bit of good karma you needed to kick you over the really-nice-guy threshold before you passed the Ring."

"I wasn't all *that* nice—"

Jean shook his head. "You wouldn't have to have been. What happened to you is a result of cumulative behavior. And don't forget, it works both ways. There are people who apply over and over again to be MicroLevelers, people who're really hot for it, and they always get turned down because their karma's not right."

"Yeah, I've heard about that."

"Anyway, there are about fifty other people who got the accolade yesterday," Jean said, getting up, "and I have to talk to at least ten of them before I go off shift. So start going over that checklist! I'll be back in touch with you in a few days. Or wave me off if you're not ready, and I'll check on you in a week. Whenever. This is *your* world."

He held out a hand; they shook again. "Thanks!" Rik said.

Jean waved, vanished. The template went out too, leaving only the glowing words hanging in the air again.

Rik stood there for a few more moments, thinking, *I should have asked him to leave the table.* But then he thought, *Naah! I'll get one of my own.*

Rik activated the in-game control that put him back in his virtual office again. The phone was ringing: he picked it up. "Hello?"

"Where the heck were you yesterday?" his friend Tom's voice said. "We missed you! Angela crack down on you all of a sudden?"

Rik laughed. "No," he said. "Nothing like that. But something came up. When can we reschedule?"

"We're all gonna be back in tonight," Tom said. "An hour later than yesterday. One of Barbara's kids cracked a tooth on the front steps; she has to take him to the dentist first."

"You're on," Rik said.

"What is it?" Tom said, sounding a little suspicious. "Seriously, has something happened? You sound weird."

Rik's office "doorbell" rang, or rather buzzed. It was an audio cue that he'd built into his space that would go off when Angela texted or e-mailed him that she needed his attention. "I'm fine," Rik said, "but that's Herself buzzing. She mentioned she wanted to get some shopping done today."

"It's always something," Tom said. "No problem. We'll see you tonight!"

"Will do," Rik said. "Best to Marsha."

"Right. See you."

Rik hung up, glancing around the office before killing his RealFeel link to Omnitopia. *The Hollow Earth,* he thought. Suddenly he could just see it in his head. The strange, concave landscape arching up around him in all directions, the bizarre little sun hanging in midair, in the center of everything. Mammoths, dinosaurs ... *But no,* he thought. *Those were in Verne. Bring something different to the table.*

Rik put the dreams on hold and killed the link, vanishing. *But not for too long!*

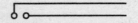

Outside the huge floor-to-ceiling plate glass windows, the Sixth Avenue traffic was pouring past as usual, and the sidewalks just outside were full of the normal crush of midtown Manhattan lunchtime pedestrian traffic. But the sidewalk traffic was moving a lot more slowly than normal due to all the people who'd pushed up against the glass to stare in at the TV lights and strobe flashes illuminating the brightly decorated, neon-lit acreage inside.

The whole front half of the huge ground-floor display space was crammed with hundreds of people—disproportionately teenage and male—crowded around neon-decorated fixtures that incorporated gaming control consoles and wide-screen plasma displays. High over their heads, completely ignored, hung slowly rotating neon-and-strobe signs declaring INFINITE WORLDS — *MAKE THEM YOURS!* Here and there some local TV station's camera crew tried desperately to push through the crowds around the gaming console, but they were making slow work of it: potential players were stacked six deep around the consoles, each one waiting for the five minute play-period that they'd been allotted on making it in through the front doors. Outside, the line went halfway around a long Manhattan block, and no one who'd made it in this far was going to take the chance of moving an inch and losing their chance to be one of the first to get his (or occasionally her) hands on the game. Thumping rock music blared over everything, even its insistent *now!now!now!now!* beat almost drowned out by the shouts of the game players as they hammered at the controllers, lost in the furious excitement of mortal combat in a brand-new world.

Past the triple line of game consoles, a wide cordon of gaudy advertising flats fronted by goodie bag tables and booth babes stretched from one side of the space to the other. In the middle of the cordon was a gap guarded by a platoon of intimidating black-clad bouncer types, most standing in faux-Secret-Service at-rest poses while a couple of their number checked press passes and hologrammed invitations and waved the fortunate few through. On the far side of the cordon there was a little more room to move and breathe. More camera crews and representatives of the print and electronic press, along with various B- and C-list celebrities, jostled for access to the bars on either side and the tables with swag bags that contained merchandise more valuable than the advertising-laden "nickel bags" being laid out for the fans in front. The contents of most of those bags—for the early possession of which the fans out front would probably have committed any number of misdemeanors—would be for sale on eBay within hours, and the host of the party knew this and didn't care. It would be great publicity that was what counted. *And thank God this is almost over.*

At the back of the exhibition space, beyond the bars, behind a velvet rope and another line of bouncers, was a dais backed with more plasma screen and holographic signage repeating again and again the trademark violet Mobius-infinity symbol, rotating serenely once every two seconds on every screen. On the dais, the last crowd of press people who would be granted admission were shouting questions, and flashes were going off with near rock-concert frequency in the face of the tall, husky, dark-haired, smiling man with his arm around the shoulders of a cardboard stand-up of himself holding a copy of the *Infinite Worlds: Threefold* game package.

"Mr. Sorensen! Mr. Sorensen!"

"Phil! This way, please, Phil!"

"How many DVD units do you expect to move this weekend, Mr. Sorensen?"

"In excess of five hundred thousand. Give or take one or two—"

"What about downloads?"

"It's hard to tell, but the projections suggest somewhere in the neighborhood of three million."

"Will you break Omnitopia's record?"

Phil chuckled. "The question is, can they match ours?" he said. "We've got a tried and tested gaming platform that eight out of ten gamers say they prefer to less structured and more unpredictable forms of gameplay. Of course dedicated gamers want something new and exciting. But they also want a robust platform that they can depend on, and a game at an affordable price point, not one that's had its buy-in costs inflated by some executive's desire for the world's most advanced filing system." Phil paused for a breath and got the laugh he was waiting for. "Serious gamers want to buy *games*— not vaporware, not research that may never pay off. And they want to know that they're going to *get* what they think they're paying for! That's what Infinite Worlds is all about. This Threefold expansion gives them the chance to have their virtual cake and eat it too— new play modalities in a landscape that's both familiar and all new, with a rock-solid game engine and dependable server structures worldwide. When other so-called innovations have gone the way of the dodo, Infinite Worlds will still be here, always growing, but always giving the world's most loyal gamers what they expect from Infinity Inc.— affordable action!"

More questions were shouted, and Phil kept answering them, smile in place— all but the one that one ill-advised reporter kept repeating: "Do you have a statement regarding the rumor that you're trying to bury the hatchet with Dev Logan and merge with Omnitopia?" Phil simply ignored that the first couple of times; but after the third repetition, he glanced off to one side, where Deirdre, his PR chief, was standing, and put one hand casually in his pocket. She instantly turned to quietly give the high sign to the stage manager and the bouncers that this final press access of the day was over. One of the bouncers immediately unhooked the velvet rope as Deirdre came over to Phil and said, "Mr. Sorensen, your four-thirty—"

"I know, Deirdre. Thanks. Sorry, folks, we're done. Thank you, everybody," Phil said, turned his back on the press, and made his way toward the back of the dais.

His own security people were waiting for him there, four large dark-suited and Ray-Banned gentlemen who surrounded him and walked him out of the back of the Infinity Inc. store's display space, past a jumble of temporarily stored display flats and shelving, then out to the utility entrance behind the building. His limo stood under the carport, its door open. He got in and pulled out his PDA as the door was closed, flipped its lid open, and brought up Reuters Financial to see what his stock was doing.

He swore as the limo's other door opened and Deirdre got in. The door was closed for her, and she put on her seat belt and said nothing as the car started up.

Phil exhaled. "Well?" he said.

"Well what, Mr. Sorensen?"

Her tone was defensive, as well it might have been. "Sorry," he said. "Not your fault. Who was that?"

"The reporter who kept asking about Omnitopia? I don't know."

"Find out."

"I will. Whoever he is, we won't be credentialing him again. I'll see who in my department gave him a pass and make sure they tighten up their requirements." Her mouth was set tight: an uneasy, unattractive look on what was usually such an untroubled face. "He was probably just some blogger . . ."

"It doesn't matter," Phil said as the limo pulled away from the building. "What I'm interested in is the source of the rumor. It's information that could be useful. See what you can find out."

"Of course, Mr. Sorensen."

He sighed and leaned back against the cushions as the limo turned onto Fifty-fifth Street. Phil gazed out the selectively polarizing smart glass windows at the traffic and the buildings, at the curious faces gazing at the limo's windows (ebony dark to them) and wondering *Is that somebody important?* It was only a few minutes' drive to the building that housed Phil's corporate offices, but all the while he could feel Deirdre getting more tense. "Listen, Deirdre—"

"I should have stopped him," she said. "I'm sorry."

"If it hadn't been that guy, it would've been someone else," Phil said. "You heard someone mention Omnitopia just a few moments before he did. This is the press we're talking about. If they can't find a fight, they'll manufacture one. It's their job. Peaceful relations between competitors don't sell any papers."

His PR chief said nothing for a moment, pretending to be distracted by the horn of a cab changing lanes and veering too close to the limo; and her tension in no way ebbed. "You're right, of course," Deirdre said, as the limo pulled up in front of Infinity Inc.'s New York headquarters.

Phil said nothing. The security guy riding shotgun got out and opened Deirdre's door. "Thank you," Phil said. "Listen, call my PA in the morning and let's make some time to look over the schedule for the next few days. I'm going to want to make some changes."

"Of course, Mr. Sorensen. Have a good evening."

The door closed. The security man got in again, shut his own door, and the limo started up. "Hartnell and Wise, sir?" the driver said over the speaker.

"That's right."

The car purred through the early rush hour traffic, stopping, starting again, turning for the journey crosstown. Phil stretched against the cushions, pulled out his PDA again, checked his stock one more time. *IICC now down four points.*

He frowned, put the PDA away, and—having nothing better to do—pondered Deirdre's uncharacteristic nervousness. After a little while, the answer came to him. *She was freaked because what happened there would normally have made me go ballistic when we were away from the cameras. And this time it didn't.*

Phil smiled—a smile that the people he worked with would normally have found most disquieting. Deirdre had no way of knowing that there was about to be a big change in her boss' attitude toward Omnitopia—bigger than almost anyone who worked closely with him at Infinity Inc. would have believed possible. *So much is going to change. And when it does, the annoying questions are going to stop at last.*

The midtown traffic now left Phil a good few minutes to contemplate, with increasing pleasure, what that was going to feel like. Finally the limo slid up to the curb and stopped. The security guard got out and opened his door. Phil stepped out in front of a Park Avenue address that looked much like its neighbors to either side: a discreet white limestone edifice four stories high with a gilt-and-iron gate protecting a beautiful beaux arts walnut door. As he crossed the sidewalk, the inner door swung open, and the gate buzzed and unlatched.

Inside the door waiting for him was the handsome silver-haired assistant who managed the outer office of Hartnell and Wise. "Miss Wise is waiting for you, sir," she said, and led the way up the marble staircase to the office at the top of the landing.

The assistant opened the door for him and stood aside to let Phil step into Morgan Wise's office. Normally in a brokerage of this age and exclusivity, the partners' offices tried to suggest a tradition of discretion and reliability by affecting a lot of leather and heavy wood paneling. But this space was light, bright, and nearly bare: white-walled, floored in blond wood, with one white desk, a single under-stated chrome-and-rattan Eames chair on each side of it, and a single white flat screen monitor standing on the desk.

Morgan Wise was standing behind the desk waiting for him: tall, slim, her shoulder-length dark hair swinging free above the jacket of a dark-skirted suit. She reached out across the desk to shake his hand as always, then sat down again while the silver-haired office assistant shut the door. "So," Morgan said in that soft, sultry voice that always made Phil think she would do well as a late-night radio host if she ever wearied of working the markets. "You have some news for me?"

Phil nodded. "The timings have come through," he said.

Morgan tapped the desk briefly and a keyboard appeared in its surface. "Is the date still the same?"

"Yes."

More tapping; then she looked up. "So?"

Phil pulled a piece of note paper out of his inside jacket pocket, handed it across the desk to her. Morgan looked closely at it and tapped again at the keyboard, pausing once or twice to check the figures written on the note. "All right," she said, pushing the note back to Phil. "I'll have my silent colleagues in the Far East start bracketing our shell companies' buy orders around those times. After that—" She folded her hands above the keyboard, rested her chin on them. "I think the twenty-first is going to be a very busy day for you. Because in the wake of the day's events, I'd say you could be majority stockholder by . . ." She studied her monitor for a moment. "Let's say midnight."

Phil smiled. "That's when their rollout party is supposed to start," he said softly. "Won't it be interesting if the company has a new owner by midnight their time?"

Morgan smiled. "We'll see how it goes," she said. "But if the share price reacts as emphatically to what's about to happen as our calculations suggest, it could happen even sooner. All we can do now is wait." She arched one eyebrow. "Always the hardest part."

She stood up. So did Phil. "You can always pass the time by thinking about your commission," he said.

"Please," Morgan said. "Some things one does for art's sake."

Phil smiled, shook her hand again, and headed for the door.

It opened before him: the silver-haired assistant showed him down the stairs. As he swung the gate to the sidewalk open and the beaux arts door shut at his back, Phil began to hum, and as the limo door was opened for him and he slipped in, he started to sing softly.

"The party's oooooooverrrrr . . ."

And the limo door closed.

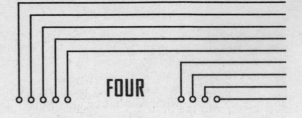

FOUR

IN A CIRCULAR ROOM directly under the pointed tower-roof of Castle Dev, the circular table of inlaid black ironwood was being prepped for a meeting. Pads were being laid out, bottles of mineral water fresh from the cooler set out with glasses and napkins, laptops brought in and set down at the places where their owners would sit. But out in the sunshine, half a mile away, a man on a black bike was pedaling slowly down a nearby path, thinking hard.

His phone rang, its ringtone singing a music-box version of "Hail to the Chief." Dev sighed, braked, and hopped off the bike, walking it off the path onto the grass under a nearby tree and then letting it lean against him while he fished the phone out of his pocket. From about fifty feet farther back along the path, Dev heard the sound of badly smothered laughter. He glanced that way and saw a couple of his employees, one male and one female, watching him as they approached. The lady was talking to someone on her own cell phone, while the guy was texting someone at high speed. The phone-talker grinned at him as they got closer; the texter looked up and smiled too.

Dev rolled his eyes at them and tried to scowl, but he wasn't really in a scowling mood at the moment and besides, they knew the joke. As he flipped his phone open, Phone Girl and Text Guy passed by. Phone Girl waved, Text Guy saluted snappily. Dev nodded, waved back, turned away. "Hi, Dad . . ."

"Morning, Son," said Joseph Logan's gravelly voice. "What the devil's that noise?"

"Noise?" Dev said. He stared around him, trying to see what his father was talking about.

"That screeching!"

"What screeching? I can't—" Then, in the tree above him, he located it. "Oh. It's one of those jaybirds," Dev said, peering up into the branches but unable to see anything: the birds in question were famously shy. "The beige and gray guys that keep wrecking your feeder."

"Nonsense. Thing sounds like one of those birds you always hear screaming in nature movies. You should get rid of them, they're probably dangerous."

"Those are red-tailed hawks, Dad," Dev said. "The TV people use that sound effect for every bird except the Bluebird of Happiness. If there *were* hawks here, we couldn't get rid of them, they're protected. Anyway, these are jays, and I can't do anything about them. It's their nesting season, and they're protected too. Was there a reason for this call *besides* you trying to save me from the local wildlife?"

"I was worried about you," said Dev's dad. "Your stock is down."

Dev rolled his eyes. His father might actually be worried about him, but the reasons would be far more complex than anything merely related to the antics of the stock market. "Jim says we'll be fine. We're hoping to hit a thousand by rollout day."

The two statements were independently true, but Dev was hoping his father would take them as interrelated—that might buy him a few moments' peace. But this was a futile hope. "Not that I don't like Jim," Dev's dad said, and Dev thought, *Bzzt! Five points off for fibbing!*—"but he's still kind of wet behind the ears at the corporate finance game—" *Bzzt! Wall Street Journal's CFO of the Year!*"—and I'm a little worried about your exposure when you have all these conglomerates sniffing around your coattails and acquiring your shares on the sly. If you—"

"Dad," Dev said, "before you get started, I know exactly what you're thinking about, and it's well nigh impossible for CapCities to do *anything* on the sly. They have as much on their plates and as many people staring at them right now as I do. CapCities wants to buy Shanghai Welter but can't do it because they don't have enough liquidity because of the jump Shanghai took on the NASDAQ last month. So CapCities has been strutting around the markets acting big for the past couple of weeks while they liquidize some of their other assets to cover their shortfall—" Dev heard his dad drawing breath to interrupt him, but he forcibly overrode his own politeness reflex and kept right on going. "And since our rollout's coming up and we're big in the news right now, it serves their purpose to pick up a little of our stock and make some smaller companies think *Wow, look at that, I bet they're thinking about acquiring a controlling stake in Omnitopia! I bet they'll want some smaller stuff, too, let's divest ourselves all over them!* And Cap'll pick up some of those little guys like Andorra Electronics and Delta V Broadcasting to cover the divisions they're going to divest, which they've been looking for an excuse to get rid of for months. Then about two days after we roll out, they'll say, *Sorry, your figures weren't quite what we were expecting after all,* which will be true—they'll be bigger, but never mind—and afterward CapCities will go off and buy Shanghai the way they wanted to, and everything will be fine. When it's all over, I'll send you the clippings."

There was a brief silence. *Maybe the clippings thing was taking it a little too far,* Dev thought. The silence stretched. Finally his dad said, "The only reason you know all that is because Jim told you."

Absolutely right, Dev thought, *and that's why you're pissed—you didn't get to tell me first. Which it's not your job to do. Why do we have to have this same conversation every day with different words?* "That's what he's paid for," Dev said. "And he's one of the best in the business, or at least that's the delusion that the *Wall Street Journal* has at the moment. So you relax, because Jim and I have it set up so that it's gonna be easier for somebody to obtain a controlling stake in the moon than in Omnitopia. Meanwhile, where's Mom? She said she was going to call yesterday evening, but I thought maybe she got busy."

"She's in the hospital," his dad said, with what sounded to Dev like barely concealed triumph.

"What?"

"For tests. Her back was acting up again."

"Oh, God," Dev said. "Do you know when's she going to be out?"

"This afternoon. And you'd know, too, if you'd just concentrate a little more on staying in touch with her instead of playing the high and mighty corporate executive—"

*Which I couldn't play hard enough for you five minutes ago. I just can*not *win, can I?* "This afternoon?" Dev said. "When did she go in?"

"This morning—"

"So she's not *in* the hospital, she's *at* the hospital. At the clinic—"

"Oh, well, if you're going to play semantics games with me—"

"Games are what it's all about, Dad," Dev said, in a voice intended to sound carelessly cheerful. If it was vengeance for his father trying to throw a fright into Dev over something relatively minor, at least it was a petty vengeance. "Who taught me to play hard? And speaking of games, you still haven't RSVP'd for the big switch-throwing ceremony."

"Uh," his father said. "Well, I don't know, it depends on your mom. If she doesn't feel like going—"

"I understand completely," Dev said. "Try to let me know by tomorrow night, okay? Otherwise I'm going to have to give your VIP seat to some minor head of state, and they'll brag about it afterward, and then I'll have to buy their country to put them in their place. It'd put a dent in *my* liquidity, and we can't have that, can we? Gotta go now. Bye-bye."

Dev punched the off button, and just stood there for a moment looking at his phone. Then he swore under his breath. *Why do we always have to be doing this to each other?* He thought. *I know he loves me but he has such* strange *ways of showing it.* Dev had trouble remembering any time in his life when the two of them hadn't been at each other's throats about something: when he first caught the gaming bug from his mom as a child, when he ditched his (dad-pleasing but ultimately unsatisfying) English lit degree program at Penn State to go study computer science at MIT, when he went on to finance his degree independently after his dad refused to pay for it . . . Endless introspection on the subject and one interesting but inconclusive bout of analysis had left Dev with plenty of theories about The Dad Thing, but no certainty. *Are we just two control freaks banging heads? Or is this a liberal-arts-versus-science argument?* Dev's dad's three degrees were all in the humanities, and his retirement from his emeritus professorship at Penn, though often threatened, never quite seemed ready to happen. *Or are we just having some kind of sublimated town-and-gown fight?* This was Dev's favorite theory at the moment, since his huge financial success had taken none of the edge off his relationship with his father, and had for some time made it rather worse. Now his dad's routine anger seemed generally to be shifting into what read as angry pride. *Who knows, maybe it'll just be pride someday. . . .*

Naaaah.

He sighed and speed-dialed his mom, hoping she was someplace where she could take the call. After only two rings, she answered. "Dev, honey!"

"Mom, are you okay? I'm so sorry, I should have called you when you didn't get back to me!"

"Oh, you silly boy, don't beat yourself up, I'm fine."

"Mom, people in the hospital are not fine! By definition! What's wrong? Is there a problem with the implant?" His mom had had a synthetic disk replacement a couple of months previously, swapping in a liquid-filled implant for a lumbar disk crushed in an old skiing injury.

"Stop fussing, it's not serious. They may need to put a little more silicone or whatever into the implant, that's all. They've got me scheduled for a scan tomorrow morning, and then they'll stick a needle in the little valve or whatever and pump the thing up if they have to."

Her tone put him more at ease than anything specific she was saying. He could just see her, silver-haired, petite but regal, those gray eyes glinting as she lounged in some clinic chair at ASU, making the place look as if it had been suddenly taken over by a small but impeccably dressed reigning queen on her day off. "Okay," Dev said. "I'll stop worrying, then."

There was a second's pause. "I know that voice. You just got off the phone with Daddy."

"Uh, yeah."

His mom chuckled, though it was a rueful sound. "More needles. What day would be complete without you two sticking a few into each other? He's just worried about the rollout, honey."

"So worried he hasn't RSVP'd yet."

"You let me handle him," Dev's mom said. "We'll be there. But it's just another needle, Devvie, this making you wait."

"Yeah, well, I really prefer his aggressive to his passive, Mom."

"So do I, but we don't always get to choose. Dev, don't you have somewhere to be right now? You must be up to your eyeballs in meetings."

He glanced at the phone's clock. "Yeah, they'll be waiting for me up in the Tower. You sure you're okay?"

"I'm not in any pain, if that's what you mean. I had a long day out yesterday, and it was bothering me then. I took an aspirin last night and it was fine. But they warned me not to ignore little twinges while the implant was bedding in, so I'm being careful. I'll be home in a few hours. You go get on with your life!"

"Yes, ma'am."

"That's what I like to hear," his mom said. "Unquestioning obedience."

Dev raised his eyebrows, for he could think of no lie more outrageous that might come out of his mother. Bella Maria Logan née DiVincenzo was a rebel at heart and appreciated rebellion in others, which was probably the only reason Dev and his father were still talking to each other at all. "Yeah, right," he said. "Call me when you get home, okay?"

"Will do."

"Ciao Bella!"

"Knock 'em dead, Devvie," she said, and hung up.

Dev put the phone away, then walked his bike back to the path and got on. As he started pedaling, the phone rang again.

"Don't answer it, Boss!" said a voice from behind him.

"Yeah, yeah," Dev said as another of his employees, a buxom middle-aged Asian woman, passed him on a pink bike, wagging a warning finger at him. The phone kept ringing, then finally stopped, the call diverting to his PA's office. Sometimes Dev suspected his people of having some kind of campus-wide warning system, so that e-mails or IMs or texts flew around campus whenever he was heading from one building to another: HE'S ON THE MOVE, DON'T LET HIM ANSWER THAT PHONE! For it was widely known that Dev couldn't ride his bike and talk on the phone at the same time: he invariably fell off. The joke, though, suited him. In fact, he'd encouraged its spread. It meant that there was at least an hour or so each day—if divided into many small pieces—when Dev didn't have to take phone calls from anybody. *If I'd known when we went public how much quiet time I was going to lose every day, I might never have done it.* But it was too late now. At least he had these precious moments, out in the sunshine or under his trees, when he could take a breath and just think—or *not* think. Dev knew that some people, not all of them his employees, thought he was eccentric—a local variation on the "bicycling royalty" of Europe—or else just calculating, trying to look homespun or nonelitist. He was happy enough to let them think that, but under no circumstance, unless he had a guest with him or the weather was genuinely foul, would he allow himself to be wrestled into a golf cart and a position where he would have to answer the phone.

On cue, the miserable thing rang again. The ring wasn't a personalized one, so Dev ignored it and pedaled on around the drive that led to the formal front entrance of Castle Dev, a wider and more overstated version of the back gate he'd left by in the morning. He rode his bike over the bridge, hopped off in front of the gate's archway, and walked it through, over to the long, canopied bike rack off to his right. As usual, there was an empty spot at the far end: he shoved the bike into it, pushed the kickstand down, and headed for the foot of the office tower.

It was actually one of seven towers—the six lesser ones

were only a story and a half higher than the corners of the building. The general effect of Castle Dev was as if someone in Renaissance Spain had seen a French chateau and decided to restate it hexagonally in golden stone, cream or ruddy plaster, and red tile. The central courtyard with its fountain and the arched, arcaded cloister spaces around it suggested that the architect had been suckered in by Moorish influences as well. Flowery vines and rosebushes clambered up the interior walls, softening the impact of the windows that overlooked the courtyard; the fountain, in full flow now that the workday was well under way, sprayed glitter high into the air. Across from the fountain and butted up against the opposite wall of the compound, the main office tower—a reworking of the castle keep concept—reached up six stories to the circular course of polarized glass that made it look as if the pointed tiled cap of the tower was floating unsupported in the air. Up there Dev could just catch sight of a few figures moving in the meeting room space. One silhouette came over to stand at the window, gazing down into the courtyard, then raised a hand.

Dev grinned and headed in through the archway at the tower's foot. The security guy in his small outdoor-duty cubicle nodded to Dev and buzzed him through.

Dev turned left through the door and got into the glass elevator, ascending through the lower rooms—his main in-house office, the game room above it, the media support level for the rooms above and below—and then, finally, the conference room with its charcoal carpet, three hundred sixty degree view, round ironwood table with its eight chairs, and—most important—the people who went with the chairs.

Typically, none of the people were *in* any of the chairs. Natasha Bielefeld, tall, elegant in yet another of her beautifully tailored skirt suits, her precision cornrows half hidden under a Hermès scarf, was standing over by the freeway side of the window, laughing one of her patented slow deep laughs at something Tau Vitoria had just said. But this was their normal configuration. Though it had been a good while since Natasha handed over her old duties as chief server engineer to Tau and became Dev's vice president of operations, Tash was still a hardware geek under the skin. Whenever they were in the same space with Dev, she and Tau always wound up telling each other hardware horror stories whenever they weren't speaking exclusively in ARGOT. Tau looked like his normal self: splashy shirt, tidy jeans, extremely expensive shoes, and those chiseled dark southern Slavic good looks, moderated by a touch of designer stubble and a tendency to sudden goofy expressions that wouldn't have looked out of place on a cartoon character.

Tash and Tau were at twelve o'clock in the room. At about ten thirty, little Doris te Nawhara, in slacks and T-shirt—the inevitable reaction to the lawyer clothes in which she spent most of her away time as Omnitopia's chief counsel and head of legal affairs—was waving her arms in apparent exasperation as she told Alicia Chang, Dev's lead concept artist, and young Ron Ruis, his blond, thin, and slightly hyperactive chief environmental artist, what was almost certainly yet another outrageous dumb-litigant story (of which Doris seemed to have thousands). At nine o'clock, drinking coffee and looking idly down from the window at something going on near the back gate, was tall thin Cleolinda Nash, Dev's head of client engineering, who was responsible for the general look and feel of Omnitopia as a whole. She was wearing dark jeans, soft suede boots, a faded navy blue first-generation Omnitopia hoodie and a weary look. And opposite her, at approximately three o'clock, was the figure who had seen Dev coming: Jim Margoulies. Dev glanced at Jim now and found it strange, as he sometimes had at other such meetings, that they were both standing in this extremely grown-up and luxurious place full of fancy machinery, both overt and hidden, and that they were *not* six, or twelve, and wouldn't get chased out if they were caught here. It was routinely a shock to look at his lifelong best friend and realize that somehow he was now as tall as Dev—bizarre, as he had been shorter until almost college—and was wearing a suit, and bifocals, and even going stylishly gray at the temples. *When did we grow up? It's so strange. But aren't we lucky? We can still play . . .*

The sound of the elevator doors brought everybody else's attention around. "Hey, guys!" Dev said and went around to exchange hugs and greetings with Alicia and Cleo and Doris, who he hadn't seen in the flesh for some days, or in Doris' case, nearly two weeks.

"Busy time, Dev," Doris said, looking him over carefully. "And going to get busier. You all right? You look thinner."

"Yeah, I wouldn't be surprised if I've dropped a few," Dev said.

"I have a message for you from Mirabel," Jim said, bringing Dev a cup of coffee. "She just texted me. It said, 'Tell him to beware the sandwich of doom.' This mean anything to you?"

"That my life's in danger again," Dev said, taking a slurp of the coffee. "Or still. In other news, your favorite 'niece' is demanding an audience with you."

Cleolinda chuckled. "The consummate financier," she said. "Always following the money . . ."

Jim looked shocked. "I thought it was my heart of gold and boyish good looks!"

General jeering and snickering ensued. "Actually," Dev said, "it was the dollhouse you gave her last Christmas. And the way you got your head stuck in it while you were working on the upstairs bathroom."

Jim gave Dev a look. "I seem to remember you standing there while I was stuck and doing nothing about it, too," he said. "That was a laugh riot. Remind me to punch you in the head."

"That approach never got you far when we were ten," Dev said. "But I'll schedule it if you insist. Have Pammie call Frank."

More snickering. Dev sat down in his usual spot at the table, on the freeway side of the room. "Okay," he said. "Let's get ourselves sorted out. We've got a lot to talk about."

The group sat down, pulled out paperwork, opened laptops, reached for notepads. One of Dev's various office laptops, all of them identical and tasked to keep themselves so, was waiting for him at his place. He popped the lid and waited for the machine to come out of sleep mode while glancing around at the friends who'd followed him from the collapse of the company he'd originally formed with Phil Sorenson seven years ago. From the ashes of that nasty and uncomfortable breakup, they'd helped Dev put together the new start-up that launched Omnitopia's immediate predecessor. It had been a shaky start. But from a very small group with limited money but big dreams, they had since grown into a power to be reckoned with, first in the gaming world, then in the corporate landscape. It was always heartening to Dev that, so far at least, his core group's tightly interlocking friendships had been sufficient to keep them all both close and effective in the face of ever-increasing challenges. It was a shame, though, that the necessities of running a worldwide business made these physical conclaves so much less frequent than they used to be. Dev and the Seven were never out of touch, but with all of them jetting all over the planet to keep an eye on things, there was little chance for everyone to get together in the same place except at quarterly corporate assessment and planning meetings—and occasionally at times like this when there was a major change coming in the game, or some kind of crisis. *Yet here they all are, chatting away as if they'd last been around this table just yesterday.*

He turned his attention back to his laptop, tapping at it until the magazine-length document that passed for his to-do list came up. "Okay," Dev said. "Let's deal with the reality-based world first. Who's got the most important thing?"

"Besides your sandwich?" Jim said.

Dev rolled his eyes. "Besides that."

"Well," Natasha said. "How about the massive online attack scheduled for between twenty-four and forty-eight hours from now that's intended to crash the game, destroy our credibility worldwide, and steal a hundred million dollars of our money?"

Dev gave Tash a resigned look. If she wasn't a drama queen *per se*, she was at least high up in the line of succession. "Yeah," he said, "let's talk a little about that. Anything new since your note the other morning?"

Natasha leaned on one elbow, picking at the keyboard of

her laptop with one hand, and shook her head. "All of you networked in? Here's what we've got." She looked around at the others. "Briefly: in-game security has been working this problem for most of a month now. Around the time we announced the hard launch dates for the rollout of the new expansion, the chatter level about Omnitopia on the major phreaker and hacker sites worldwide started going up. Lots of the—for lack of a better word, let's call them people—on those sites started suggesting to each other that the period when we would be migrating the game software and ancillary routines to the new servers would be a great time to attack us, if they could just figure out exactly when the move was going to happen."

Tash looked up from her laptop, scowling. "Those interested in attempting this kind of attack would know that the migration needs to be complete by at least a day or two before the hard launch. There's no way any company in our situation would try to deploy a new version and sign up possibly millions of new users without actually having the new servers up and running. The hard copies of the games go on sale in the stores at midnight oh one on the twenty-first. That's been public knowledge for months. What everybody around this table now knows, and what the naughty people out in the hacking community don't know, is that most of the migration has already happened and that its most crucial phase is scheduled to begin tonight at nineteen fourteen local time, or oh three fourteen Zulu. That being the latest some of us could get it moved to." She gave Tau a look.

"And the soonest I can guarantee it'll go off without a hitch," Tau said. "Which is something of an issue."

Tash dropped her gaze to her laptop again in a way that somehow managed to imply that such a delay was something that never would have happened on *her* watch. "Testing will occupy another twenty-four hours," she said. "The mythical 'switch' will actually be thrown about twenty hours before the ceremony, which is at eight P.M. local on the twenty-first."

"And that's when we're expecting the trouble?" Jim said.

Tash shook her head. "It would be nice if we could be so sure. But there are two things these people want, as far as we can tell. They want our money, and as much of it as they can get. But even more than that, being hackers, they want to make us look stupid. That means they have to hit us as close to throw-the-switch as possible, so as to be able to break their exploit to the news media at the same time we're doing our main publicity blitz, thus maximizing the appearance of their cleverness and our stupidity. However, they also want to execute the actual exploit, whatever it may be, sufficiently early so that they'll have time to successfully go into hiding and not get caught with what they've stolen. That works slightly in our favor. It gives us time to either catch them in the act, or to undo whatever damage they've done before the 'switch' is officially thrown."

"So," Alicia said, "the vulnerable time starts . . ." She checked her watch. "Any minute now."

Tash nodded.

"What kind of attack are we looking for?" Ron asked.

"Something intended to compromise one of the main game structures," Tau said. "Early indications suggest that it won't be anything crude, like a distributed denial-of-service attack. Or not *merely* a DDOS. The focus of the main attack is most likely to be player management, but that'll probably just be a blind for an attack on the financial structures."

Doris te Nawhara shook her head. "Why bother with player management?"

"Massive identity theft?" said Alicia.

"That's what I've been worrying about," Dev said. "Even if they fail at the money theft, it would still be incredibly damaging to us as a company if they made off with the credit card data and banking and personal profile info we hold for millions of players. The subsequent lawsuits would destroy the company in a matter of months." Dev let out a long unhappy breath. "Fortunately, one of the main purposes of the Conscientious Objector real-time proxy implants in our users' machines is to prevent that kind of data theft. And I take it—" he looked over at Tau "—that the CO routines are functioning normally."

"They were the very first part of the old game substructure to be migrated into the new servers," said Tau. "They're operating exactly as they should. But you should know that as well as I do."

"Well, yeah, I should," Dev said, "but I haven't looked at them yet today."

Everybody around the table glanced at each other. "You haven't been online today?" Alicia said incredulously. "Are you feeling okay?"

"I'm fine," Dev said. "It's just been busy. Anyway. We need to continue to keep the data about the expected attack exactly where it's been—under wraps, confined to the most senior people in the departments involved, and only those people and departments. There are entirely too many ways for this to leak out into the public domain."

"Any of which," Jim said, "could damage our share price badly."

"We'll get back to that," Dev said. "Now, the news *will* leak, of course. Sooner or later that's more or less inevitable. But the longer it takes, the happier I'll be. Meanwhile, we're not just going to sit around and wait for this to happen. We have a fair number of options open at our end. Tau?"

"Offense," Tau said. "The best defense, after all. System security has spent the past ten days doing heavy interactive port scanning on all our user accesses, assembling profiles on users who seem to be changing IPs or Internet gateways unusually frequently. We've assembled a list of some eighty-six thousand suspect gateways and machines that are reporting open relays or other similar vulnerabilities that can be exploited by the attackers. With machine assistance, we've been erecting 'trap-door spider' logic sieves around all of those gateways. Kosher logins slip through with no trouble. Dodgy looking ones are rerouted into barbed-wire extended loop structures that never allow them access to the Omnitopia servers. Or else the inbound dataflow in those connections is frozen, and they're then locked open so that we can feed them grenades."

Alicia gave Tau the kind of look a little sister gives a braggy older brother. "Could these geekspeak idioms get any *more* militaristic?" she said.

"I didn't make them up," Tau said. "Don't blame me! But this is going to be at least a series of skirmishes, if not a war, so logic bombs, Trojan horses, and virus attacks are all perfectly in order. The machines that attack us are going to find themselves coping with a wide spectrum of very nasty bugs. Some of them are quite simple keystroke loggers that will embed in the attacking machines, record a few days' worth of data, comb their hard drives for more, and then report in to our security staff as to the whereabouts of the machines and the people using them—login times, genuine IP addresses if we've been dealing with aliases, phone company account info, you name it. If those routines fail, our people monitoring the attack processes will let loose tailored command viruses geared toward burning out the brains of the machines trying to attack us. Wipe their drives, fry their chips . . ." Tau got one of those slightly feral looks that Dev had seen over the course of many a late-night programming fest. "Surprising what you can do to a motherboard by just telling the operating system to turn off its processor's fan."

"Some legal implications there . . ." Doris said, scribbling on her tablet.

"Considering that the people who'll be attacking us will be attempting to destroy private property and proprietary data," Tau said, "it should be fun watching them try to sue us, don't you think?"

"Not arguing the point," Doris said, still scribbling. "We just need to start planning what our countersuits will need to look like."

"How many personnel have you got assigned to this?" Dev asked.

"More than five hundred right now," said Tau. "As I said, the attack instrumentalities proper are very self-driven, but they yell for help when they need it, and we've got a lot of very smart on-the-fly programmers worldwide who've signed up to do kamikaze duty where needed—'riding' the programs in and directing the routines to where they can do the most damage."

Dev nodded. "All right," he said. "If you need more people, borrow as necessary from security worldwide. Or other departments." He scrolled down his to-do list. "Anything to add to this right now? Then let's move on. Media?"

"I heard from Mikal in PR a little while ago," Tash said. "He said Joss has picked up your *Time* magazine journalist and passed her on to his staff."

Dev raised his eyebrows. "Any word on how she was?"

"A bit prickly, Joss said."

Dev shrugged. "To be expected, I guess. An article about how wonderful and shiny-sparkly we are isn't going to sell them a lot of copies. They want dirt." He smiled, but the smile was thin. "Who owns *Time* this week?"

"G.E.?" Alicia suggested.

"Warner?" Cleolinda said. "I mean, it's TimeWarner, right?"

"I know! Bertelsmann!" Doris said.

"You're all behind the times," said Jim, leaning back in his chair and tapping idly at one of his laptop's cursor keys. "It's CBS."

"Just as long as it's not Phil," Tau said under his breath.

"Not this week," Jim said, "or any other. Which is of course part of the problem."

"Not ours," Dev said. "Or at least not today. Other media?"

"The new prelaunch commercials are rolling out nicely worldwide," said Tash. "All the major broadcasters are showing good overnights. The new streaming ads on the major search engines have been getting good hit percentages—better than the last batch."

"Okay," Dev nodded, hitting the scroll key on the laptop again. "Meanwhile, the reaction over in our competitor universes. . . "

"The reaction consists of attack ads," Jim muttered. "And it's a pity you're not running for office so we could call them that in public."

Dev gave Jim the don't-start-this-one-again look. Every now and then Jim suggested that Dev was wasting his talents merely running a virtual country and should try his hand at participating in the management of a real one. On days when he felt like arguing about it, Dev would suggest that Jim needed to find out how to make him some more money, and he would simply buy a country rather than go to the trouble of campaigning. Today, however, he didn't feel at all like arguing. "Tau?" he said.

Tau raised his eyebrows. "Game Dynamics has started a big push on *Visions of Otherwhere: The Burning Moon.*" He shrugged. "It's gonna be a wet firecracker at best. The magazine and Web site critics have already been all over it for being more of the same but different. And the new game engine is a wash too. The whole thing's a dud—I could almost feel sorry for the development teams: it's their reputations that're going to suffer. But their boss made them push the boat out before it was ready to do anything but sink. Typical: Ross Lyman has never been a big one for giving a damn about his employees."

"Or anything else," Dev said under his breath. "WonderWorlds?"

"Lots of TV ads for *Terminus VII*," Tau said. "And a lot of static stuff all over the blogs and dynamic Web sites. Not to mention a ton of astroturfing with about a million commenters doing fake grassroots stuff pumping Terminus' new character system and running down our new product, despite the fact that no one's seen it."

Dev's smile felt a bit crooked. "Well," he said, "that's entirely Elaine Shannon's style. Never use a clean trick when a dirty one will do."

"What *is* it with that woman?" Tau muttered. "Did you turn her down for a prom date or something?"

"I truly wish I knew," Dev said, shaking his head. "Are we likely to be at the same trade show or something in the next six months? I really ought to set up a meeting and ask her what her problem is." And now that he thought about it, it was a little strange that two major players in so small an industry had never met physically or even had any business dealings with each other. *Though is that it, I wonder? The gaming world's so little and inbred. Maybe Shannon thinks I've been shunning her for some reason?* There was no telling. But WonderWorlds' CEO seemed to consider Dev her very own personal archenemy, and Elaine Shannon's famous temper flared up spectacularly when anybody brought up the subject of Omnitopia in even the most bland or banal context. It wasn't that her company wasn't successful enough in its way, and the fan base of the *Terminus* game series was famously noisy and loyal. *Unless for some reason she feels that the loyalty might start slipping.* He glanced over at Jim. "How's her stock doing?"

Jim shrugged. "Up a little this week."

"Because of that rumor that Sony was sniffing around them with an eye to a buy?" Cleolinda said.

Jim shook his head. "Don't think so. More likely there's something to the theory that big news for any one game floats all the other boats a little higher."

"Not that she'll like that, either," Dev said, resigned. "Any success that she hasn't personally achieved just seems to make her madder. A concept which brings us, more or less inevitably, to Phil."

"Infinity Inc. is going full steam ahead with the publicity for the *Infinite Worlds: Threefold* multiple-expansion launch," Cleo said. "Exactly as scheduled, directly opposite us." She shrugged. "A wasted spend. It's like Phil *wants* to poke his own eye out."

Jim threw Dev a look that said, *It's your eye he wants to poke out, but he'll split the difference as long as you get the message.*

Dev grimaced. "More attack ads?"

"Yes indeed," Cleo said. "Nasty stuff."

"How nasty?"

"He doesn't *quite* accuse you of child abuse," said Cleo. "But there are veiled references to the Playground incident. A lot of buzzword-loaded stuff about 'player safety.'"

Dev shook his head. "How long are his attack ads going to run?"

Tash glanced at her notes. "Joss spoke off the record to a couple of the agencies, and they said two weeks with an option for three."

Dev sat playing with his pen for a few moments, staring at his laptop's screen. He could just hear Phil's voice, a long time ago. *Where were we at the time?* he wondered. Probably it had been yet another of those late-night beer-soaked student union bull sessions that they'd both loved so much in the ancient days. After class, after work, night after night, they had stayed up to talk about anything and everything way into the wee hours: their hopes, their dreams, the company they'd start, how life would be when they were rich and the world was at their feet. But those days seemed as far away now as the other side of the world, and as long ago as the Cretaceous. And Dev had been warned, and had ignored the warning. *I'm a good friend, but a bad enemy, Dev, my boy,* Phil's voice said in that particular dim-lit memory. The voice had been almost resigned, sounding as if this was a problem that Phil would really have liked to do something about, but couldn't figure out how. *Give me a reason for a grudge, and I'll hug it to me until the last trump blows.* The phrasing had been curiously antique, and Dev had laughed at it, way back when. *As if we would ever be enemies . . .*

Dev looked up out of the memory. "Well, keep an eye on their numbers," he said. "And tell Joss to keep an eye on anything that needs handling in the press. And as for legal . . ."

"I'll keep an eye on it," Doris said. "If he steps over the line, he's going to wish he hadn't."

Dev rubbed his face. "Okay, any other real-world stuff that merits our attention?"

"Just this," Doris said. "The *Journal of the American Medical Association* is about to come out with an editorial on the RealFeel system. Their experts don't think we gave it enough beta."

Dev rubbed his head. "I thought our experts said we did."

"You want a laugh?" Doris said. "Some of them are the same people."

"Now that's just *wrong* . . ."

Doris shrugged. "Are you kidding? You put ten medical researchers in a room, you get fourteen opinions, three-quarters of them paid for by somebody besides whoever owns the room."

"Yeah, well, we paid for ours," Dev said. "Question is, were our researchers following the money or the science?"

"As far as I can tell," Doris said, "the science."

"Dev," Jim said, "at the end of the day, you know that

everything we do is about risk. We're all sliding down the same razor blade together: without risk there's no growth. Nobody held a gun to our players' heads and made them buy this technology."

"Their lawyers are going to say we did," Dev said, "when they get around to suing us for some obscure cognitive disorder they come down with after using RealFeel. Or because they spilled boiling coffee in their lap one morning in the drive-through after they were up gaming late."

"As far as we can tell, the technology's safe," Doris said. "Don't forget, the military was testing it first."

"I am so vastly reassured," Dev said, "to have the results of the low bidders in a potentially slanted testing regimen to rely on." He leaned back in his chair, looked at Jim. "We need to be doing something to protect the corporate side of things."

"We have," Jim said. "There's a heading for this kind of issue under the general contingency fund in the conglomerate insurance arrangements."

"Ooh, corporatespeak, Dev said. "Translation please?"

"Wait till someone sues us, and handle each case on its own recognizance. But the insurance company judges the risk of suits as only marginally higher than that of suits from players using more standard input/output software, so the underwriters have rolled it into the broader coverage for this premium period. Additionally, RealFeel is only on offer in the United States and Canada at the moment, so our exposure's limited. The situation will be different when it goes on release in the UK, as then EU regulations come into play. But our legal reserve has about five hundred mil in it at the moment, so . . ."

"Okay," Dev said, "we'll see how it goes. But let's be clear: this is a *game* we're selling here. It's supposed to be for people to have fun with, not for them to get hurt. If lawsuits start, there'll be no jerking our players around. If they're harmed, I want them compensated."

Doris nodded.

"And my last real-world thing," Dev said. "Or at least, something on the interface between the real estate and the unreal. Tau, the bug list . . ."

"And bug number three," Tau said, sounding profoundly unhappy.

"It's something going on in Conscientious Objector," Dev said, "isn't it? That's the only conclusion I can come to."

Tau nodded. "Without starting to spew code all over the table," he said, "I'm pretty sure the bug is something to do with the way the basic CO structure and routines are interacting with the new hyperburst memory."

Dev swore. Tash tutted at him. "You keep talking like that," she said, "you won't have anything left to say when you hit your thumb with a hammer."

"If we don't fix this in two days," Dev said, "it's gonna be *exactly* like hitting my thumb with a hammer. About twenty million times. Dammit, we were *promised* that the memory was going to be a hundred percent backward-compatible." He scowled at the table. "And it's not like we can just unhook the CO routines from the game until we work out what's the matter. They are absolutely vital to the security subroutines that, theoretically, are going to keep the incoming attack on the game from succeeding."

He started playing with his pen again, considering possibilities. "I would ask if we can set aside an 'island' of the old legacy memory, move the core CO routines onto it, and attach the island to the main body of new memory with a logic causeway. But already it sounds too risky."

"There are fifteen ways that could blow up in our faces," Tau said. "Now never let it be said of me that I'm not willing to defer to superior experience—"

He glanced at Natasha. Like everyone else at the table, she was now gazing at Tau with an expression of total incredulity, as no one there had ever heard Tau defer to anybody but Dev about anything. But seeing that he was serious, Tash thought about it for a moment, then shook her head. "I think your first instinct's right," she said. "It's a recipe for disaster. Besides, it would mean migrating the CO routines back onto this theoretical island, and that would take time that we don't have. Especially since if it doesn't work, we'd have to migrate it right back. I wouldn't dare try holding both versions in memory at once, even if we could."

Tau looked unfocused, then shook his head. "Impossible. Forget about it."

He joined Dev and Natasha in looking grim and unhappy for a moment. "At least," Tau said then, "the ways the routine have been failing aren't *serious* ways. In fact, they've almost all been in Microcosms so far."

"I don't find that reassuring," Dev said. "Even though I know what you're thinking: the Microcosms are more likely to show peculiar symptoms than the Macros because they routinely have more nontypical things done to them, and by people who don't always understand what they're doing." He sighed. "And I hate not knowing why the Conscientious Objector is misbehaving, because if it starts doing it somewhere else, somewhere much bigger, it's likely to blow up in our faces."

There was quiet around the table. "You're all being very nice not to say what you're thinking," Dev said, "which is that the CO routines are my invention, that I've been the one who's been all paranoid over the past couple years about keeping them away from almost everybody else at the company—"

"Except that the paranoia's paid off," Tau said. "Remember when we expanded all the virtual real estate in the Macrocosms to 'real-world' size? Without the CO, we'd never have caught the guys who tried to use that event to divert all the Telekil logins on launch day and steal our users' private info. And we caught the moles who'd been trying to get inside the Conscientious Objector's guts. The only reason they failed was because you'd made sure the CO's inside code was kept so inaccessible to everybody but you and the Chosen Few."

"Meaning you," Dev said. "All right. Unfortunately the downside of that is that there aren't many of us who can work on that problem. So let's you and me do some old-fashioned hacking tonight. Got time?"

"Nothing else more important on my plate," Tau said. "I'll alert the software implementation groups to lock down what they're doing and get all today's changes stable before six."

"Okay. Pass whatever else you've been working on to

your trouble teams, okay?" He sighed, scrolling down past the bug list. "Enough of the so-called real world, which is really annoying me today. Unreal estate, ladies and gentlemen! Tell me of my worlds!"

A rustle went around the table. "Macrocosms!" Dev said. "What's buzzing in the Hundred and Twenty-one Universes?"

"The rollout, mostly," Ron Ruis said. "The pace of gameplay has slowed a little everywhere. It's the usual let's-see-what-happens thing." He grinned. "Rubbernecking."

Dev nodded. "That we were expecting. Ongoing conflicts?"

"Running in sixty-four percent of the Macrocosms today," Alicia said.

Dev frowned. "Seems a little low."

"Design planning mandated a 'cosm-wide 'peace percentage' for the pre-rollout period," Ron said. "We can go down as low as sixty. It lets the newbies travel a little more widely without getting stomped on too much. Also, some of the marginal 'cosms have had their conflict constants dialed down a little so that players can do more exploring without getting jumped by game-generated characters every other minute."

"It's not a bad idea," said Cleolinda. "A lot of people have the rollout on their brains right now. It's impairing play somewhat, so it's just good business to have the GGCs cut them a little slack."

"New conflicteds today?"

"Fifteen. There's the full list." Alicia brought it up on all their laptops.

Dev glanced down at it, nodded. "Okay. Dasheth Prime, Pandora, LongAgo Three . . . Oh, good, TwoMoons finally got their act together. I was starting to worry—thought we gave a war and nobody came."

A chuckle went around the table. "Every world to its own speed," Alicia said. "Can't rush these things, sometimes, and the Moonies are a breed unto themselves." She left unspoken the other strange truth about that 'cosm, which was that its income had been five percent over the Omnitopian average for the past three years—and despite intensive study, no one really understood why.

"Heaven forbid I should fix what's not busted," Dev said. "Nothing else in the Great Worlds? Fine. How're the Microcosms?"

"Eight thousand four hundred twenty-two running today," Ron said promptly. "They paid—" He glanced at his laptop. "—just north of one point two million dollars in royalties. Of nonrunning 'cosms, we had twelve deactivations and forty-one formal abandonments—those are being fostered out to other MicroLevelers as usual. Three crashes due to bad or strange code—those are being debugged. Thirty-four new Levelers came in, twelve by system-initiated upgrades. The rest got the accolade from staff, either independently or by nomination."

"Those deactivations—anything new that's going to get us sued?" The Playground fiasco was still very much on Dev's mind. The idea that someone might have been using his universe for such evil purposes made his flesh crawl.

Ron shook his head. "ToS violations, but nothing like *that*. One of them was a stolen-gold laundry. Very clever; it exploited a loophole in ARGOT. I'll pass you the details."

"That loophole plugged?"

"It will be by tonight, temporarily at least. It's been moved way up the list of things to fix for the next release of the language."

"Okay. Copy me the new 'cosm details as usual." He turned to Jim. "And one more so-called real world thing I forgot. I had a phone call just before I came up. Our most reticent shareholder is very concerned about our share price. I have a feeling you may be hearing from him."

Jim covered his face with his hands. "Oh, Bog preserve me!"

"He's just following the money," Dev said, "like your other biggest fan. But the sentiment he was expressing is popular. I really, really want us to break a thousand during the launch. It'll leave a welt on Wall Street's hide they won't soon forget."

Jim shrugged. "Better go sacrifice a goat to the great god Fed," he said. "No guarantees."

"Really? You don't think we'll do it? We've moved heaven and earth to get it to happen . . ."

"Heaven and earth have their own motions," Jim said, and leaned back in his chair. "You think I wouldn't like it too? I want to redecorate my office." A skeptical snicker ran around the table, as Jim had not been known to redecorate any space he'd occupied since he joined Dev in the company: he preferred to be moved into an entirely new building.

"Okay," Dev said. "You're hedging your bets. I can understand that."

"It's how I made us the unstoppable financial force we are today," Jim said and there was no snicker this time, because the statement was incontestably true. Along with his ancient friendship with Dev, forged in the fires of that never-to-be-forgotten fistfight when they were six and rock-solid ever after, Jim had brought to the Omnitopian round table, along with his Harvard MBA, a near-Machiavellian understanding of the markets. "Dev, never mind the goats. If I see us ready to go over the top, you'll be my first call. But it's too soon to say."

"Three days before the launch is too soon?"

Jim nodded. "Three days in finance is like a week in politics," he said. "Or two. Ask me again in about forty-eight hours."

"I will do that," Dev said, and turned to the others. "Anybody else? Last thoughts?"

Heads shook all around. "We're done," Jim said. "Better go get online before your world crumbles."

Dev nodded, stood up. "Okay, troops," he said. "Let's go play!"

Everyone else got up. "We doing a Great Wall tonight?" Doris asked. It was code for a group dinner, just as it had been seven years ago when such dinners took place not in an Omnitopian executive dining room, but in the back room of a little Chinese place in Phoenix.

"Yeah," Dev said. "My place?"

The sound of general agreement ran around the room as people packed up their things. "Great," Dev said. "I'm going home for lunch. Jim, come on with; you can see She Who Must Be Obeyed before you go back to work."

"Do I get to ride on the back of the bike?" Jim said, shutting his briefcase.

Dev rolled his eyes and headed for the elevator.

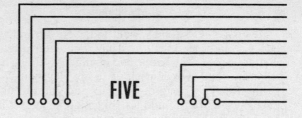

FIVE

RIK DID HIS BEST TO BE GOOD that day. It was hard work. He made lunch for the family, he tidied the master bedroom, he vacuumed the upstairs hall. Granted, the upstairs hall really needed it. Mikey, too, had been good that day, and had spent the better part of an hour cleaning out the hamster cage. As a result, the upstairs hall between Mikey's room and the bathroom, where the upstairs garbage can lived, was liberally scattered with cedar shavings and other slightly less salutary detritus. Rik had busied himself making sure he got every shaving up, while thinking slowly and carefully about a lot of the reading he had done online earlier that morning. It came almost as a shock to him when somebody came up behind him and took the vacuum out of his hands.

"Enough," Angela said to him. "You're going to give me a guilt attack. Go play with your toy."

He looked down the hall, satisfied that it was clean, and smiled at her. "You really are the best woman on the planet, you know that?"

She rolled her eyes at him. "Yes, I do. Now please, get in there and close the door. Your halo is blinding me."

He smiled at being let off the hook. "What's for dinner?"

"Spaghetti and meatballs," Angela said. "And no, you don't need to help. I don't wanna see you until six."

"Can I have an iced tea first?"

"Anything. Just go away and stop being so good! I'm beginning to wonder what pod person removed my husband when I wasn't looking."

He kissed her soundly, went to the fridge, and got himself a very large iced tea—he'd have beer later, after he successfully pulled off what he had in mind, assuming he *could* pull it off—and took himself up to the playroom. When he got the RealFeel headset on again and got into his workspace once more to find that golden apple logo still showing in the status window, he had to shake his head. It was hard to believe. *But there it is.*

And how am I going to explain this to Raoul?

Sitting there in his little private eye's office, he rubbed his face, shook his head. Raoul was a problem for later in the day. *And not that much later in the day, either. What is it now? Threeish, here. Which means it's . . .* He tried to do the time zones in his head. Fortunately, everybody was on the same continent. *It's okay. I may actually have enough time to get this to work. At least enough to paper over the cracks and show them that I've actually been giving this thing my attention.*

He walked out the door of his little office inside the Omnitopia gaming system and straight into that vast darkness. There Rik stood, staring up at the THIS SPACE FOR RENT sign that still hung there. Rik was tempted to leave it there while he worked, just as a reminder that all this was still real. But it was time to get past that now—what was he, a kid who couldn't get used to reality? —and anyway, it might screw something up. *Better to get rid of it.*

He didn't want to be standing there in the dark, though, so first he turned on the sun.

It was small and fiercely bright, and somehow looked much closer than the real sun would, even though from where he was standing, its diameter looked the same. That was one of the first things that had occurred to Rik about a good-looking Inner Earth: a sun about six hundred miles wide, hanging in place and rotating as if it was made of hyperdense matter, as heavy as the whole Earth's core so that everything stayed in balance. *No point in having an Earth that wobbles in its orbit, after all. You want it so that the people supposedly living on the surface will never notice. Not that they're ever going to be my problem.*

The sun had been surprisingly easy—even easier than

the structure for the world in which it was now hanging. With only a little searching in Omnitopia's forums, archives, and Web spaces, Rik had found that there were a lot of Microcosm templates available that started out with hollow spheres for convenience, and then constructed various structures inside them—caves, castles, you name it. After some browsing, Rik had found one that had suited his purposes particularly well, being nothing else but a hollow crystal ball meant to hold genii or demons. The sphere's outer dimensions were variable, but didn't impair the hugeness of the inside, which was meant to be as big as a world to the creatures held inside it, even if it seemed small to those outside. Rik wasn't particularly concerned about the outer dimensions—the first thing he'd done with the WannaB language was describe the outside as out of bounds. The access to Rik's 'cosm via the Ring of Elich was going to be on the inside of the sphere, not the outside. It would take only a sentence or three in WannaB, he thought, to opaque the crystal. Then it would just be a matter of starting to lay terrain down on the substrate.

The terrain, Rik thought. He couldn't wait for the others to see this place. *Well, I can't wait for* most *of them to see it. But not bare, not like this. It needs a little work first.*

"Okay," he said to the darkness. "Uh, meta, please?"

A screen like the one he worked with inside the normal game spaces rolled itself down on the air, showing him a window into the virtual 3-D storage where modules of the WannaB language, shining and round as DVDs, were stacked up like so many flat coins. He reached into the window, took one out, turned it over in his hands. Each module was a number of words, a phrase in WannaB. Each one had a number of receptor sites where it could be made to adhere to others, changing the structure and behavior of the virtual space around it. Jean-Marie had been right: working with these was easier than it sounded at first, and the resemblance to working with TinkerToys, once you got started, was strong. The difference was that these modules were worth a lot more than TinkerToys.

Rik flipped the module he was holding up into the air, caught it, looked at the way the words swam and swarmed underneath the surface of the disk. Anybody who had followed the Omnitopia feeds for long would have heard that there was a black market trade in stray words of the ARGOT language. Even in this simplified form, tamed and made less complex so that average players could handle them, there was a demand for the virtual version of words of power. It didn't matter that the minute the Omnitopia system security people caught a 'cosm builder passing code on the black market, that 'cosm would be confiscated and the player thrown out of the Great Game on his ear. There were still people who were tempted, who thought they could get away with it. And the buyers, it was whispered, would find you. You'd be sitting in some bar in Omnitopia City, some tavern in one of the basalt-cliff towns of Onondaga, a spaceport dive on Kweltach, a downtown cellar dance 'n' smoke place in Napoletaine, and someone would sidle up to you, sit down by you, and whisper, "Got code?" The sums that would change hands—usually in real-world money, as game gold was too easy to trace—would be very tempting indeed. Especially if you had a 'cosm that hadn't been earning. You could make serious, serious money on the side—

Rik grimaced. *No sooner trusted than tempted,* he thought. *What kind of person am I?* He breathed out. *But I'm never going that way. I'm too chicken. Which is a good thing.*

He put the disk back where he found it and said to the space around him, "Can I have the wireframe, please?"

The darkness all around Rik vanished, replacing itself with a grayed-out charcoal background which was rather like being trapped inside a turned-off lightbulb. High above him hung a little pearly sphere: his sun, no longer blinding now that it was running in schematic. Against the far-flung background of the larger sphere, the basic curvature of the space as Rik had established it so far defined itself in glowing white lines of latitude and longitude. Rik was standing at the bottom of an empty globe that was waiting to have a world written on it.

He got to work. For the next two hours he lost track of time almost entirely, stacking up terrain structures and watching the basic 2-D wireframe landscape spread out around him, then having the structures fall apart on him, and the whole thing wiped out. The modules continually did things he didn't expect, and also things that he did, but in ways that foiled his original intentions. Nonetheless Rik began to get a feel for this mode of construction, which started to feel like putting together a puzzle (though one without a predetermined pattern). The different modules, he found, actually were programmed to give you a hint when something was going to work: there was tactile feedback as well as visual, and the "puzzle pieces" themselves would shift subtly in the color or intensity of their internal light, the cues suggesting which pieces of code were meant to work together and which were likely to cause a ruckus if you insisted on forcing them together. Finally Rik wound up with a stack that had everything he wanted to start with and that was correctly balanced, in which all the colors seemed to be flowing correctly and the sticky bits were sticking together soundly. "Okay," Rik said to the meta window, glancing over the control panel that was displayed in it. "Turn on live display." And he held his breath.

High above him, the sun came on. For yards and miles, and then apparently thousands of miles from where he stood, in a truly amazing imitation of distance, landscape went rolling out. It was very generic landscape—forests and fields, occasional mountain chains, a few large and small oceans automatically generated by the fractal routines built into the code. Underfoot it still felt flat as a floor: there were no textures in place as yet. But that could wait. Right now the landscape ran right up around the insides of the sphere, as he'd told it to, and right up to the top of the sky, where a particularly large ocean was covering the entire "polar" region of the inside of the sphere, looking and acting as if gravity was holding it there. Rik let his breath out slowly, watching with wonder the sheen on the water at that great height from the little hot sun seemingly hanging eight and a half thousand miles or so below it. *This is so cool! At this "distance" the upper surface looks like sky, even though it's not. A little darker, maybe. More indigo. But all the virtual air between here and there is scattering the light just fine. Might want to turn the sun up a little—*

He grinned at himself. *"Turn up the sun."* Hah. *What a little tin god we are all of a sudden.* But that was another question. This 'cosm, this world, was going to need a name. And the name would have had to come from somewhere. *This world needs a mythology. And a history. And people, obviously people. But what kind? And animals. And a goal. What's a world without a goal? There has to be a game in here, something worth playing, something worth striving for.*

Suddenly Rik actually broke out in a sweat as he realized the sheer size of the endeavor he'd walked into. He took a deep breath and slowly turned, taking a look at the parts of the globe that had been behind him. He was going to have to turn this from just a shell into a real world. He was going to have to people it, infuse it with life ... and then market it. Because, as he turned, he now saw something hanging in the sky as a replacement for the FOR RENT sign. It read

ROYALTIES EARNED TO DATE:
0000000.00

Very slowly he smiled. *The heck with creation anxiety,* Rik thought. *This is going to be an absolute blast. I can't wait to see that thing tick over for the first time.*

And I really can't wait to show the guys!

"Door, please," he said to his space. The door back into Rik's private eye office reappeared. He went through it and headed straight over to the coatrack in the corner by his desk, where the robes of his art were hanging. He snapped his fingers, changing instantly out of virtual street clothes into his normal Omnitopian character kit—boots, breeches, linen shirt and undertunic, the quilted tabard lined with spearproof dragon hide, and finally the belt pouch with the bags of simples and Rik's special medical tools. For a moment he considered wearing something more formal. *But no. This is just another of our usual meetings. I don't want them to get the idea I'm getting all stuck up on them or something.*

Rik reached up to get his cloak, swung it around his shoulders, and paused for a moment. *This is so strange,* he thought. *One day everything's going on as usual and the next day suddenly it's a big deal what you wear, what you say.* He thought of Raoul. *And who you see—*

He let out a breath. There was nothing that could be done about that, but it'd be a lie to say that Rik would have been relieved if he'd found that Raoul couldn't make it tonight. *Never mind,* Rik thought. *Other things to think about today.* And he couldn't help grinning again as he reached around behind the coatrack, got his swordbelt and buckled it on, slinging it in the over-the-back carry position. *It's still so neat. Let's go—*

He went back to the door. "Close the Microcosm, please," Rik said to the game management system. The doorway went cloudy and vague with the same kind of swirling gray-out that the Ring of Elich used for doorways that were out of commission or waiting for an incoming transit.

"Omnitopia City," Rik said. "Quarterlight Street, by the Great Ring, please."

The swirling in the doorway cleared away to show him evening light. Rik glanced around his office, waved the lights off, stepped through the door—

—into absolute chaos. *What the f—!* Rik thought in shock as the sound came on with his passage through the doorway, and he heard the roar of people's voices, shouting, screaming, the hubbub of running feet, and saw the stuttery flash of magelight all around in the twilight.

The Plaza of Exploration was a battlefield—literally. It was hard to make out at first who was doing what to whom. There was one large group, not human, who seemed to be operating in concert and chasing most of the other people Rik could see in the plaza, striking at them with clubs of ironwood and carved stone. *Trolls?* Rik thought, astonished. *They look like it, anyway. Liveried—*At least it looked like a livery they were wearing, something dark purple. *But what the heck's going on here? You can't have a battle in Omnitopia City!*

Nonetheless, somebody seemed to have forgotten to tell the trolls that. There were maybe five thousand of them in the plaza, scattered all over the place and bashing anybody they could catch. Things weren't all going their way: here and there flashes of magelight from characters and players of all styles struck them down as Rik watched. The trolls were trapped in this world, too, as Rik could see from here that the Ring of Elich had shut itself away behind a secondary ring of impenetrable blue fire.

Then his head snapped around as, from not too far away, he heard the yell *"MEDIIIIIIC!"*

Rik's eyes went wide, but he couldn't help grinning. Even unprepared as he might have been for this particular scenario, dealing with that kind of shout was what Arnulf Manyfaced lived for. Hurriedly he whipped off his cloak, flipped it inside out so that the squared white cross and crossed swords showed clearly on his back. *But what the heck am I going to say to the guys? They're going to say I'm avoiding them. Well, never mind that now . . .*

He plunged into the fray. All around him magical blasts of multicolored fire were shooting in every direction, kicking up paving stones, knocking plaster off walls on the buildings closest to the Ring, blowing out windows. Arnulf plunged through an insane melee of shrieking and cursing and the yells of men and women and beasts of every kind, dragons howling, somebody's leashed hellhound yelping where somebody else had stepped on it. Arnulf paused only long enough to let a very large crowd of angry Gnarths muscle past him in pursuit of the trolls, their armor in shreds and their independent liveries indistinguishable from one another in the coating of city muck and blood they'd acquired during the beginning of the fight. Then he ran on again, trying to see where the shout had come from.

"Over here!"

He angled to the right, where a big hairy guy, some kind of drow or ogre at first guess, was waving at him past the body of a battle mammoth. Rik shook his head as he dropped to his knees beside the huge bulk: it took a lot of ergs or magic to bring one of these down, as most of them availed themselves of magial engineering as soon as they could afford it, buying themselves an augmentation of that already redoubtable hide.

"What happened?" Rik said, unfastening one of his simples bags and dropping it in front of him.

"Guy caught a blast of trollfire right in the chops," said the ogre. He—no, she, sometimes it was hard to tell with ogres—was a huge red-haired type, horny-hided and with the typical big blunt face. "Then a troll hit him from behind when he went down—"

"Friend of yours?"

The ogre shook her head. "No, just saw him go down. Thought he blundered in here by accident, maybe—"

"I bet a lot of people've been doing that," Rik said. "Did it myself. How long ago?"

"Maybe five minutes."

"Great. Thanks."

The battle mammoth stirred a little, a feeble jerk of the legs. "What happen?" it said. "Can't move—"

The translation sounded a little stiff. "Game management," Rik said as he got up and hurriedly looked the beast over, "display original language."

The translation obligingly displayed in a split frame above the stricken character's head. It was Chinese of some kind, Rik thought. "What is that?"

"Mandarin," said the game management voice.

"Okay," Rik said. "Lie still, it will be all right." He kept his wording a little more formal for the moment. The game translation matrices famously had trouble with slang and casual usages when the servers were overloaded, which Rik could just bet they were at the moment. "I am a medic, I will help."

He circled around and did the quickest assessment he could when the client was so very large. Head and chest were okay, but there was definitely considerable damage to the rear: a big crushing injury of the back right leg, a lot of blood loss from a torn vein. Arnulf got busy, as there was no time to waste when there was damage of this kind—not if he was going to keep this player from losing his character entirely. There was no telling how much of the guy's monthly—or yearly—income was wrapped up in this persona. Game display would show that data later, if Arnulf had the time or inclination to look.

Arnulf held his hands out over the massive body and invoked the medspell routine that would give him a more detailed diagnosis. He heard in his ear, without really noticing it, the soft stylized *ka-ching!* cash-register chime that told him the system had docked his game gold total for the performance of this spell. The spell graphic proper ran with its usual speed and showed Rik the details of the tear in the vein—fortunately a fairly clean one—and the smashed muscle. *Aah, whatever hit him got the tendon too. Damn it. Probably one of those nasty big stone clubs with spikes sticking out all over it. Never mind, let's get him patched up—*

Rik did some quick sums in his head as to how much spell energy it was going to cost him to reknit the tendon and regrow the muscle. *There's so much of it, that's the problem.* But it was *his* problem, not the client's. Other medical mages might go around requiring payment in advance, but that wasn't how the MediMages Without Frontiers guilds operated. *I get to forgo those fancy new robes until this guy pays me off,* Rik thought. *Whatever.*

He okayed the payment for the spell, heard that soft *ka-ching!* again, and held out his hands. Under them the magefire bloomed. The muscle began reinflating itself: the tendon rewove its core, then its sheath. Arnulf glanced up only briefly during this, noting that there suddenly seemed to be lot of movement around them, big dark forms blowing past across the plaza.

"Don't worry," the ogre said. "Looks like the citizenry and the tourists're getting rid of the trolls. I'll make sure you don't get trampled."

Arnulf saw one massive black form rushing toward them gather itself and leap right over him, the ogre, and the battle mammoth. It was one of those giant flesh-eating doomsteeds from Palomino, followed by several others of its kind. *That's gonna be fun,* Arnulf thought, as the huge angry creature and its fellows went plunging past and headed for a group of trolls running out of the plaza on the south side. *Be interesting to see one of them eat a troll. Probably crunch the thing right up like hard candy. Maybe later.* He kept his eye on the mammoth's muscle: it would be a shame to spend all this energy on a crooked heal.

But it was coming along nicely. After a few more minutes of making sure that both ends of the muscle knit out equally, it was just a matter of sealing the torn underskin fascia membrane and regrowing the red-brown fur over the healed injury. "Would you try to move that leg for me now, please?" Arnulf said.

The mammoth moved the leg jerkily: moved it again. "Feels better," it said.

Arnulf stood up, dusted himself off. "Okay," he said. "I mean, all right. Try to stand up now."

Shakily the mammoth stood. It swayed a little, but didn't fall again. "You feel all right otherwise?" Arnulf said. "How is your head?"

"Head's all right," said the mammoth. It turned its head, felt the leg with its trunk.

"Good," Arnulf said. "Is everything else all right?"

The mammoth turned back toward Arnulf, patted his face with its trunk: a clumsy but friendly gesture. "All, all right. Thanks, thanks many."

"Great." Arnulf went over to it, patted the mammoth's shoulder. "My card."

Instantly the mammoth was painlessly branded there with the mark of Arnulf's guild, his own set of ID sigils, and the Omnitopian date and time. When the player handling this character was ready, or could afford it, he'd credit Arnulf's game account with the basic healing payment, or more if the player could afford it—healing was always assumed to run on a sliding scale, so that those who could afford it paid a little more and subsidized those who might have more trouble paying. Once the healing was paid for, the brand would vanish; in the meantime it served as a free ad for Arnulf's services and for his guild.

The mammoth felt the brand curiously with its trunk as the ogre got up to have a look at it as well. "We're all done," Arnulf said. "Go on, better get out of here till they clean this up. And keep your head down, guy."

The mammoth nodded and lumbered off toward the Ring. "Hey, thanks for helping him," said the ogre, heading that way too.

"It's what we do," Arnulf said. "Thanks for making sure he got help. That was the important part."

Arnulf packed himself up, dusted himself off, and looked around to see what seemed to be the safest direction in which to make his escape.

He found that four or five other practitioners had hit the field of battle while he was busy with the battle mammoth. There wasn't really anything much for him to do: "complete" casualties, character deaths, had already vanished from the field of battle. Others, not so badly hurt or just shaken up, were getting to their feet, checking themselves out. There was no more fighting going on in the plaza. The trolls had all been chased out of it, and even as he watched the doomsteeds and various others pursuing them, Arnulf could see some of the trolls vanishing into thin air, as if simply plucked out of play. "Looks like the cavalry's come over the hill," he said under his breath.

He watched the plaza for a few more minutes. The Ring was still closed off. *Got a few minutes to kill here, I guess,* Arnulf thought, and glanced around. Off to one side was a group of Elves and humans and other creatures, leaning against one of the buildings that surrounded the plaza and surveying the former battlefield.

Arnulf made his way over to them. "Everybody okay over here?"

There was a general chorus of agreement. "Thought we'd stay out of the way while the management tidies things up," said one of the smaller creatures sitting by the wall, a black witch's cat with a British accent. "No point in getting stepped on."

"No," Arnulf said, leaning against the wall as well, watching idly as the plaza started to clear out. "But I got here in the middle of the brouhaha. When did it start?"

"About half an hour ago," said the cat. "Big charge of trolls came out of the Ring from about twelve different portals over a few seconds. Trashed anyone who got in their way." Its tail lashed. "There were a lot of people waiting for access—it turned into a real mob scene. Then the word got out on the City nets and half the town came pouring in here, all indignant and looking for a fight." The cat smiled.

"Transient population's bigger than usual, what with the rollout coming. Whoever those trolls were representing, they didn't have it as easy as they thought they were going to."

Rik shook his head. "Well, 'indignant' I can understand," he said. "I thought there couldn't be wars in Omnitopia City anymore. The City outlawed that kind of thing years back!"

The next player over along the wall from the cat, an Elf leaning wearily on a bow with a broken string, got a bemused look. "Well, yeah, it did," he said. "But have you been hiding under a rock or something? The mayor got killed last night."

"What?" It came as a shock. The charismatic Dwarven politician Margon k'Pellish had held the Omnitopia City mayoralty, it seemed to Arnulf, for the guts of forever. Everybody had gotten used to him as a likable, laissez-faire kind of character with brains enough to run the city and also to stay out of its way. Then again, that long a time spent in office was probably reason enough for whoever was playing old M.K.P. to have gotten a little careless.

"Yup," the Elf said, leaning his bow against the nearby wall and patting himself down for a moment, then coming up with a scented smokestick. He tapped it against the wall; the tapped end lit. The Elf took a long drag and blew out purple smoke that wove itself into rings, linked through one another and went floating off into the evening sky. "Manticore got him," the Elf said. "Nasty. Someone smuggled it into his office."

Arnulf blinked. A manticore stood six feet high at its leonine body's shoulder, and might be four or five yards' length between the nose on the beast's ugly man-face and the scorpion-stinger tip of the long tail. And then there were those big sharp-edged wings to consider, spanning some eighteen or twenty feet even on a small animal. "Must have been some determined smuggler," Rik said.

The Elf nodded, took another drag on the smokestick, then stubbed it out on the wall and dropped the butt. A mallrat scampered down out of the side street, caught the butt before it even hit the ground, and ran off down the street with it. The cat eyed it and closed its eyes, unconcerned. "Thing got around the guy's security spells, apparently," the Elf said. "After that, in came the trolls."

Arnulf frowned and shook his head as he looked across at the Ring. "Anything on the feeds about who might have been running them?"

"Nothing definitive," said the Elf. "The usual rumors. I saw some people suggesting this was something to do with one of the 'wealth redistribution' guilds." He gave Arnulf an annoyed look at the name. Arnulf rolled his eyes, agreeing. The various thieves' guilds were always trying to position themselves upmarket—at least organizationally—with poor results: a thief was still a thief, no matter how they tried to portray themselves as downtrodden blue-collar types who only needed collective bargaining powers to make the world work perfectly. "A lot of smash-and-grab action started going on just after the trolls arrived, apparently."

"Great," Arnulf muttered.

"Well, it won't last," the Elf said. "But in the meantime, no more mayor, no more government. No more rules. At least until we get a new mayor." He smiled a grim, amused smile. "Election by combat, as usual."

"Hoo boy," Arnulf said, making a mental note to stay out of the City for the next few days. "Wonder what upper management's going to make of *this* development."

"What, you mean in terms of the rollout?" The Elf shook his head. "No idea. I suppose Dev Himself could always drop out of the sky and calm things down. Appoint a mayor or something. But that's not usually his style, as I understand it. He seems to like to let things run."

"Yeah, but now?" There had been so much publicity about the rollout that Arnulf found it hard to believe he'd let the centerpiece of the whole Omnitopia project turn into the epicenter of a civil war at such a sensitive time.

"No idea, man," the Elf said. He picked up his bow, started to sling it over his shoulder, and then remembered that it wouldn't stay slung. "I'm gonna be watching the feeds, that's for sure."

"Yeah," Arnulf said. "Me too."

As they watched, the blue fire surrounding the Ring vanished. "There we go," said the Elf. "business as usual."

"You think?" Arnulf said. "After something like this?"

"Gonna have to be," said the Elf, "if upper management wants their rollout to go as planned." And he bowed to Arnulf, the exaggerated courtesy of one denizen of the Hundred and Twenty-one Worlds to another. "Play fairly, Brother," he said. "Play well."

"Yeah," Arnulf said as the Elf and some others who'd been leaning on the wall by him headed down toward the Ring. "You too."

The crowd around the Ring was already getting pretty thick. Rik relaxed against the wall for a few minutes longer, his gaze lingering on the huge shape of the battle mammoth, which had been standing down in the plaza all this while, and now was making its way slowly toward one of the portals of the Ring. Arnulf watched him—"him"? Well, the mammoth had been male, but that didn't guarantee anything—until he passed through the portal and vanished into what from this distance looked like a mountainous landscape. *That,* Rik thought, watching the mammoth's gait with satisfaction, *was a nice piece of work.* It was going to be interesting to go to the next Guild meeting and talk to some of his mage buddies about what he'd discovered about the anatomy of the mammoth. *But in the meantime,* he thought, *I really should get along to Meruvelt. They'll be waiting.*

Arnulf dusted himself down again, made sure that his pouches were intact and his sword slung in a position where he could drop it to drawing level if he needed it. Then he headed down toward the Ring.

The post office box place sat in the middle of the forlorn little strip mall on lake Mirror Road, with an orthodontist on one side and a falafel joint on the other. As far as Danny was concerned, though, the real jewel in that strip was the pizza place down at the end. He valued that maybe even more than the ATM between the pizza place and the dry cleaners.

The crusts on the pizzas were pretty good in there; the guy behind the counter had a light touch. Those pizzas, and the beer from the pizza place's cooler, kept Danny sane while he worked in the Hartfield branch of Post Boxes Unlimited. What was even better for his mental health, though, was the certain knowledge that the pizza place wouldn't need to be part of his life's landscape for very much longer. *Two more days,* he thought. *Three, tops. After that—*

Danny pulled the car headfirst into the parking place right in front of the PB Unlimited shop, got out, and slammed the driver's side door with what was probably unnecessary force. This was the third of these runs he'd had to make today, but when his boss Ricardo got it into his head to restock on packing supplies, his enthusiasm tended to get out of hand. At such times, no trip to the wholesale cardboard box place ever meant less than a car absolutely stuffed full of bubble wrap, flat-pack boxes, strapping tape, folder tabs, and other junk that could surely have been bought in smaller quantities, or at least bought when it was actually needed. But that wasn't Ricardo's way. Ricardo tended to stock as if he expected a flood or tornado or some other natural disaster to descend on Big Joe's Office Supply and Cash and Carry and blow it into the next state.

Danny went around the back of the car, pushed the button that popped up the hatchback's rear door, reached in, and pulled out the first batch of flattened, unassembled boxes. *This too shall pass*, he said to himself. *Only a few more days. Then Ricardo, and the pizza, and all these boxes, they'll all be just memories. Saturday*—Danny smiled to himself—*Saturday, I quit.*

He staggered up to the front door, paused, turned around, put his butt against the door, carefully pushed backward, and let himself in. As usual, Ricardo was too busy taking inventory, or wrapping something up, or just sitting behind his desk contemplating the cash register, to ever come over and actually open the door. If the boss hadn't felt like doing it most of the time, even if he'd done it only very occasionally, Danny could've coped with that. But Ricardo *never* opened that damn door for his overburdened employee, not once. *The man just does* not *give a good goddamn about his staff.* Not that this was exactly news, either; Danny had known it since he first came down and applied for this job. The wage he was being paid was not the wage anybody paid to a valued employee. It was, in fact, just barely over the wage paid to the kids down at Mickey D.'s for asking people if they wanted fries with that. *But never mind,* Danny thought. *Just keep saying it: "This too shall pass."* He turned around very carefully and let the door fall closed behind him.

For a moment he just stood there enjoying the air-conditioning. The temperature difference between outside and inside, this time of month, was considerable. *And God knows what it's gonna be like this time next month,* Danny thought. Or rather, God might know, but Danny wasn't going to. Danny was going to be somewhere else. Ideally, somewhere cooler.

He walked over to the far end of the shop, heading for the spot where the counter divided and left a path open toward the storeroom in the back. Ricardo, sitting on his high stool behind the register, threw a passing glance at Danny and then went back to making notes about something or other on one of the store's lined pads. *Then again,* Danny thought as he went through the space between the counters as carefully as he could when his arms were piled high with flat-folded boxes, *the heat itself isn't really the problem. This same temperature might not be such a terrible thing, if you had a beach right in front of you. White sand, blue water, and a breeze.* But if anybody in this part of greater Atlanta had seen or heard of a breeze recently, they were keeping that news to themselves. And the beach was a long, long way away. Lake Mirror Road might promise all kinds of things with its name, but the lake in question was lost among the big buildings of the local industrial estate, just a mucky little pond behind the FedEx depot and slightly offset from under the main approach paths for the airport.

Danny maneuvered his way into the back room and put down his pile of flat-fold boxes with great care next to the two other stacks already pushed up against the painted white concrete blocks of the back room wall. He lined them up carefully with the other two stacks, tucked them in snugly against the wall, and squared off the stack. Then Danny straightened up, examining them. There was no harm in being methodical and tidy. That approach worked in other parts of his life—and being tidy tended to distract the boss from other things that might be going on.

He glanced through the door to the front. As usual, Ricardo was so deeply sunk in the ins and outs of lower corporate management—a heavy bout of catalog reading at the moment—that he rarely noticed anything Danny did as long as it looked vaguely like something he'd told Danny to do. And every time Ricardo actually got off his butt long enough to check and see the work was actually getting done, it reinforced this impression of Danny as a willing—or at least uncomplaining—wage slave. That suited Danny fine. He headed out through the store, making his way to the car again. The customer area of the store was not much to look at—it was as desperately plain as most of its fellow PB Unlimiteds. One wall was loaded up with wire racks of commonplace office supplies—padded envelopes, twine, tape, packing labels, receipts, and air bills for all the major courier companies, and a long table to work on when getting a shipment ready. The other wall had the locked post boxes built into it, large and small. In front of it, by the window, was a long, high ledge to sort your mail on, with garbage cans underneath the ledge to take all those "You May Have Won A Million Dollars!" letters, the junk mail and catalogs and leaflets. Between the ledges and the counter and the register were the scales, and most important of all, two simple desks with very basic PCs on them, hooked up to the store's broadband. Those were the meat of the matter for Danny: the main reason he was here and what made work here at least tolerable. *Well,* he thought, *that and the air-conditioning . . .*

He headed out the door into the humidity, making a face. It was astounding how fast you could go from being relatively cool and comfortable to being sticky and annoyed. It was as if the water in the air wrapped itself around you and clung like a badly wrung out washcloth. Danny wiped his brow as he went to the car, popped the back hatch open, and got out the last stack of cardboard boxes. He juggled them a little, getting them balanced in one arm so that he had the other arm free to close the hatch. Not that there was anyone here likely to take anything out of the back of the car. During the daytime, at least, this was the most boring, little-trafficked strip mall for miles around. *But still,* Danny thought, and shut the hatch. *Let's not take a chance that something might happen now, just before it's all over, to ruin everything. Be methodical.*

He went through the maneuver with the store's door again. His boss, sunk in the delights of the big fat stationery wholesalers' catalog, never even bothered to look up. One more trip to the back room, the next stack placed neatly on top of the last one, squared off, straightened up. Danny rubbed the small of his back, wiped sweat away. Out in the front, Ricardo turned over yet another page of the catalog and sighed, a desperately tired noise for someone who had done so little actual physical work during the course of the day. *It's only a matter of time now,* Danny thought. Fortunately today had been a slow business day, and now that it was so close to noon and Danny was back and finished with the supply run, the boss was feeling more imperative urges than that of work. Danny could hear the rustle as he turned over a few more pages in the catalog, each one more slowly than the last. *You'd think they weighed tons,* Danny thought, amused. Finally there came the sound he'd been waiting for: the creak of the legs of the behind-the-counter stool as Ricardo got up.

"Gonna go out and get a sandwich," Ricardo said, hitting the ground with an audible thump. In the back room, Danny smiled; he knew that Ricardo's lunch would not stop at a sandwich. There would be beer, probably a few beers; and if Danny gave any sign whatsoever of noticing this afterward, Ricardo would frown and growl and make "shut up, you should be grateful for your job" noises. Danny, however, had no plans of noticing, no matter how many beers the boss had. He planned to keep his head down and appear to be grateful for this job for exactly three days longer. Then . . .

White sand, blue sky, and a breeze in between. For the moment, all Danny had to do was look innocently industrious as Ricardo put his head through the door from the front, looking at him with a frown. "If the phone rings," he said, "don't you miss it."

"No, sir," Danny said. It was a laugh—the odds of any phone call over lunch hour were almost as low as the odds of one any other time of the day. Most of their customers were drive-ins, not given to calling ahead.

Ricardo lumbered toward the front door. "Be back in an hour," Ricardo said. The door squeaked opened, squeaked shut.

For the look of the thing, Danny went out front and spent the next few minutes tidying the racks. It was just as well he did; Ricardo hadn't been gone a minute and a half before he came back in that door, apparently for no other reason than to see if Danny was going through the cash register. Danny, then busy straightening out a wall display of rolls of Scotch tape, simply looked at Ricardo and didn't say a word. Ricardo let out a long breath of annoyance, as if it were somehow Danny's fault that he had *not* been stealing when Ricardo came in. Then out he went again, making his large, slow way down the strip mall.

Danny finished straightening the racks, then threw a last glance out the plate glass windows at the front. The air over the surface of the parking lot was wavering in the midday heat; out on the main road, sparse lunchtime traffic went by as usual. Danny turned away, making his way back to one of the computer desks, and sat down.

He slipped on the headset and wiggled the mouse to stop the screensaver. On the computer screen's desktop were the usual icons—word processor, calculator, business suite, image editor, Web browser, and some document folders. Danny clicked on My Documents to open it, then went to a folder that simply read "New Folder," as if it had nothing in it. He double-clicked on it. *Password? said the text box that came up.*

Danny gave it the combination of letters and numbers it was expecting. The folder opened to show what looked like a standard Web browser icon. Danny double clicked it, waited for the security window to pop up. After a few seconds, it appeared. *Passphrase?*

Danny glanced around, entirely out of reflex, then typed

quickly. He paused at the third group of characters to think what day today was. The passphrase did not remain the same; it changed each day, the last six-character group expressing the day's date in hex. *Eighteenth, let's see...* He typed the six characters, hit enter.

A custom browser window popped up. It could've been mistaken for the machine's own browser, and indeed was meant to be; but its pulldown menus were much different. Danny clicked on one of them, then clicked on the connect choice that was offered.

Another few moments' wait. From here on in, things would slow up a little bit due to the encryption. Danny didn't mind; he would sooner know that the communication was secure—especially considering who was on the other end of it. Not that he had any real idea who those people were. From the very start, when he had run across the masked figure in one of the clandestine hackers' playrooms on Omnitopia, there had been no names mentioned, no hints given as to real identities. Once he understood what was going on, that secrecy had made perfect sense to him, and he was happy to cooperate. It meant that if something went wrong and the cops—whatever cops—descended on the operation, no one would be able to give away any of the others.

Danny drummed his fingers idly on the desktop, shooting a glance at the front windows. Nothing moving out there, which was a relief; it would be annoying to be interrupted in the middle of this—

Typically, the phone rang. Danny cursed under his breath. *Is that Ricardo just calling to yank my chain?* He pulled off the headset and hurried over to answer it. "Post Boxes Unlimited, this is Danny, how can I help you?"

"Hey, man, it's Jackie."

Danny relaxed a little. It was the guy behind the counter down at the pizza place, who he saw occasionally after work at one of the local bars near the airport. "Hey, man, what's up?"

"Just wanted to let you know—" A pause, a clash of metal; it was the sound of an oven door being opened, then shut again. "The big guy's in here for his lunch—"

"Yeah, he headed out a few minutes ago."

"Yeah, well, thought you might want to know he's on his second beer already, and he's ordered two pies. Don't think he's gonna be back anytime soon."

Danny breathed out a small sigh of relief. "Thanks, man, I owe you one. Do me a favor? When he walks out the door, gimme a call?"

A chuckle at the other end. "No problem, man," said Jackie. Danny knew that Jackie wasn't particularly fond of his own boss and almost certainly assumed—correctly—that Danny didn't care much for his, either. Wage slaves knew each other on sight. "No point in having a good day interrupted by work."

"You got that, man," Danny said. "Thanks much."

"I'll be down with a bunch of the FedEx guys at the Smokestack on Sunday afternoon," Jackie said, "if you wanna buy me that beer you owe me."

Danny chuckled, mostly because he had no plans to be anywhere near here on Sunday. "We'll see how it rolls, man," he said. "Talk to you later."

"You got it," Jackie said, and hung up.

Danny hung up, made his way back to the desk, and sat down. The screen was still thinking about what to do next. Sometimes the cryptography took longer than usual for some reason or other—*Ah, here we go.* The browser window cleared, then went black. Danny waited for the text input window to come up. A few moments later, a word came up on the screen, all in caps. HI.

Hi there, he typed back. There were moments when it bothered him not to have even a handle to call the other guy by; it was strange, especially when your normal online-world dealings left you so used to having at least a fake name to grab hold of, if nothing else. But again, anonymity was key here. He'd sooner not have a name to use, especially if it meant making it harder for some cop here or in some other country to chase him down. Yes, they were all using anonymizers to conceal their locations—the address masker was built into this custom browser—but Danny knew that those could and would be broken by the people who'd eventually get onto their trail. By that time, Danny intended to be somewhere far away where he would never have to touch a computer again. He would be conducting his life on a cash-only basis in some country with friendly banking laws. In fact, he was still conducting the argument with himself about which country that would be. Switzerland was overrated, a spent force now, what with the new banking disclosure laws there that came along in the wake of the war against terror. But there were lots of other places to consider—newer, smaller, less cooperative. Some of them were in the Caribbean, some of them in sunny southern seas elsewhere.

GOT NEW TIMES FOR YOU, said the text on the screen.

Danny reached for one of the copy shop's branded pads, tore a piece of paper off it—during one of the earlier security briefings, he had been warned about the readability of any notepad's lower sheets—and started writing on the single piece of paper on the hard table. YOU READY? said the screen.

Danny put the pen aside. *Go,* he typed.

The screen spilled out a series of six letter and digit sequences, which Danny diligently and carefully began to copy. Each of these looked like one of the standard six letter and digit codes in hex that stood for a color that could be used in a Web page's code to paint in a background or color a type font. But at home, Danny had a neatly-printed little codebook in which each of those 256 groups had been assigned a different meaning—most of them having to do with times. Each code group changed in meaning depending on which other code group it was near. Anybody who happened to be intercepting this message, and anyone trying to figure out later what it meant, would easily mistake it for a set of directions for the design of a loading Web page. But the codebook meanings were far different. Danny had laughed, just once, when he finished reading that little book through—a boring read, most of it—and came to the last group, the "#000000" code for the color black: it translated as "flee at once, all is discovered."

At least there was no sign of that in *this* message. There was nothing else, either; the person typing at the other end was never chatty. When the code groups stopped, the only thing that came up on the next line was the single word: REPEAT. Danny typed in the six-digit sequences exactly as he had noted them down. He understood the other guy's concern about making sure that it was right. The code sequence described the times when Danny and his many coconspirators in this hack would be hitting a lot of different servers worldwide, a lot of different player groups in Omnitopia, with the goal being to overwhelm them while accounts were being raided for money. This business would require split-second timing in acting as one character, dumping it, signing out, signing in as someone else, on some other server entirely, and then acting as that person. It had been four or five months ago now that Danny had been sent the software with which to do this work on his own home computer and various others. Those other computers— including the poor dim ones here at work—were now all latent zombies. They would be transformed into willing slaves of his own machine at home as soon as he activated the program there and sent them the necessary command down the broadband line. This was a technique that spammers had been using for years to confuse large systems, and even occasionally to break into military or other classified sites by the sheer weight of numbers overwhelming their gateways to the outer world. In this particular case, the group that Danny was working with had brought the concept of the distributed denial-of-service attack up to a whole new level.

They'd had to. Omnitopia's Conscientious Objector routine was too damn smart to be taken in by the simple botting techniques of an earlier, kindlier age of spammers. It could immediately recognize a computer that was acting like a bot and freeze it out—shutting down any access from that computer's network address, and incidentally calling the local cops. The people behind this plan had had no intention of wasting their time on so old and predictable a technique. Instead they were basing the attack on sheer numbers of genuine human beings, which the CO routine shouldn't be able to profile so easily. If a lot of these logins would be coming from China and other parts of the Far

East—places where labor was cheap and there were lots of willing people sitting at keyboards who didn't care too much about the details of what they were doing as long as they got paid something better than their weekly wage—that was entirely to be expected: it was a resource worth exploiting.

Each person would activate his own or her own share in a pulsed wave of attacks that would come from all over the planet, clogging the Omnitopia servers with resource-heavy demands that would leave certain accounting and cash-inventory routines starved for resources, taking seconds to execute instead of milliseconds. And during those vital fractions of a second, from all over the world, many hands would reach into the virtual cash register while its drawer was stuck open and pull out wads of the green stuff.

Danny smiled to himself in quiet appreciation of the elegance of the scam and its simple audacity. His own nameless and faceless handler had been cagey about the details, but the number of keyboard slaves involved in the attack sequence was apparently somewhere up in the millions. There was no way the Omnitopia people would be able to defend against that completely—especially not at this time when their inside sources had confirmed that the new Omnitopia servers would be vulnerable.

And they were coming into that magic time now, Danny knew. The attacks would be taking place very soon—he'd known just how soon once he got these code groups home. But one way or another, within three days it would all be over. Omnitopia would be looking very stupid, and the Black Hat Ring who'd hatched and carried out this exploit would be famous—or infamous—worldwide if anonymously so. Danny wasn't particularly concerned about the fame: all he'd wanted was a chance to get out of this loser's life of minimum-wage jobs and into a life of lazing by some seaside with a cold drink in his hand, partying when he liked, and never doing anything that looked like work again. *And by Saturday, I'll have it.* By Saturday afternoon, having been given lots of helpful instructions about how best to lose yourself in the system despite its best attempts to keep track of you, he would be on his way out of Georgia, on the first of a number of planes, trains, and automobiles to anywhere—and finally on his way to the place in the sun that life owed him.

Danny waited, watching the black screen. Momentarily, the type came through. FINISHED.

And that was all there was. This was the only sad thing about the plan for Danny. He'd always been a gregarious type; he enjoyed playing the Great Game with others, talking about it, laughing about it. But there was no one, absolutely *no one* he could share this with. And of course, he understood the reasons; but it was sad all the same. Brag rights would be so sweet. Even afterward, if he wanted to stay free and wealthy, he could never say anything about having been part of The Day the Black Hats Won. It was really very, very sad. In fact, his handler had advised him to give up Omnitopia entirely. *It's a goddamn shame,* Danny thought. *After I finally got my mage up to level thirty-five.*

A little sadly, *Finished,* he typed.

The black screen went white: the browser window closed itself. Danny reached down and punched the computer's reset button to make sure the broadband router's logging function failed to shut down correctly. That would mean that all the morning's sessions on this machine would fail to log as well. Ricardo would give him grief about it, but the machine occasionally committed this error on its own, so Ricardo wouldn't be able to specifically blame Danny for it.

The machine started rebooting. Danny got up, stretched, and went to the window to look out at the sun blazing through the smog, and the lunchtime traffic, and the hot air dancing over the parking lot. In his mind he could already see a much different sun, shining down on white sand, a blue sea beyond it, a cold drink in his hand. *A mint julep,* he thought. *I've never had a mint julep. But I'm going to have one soon.*

Danny turned away from the window and, methodical as always, started straightening the padded envelopes in the bin by the scale.

The employees called Infinity Inc.'s main New York-area manufacturing and R&D facility "The Flats," not so much as a reference to the wilderness of North Jersey salt marsh all around it, but because it was (they said among themselves on the company infranet's chat area) just a little too small inside for you to be able to see the curvature of the earth. Phil—checking on the infranet chat under a pseudonym, as everyone knew he sometimes did—had at first been slightly offended by the nickname when he'd heard it. But the reaction had worn off over time, as none of his employees seemed eager to dump their jobs just because of the facility's size.

He was standing on the balcony outside the executive office suite at the building's west end, looking down over the shop floor—a sprawling quarter-mile long vista of cubicles grouped in nodes of four, eight, and sixteen, depending on how many subteams, teams, or groups they were housing, along with various "pick up and go" group meeting modules for employees whose job descriptions made it more sensible for them to move from area to area in the course of the day's work. Some of them were making their way around the floor even now on razor scooters or on one or another of Infinity's little fleet of Segways, and the huge place hummed under the high roof with a soft clamor of conversation, the sound of people getting on with business in a place designed to keep them on track. It was a heartening view. Phil liked his people working where he could walk or ride around under one roof and see them all without having to run all over the landscape, at the mercy of the traffic or the weather.

Where is he? Phil thought, pulling his phone out of his pocket to see if he'd missed a text. But nothing new showed on the screen. *He's not going to like it if he makes me come looking for him. Well. Give him another five minutes.*

Phil wandered down to the end of the balcony and looked out the floor-to-ceiling window at the northward view, over the huge parking lot and beyond. Infinity Inc. Kearny had been built just inside one of the major loops of the meandering Hackensack River, on land Phil had acquired five years previously when the company started getting a good head of steam and he foresaw the need for a far bigger facility that would be able to hold both his development and manufacturing requirements under one roof. Even then, undeveloped, the property had been a good bargain: reclaimed land, cheap even after factoring in the price of detoxing it from the waste chemicals, heavy metals, and so forth, that had seeped into the ground and the water table beneath it from the older industries that had occupied the area prewar. All those industries, shipbuilding and small-scale light manufacturing and so on, had expired of capital loss during the Great Depression, or of inability to keep up with consumer trends in the postwar boom, leaving the local communities chronically short of employment opportunities and desperate for inward investment of any kind. When Phil had come along and offered Kearny Township money for land that until then had been essentially worthless, they'd grabbed the offer with both hands.

And they hadn't been sorry afterward, especially when this facility opened and hiring began. Infinity Inc. had become one of the major employers in northern New Jersey, and had been able to pump a lot of action into the local economy simply due to I.I. Kearny's location. It was handy for cheap transport, right by the Jersey Turnpike and the rail yards outside of Newark, and close to the courier and parcel shipping companies that clustered around the fringes of Newark Airport. To Phil's way of thinking, a tightly consolidated facility like this made far better economic sense than some splashy purpose-built greenbelt facility, more style than substance.

Back at the middle of the balcony, he heard the elevator go *ding!* Phil turned to see his operations manager Link Raglan step out of it—

"Link? Down here."

He came hurrying down to Phil, a bland-faced blond guy who looked more like a professional wrestler than anything else: burly and massive across the shoulders, with wrists as thick as some people's forearms, and a neck so big it could be detected only by the presence of a collar and tie around it. Unfortunately these were always under a suit that looked like Link had been shoved into it under pressure. Even on his salary he insisted on buying his suits off the rack, and his notion of what constituted a fit was uncertain at best.

"Sorry, Mr. Sorensen," Link said as he came up to Phil. "The turnpike was a mess, and I couldn't stop to text."

"It's all right," Phil said. "Just don't make a habit of it: I'm going to need you accessible at a moment's notice when things heat up over the next few days." They started toward the staircase at the end of the balcony. "Are the people we're supposed to be seeing ready for us? I can't stay long. I have to get ready for that charity thing tonight before I head out to the Island."

"They're ready," Link said as they headed down the stairs.

"Good. How are the preload numbers looking?"

"Busy. The download servers are getting hammered with thousands of logins, people trying to hold download slots open."

"But the system's dumping them on six-minute latency?"

Link nodded. "To favor the high-speed broadband users, as we planned. The dial-up and ADSL people will be getting a download manager pumped downstream to them in the first five minutes, and when they get dumped, they can log in as many times as they have to in order to pick up where they left off."

"Good. I don't want the system getting bogged down in slow downloads like it did on the last expansion. It made our first-day numbers look like crap."

"No danger of that now, sir."

At the bottom of the staircase, the usual golf cart was parked. Phil climbed in. Link got behind the wheel, started it up, and hung first a right, then a left to drive down the vehicle-and-mail-cart access path along the south side of the building.

Phil pulled out his PDA and flipped it open for a moment, glancing at the Bloomberg page for Infinity's stock and noticing with satisfaction that the graph for the day had edged up slightly. *Good. All we need is a nice fat hit on the numbers today to make Omnitopia's splash look a little less splashy. Three points would do; five would be better. But we're already in a position even just on prelaunch buzz to take the first shine off Dev's day in the sun. And then, after those first clouds move in, the deluge.*

About a third of the way down the facility's floor, Link hung a left. In all the cubicles they passed, Phil saw interested eyes peering out at the sound of the oncoming cart's beeper or the sight of the rotating light on its back. The looks, though interested, weren't particularly surprised, for Phil was here at least a few times every week—sometimes just wandering up and down among the cubicles, sometimes being driven around, or driving himself—and looking in on this or that department to keep them on their toes. The company HR and psych people had repeatedly emphasized to Phil the importance of being here and being seen to be part of the team. He did it because he knew it was good business to do it, but sometimes it got on his nerves. *Whatever happened to just doing your job because you were being paid to do it? All this I'm-one-of-you stuff, they know it's a sham, I know it's a sham, why do we need to bother? They're my employees; why should I have to bribe them to perform?* But such was the corporate culture in which Phil now found himself, and rather than incur the bad publicity that would come along with not being seen to be playing the game, he played it. *That's what we're all about, here, anyway, isn't it?* he thought, resigned. *Games.*

Link was slowing now. He pulled the cart over and parked. Outside the next island of cubicles on the right, a crowd of ten or twelve employees were standing, all dressed in identical violet II T-shirts emblazoned with the new *Infinite Worlds: Threefold* logo and the legend ROLL-OUT FEVER—BE THE FIRST!

Phil climbed out of the cart and went to meet them. They broke into applause as he headed toward them, and Phil had to grin, even though he suspected the response of being coached rather than spontaneous. *Doesn't matter, be sincere even if you have to fake it.* "Hey there!" he said, and made the rounds of the group, shaking everyone's hand.

"Okay!" Phil said when that was done. "So you guys are the team leaders for the Social Networking Download

Stimulus Initiative. Or SNDSI for short . . ." His attempt to pronounce the vowel-less acronym made them all laugh. "Who makes these names up, anyway? Never mind. Whatever we're calling it, your section managers have pulled you out of the ranks for this opportunity because they think you and your teams have got the best chatting and blogging and tweeting skills in the company. So today your job is to get out there and chat and blog and tweet up a storm about *Infinite Worlds Threefold*. And we've made it even easier for you by building custom chat, blog, and tweet clients for you. Now, as I understand it, you've all had a week or so to break those in?"

Heads nodded all around the group. "Great. All over the world, people are already excited about the hot new product we're rolling out today, but your business today starting at six P.M., and tonight, and tomorrow until six P.M., is to get them five times as excited as they thought they were! Every time you and your teams blog about the game and someone follows the URL to the download site, every time you tweet about it and they jump to the Twitter-linked address, every time a chatter follows the link you point them to—that login and download will be credited to your account and your team's. Then, at the end of the twenty-four hours, we'll total up the logins and downloads. The winning team will be getting not only the place of honor at the rollout party here tomorrow night, but also an extra week of paid vacation this year." The whole group cheered. "And an all-expenses paid vacation in Hawaii for that whole team and their families to use it on!"

The expressions of shock and delight, the shouts and the sudden outbreak of inter-employee hugging, went well beyond Phil's expectations: for a moment he was caught off guard and lost the thread of what he'd been saying. But after a few seconds he recovered. "So what you need to do is motivate each other like crazy today and tonight and tomorrow, and remind the gaming world and the whole Internet that Infinity Inc. is the original nine hundred pound gorilla, no matter how many other hairy apes may be running around the place!"

More cheers. One of the employees, a little pigtailed

lady, had actually burst into tears at the news about the vacations, and was still wiping them away while jumping up and down for joy. Looking at her, Phil started feeling more uncomfortable than ever, and couldn't work out why. *Doesn't matter. Time to go . . .* "Okay, people," he said, "good luck! Go for it, and make me and your teammates proud!"

The employees all burst into applause again. Phil waved at them and headed back toward the golf cart, trying not to look like he was hurrying.

Phil climbed back into the cart's backseat and kept waving at the employees while Link got in, started the cart up, and turned them around. Then he looked over his shoulder and kept waving at the still-cheering crowd until they turned the corner and were out of sight. Annoying as he found the need to "incentivize" his staff, it was still amazing the enthusiasm you could generate by diverting no more money than the company spent for bottled water over a couple of weeks.

Phil let out a breath. "Okay," he said. "On to other business." He pulled a little bottle of hand-sanitizer out of his pants pocket, squirted a bit of sanitizer gel into one palm, and gave his hands a scrub. "Is the car back yet?"

"Right outside the west doors now, Mr. Sorensen."

"Good. I want hourly reports on how they're doing as soon as they get started. I won't be turning in until late, so don't skimp on the post-midnight reports, understand?"

"Yes, sir."

"Excellent. Now get me out of here." Phil sighed. "I have to go be charitable."

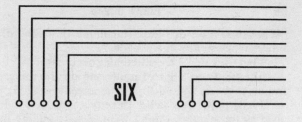

SIX

LUNCH, OF COURSE, did not happen on time, for this was Dev
Logan's life, in which nothing during these three days was
going to go according to plan. He hadn't made it more than
halfway across the inner courtyard before his phone went
off, and this time it was one of the tailored rings he never
ignored, his assistant Frank's. "Boss—"

"I know, I know," Dev said, feeling faintly guilty. "I'm
supposed to be having lunch with Lola, I'll be—"

"No, it's not that! 'Trouble at t' mill,' Boss."

It had started out as old code between Dev and Jim for
times when there was a fairly serious problem. Now many
of the other staff close to Dev had adopted it despite not
having been born when the joke was first made. "Oh, no,"
Dev moaned, covering his eyes with one hand. "Not the
server attack already, at the worst time, *please* tell me it's
not the server attack!"

"Boss, not on an open line!" Frank said. "Not something
I'm not supposed to know about! Not not not . . ."

"Sorry, yes, of course, *what is it?*"

"We seem to have been having a little dustup in Omnitopia City—"

"A *what?*"

The conversation went on for some minutes while Frank
gave him the earliest details. Dev went from muttering to
swearing in the first five of those minutes, was immediately
lectured on language by Frank as usual, and spent the rest
of the briefing fuming.

Finally Frank fell silent. "So?" he said after a moment.

"What should we do? Inquiring minds down in infrastructure management want to know."

"I bet they do," Dev said under his breath.

"There's been a lot of muttering on the gameside infranets that you should appoint a new mayor."

"I hate that," Dev said. "The city's supposed to be managed by the players. I don't want to start pulling their autonomy out from under them at this late date."

Dev sat down on a nearby bench and started moodily pulling the tiny spiny leaves off a branch of a nearby shrub, shaking his head. "I still can't believe they *did* that," he said.

"Did what?" said a voice from behind him.

Dev glanced up. Tau Vitoria had come up behind him, his arms full of his laptop and some folders. He sat down next to Dev, looking concerned.

Dev rolled his eyes. "Frank, tell Tau what they did." He handed Tau the phone.

Tau listened, expressionless. Dev watched him for a few moments, impressed yet again at Tau's strange gift for being able to listen to a conversation with this totally unreadable face, like something carved from stone. *Some weird European superpower,* Dev thought, *or something he inherited from one of these kings he's supposed to be related to.* He gazed across the courtyard toward the family wing's windows and thought he saw something moving behind one of them. The way the sun caught the windows at this time of morning, the reflections made it tough to see detail, but whatever was moving was down low— Then the moving object got closer to the window, and he could see it was Lola waving to him. *I should be up there having lunch with my baby,* he thought, *not having to deal with this right now!*

"Yeah," Tau said, "I heard all about that. Yeah, just now." A moment's silence. "No, it's okay, it's being managed. Yeah. No, Randy called me first—he and Majella are waiting to talk to you right now, they've got some strategies. You just caught the boss before they could catch you. Yeah. Okay. Anything else for him?" A pause. "Okay. Bye."

He closed the phone and handed it back to Dev. "I heard about this about thirty seconds after you walked out of the room, and it's being handled," Tau said. "Infrastructure is adding some stopgap manpower solutions to deal with this situation and the aftermath until we have time to solve it more thoroughly after the rollout. They'll be briefing Frank in a bit. Right now the only thing that's needed is a little more human oversight. After that we'll teach the system how to prevent this kind of thing itself."

Dev took the phone back and put it away, shaking his head. "I still can't get why they did it."

"Because they could?" Tau said. "And I warned you they would! Remember when I told you that you should have inserted the no-warfare stricture via code fiat? But you didn't want me to, you hate doing that. 'They'll behave,' you said to me. 'Omnitopia City is the major cross-world commerce center, they know better than to mess with *that*.' Well, no they don't!" And Tau snickered at him.

"Okay," Dev said after a moment. "Okay, I take your point."

"And after this you will *listen to me* on stuff like this? Because frankly it's a miracle that this took so long to happen."

"Yeah, yeah, just shut up, Mr. Smugness," Dev muttered. But he had to smile. Tau could be infuriating sometimes, but he had never yet failed to have Dev's and Omnitopia's best interests at heart. "So I take it you have newer news than Frank's about who was at the bottom of this little fracas?"

"A troll guild from Jormundr," Tau said. "They steamed through the Ring Plaza, did some damage, and were getting ready to steam on out the other side when the inhabitants of the City decided to get cranky about them. Didn't seem like a good idea to stop that. After all, civic virtue is something we do try to inculcate."

"Was this an independent operation, or were they bought?"

"We're looking into it," Tau said.

Dev dropped his face into his hands, rubbed his eyes. "See that," he said. "I leave my universe untended for one day, and look what happens!"

"Ahem," Tau said. When Dev looked up again, Tau gestured around him to the bustle that was Castle Dev, and by implication, to the hundred acres around it—thousands of people coming and going, all with one thing in mind: that universe. "Hardly untended," Tau said.

"Oh, please," Dev said. "Don't soothe me. I hate being soothed."

"This would be obvious," Tau said. "Come on, Big D, calm down. You have to anyway. Because guess who's on her way?"

Dev looked around him, startled. "What? Is Miri done with her dress fitting already?"

Tau rolled his eyes. "Oh, no, Boss. Much better than that. *Time* Magazine Lady is about to arrive."

"No way," Dev said. "Not right this minute! I have to get online and have a walk around before my universe gets really cranky with me and breaks something else. Put her off for me. Better still, you talk to her."

Tau acquired an expression of sorrowful self-sacrifice. "Well. If I have to—"

"Yes, you do!" Dev said, jumping up from the bench. "I've got to get in there."

"This is just superstitious behavior," Tau said as Dev headed for the family side of the building. "You're a techie, Dev, you should know better—"

"Oh yeah? Remember the *last* time I didn't go O-side until after lunch? That was the day we had that big attempted break-in! If I don't get in there—"

"Go on, go on," Tau said, "I'll stall her for you. But you owe me one."

"More than one," Dev said, and headed at his best speed toward the doors that led upstairs from the courtyard to the family wing. But something was niggling at him: and right in the doorway he stopped and shouted back at Tau, "Wait a minute, what the heck are you trying to pull? *You're* the one she's scheduled to be seeing now anyway!"

Tau merely grinned at him and made a bye-bye wave.

"You're fired!" Dev shouted.

Tau checked his watch. "Twelve-fifteen," he called back. "Possibly a record."

Dev, muttering in amusement now, headed through the doorway and toward the elevator. A few moments later he was walking through the doors into Lola's suite, annoyed that he had to disappoint her, and himself, by not having lunch with her. The annoyance was sharpened by the sound of her laughter coming out of the living area. But then the annoyance fell off somewhat as he saw someone in a three-piece suit sitting cross-legged on the floor with a picture book in his lap. It was Jim Margoulies.

"How the heck did you beat me up here?" Dev said, heading over to them. Lola was sitting on the opposite side of the low table, stuffing a frankfurter into her mouth—one of several that sat on the plate in front of her along with some dunking mustard—and grinning at her Uncle Jim.

Jim shrugged. "You were on the phone. I was getting ready to come over anyway when Tau told me to step on it, as you would probably have a problem in about two minutes. Oh, thanks, Pops—"

Poppy had come in and now handed Jim an iced coffee. Lola extracted half the hot dog from her mouth, waved it at Dev, and said, "Uncle Jim is reading me about Wuggie Norple!"

Dev grinned. It was Lola's favorite book, one which at present she never stopped insisting she wanted read to her—with the result that Dev and Mirabel now both knew it by heart. Dev was more than relieved to let Jim handle the torture for the moment—assuming he knew what he was getting into. "That's great," Dev said. "Jim, you sure you have time for the literary life right now?"

"Yes I do," Jim said, "and right now *you* should go take care of what you have to before you start getting stressed."

"'Start?'" Dev said. But he smiled at his friend and got down by Lola. "Got a hug for Daddy, Lolo?"

She stuffed the hot dog back in her face and put her arms up. Dev smooched her, participated enthusiastically in the rather mustardy hug, and said in her ear, "You know what Mommy said?"

"What?"

"If you're a good girl, she's gonna take you to Coldstone later."

Lola emitted a shriek of joy that was deafening at this range, not that Dev minded. She disentangled herself from

Dev and turned to Jim with utmost seriousness. "Unca Jim," she said, "can you come to Coldstone? I'll buy you an ice cream."

"Hmm," Jim said. "Well, we should consider the financial side of this carefully before we make any overt moves."

Lolo put down her hot dog, jumped up, and vanished into her bedroom. A few moments later she emerged carrying her piggy bank, a fat pink earthenware business with a pronounced smirk, which had been a gift from Jim.

Dev gave Jim an amused look. "I'm going to leave you fiduciary wizards to sort this out among yourselves," he said. "If you need me, I'll be O-side."

"I'll catch up with you later," Jim said.

Dev headed out past Poppy, who was standing in the doorway looking on with amusement at the energetic shaking and jingling now underway. "I've gotta cure her of this impulse buying," Dev said.

Poppy chuckled. "No impulse about it, Daddy Dev," she said. "She's been plotting this assault on the marketplace ever since you mentioned Jim this morning."

Dev shook his head, smiling, as he headed out. "When her mom turns up," he said, "tell her I'm online, okay? Got some things to see to."

"Will do, Dev."

He left Lola's suite and headed down to the far end of the family wing proper. Dev had offices all over the campus, in every major "village of the like-minded," but his main one took up about a third of the north side of Castle Dev. There three floors of the north wing had been interconnected with spiral stairs and old European-style open passenger lifts. The doors at the end of the family wing opened on the third-floor executive office, the most comfort-oriented one, which was more like a giant living room than anything else, and childproofed. Couches and comfy furniture were scattered around the big central desk, most of the walls were lined with railed bookshelves, and all the windows looked inward. The outer windows on this level were replaced by a FullWall macroplasma screen for teleconferencing and other purposes. Right now it was showing an image that was one of an endlessly changing set of webcam views—in this case, some Mediterranean city he couldn't identify off-hand. "Household management," he said as he opened the door of the glass-enclosed niche for the paternoster lift and waited for the downward-moving step to reach floor level.

"Yes, Dev?"

"What's that on the wallscreen right now?"

"A view of Split Harbor," said the management computer.

"Thank you. Boot up the second floor online suite, please?"

"Booting now."

Dev stepped onto the lift step as it came level, keeping an eye on the niche's glass door to make doubly sure it closed and locked properly behind him, as Lola sometimes came in here with one or another of her PAs. *City security,* he thought as the lock snicked home. *Manpower isn't going to solve it. I wonder . . .* But there were other concerns right now. Item three on that list kept coming back to haunt him, and the Conscientious Objector routines, which he was sure were somehow at the bottom of that particular mal-function. *Well, we'll see what Tau and I can brainstorm later. Meanwhile . . .*

He stepped off the lift on the second floor. Here was the place where Dev got most of his daytime work done: another neutrally-furnished place like the tower meeting room, but this one featuring several huge desks—one of which was Frank's, though Frank also had numerous offices and cubbies scattered around the campus linked together by teleconferencing and online-access facilities. Various solid filing facilities, more bookshelves, and another smaller FullWall alternated with both outside and inside windows on this level. Off in the northeast corner sat a black glass cube twenty feet on a side.

Dev headed for it, and the access cube's sensors, check-ing his biometrics, cleared the glass and swung the cube door open for him. Inside was a big comfortable zero-G chair, its intuitive gel cushions and built-in counterbalance functions meant to keep a heavy online user's body from feeling the strain of all that sitting-still time. Dev sat down, reached into the chair pocket, and pulled out the RealFeel interface. "Close up," he said to the cubicle, "and go dark. Interior lighting on low. Frank?"

The household management computer said, "Finding him." A moment later came the soft *burr-burr* of an on-campus phone ring. "Yeah, Boss?"

"I'm in the second-story cube," he said. "Need to have a quick look around at some things online. I should be done in an hour or so. Are we clear?"

"No problems at all, Boss," Frank's voice said. "Except for the one you're gonna have with certain parties if you're not seen to eat something pretty soon."

Dev smiled wryly. "Tell her what happened to my lunch hour."

"I'll tell her," Frank said, "but don't think it's gonna spare you what you've got coming. Just go over to the cantina when you're done and eat a sandwich, will you?"

"Yes, Mommy! Bye-bye."

The connection went quiet: from long analysis of his voice patterns, the household management computer knew when Dev was done with a call. He sighed, slipped on the RealFeel headset, got the eyecups in place, and looked into the darkness.

There was the usual faint flash as the headset's hardware got into sync with his optic nerve and engineered the necessary connections. A second later Dev was sitting in his online workspace, which was a twin of the second floor office—with certain differences.

He got up out of the chair. The glass of the cubicle cleared around him, and the door opened. Dev headed out into the office, making for the central desk. What in the physical world had looked like a huge and fairly tidy expanse of ebony, featuring only some paperwork awaiting signing and some bric-a-brac surrounding a small brass cannon, was here a huge black glass slab around which hung hundreds of vertical sheets of light. Most of them were pale almost to the point of transparency, some of them brighter and more visible, a few of them opaque and glowing; in one case, the glow was throbbing brighter and dimmer, brighter and dimmer, like something that urgently needed to be looked at. Beyond the desks and the documents there were no walls: the view stretched straight out over the streets and rooftops of Omnitopia City. The floor was glass nearly as black as the desk, and through it, away down a couple of hundred feet or so, could faintly be seen the upper surfaces of the lintel stones of the Ring of Elich. Farther down, Dev could see the plaza around the Ring, busy with players as always. He paused to study it for a moment. If there was any vista in Omnitopia that Dev knew how to read, it was this one; and to his eye it looked a lot more agitated than usual.

Well, they'll calm down, he thought. *But meanwhile—*

Dev went over to the most brightly throbbing document, reached out, and tweaked its lower corner. The doc expanded to a sheet a couple of feet long by a foot: it was Frank's initial written debrief about the streaming attack on the plaza, now with a couple of attachments. One of them was a complete census of players involved in it as attackers, victims, or other participants; another was an initial analysis and list of suggestions from the infrastructure management people. Dev flicked the surface of the document a couple of times with a forefinger to make it scroll up as he looked over the suggestions. He thought about them for a moment, then scrolled back up to the top again and poked one of the names on the document's cc list. "Randy?" he said.

A window popped open on the document. In it there appeared the webcammed image of Randy DeNovra, the chunky dark young senior manager in infrastructure management. He was sitting in front of his monitor and typing something by hand, yet another of a series of endearingly retro office habits. "Hey, Mr. Dev—"

"I've just been through your recommendations. Thanks for getting those in so quickly."

"Like I wouldn't have done it even if I'd had a choice," Randy said, "which I did not. Majella's been running around screaming at the top of her lungs for the last hour about being terrified of some kind of copycatting attack. And it could happen, so the sooner we have some kind of measure in place, the better."

Dev listened. "Don't seem to hear any screaming now."

"Her PA made her go have a latte," said Randy. "When she comes back, she can claim it was her blood sugar talking."

Dev smiled. "Okay," he said. "Just quickly: suggestion one sucks, so don't do that. Suggestion two sounds kind of okay, but let me think about it for a while, and if I haven't come up with something useful in the next twenty-four hours, go ahead and do what you're planning. Suggestion three— How much manpower are you intending to spend on this particular solution?"

"About a hundred people," Randy said, "scattered around the various time zones, until we get the new code in place that will sniff out this kind of attack anyplace in Telekil, not just the City. We've got a lot of volunteers already, people who're willing to retask their personal-project time. They'll screen large-scale player movements in real time, assessing the weapons and other assets that the players are carrying, and assigning live assets from proctoring to keep an eye on anything that looks weird."

"How long for the code?"

"A week and a half, I think. Might be two. We've got a lot of interleaving to do with the basic Ring routines; you don't want it mistakenly outlawing legal movements of large groups."

Dev thought for a moment. "Okay," he said. "Don't try to cover more than half of your personnel assignments with PP time, though. I'll have personnel authorize double time for those who're interested. Spread the word around in the assignments infranet and see who picks you up."

"Probably a lot of people, Mr. Dev. People feel protective about the City. A lot of folks are in shock."

Dev's grin went a bit sour. "They're not alone," he said. "Anything else we need?"

"Not unless you have more notes on our notes."

"Okay, then we're done," Dev said. "Thanks, Randy. Tell Majella I said to calm down, she's doing a great job."

"Will do."

The window closed. Dev sighed, looked over the document one more time, and tweaked it again to take the throb out of its glow. He was about to turn away from it when he remembered to ask the usual question. "Any correlations between this and other pending material?"

One of the attachments to the document he was still holding started to throb. It was the census list. The other was some feet away, closer to the desk. When Dev beckoned it closer, he found that it was Ron Ruis' Microcosm status report for that morning.

"Huh," Dev said, enlarging that document and scrolling down it to find a name that also appeared in the census list. "Really ... ?"

He poked the name. "Sticky that for me," he said. "Tag the sticky as 'investigate.' Meantime, show me the rack, please."

At the other end of the office, away past the festoons of documents hanging around the central desk, a wrist-thick horizontal beam of white light appeared. From it hung many shadowy forms which, as Dev made his way over to them, resolved into what at first glimpse could have been taken for bodies. Male and female, human and nonhuman, monstrous and ordinary, they were all shapes that Dev had invented for himself, or which his staff had invented for him, so that he could walk his worlds undetected and get a sense of what was really going on in there.

He stood there irresolute for a moment, then waved the rack along a little. The shapes fled out of sight to be replaced by new ones. "No," Dev said. "No, no, no ..." The display changed again, then again. Finally Dev's eyes lit on one seeming that he hadn't seen before. "What the—"

He pulled it off the rack, looked at the front of it, turned it around, snickered. *Okay,* Dev said, and shrugged into it as if into a suit jacket. "Mirror, please?"

A reflective sheet appeared out of nothing in front of him. Dev snorted, amused. "Fine," he said. "Kill that. Omnitopia game management—"

"Good afternoon, Dev," said the dulcet control voice.

"And the same to you, game of mine," Dev said. "First things first. I want a playback of the incident referenced in Frank's précis document. Then a walkthrough of the incursion and excursion sites. Meanwhile, screen all in-game feeds and news services for references and reactions to the

referenced incident. Plot against this month's emo index
and the baseline index from a year ago, and while I'm on
walkabout, start showing me the twenty highest, twenty
lowest, and a Monte Carlo sampling from the middle of the
bell curve."

"All right, Dev," said the control voice. "Where do you
want to start the walkthrough?"

"West side of the plaza," Dev said. "Best view of the incursion route."

Part of the black glass floor peeled itself downward
from the floor level and folded itself into steps. Dev headed
down them, whistling softly and feeling a sudden relief as
the darkness of Omnitopian night washed around him, the
plaza's torches and magelights throwing shadows away in
every direction from the stones of the Ring of Elich. *Okay,*
he thought, *let's see what needs to be done.*

Rik heaved a sigh of relief when he finally stepped through
the gateway into Langley B. It was starting to seem as if
he'd been trying to get here for days, but now he stood at
last in the midst of the White Arcades at the heart of the
City of Artificers, the arch-surrounded plaza at the hill-
town's top that was Langley's primary access to the Ring
of Elich. As usual, the marble-paved space inside the arcades was full of midweek traffic: the stalls and stands that
belonged to the casual traders were being cruised hard by
various people and creatures in mystical robes and wizard's
hats, long black trench coats (usually hiding samurai swords
glowing a dangerous blue from inside their scabbards, and
sometimes right through them), and in a few cases, motor-
cyclists' leathers or ornamental ladies' armor with about as
much coverage as your average bikini.

Rik skirted carefully around one such lady—he'd run
into them in the past and they could be testy: something
to do with cold chain mail against the skin, he'd always
imagined. *Must give you some awful kind of rash.* But, leaving the predictable wizards and mages aside, you got a lot
of aligned and unaligned warrior types here as well from

Macrocosms and Microcosms everywhere. Langley B was famous right across Omnitopia for the quality and variety of its magian and wizardly gear, everything from the simplest basic outfitting—robes and so forth—up to the fanciest custom magic weapons. Almost everybody who worked in one of the feudal or magical scenarios came here to shop or commission materiel eventually, as there were more arms- and magic-devoted Ivory Towers here than in any other Macrocosm. Some people suggested that the special protective status that went with Tower facilities should simply be extended to the whole 'cosm to save time and cut down on red tape.

Rik made his way leftward around the curve of stalls, which matched the curve of the surrounding arcades, and went on down the small winding street that led to his preferred robier's. Calling it a street was possibly an error: it was more of a stairway, its path switching back and forth as it made its way steeply down past the houses and shops set into the hillside or perched precariously on stilts and pillars on the street's far side. All the narrow buildings had the typical steeply-pitched Langley blue-tile roofs with extended, curved eaves; what they lost in width they made up for in depth, normally extending several stories up or down, depending whether they were on the hill or valley side of the street. As usual, Rik got a little confused about which one of them was his robier's place, as it wasn't signed, and its front had the same wide, closed shop-shutter and was plastered in the same worn, gray-blue stucco as its four immediate neighbors on the hill side of the street. Rik paused for a moment in front of them, and then remembered the weird spider-shaped boot scraper next to the wooden door he wanted. He went over to that door and knocked on it.

Nothing. Rik knocked again, louder.

Still nothing. Rik stood there in the morning sunshine and wondered, as he often had before, whether this house's owner was a real player or somebody game-generated. The high quality of Omnitopia's GGCs was either a source of joy or a serious annoyance, depending on what you were trying to get done at any given moment. Lal the Robier's profile, which he'd looked at any number of times, did not show any out-of-world contact info or other personal details. Not that this by itself was unusual—lots of players preferred to keep their in-Topian and out-Topian lives strictly separated, either for personal reasons or the normal concerns about identity theft, persona-jacking, and so on. Still, it was annoying not to know whether his knocking was simply leaving a "Rik tried to reach you" message in the in-game message box of someone who was busy with their real life at the moment, or whether the game was just making him wait because that might be a thing that the character who lived here would do—

With great suddenness and a deafening creak almost like a gunshot, the shutter next to the door abruptly dropped, bouncing down flat at the end of the iron chains that normally held its top edge up against the house. Inside, in the darkness, a little dark-shawled shape with a tangle of white hair glared out at him, blinking in the brightness. *"What?!"* she yelled.

"Uh, fair morning to you, Lal," Rik said. "'Tis Arnulf Manyfaced. I've come for my robes."

"You were supposed to be here two days ago!"

"Uh, yesterday," Rik said.

She came farther into the light and scowled at him. She had a round wrinkled-potato face and little sharp black eyes half hidden among the potato wrinkles. It was not a face you could ever imagine smiling; or if it did, you might be tempted to back away before something untoward happened. "You might have sent me a messenger to tell me you were going to be late!"

He might have, but it had completely slipped his mind in the madness of the last day or so. And it was true that the service-driven economy of real life could sucker you into thinking that just because it was a business day in a given Macrocosm, the person with whom you had business could be expected to be there. "I'm sorry," Rik said, smiling at her in an attempt to get her off the shouting jag he had a feeling was about to start. "It was completely my fault, Lal. Please forgive me."

She scowled at him. "Huh," Lal the Robier said, and disappeared back into the darkness of her shop.

Several moments later she appeared with a bundle done up in rough handmade brown paper and string. "I suppose you're going to want to try them on," she said, and sniffed in disdain, glaring at him again.

Actually there was nothing he wanted to do less right now. His friends were waiting for him in Meruvelt. "Uh, no," he said, "it's all right. If there's a problem I'll stop back another time and we can do the alterations."

"Very well. Take them with or have them sent?" the little woman growled.

Do I really want to cart these things all the way to Meruvelt? Rik thought. You did pay slightly less for moving artifacts from one 'cosm to another if you carried them yourself. But then the group would be heading back to his own Microcosm as well, and Rik would have to bring the robes along. *Do I, Come to think of it, do I incur any extra charges for that?* Rik sighed, decided to keep it simple for the time being. "Send them, please."

"Fine. You owe me twelve in gold, plus one gold six minims shipping."

Rik fumbled around in his waist pouch for the right coinage while trying to convert Langley gold ducats to Omnitopian game gold units in his head, wondering whether he was about to be overcharged for his shipping. But he was in a rush. "Thank you," he said, and handed over the necessary gold.

Package and robier vanished into the darkness of the shop together. A second later chains rattled and the shutter was hauled up and slammed closed against the wall. Rik stood there, slightly bemused. But only a second later, the game management system said in his ear, "A delivery for you, Rik. Do you want to hear storage options?"

"No thanks," Rik said. "Store it in my office space."

"Done," said the control voice. "A confirmation of this operation has been stored in your inbox."

"Okay," Rik said, and turned to make his winding way back up the street. *Well, at least I've got them now, and I can show them to Angie. Still have to wonder, though: is Lal real . . . ?*

On the way back up the hill, Rik stopped once or twice

at the switchback terraces to get his breath. The view down from here was fantastic, especially on a nice day like this when the weather was clear: endless vistas of hilly green forest and countryside rolling away into the misty horizon, a morning sky streaked with filmy mares' tails, the high pink sun warming it all. But to his mild horror, Rik now found himself unable to appreciate the view simply for what it was. In the back of his mind, he kept seeing wireframes. *I wonder how they got that effect,* he thought, looking up at the mares' tails and trying to work out how the pertinent ARGOT or WannaB modules would have to be stacked. *You'd have to fiddle with the wind variables, I guess. Or who knows, it's probably a macro: they have to have the Macrocosms completely automated . . .* As he climbed back up in to the Arcades plaza, Rik found himself debating whether it wouldn't really be more fun to control the weather yourself, day by day. *But probably that gets to be a bore after a while. Or you're busy with all the other things you have to do to keep a world running.*

Or counting all your money, said one hopeful part of his brain. Rik snorted at himself in amusement: it'd be a long time yet before he had *that* problem.

He went over to the center of the plaza, where the paving stones outlined, in dark stone and crystal, a broken circle that mirrored in small the stones-and-openings pattern of the Ring of Elich. All over Omnitopia, broken circles like this marked each 'cosm's access to the master gating system. Rik picked an opening, waited for the crystal to go from gray to clear, and stepped through.

He came out of the Ring of Elich, stepped clear from the gateway he'd just used, and then said, "Gate management?"

"Listening," said the control voice.

"Preprogrammed gating to Meruvelt, please?"

"Found. Laid in," said the voice. "Approach at will."

Rik picked a short line—not even a line, really, just a group of she-Gnarth laden with shopping bags—and waited for them to go through while glancing around to see whether things were now looking a little more normal. The gate before him swirled gray, cleared, and there was the broad green City Meadow at the edge of Meruvelt's main city, Dunworn.

Rik moved through, stepped away from the ring of flat black and white flagstones laid in the meadow, and took a deep breath of the evening air as he looked out over the low wall that bounded the meadow on its east side. This was another place that had a great view. Dunworn was a walled city built at the top of a plateau in the broad, gently rolling plains country of Meruvelt's northern continent. It was cavalry country, this whole continent—chariot country, too—and had become a favorite playground for gamers from all over Omnitopia who preferred mounted feudal or Renaissance-era combat. That also made it a good place for medically-minded players, as there was always a battle of some kind going on here, and plenty of casualties to treat.

For the time being Rik turned his back on the view and headed toward the town, which rose up in the middle of the plateau, surrounded by parkland and stabling. Stable Circle smelled as warm and brown as usual as Rik made his way through it. The whinnies and snorts of hundreds of horses, and the roars and grunts and whimpers of other beasts less horselike but no less useful as cavalry, were all around him as he zigzagged through the shanty stabling of the outer ring toward the more permanent and better-built facilities, the long-term stabling, livery, and short-rent barns. Past them was the ring road around the town proper, along which were the usual snack stalls set up to tempt the stabling crowd and the steed owners making their way back and forth. The smell of grilling sausages and frying breads made Rik's stomach growl as he headed for the gates that pierced the town walls on the east side.

Something to eat, he thought, *would definitely be on the agenda at this point.* Rik normally tried to keep his in-game eating to a minimum, as it could get you into bad habits out-of-game—and there were always the stories of people whose brain/body relationship had somehow left their bodies too amenable to believing that the virtual food had been real, so that they gained terrible amounts of weight even though their diets in the real world continued as usual.

Rik went through the gate and headed across the cobbled plaza, shuddering at the thought. He wondered yet again how some people could spend all their spare time in Microcosms like SinTwo and GulaGula—which were all about not just eating, but eating entirely too much—and come out again still able to cope. The thought of places where you could purposely turn off your appestat and eat constantly, for hours, without any side effects, always struck him as faintly disgusting. But no laws were being broken there, and it was people's own business what they did . . .

As for me, he thought, turning into one little street that was lined with cookshops and restaurants, *a sausage or two won't do any damage at all.* About halfway down the street Rik could see the glow in the windows of the House of the Last Man Standing, his crowd's preferred tavern. It was well away from the busy heart of town, but the prices were better down here, and the Last Man had a name for being popular with the locals as well as with the quick-turnover battle-following crowd.

He pushed in the broad iron-bound door and glanced around. The Last Man's front room was high-ceilinged for an in-town inn, with the second floor apparently converted to a gallery in some earlier era: some people thought this might have been a coaching inn at some earlier time and had had its courtyard enclosed. At any rate, now there were two levels to drink and dine on—the big downstairs floor and the upstairs gallery level, where you could hang over the railing and pelt people you didn't like with beef bones.

As the door closed, a bone whizzed past Rik and bounced on the flagstoned floor in front of him. Instantly a mereworm dashed out from under one of the nearby tables, snatched it up, and made off with it, roasting the bone with a tiny jet of firebreath as it went. Rik looked up at the sound of laughter and saw Tom and Barbara and Raoul, all in MediMages Without Frontiers post-battle garb, sitting at a table for four up in the gallery wing nearest the door. "You're late!" Barbara shouted.

"Two *days* late!" Tom called down.

"Oh, come on, it's only one," Rik called up to them, and headed for the stairs.

When he got up into the gallery, his mouth started to water immediately, because they hadn't waited for him, and the order had just arrived. The fourth place setting, with the typical oversized napkin and the Meruvelter two-tined fork, had a big sausage platter on it, and a hunk of brown fennel bread, and beside it was a huge mug of the local whitebrew beer, like one of the Belgian wheat beers. "Oh, you guys," Rik said as he plunked down on the bench beside Barbara, "you have no idea how good this looks. Barb, how's the little one?"

Barbara rolled her blue eyes and pushed the long braid of blonde hair back. "Not a big problem," she said. "We got the tooth capped. Just a temporary—it's too soon to put a permanent one on, apparently. Where have you been? Did they make you go back to work or something?"

"Uh, no—"

"Hey, let him eat something," Tom said. Here and in the real world he was a big broad dark-haired guy with a mustache, always jovial: Rik couldn't recall ever having seen him frown, not even in the middle of a battle when people around him were bleeding and screaming. A look of intent interest was all he ever showed. "Mustard?"

"Thanks—"

For a while they settled into small talk, which relieved Rik as he tucked into his sausages. There was some discussion of the last battle they'd all been in together, down in the Kargash Peninsula, where forces of the Southern Oligarchy, which was trying to consolidate the other sovereignties of Meruvelt's southern continent "You mean 'annex,'" Barbara had said once, "or 'overrun—'") had come up against a cavalry force of the South Outlands Union, a united force of various small kingdoms or sovereignties which were not up for being overrun just yet. The Oligarchy forces had come off badly, having been tricked by their enemies into attacking under less than ideal circumstances ("Uphill?" Tom said, incredulous. "What kind of noob thing is *that?*") and were now spoiling for another encounter with the smaller and more mobile force that had made them look so stupid.

"So where are they thinking of having it?" Rik said.

"You haven't seen it on the feeds already?" Raoul said. He had finished his food and was leaning back in his chair, idly stabbing his wine-stained cork place mat with the two-tined fork.

Rik shook his head. "Been a little busy," he said. *And now you're going to have to tell him why,* he thought, reaching for the mustard pot again as he started dismembering his second sausage. It wasn't as if he didn't like Raoul. He was one of the original members of their MediMages circle, part of it for nearly three years now, a tall, lean, rangy, red-headed point of stability in a gaming world where people could slide in and out without warning when real life interfered. He was a nice enough guy, affable enough off the battlefield, only irascible when on it, and effective at what he did regardless of his mood. But there was always something strangely guarded about him, and Raoul didn't talk much about his home life or his business in the real world.

That was of course his privilege: but the way he slid away from the subjects just bothered Rik sometimes. What Raoul did want to talk about was in-game life: especially all the research he'd been doing, all this while, for the Microcosm he was going to build someday. The plans for his 'cosm changed repeatedly, but the enthusiasm never did. None of them rode him too hard about this, and all of them nodded enthusiastically and pretended interest whenever the subject came up, because they all knew for how many, many months Raoul had been trying to get the Microcosm people to notice him . . . without success.

"What?" Tom said. "Nothing bad, I hope."

"No," Rik said, spearing another bit of sausage and dunking it in the mustard. *Might as well get it over with, because it's not gonna get any better . . .*

Barbara looked at him oddly. "What?" she said. "Nothing's wrong with Angela, is it? Or the kids?"

"Oh, no! No. It's just that—" He popped that last bit of sausage in, chewed, swallowed. "I got knighted," he said.

Tom's mouth dropped open. Barbara's eyes went wide. Raoul—

—smiled. There was a deliberateness to the expression that instantly creeped Rik out, but there was nothing he could do about that now. Tom's grin was spreading from ear to ear. "Knighted as in *Microcosm* knighting?" he said. "As in *MicroLeveling?*"

"Uh," Rik said, "yeah."

Barbara whooped and then waved for the attention of one of the servers down on the floor level, a lady in standard "wench" garb. *"Beer!"* she shouted.

The serving lady made a bored "yeah, yeah, be there in a minute" gesture and went off toward the kitchen. Rik glanced from her back to the others, and finally to Raoul. That smile was still there. It looked tight. Rik forced himself to smile too, as if he wasn't seeing anything wrong.

"Good God, congratulations," Raoul said. "How the heck did this happen?"

"I don't know," Rik said. "I swear! At first I thought they'd made a mistake, mixed me up with someone else—"

He started telling the story, trying not to sound too excited about it, because all the time there was Raoul with that smile. Yet at the same time the excitement started to get the better of him eventually as the others pressed him with questions, as the new pitcher of beer arrived and flowed, and as even Raoul started to get into the spirit of it, curious at first then eventually even starting to look approving. Rik tried to keep away from the technical details, at least partly because he wasn't too clear on some of them himself. But Tom and Barbara were interested in far less technical matters.

"Gonna build yourself a Philosopher's 'cosm?" Tom said and grinned.

Rik shook his head. "Oh, please," Rik said. He caught the eye of another of the servers down on the floor and gestured at her—they'd already run through that second pitcher of beer. Then he grinned at Tom, because he'd felt it was inevitable that somebody would bring this up eventually. The Omnitopia message boards were full of stories about people who'd supposedly succeeded in building Microcosms that were secretly and cunningly engineered to produce abnormal amounts of gaming gold. "It's an urban myth. You ever actually talk to someone who personally knows a player who's done it? It's always a friend of a friend of a cousin of a coworker halfway around the planet. Anyway, like Omnitopia would let people mess with their economy like that!"

"Yeah," Barbara said. "The Gnomes'd come after them."

There was snickering around the table, for the Gnomes at least were no urban myth. They were the inhabitants and guardians of Rhaetia Secunda, a Macrocosm devoted entirely to gameplay in the fiduciary mode. There wannabe brokers and tycoons could play with a duplicate virtual version of Earth's finances, riding the so-called Real-World markets as if they were a game and collecting percentages of game gold for correct prediction and manipulation of stocks and futures. But attempted cheating was very much frowned upon, and the fighting skills of the savage bankers and killer accountants of Rhaetia Secunda's capital city Turicum were legendary across the Macrocosms. Rarely a month went by without some fraudulent Microcosm being invaded and ravaged by hordes of Doom Brokers under the command of the dreadful Chief Gnome, Bloomberg the Terrible.

"I hear," said Tom, "that the Gnomes aren't GGCs. They're employees from Omnitopia financial security." He grinned. "The kind of people who feel about red ink the way everybody else does about blood."

"Yeah, and isn't Bloomberg supposed to actually be the chief of Omnitopia financial or something?" Barbara said. "What's the word I'm looking for? The head honcho."

"CFO?" Tom said.

"That's it."

"Heard that," Rik said, "but the PR types won't comment. Probably wouldn't even if it were true. *Especially* if it were true." He shrugged. "Anyway, I don't care about Philosopher's 'cosms. I don't even have that much time to think about the Microcosm right now. I was going to sit down and have a think about it when I wound up in the middle of the craziness down by the Ring of Elich—"

"What?" Tom said. "What craziness?"

Then *that* story had to be told, leaving general astonishment and shock in its wake. "I never thought something like that could happen!" Tom said. "City ought to do something. What a mess!"

"Yeah," Rik said. "It's not something you'd want to get caught in on your way somewhere serious, like a battle elsewhere."

Raoul was shaking his head, looking bemused. "Can't believe it," he said. "You mean that now you've got a 'cosm, you're still going to have time to waste patching people's characters back together?"

There was something about the tone, or the phrasing, that got under Rik's skin a little. "Hey," Rik said, trying hard to keep his tone even, "give me a break, huh, Raoul? I'm a player. That's not going to stop."

"Probably why he got the accolade in the first place," Barbara said, sounding as nettled as Rik felt but would not show that he did. "They notice things, I hear. Have the cojones to be happy for him, why don't you?"

There was a little silence after that. Raoul got interested in his beer. "I want to see," said Tom after a moment, and called up a feed window to hang at the end of the table. News of the attack was all over the feeds by now, so there was no problem in finding a replay of it from one of many gamers who'd been in the area when it happened. Then Barb caught sight of Rik in one of the feeds, and some more time was spent hunting down other player POVs to find ones that showed a better view of what Rik was doing.

"You could always ask *me!*" Rik protested, starting to feel a little too much like the center of attention at this point. "I was there."

"Yeah, no argument," Tom said, "but how often do we get to see somebody we know make the news? Just shut up and let us enjoy it."

Fortunately that didn't go on for too much longer. Barb started getting a yen for dessert, and one of the Last Man's famous skyberry pies with hot cream was called for, divvied up, and demolished. "This is wild," Tom said as they were finishing it. "We're gonna have to schedule *another* meeting to get our planning sorted out for this next campaign. Have to be in the next few days, too: the Union isn't going to wait forever to hit Southern again—they've got the initiative now. And if I was Southern, I'd want to hit them first."

Then the business of syncing everybody's schedules came up again, never an easy one: work nights were always problematic, and family commitments had to be worked around. More windows were called up around the table, showing appointment calendars and schedule spreadsheets, and the normal squabbling and bargaining ensued.

"Okay," Tom said at last. "Two days from now?"

"That's the big new-rollout night, isn't it?" Raoul said.

"Yeah," Barbara said. "Good night for it, though. The City'll be crawling with noobs, and a lot of people will be staying out of the 'cosms to avoid the crowds. Or because they don't want a sensitive campaign to get caught in some giant disk crash if the rollout doesn't work out right." She grinned. "We can meet here, out of the way, and take our time figuring out who we're going to sell our services to."

That met with general agreement, which was good, as it was getting to be time for Rik to head back home to real life. But it also gave Raoul the opening to ask the question that Rik had been both eagerly awaiting and dreading: "Well, Mister Leveler, when do we get to see it?"

"Well—" Suddenly Rik was a mass of second thoughts. "It's barely even started. Just a shell."

"Oh, come on, Rik!" Barbara said. "You know you want to."

Tom gave Rik a wry look. "Might as well get it over with," he said.

Sometimes, Rik thought, *he can be unusually perceptive.* "Okay," Rik said. "Let's finish up here and I'll show you what I've got."

Raoul shifted uncomfortably on the bench. "Gotta take a real-world leak," he said. "I'll be back in a minute."

"Sure," Rik said. "You've got the address for my office. You can get into the 'cosm from there. I'll leave the door open."

"Right, be there in a sec." Raoul vanished.

The others got up, gathered their things together. Tom called for the slate and scratched out everybody else's tallies. There was a not very enthusiastic chorus of protest from Rik and Barbara. "No, no," Tom said, "I did good on our last medivention. Still haven't finished sorting out all the bonus points. Let me get this one."

Rik thanked him: Barbara did her usual you-can't-pay-for-me-against-my-will thing, then grinned and thanked him too. They made their way down the stairs, pressed a fifteen percent largesse in Meruvelt cashplaques on the chief wench, and headed out into the evening, making for the City Meadow ring.

Once they got there Rik paused for a moment in front of one grayed-out flagstone. "Game management?" he said.

"Good evening, Rik," said the control voice, for his ears only. "What do you need?"

"Transport for four to my Microcosm," he said. "Barbara and Tom here will come through with me. Raoul will be coming into my office in a few minutes: please let him into the Microcosm when he gets there."

"Transports laid in," said the control voice. "Access is open. Please step through."

"This way, guys," he said as the flagstone swirled gray, went clear. He stepped through.

The next moment he was standing to one side of his own small broken ring, a series of steel-and-electrum plates set into the solid stone shelf at the bottom of a broad cliff. He moved aside as first Barbara, then Tom, stepped into the space. They looked around them, and up, and Barbara gasped.

Something inside Rik leaped with pleasure. *Exactly the response I want from people in here for the first time,* he thought. *That's* exactly *right!* And it had to be said that the inside world looked much better than it had originally. There was less land inside the hollow world now, and more sea: Rik had started to find the rich color of the oceans on the far side of the inner-world shell more and more seductive the more he worked with them. The brassy little sun shone down on the first piece of heavy furnishing Rik had done: away along the ridge of which the cliff behind them was part, perched on the ridge crest, stood a sheer-walled brazen castle keep, spired and towered, glittering in the eternal day.

"This is so . . . weird!" Barbara said. "But in a good way!"

Tom was looking around, nodding, at the endless expanse of fields and forests reaching away from them in all directions. "This is spectacular, man," he said. "You built this in two *days?*"

"Well, a lot of it's modular," Rik said. "I still don't have the slightest idea what to do about the GGCs, let alone what gameplay in here is going to look like or what it's about—"

"Oh, you *have* to have wars," Tom said. "Can you *imagine* what wars in here would look like? At night the sky wouldn't have stars in it. It'd have *battles.*" He pointed up past the sun. "Think about it! All that way away—the enemy campfires, glittering—" He paused. "Wait a minute, do you ever get night in here?"

"Uh, I'm working on that. Some kind of selective screening."

"What are you calling it?" Barbara said.

This was something that Rik had been arguing with himself about practically since he started, and had changed his mind a hundred times. He took a deep breath. "Indigo," Rik said.

Barbara, looking up into that deep rich sky, nodded. "It works."

"Well, it's temporary," Rik said. "I may come up with something better. It has to have its own history: the characters may not want their world to be named something that doesn't make sense to them—"

Tom chuckled. "Secondary creation syndrome already," he said. "They picked the right guy for this job, that's for certain."

"Wow," said Raoul behind them.

They all turned as he walked out of the broken ring. Raoul was looking up into that astonishing sky, and for once his face was wearing an expression that Rick didn't mind seeing there: it was unalloyed amazement.

"Wow," he said again, as he came up with them. "What is it? A Dyson sphere?"

"No," Rik said, "just a hollow Earthy kind of thing."

"He's calling it Indigo," Barbara said. "Isn't it fabulous?"

"What are you going to game in here?" Raoul said. "SF or fantasy?"

"I haven't even started to get close to working that out yet," Rik said. "It may take a while."

"Rik?"

Barbara's suddenly confused tone of voice surprised him. He turned to see that she was squinting up at the sky with a peculiar expression. "Is it just me," she said, "or is the sun doing something?"

Rik squinted up too and was horrified to see that it was. It was flickering. Then the sun began very slowly to go dim, as if in the early stages of a brownout.

"You have an eclipse scheduled?" Tom said.

"No," Rik said, "believe me! Just getting it turned on and looking the right size and shape took a little figuring. I wasn't going to start playing around with dimmer switches at *this* early stage—"

Rik went on talking to them a little about the complexities of the WannaB language and the way the little modules didn't always stick together the way you thought they should. But he was talking to distract himself from what the sun was doing. What he had hoped was some kind of momentary glitch was now proving to be no such thing. The sun was getting dimmer and dimmer, going almost ashen now . . .

It went out; and as it did, in its last pallid gasp of light, the landscape surrounding them dissolved itself. With a strange fizzing popping noise, like a lightbulb blowing out, everything went completely dark. Then, slowly, words of light stuttered back into existence up in the darkness:

THIS SPACE
FOR RENT

Rik was so chagrined he couldn't even bring himself to curse. Tom chuckled, though the sound was sad and commiserating. "And all our dreams vanish into air, into thin air . . ." he said.

"Well, crap!" Rik finally said. "I thought I had it at least a *little* under control . . ."

"Possibly premature," Raoul said. He clapped Rik on the back, not that the gesture made Rik feel all that consoled. "Well, you'll get the hang of it. Or if you don't, you can always sell it to a third-party broker. Assuming they don't take it off you first . . ."

"They don't do that," Rik said. "Or so I'm told."

"Well, this isn't your fault!" Barbara said. "You just wanted us to see it right away. And who could blame you? Besides, we talked you into it. Doesn't matter. It's exciting, Rik! Keep us posted and let us know when you get it working again. I want to pop the virtual cork at your opening."

"Yeah," Rik said. "I'll do that. Game management?"

"Here, Rik."

"Can I have the door back into my office, please?"

In the darkness, a door opened on muted afternoon light that now seemed very bright indeed. Rik headed for it, the others following. In his office, they said their goodbyes for the time being. "If there's any problem with the meeting schedule," Tom said to him as he made his way toward Rik's outer office door, "give me a call."

Rik shook his head. "Shouldn't be a problem," he said. Barbara smooched him as she went past: Raoul patted his shoulder, heading after her. "See you guys later . . ."

"Later," they all said. The door shut.

Rik stood there, looking at the shut door, and sighed.

He was tempted to go straight back into the Microcosm and start tinkering again. *But no,* he thought. *I promised Angela I wouldn't be in here all day.*

Damn it!

"Game management?"

"Here, Rik."

He was about to say "Log off," but stopped himself. *Not just yet.* "Ring of Elich, please."

His office vanished. He was standing near the Ring.

Rik sighed and looked around him again. The plaza was back to normal, as far as he could see. Despite it being the middle of the night, the usual unending traffic was passing in and out of the Gate. He took a deep breath, turned his back to it and started to walk back to his normal ingress spot. *A few minutes' walk,* he thought, *just to get rid of—*

Of what? Of being pissed off at the Microcosm for crashing in front of everybody? *Well, yes. No point in taking that annoyance home and dumping it on Angela and the kids.* But that wasn't all of it.

He paused briefly by the great statue of Lahirien the Excessively Far-Traveled, feeling the spray from the fountain, and then moved on. *Oh crap,* Rik thought, *why couldn't Raoul have come in a few minutes later? Then he wouldn't have seen anything but the bare substrate.*

Of course the others would have told him what happened—

But as he thought about it, Rik became less sure. He remembered particularly that strangely sympathetic look from Tom. But in any case, Tom and Barbara would have been, *had* been, more understanding about it.

Anyway, it's just some kind of software glitch! Get over it. It's stupid to feel down about it. Yet he *did* feel down. And worse, he felt obscurely like some kind of traitor. He couldn't get Raoul's initial expression in the Last Man out of his mind. *Betrayed!* it seemed to say. *How come you and not* me? *It's not fair!* And even now Rik wanted to shout at him, *How should I know how come me? It doesn't make any sense to me either!*

But Jean-Marie had been clear enough about how many different factors were involved. *And it's not my fault if Raoul is getting something wrong. He's been so intense about what he's been planning, about how it's going to make all the difference for him when he gets a Microcosm. But does he ever really have* fun *in here anymore? Sure, we see him at group meetings, but he never has an independent campaign story to tell anymore. Who knows what he's doing? Does he even campaign by himself anymore? And does anyone even ask?* And maybe that was part of the problem. *Are we just feeding into that attitude by letting him concentrate so much on his Microcosm obsession?* For that was exactly what Barbara had called it, once, before Raoul had turned up for another of their nights out.

He sighed as he made his way up through the beast market, empty and dark now, on up Hook Street in the torchlight, and onward into the quiet and dark of Troker's Lane. There, at the mouth of Troker's Lane, Rik paused, seeing something moving in the shadows.

What the heck? Rik thought. He peered down into the darkness, but the flutter of the guttering torchlight was hard to see by. An animal? *No. Well, maybe not—*

"Do you believe this?" said a grumpy voice down in the darkness. "The mess people leave behind them, you wouldn't believe it. Didn't any of them have mothers, do they just throw stuff around like this at home? I ask you—"

There was no telling who the little scratchy voice was asking, unless maybe it was Rik. "Uh, excuse me—" he said.

"Yeah, you too, probably some of this is yours," said the little voice, "and now what, am I supposed to think you're coming back here to pick it up again? I don't think so—"

Rik blinked—not that he wasn't doing enough of that in this bad light—and headed down toward the source of the voice. But all the time, his hand was on the knife at his belt; he was thinking that if things could get as broken loose as they had in the plaza around the Ring, what could happen in some back alley? He got closer to the shape, and with his free hand pulled loose one of the cressets from its wall holder, held it high—

Upturned eyes gleamed in the torchlight, then went dark again as the eyes turned away from him. Rik suddenly realized that he was looking at a little man who was busily picking up garbage from the street and tossing it into a rickety-looking wheelbarrow. He was wearing what looked like some slightly crazed attempt at a uniform, but one all made up of rags and tatters stitched or even tied together, as if the whole business had been assembled from the pickings of many rubbish heaps. Hanging by two pieces of frayed hempen rope over his shoulders, on his chest and his back the man wore a pair of crude cardboard signs on which had been scrawled the words OMNITOPIA SANITATION, and in smaller letters, YOUR GAME GOLD AT WORK.

Rik burst out laughing. "Guy," he said, "why are you doing this? How hard up for gold *are* you? I'll make a donation."

The little old man gave him a cranky sidelong look, made a "Hmf" sound, and turned back to picking up garbage. After a moment he said, "Do I look hard up?"

"Well, jeez, man, this is hardly a high-end job," Rik said. "Even a noob player wouldn't do it for long. You run through your grubstake already?"

"Fifty thou doesn't go very far in this world," the little old garbage guy said, methodically picking up garbage and dropping it into his sack. "Every time you turn around, somebody's hitting you with another fee. Subscriptions, virtual food, virtual booze: drip, drip, drip, it's gone in a few weeks. You want clothes? Gotta pay for 'em. Want a horse? Want a magic flying unicorn? Somebody's gonna soak you for 'em. A suit of armor? A really good sword? There goes ten thou. Want to join a decent guild so you can make some money? Bang, you wind up paying some other game grubber a big fat initiation fee. Might as well be in the real world."

"One big difference," said Rik. "No taxes here."

The garbage guy made the "Hmf" sound again. *"This* month," he said. "Read the news lately? State of Arizona's trying to change that. Only thing slowing them down is they can't figure out whether to try to tax it as player income or virtual property. Either way, you and I wind up paying. Bastards." He straightened up, groaned, and looked down the cul-de-sac with a critical eye.

Rik raised an amused eyebrow, for the Garbage Guy seemed to have his curmudgeon levels set on high. Regardless, there was no arguing that the lane certainly looked much cleaner than it had when Rik had come down it last. "You ever find anything worthwhile in all this stuff?" he said.

The Garbage Guy shrugged, looking at Rik with watery blue eyes. "Sometimes you pick up a gold piece someone dropped after a bar fight," he said. "Some little weapon they don't care about, a piece of jewelry . . ." He shrugged again, dropped the bag into the wheelbarrow. "It's a living."

But is it much fun? Rik wondered. Though you did meet some strange types in Omnitopia: people who had trouble interacting . . . even some who seemed to have no real world life at all. Some of them were best avoided: there were entirely too many online panhandlers, creep-out cases looking for a way to walk off with some of your gold. Other people, less creepy but just sadder—poor players, unlucky ones—sometimes you wished you could find a way to help. A lot of the time there was nothing in particular you could do.

But now Rik thought of that sign hanging glowing in the sky, and started to wonder whether that was strictly true anymore. "Listen," he said. "I'm building a Microcosm. Maybe I could use some help. Come on over and work for me."

Garbage Guy gave him a funny look. "Sure," he said, utterly skeptical. "Funny. Very, very funny."

"No, I'm serious! I'm really a MicroLeveler. You can check my game profile." Rik grinned: this was the first time he'd told anybody in the game but his own group about it. "Just getting started. You can help me beta it."

The Garbage Guy stuffed his hands into a tangle of rags: Rik assumed there were pockets in there somewhere. When Garbage Guy looked up again, there was an odd look in those pale blue eyes: like someone who'd forgotten what kindness sounded like. The expression was half startled, half sad. "Why?" he said. "Why me?"

It was the question of the day, it seemed. Rik found himself having to search for an answer that didn't make him sound snotty or stuck up. "Uh, I don't know," he said after a moment. "You seem like a smart guy, and I don't see why you should be doing *this* for gold when you can do something more interesting."

Garbage Guy's odd look didn't quite go away, but it looked a little less sad. "I don't know how much I'm going to make off this," Rik said, "but if you're going to help me beta, I'd certainly pay you what your time is worth out of what I make." And no sooner had he said it than Rik was tempted to laugh at himself in sheer scorn. *One percent of infinity,* he thought. *Right. What's one percent of nothing?* For there was absolutely no guarantee—especially at the rate he was going at the moment—that he would ever make anything from his Microcosm at all. One newsfeed story Rik had seen had suggested that one out of every three new Microcosms survived for less than a year: and Omnitopia Inc. wasn't forthcoming with data on the subject, at least not to gamers at Rik's level.

He was startled out of the sudden fit of downheartedness by a cackle of laughter. Garbage Guy was laughing at him, those watery eyes actually tearing with amusement.

For just a moment Rik wondered once more whether he was dealing with a game-generated character. But there was something about this man's face that made Rik wonder whether he was perhaps dealing with the kind of player who used their own genuine face as part of their game presence, certain that as long as they kept the rest of their identity properly concealed, you would never find out who they were.

"What's so funny?" Rik said.

Garbage Guy wiped his eyes and got control of himself. "Never had a real steady job before," he said. "Before this one, I mean. And now somebody offers me another one."

"Well," Rik said, "will you take it? It's going to take me a day or so before I can get back in here, but I've got some troubleshooting to do when I do."

Garbage Guy sniffed and wiped his nose, then reached back into his raggy clothes and came up with a blue-glowing profile token, the kind of electronic business card you gave other players who you wanted to meet again. He handed it to Rik. "Here," Rik said, and dug around in his pouch to find a similar token to give Garbage Guy. *And I can't keep calling him that—* He eyed the token he'd been given as he passed his own over: but it had no sigil or name branded on it. "What's your name?"

The Garbage Guy gave him a shocked look. "I didn't mean your *real* name!" Rik said hurriedly, for in his experience the vast majority of gamers guarded their privacy jealously: their bosses or families didn't always approve of where they spent their time and money.

Garbage Guy relaxed a little. ". . . Dennis," he said finally.

"Dennis? Hi. I'm Arnulf. Arnulf Manyfaced." He put his hand out.

The little man reached up and clasped arms with Rik. Rik caught a whiff of what Dennis had been rooting around in, but kept his face straight. "Arnulf," said Dennis. "Well, young Arnulf, when do I start?"

"Uh. Tomorrow night?"

Dennis paused to consider. "All right," he said. "You're on. Now would you put that back where you found it so I can see what I'm doing and finish this up?"

"Sure." Rik stepped back to the cresset holder, shoved the torch back into it, then tried to wipe his arm clean of what had gotten on it without the gesture showing. "I'll, uh, see you tomorrow, then."

"Fine, yeah, tomorrow," Dennis said and got back to business with the garbage again.

"Game management?" Rik said.

"Listening, Rik," the control voice said in his ear.

"Egress to home space and logout, please."

"Thank you. Exit recorded at seventeen forty-one local time, and come back soon to Omnitopia!"

Troker's Lane vanished. Rik pulled off his headset, blinking at the early evening light coming in the den's windows, stretched in his chair, and got up to go find Angela and tell her about his "day."

In Troker's Lane, eyes glittered with amusement in the torchlit darkness, then turned their attention back to the garbage.

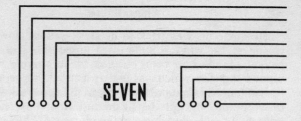

SEVEN

THE SHADOWS OF THE SKYSCRAPERS were leaning low and eastward over the river. It had been an unseasonably hot day down there; in the canyons between the steep cliffs of glass and steel you could see the heat haze wrinkling silvery against the sidewalk, if you cared to look at it. Phil didn't care to. He wouldn't have to feel that heat for more than the ten seconds it took him to get across from his building's front door to his waiting car. All the same, he was already thinking of the weekend out at the Hamptons: the cool wind, the gray-bright glitter and dazzle of the surf, the dry crunchy squeak of the pale sand underfoot as he walked eastward along his beach. Yet at the same time, even now, Phil already knew that when he got there something would inevitably go wrong with the weekend perfection. The Hamptons just weren't what they'd used to be when he first bought the house. Something was missing. Once again, as he had many times this last year, Phil thought about selling the place; trading up a little for an area up the coast somewhere, possibly a little less well serviced but also less tony, less full of posers. *Anywhere the chopper can get to an within an hour,* he thought—*no, make that three-quarters of an hour—would be fine with me. Something to talk to Dean about next week—*

Phil gazed out at the river, hardly seeing it for the moment. "You were always a hippie, goddamn it," he said under his breath, finally turning away from the window with a frown. "Even after all the hippies were *gone* you were still a hippie...."

He made his way back to his desk and sat down at it, gazing out the window, still mostly unseeing. All of today's inconsequentia had been cleaned off its shining granite-topped expanse: which was just as it should've been, since he had four assistants whose job was to keep his desk clean of everything except the most important business. And right now, that boiled down to the phone call Phil was waiting for.

He stared at the phone, already getting angry at the way the call he was expecting was taking so long. Unfortunately, that was the nature of working with some of these hired-in people; they weren't old-school business types and couldn't be depended upon to manage an owed-call list correctly. Also, in their small, nasty ways, they were not above a few high school power plays, tiny passive-aggressive attempts to make you understand who was really running things, based on the idea that you should somehow be grateful to them for getting down in the dirt and getting the work you needed done. Phil smiled thinly. *Well,* he thought, *let them think that's the way it is.* For at the end of the day, it was all about getting the result.

That was the only thing on Phil's mind, and it surprised him sometimes that some of his allies and some of his enemies never fully wrapped their brains around that concept. He glared at the phone, got up from the desk again, and went up the stairs to the gallery level of his office, where he began to pace. Phil's office had been built to accommodate that pacing; it was how he did his best thinking, and his desk stood a few feet below the gallery walkway, which wrapped around inside the corner of the building as the rest of the office did. Here he could keep an eye on the desk, and any visitors—not that many people had entrée here—while also being able to gaze out at the river. Here Phil could wander up and down, thinking on his feet, dictating to the office note management system or to his assistants, while at the same time keeping a weather eye on the view southward toward the Battery, and the wrinkled flow of water where the Hudson poured out into New York Bay. "The widow's walk," some of his assistants called it, joking, though never to his face. *When did they stop telling jokes around me?* Phil thought briefly. Then he shrugged the idea away. *Not a problem, not for here and now, anyway.* There were too many things to think about today.

He paused in the walk, glaring down at the phone again. It still hadn't rung. *It's almost end of business here,* he thought; *they know they were supposed to be in touch with me by now. How am I supposed to make my final assessments on this move if they don't—* Then Phil shook his head, went back to walking. There was no point in getting all type-A about it. The whole purpose of this business was to make other people sweat . . . one in particular.

The phone rang. "Sorensen," he said immediately.

"Mr. Sorensen," Brandy's voice said from the outer office, "I have Link Raglan on the line."

"Put him through."

"Mr. Sorenson," Link's voice said, "I've got those end of day download figures for you."

"Go," Phil said.

"Total downloads to five P.M.," Link said, "four million, three hundred and eighty thousand, two hundred and twelve."

"That's great," Phil said. And it really was, though it was strange how flat he found this small triumph in the actual moment of its achievement. Those numbers were nearly half again what he had expected—half again what even the most enthusiastic and optimistic of his trend-trackers had suggested they might achieve this week. Phil smiled again at the thought that Omnitopia was not going to have everything its own way. "So go ahead and issue the statement we prepared. Just make sure you swap in the new numbers."

"Yes, sir, of course."

"And while you're at it," Phil said, "you might want to add a little something to it along the lines of how even our most ambitious competitors couldn't have predicted such a jump in product interest. How plainly the players are as interested in established, reliable platforms as in new, unproven, blah blah blah . . ."

"Got it," Link said, and Phil could faintly hear scribbling in the background. "You want to see it before I pass it on?"

Phil thought a moment, shook his head. "No need," he

said. "Just make sure you copy it to me and the usual PR
people in e-mail. Meanwhile—" He looked out and down
through the wall-wide window at the skyscraper shadows
moving slowly out across the river, gnomons of a sundial
that he watched every day. *Almost five-twenty now,* he
thought. *Over there it'll be*— "Any news today from our
normal inside sources?"

There was no question what he meant when he said "inside." There was only one other inside that mattered to Phil.
"Nothing that we weren't expecting," Link said. "They're all
scrambling around trying to patch software holes, exactly
as we knew they would be." There was a pause. "Obviously
you were right about this. They got a little too ambitious for
• their own good. Got themselves married to this particular
date because of some weird symbolic quality—"

Phil nodded. "It's the solstice," he said. "And Dev always
was hung up on winter solstice this, spring equinox that, all
these artificial, outwardly imposed due dates. It's a weakness, and it's strengthened by the fact that we know about
it. Never mind." Phil was still amused that he'd known the
new Omnitopia's most likely rollout date long before any
of his people inside had been able to bring in the news, long
before any press release had been issued. The man was just
too predictable in some ways, and the fact sometimes made
Phil sorry for him. "Meantime," Phil said, "make sure you
and your team keep a close eye on what's going on over
there in the next forty-eight hours. If anything happens or
goes wrong that we can exploit, I want to hear all about it,
and I want a press release ready to go within minutes. Any
of their publicity that we can attach ourselves to over the
next three days, that's fine with me. Dev may have paid for
it, but we'll reap the benefits."

"Yes, Mr. Sorensen," Link said.

"All right," Phil said. "That should be it for today. You
and your team be in early tomorrow. Things are going to
start speeding up."

"Yes, sir."

"Good-bye."

The connection shut down. Phil stood there for a moment, went on looking out and over the river. One of the

Circle Line cruise ships began creeping across the reflection and shadow of his own skyscraper's tower, turning it briefly into a bright hash of interference patterns and wave crests. *That release will come out in* . . . He glanced at his watch. *Maybe an hour.* And whoever in Dev's organization was tasked to keep an eye on *him* and *his* company's business would see the article, make a note of it, and bring it to Dev—

Phil shook his head. *Or maybe not.* Phil always insisted that his own people bring him in all Omnitopia-sensitive material for his own personal examination first thing in the morning. But it was more likely, knowing Dev's organizational habits, that Dev had delegated someone else to make that judgment call for him, deciding on his behalf what needed to be read and what didn't. Phil shook his head, scowling. *Too like him,* he thought. *Always taking his eye off the ball. He never learned that the really important stuff you don't dare delegate.* But it was entirely an aspect of Dev's too-easygoing management style to delegate these most important judgment calls. *That damned fake populism of his, that weird egalitarian streak. You'd think he'd have grown out of it by now.*

Yet once upon a time, that had been one of things about them, about *him,* that had made Dev fun to work with . . . And the thought began to intrude itself: *Just when did it change?* But Phil pushed that thought away half-formed. It *didn't change,* he thought. *I changed. I learned to see those traits for what they were and are: fecklessness. An unwillingness to accept the consequences of one's own actions. Shove it off on somebody else, and then forgive them in that good-natured way of his when something goes wrong. Pretend to be Lord Bountiful, the free-and-easy employer, the all-around nice guy.* Phil shook his head again. There was no room for nice guys in this business. And sooner or later, *that* one would finish last. . . .

The only problem was, for the last couple of years the Nice Guy had kept finishing first. And there was something wrong with that.

It was very strange. Had Phil been thinking about anybody else, he'd have suspected that they had something

illegal going on—and he'd have torn into the situation to
find out just what it was, so he could use the information to
trip his enemy up. But Phil knew Dev too well. Whatever
was causing his present success would not be anything illegal . . . or, at least, nothing he knew about.

That was one reason Phil was investigating other possibilities in that direction. No matter how charismatic you
might be, you couldn't have forty thousand employees who
were *all* on the straight and narrow. Somewhere in the organization, somebody was doing something underhanded, and
when such errors of judgment or purposeful misbehavior
came to light, it could be publicized to best advantage. *You
give them too much rope,* Phil thought to as he went back to
pacing. *Much too much rope. One of them will hang you with
it. The only question is, how much will we have to help them?*

Phil walked all the way down to where the "widow's
walk" ran into a V-shaped railing that faced the corner of
the building's window-wall. Around the corner, the walk
went on above his lounge pit: a handsome, sleek executive getaway space with entertainment center, screen table,
and VR gear, linked into all the networks and all the news
services, and tied into a broad array of screens where he
could see what he needed quickly and without fuss. On
any normal day, Phil spent a lot of time in the Pit, watching how his games were doing, descending into chat rooms
and trolling Web sites for evidence of how his publicity was
working, and personally examining the output of the many
paid flacks who were out there astroturfing the endless
gameblogs and numerous major social networking Web
sites. You could never keep too close an eye on such things.
While his hired turfers held their jobs on the understanding that they were to do strictly as they were told, there
was always the chance of the occasional slippage. Phil had
already caught several of these this week, and as a result
two of his online personnel managers' heads had rolled because they had not been keeping a tight enough watch on
the paid acolytes. It wasn't that Phil liked firing people, but
paid work needed to be done correctly. And if you didn't
do it correctly, Phil Sorensen was not going to waste any
further paychecks on you.

He frowned, leaning into the railing and gazing out through the corner of the building. Phil had learned entirely too many lessons about money and how to waste it in the ancient days when he had been working with Dev. There had never been such a guy for saying he understood about not blowing money on impulse projects, and then going off and doing it anyway. Worse, it sometimes seemed as if coincidence and circumstance were cooperating with Dev to raise Phil's annoyance level by making Phil look stupid when Dev said their company should do something and Phil said no . . . and then crazy blind luck or unpredictable circumstance stepped in to make it seem as if Dev had been right all along, and Phil dead wrong. *You can only take so much of that kind of thing,* Phil thought. *It had to stop.* And so it had, when Dev bailed out.

He'd taken little joy in the solution at the time. And for some months Phil had cherished some damned fool's hope that eventually Dev would see sense, come back to the firm, admit that Phil had been right all along. He'd waited a year, two years, two and a half . . . and it hadn't happened. It had never occurred to him that Dev could possibly be so stubborn. *Or so angry?*

Phil turned away from the corner railing, at which he had been standing like the captain of a ship at sea, and started pacing up and down on the Pit side of the office. *Now when will that damned phone ring,* he thought. . . . *And angry? No. Dev doesn't get angry. And he doesn't get even, either. The damn universe just seems to do that for him.* The thought was bitter. Time and time again, even back when they were still friends, he had tried to understand what Dev was up to; what made him tick, what made his decisions keep working out right even when logic and the cold probabilities said they shouldn't. He'd never managed to find an answer. It hadn't made Phil angry, as it wasn't worth getting angry about. But frustrated. And when the parting of the ways came at last—when it became plain that despite being a programmer and theoretically a logician, logic was the last thing Dev wanted to bring to bear on this particular problem—after the break, Phil had spent a good while wondering why he himself had found it so difficult. There'd been months during the restructuring of the company when he had found it hard to focus. And he hadn't been helped by the wave of employee resignations that followed.

Phil shrugged now as he had shrugged then. It was understandable, he supposed. Some of the ways people assigned their personal loyalties in a big company made no sense when you examined them closely. The original crew—people like Jim and Cleolinda—they were such cult-of-personality types, so easily swayed by a personal manner, the perception of intimacy. Whether that intimacy was ever actually there, they either weren't able to see or were unwilling to evaluate. Phil was probably well rid of them. During those first couple of years, when none of them had seen that they'd made a mistake and come back to Infinity, he'd kept saying to himself, *Who cares? Good riddance! Let them find whatever minor success they can with him. Over here, we have work to do.* And the team who had replaced them were the best people— crack talents in code and finance, hired away from top firms all over the planet, well-paid and worth their pay. The company now had the structure it had lacked in the ancient, sloppy days when Dev had still been here, swinging crazily day by day from one piece of business to another, flinging himself into the unknown like some kind of programming-enabled orangutan, always expecting that there would be something there to grab onto at the other end of the leap—

—and always finding it.

Luck, Phil thought: *sheer, blind luck. What else could it be? It's not like he has some inherent ethical superiority, there's nothing so all-fired advanced about his business model, it's not as if—*

The phone rang.

"Finally," he said under his breath. "Sorensen!"

"Is this a bad time?" The voice that spoke sounded male: but of course these days that guaranteed nothing, what with the various voice-masking or frequency-stripping technologies you could buy if you had a mind to.

"No. But you're late," Phil said. "What've you got?"

"Our on-campus contact has handed me exactly what I

needed," the voice said. "And I've been looking into back-channel stuff all morning."

"And?"

"I've been promised a data delivery at local end-of-business," the voice said.

"Damn it," Phil said, "is that the best you can do? We're putting a lot on the line here. If anyone gets the idea that there's any connection—"

"Not the slightest danger of that," said the voice at the other end. "They're all so inward-looking, it's genuinely never occurred to them. It's exactly as you predicted; they're all so busy trying to look good, to look like the nice guys—"

"All right," Phil said. "Just keep your eyes open. How was your contact with the big fish?"

"Delayed. About an hour."

"Fine. Send your debrief to the car, I'll read it on the way to the heliport. Or, no, I'll probably be in the air at that point. Just send it to my PDA."

"Will do." The connection went dead.

Phil swore softly under his breath and turned, making his way down the hardwood steps into the Pit. *Must make a note to have someone here see if they can't be a little more proactive with what we've been so generously given . . .* He sat down in front of the big black table-sized slab of WindowGlass that was the heart of the entertainment system and leaned across it, glancing down into its darkness. *How is it fair,* he thought, meeting the eyes of his dark reflection there, *that he looks like he does, and I look like this?* You could say all you liked about the distinguished look afforded by going prematurely gray: it said other things about you that merely seeming distinguished couldn't offset. Phil let out an annoyed breath, touched two or three patches on the table's surface. Across from him, the wall lit up with a scrambled and anonymized Internet access screen—just a browser window, blank.

Phil put his hands down on the glass table and started typing. He was still a coder at heart, uncomfortable with some of the more newfangled input types—especially Dev's much-touted optic nerve interface. *God knows what that's doing to people's retinas,* Phil thought. *I should ask R&D what they make of those last few articles in the* Lancet— He kept typing. In the browser window before him appeared a long string of letters and numbers. Phil hardly even had to look at them: he'd typed this particular string so many times over the last year or so that it was probably going to be found engraved on his heart when they embalmed him.

The browser window cleared, went white. Then, after a long pause, an icon started flickering in the toolbar at the top of the window; a little pen and pad. Someone was typing at the other end.

Phil waited. A second later, in the browser window, a single line appeared. *We are kind of busy right now.*

Phil rolled his eyes at the other end's effrontery. *So am I,* he typed. *Report.*

Ninety-five percent of all preset logins now achieved and confirmed, said the screen. *Pingbacks confirm that the installed software is ready to go with an estimated two percent failure rate.*

Phil frowned at that. He typed, *Why so high? Estimated failure was 1.3 percent last week.*

There was a few moments' pause—the person at the other end was apparently not as fast a typist as Phil—and then the answer appeared: *Norton changed its antivirus update rollout day this week, expecting network/backbone trouble on June 21. Last-minute decision, and we had no warning. Failure rate is still within acceptable parameters, as it suggests a maximum of 180,000 plus/minus consoles failing to respond.*

Phil shook his head: this wasn't good. It was a basic tenet of logistics and tactics in warfare to make sure that your overwhelming force was genuinely overwhelming; in a situation like this, 180,000 consoles one way or another might make all the difference. *Understood,* he typed, making a private note to himself to make sure this particular lack of insight on that organization's behalf would not go unrecompensed. *So talk to me about risk-distribution management—*

Going forward as planned, the answer came in the

browser window. *Approximately 200,000 identifiable risks are in place and timed to begin revealing on June 22nd. Effect will snowball through the 26th and then die back before the secondary peak on June 30th and the tertiary on July 8th. They will be snowed under with investigations well into fourth quarter. Local LE will have its hands full.*

Understood, Phil typed back. His private intention was to make sure that law enforcement had its hands at least a few cases fuller if these people slipped up as far as execution was concerned. And if they thought they might try anything in the way of payback after the fact, they would find him amply protected; he had been dealing with corporate espionage and ways to prevent it for some years now, and his own effectiveness in this regard had become, to his pleasure, something of a legend. *Finally,* Phil typed, *execution time still as stated in last communication?*

Yes, the answer came back, *subject to operational conditions. Final determination will be made here, and we will text you as agreed on inception.*

OK, Phil typed. *Good luck.*

Don't believe in luck, the answer came back. The connection ended; the browser window closed itself.

Phil stared at the screen a moment longer . . . then smiled again, a slightly rueful look. That much, at least, he and his invisible correspondent had in common. Though he thought casually about luck, as most human beings did, he knew at heart that the concept didn't mean to him what it meant to others. Always underlying the word, for him, was a clear sense that the universe tended to play favorites. Not with him, though, who deserved it: with someone who really didn't, who hadn't done enough of the kind of hard work that he had. *Well,* Phil thought, *Dev, my boy, your luck is about to change.* He actually thought this with some sorrow. They really had been friends, once. That friendship had been the rock and solace of his life. And then Dev had walked away from it, and from the business that had united them, the business they could really have made something of together. What had happened since, at Dev's end, could only have been the result of an unusual confluence of circumstances that had, however briefly, functioned in Dev's favor. But Dev was going to find out that statistical improbabilities couldn't go his way forever: that the world was full of little surprises—sudden stumbling blocks set in the way, just waiting for you to take a spill over them.

It would be Dev's lack of foresight that would now make him take that spill. He would never see Phil's influence behind what was about to happen to Omnitopia's market value, for Phil had been most fastidious about covering his tracks in regards to the painful but necessary object lesson he was about to deliver to his old friend. The massive raid on Omnitopia's liquidity and the destruction of the data in Omnitopia's servers would cause the company's share price to crash in the inevitable sellstorm, and Morgan Wise and her silent brokerage associates scattered around the world would swoop on the devalued shares and buy them up by the million for Phil at fire-sale prices. Then Dev would discover with terrible suddenness that luck would take you only so far. At what he surely expected to be one of the high points of his career, Dev would go sprawling on his face in front of the world's media as a result of his own hubris. *Then* Dev would finally understand that you cannot go it alone—that you need your friends, and turning your back on them is a mistake.

After that, if (as all the PR made it seem) Dev was big enough of soul to admit his error and accept his new position as Phil's junior partner, then all would be forgiven, and a new start could be made. But first there had to be the admission that Dev had lost, and Phil had won. First there had to be that vital understanding on Dev's part that you could not go it alone . . . for that way lay tragedy.

Phil typed briefly on the black glass, wiping the computer's logs, instructing the anonymizer to handle and reroute any further communications that came in appropriately. Then he stood up and headed for the door. "Brandy," he called.

"Yes, Mr. Sorenson?"

"Have the car brought around. I'll be down in five minutes."

"Yes, sir."

And it'll be a new beginning, Phil thought as he headed

around the corner of the walkway again, making for his office doors. *A new beginning for both of us. I just hope he has the sense to avail himself of the opportunity.*

Otherwise ...

And the doors closed behind him.

The room was windowless, its walls painted in institutional beige well ornamented with brown and yellow Scotchtape marks, and the air-conditioning was broken; but nobody working there minded in the slightest. In fact, Pyotr thought as he looked across the tightly-packed logjam of secondhand steeltop desks, it was a question how many of them even noticed. All heads were down, all eyes stared into screens—at least, all the eyes of those who were using them in non-virtual ways. Yes, the place did presently smell rather like a comic book store on a ripe summer afternoon, but most computer facilities got to smell like that eventually. And within the next week or so, no one would care how the place smelled, as the present inhabitants would never have to come back to it again.

Off in the corner was the circle of VR chairs, every one occupied. There was always some fighting over these, but that too would stop quite soon. Pyotr looked absently at his watch, comparing its calendar against the one in his head. *Bug out time,* he thought, *will be in no less than forty-eight hours, no more than seventy-two ... and not a moment too soon.* He would be one of the first out the door, once he'd made sure that the various servers scattered around the globe were each running the complex set of custom scripting that he had hand-carried to each one and privately hand-installed.

Pyotr started ambling around the desks, often turning sideways and sidling between chair and chair, because there was no other way to get around. Guys and girls were jammed cheek by jowl as they made contact with Topers all over the planet, passing them information, making sure that they were clear on their own timings and what their role was in this operation. The sheer number of Topers they were dealing with had seemed daunting at first, but automated scripting for login and logout management had made at least that part of the process manageable. This was—Pyotr checked his watch again, comparing it against the time sheet in his head—the second to last rolling watch of operators. The next four-hour watch would turn up in about three hours; these guys would log out, their replacements would log in and the last five or six thousand remote proxies would be verified, tied into the network, and briefly awakened, then would have their "deadfall" scripts activated and be shut down again.

I can't believe we're finally almost done with this, Pyotr thought. The sheer size of the vast pile of zombie-management scutwork had been daunting, but its conquest had become the core of this whole operation. Pyotr had been astonished, when he'd first started trying to assess the plan's viability, how very many thousands of people were willing to cheat on a game, or in it, when offered a chance. *Everybody wants something for nothing,* Pyotr thought. *So many people absolutely believe that it's the universe's business to give them stuff for free—hundreds of thousands of people. Millions.* The master plan he'd devised was absolutely dependent on this vital feature of human nature . . . and so far, human nature had done nothing to disappoint. Pyotr was betting that things would keep going that way.

Afterward, of course, some of the players in this vast game would discover that other universal human principles were also operating: especially the one that said *There Ain't No Such Thing As A Free Lunch.* Some hundreds of thousands of would-be cheaters would satisfy an important part of this plan, involving the concept that it was expedient that every now and then some one person should be sacrificed for the greater good. Naturally this meant Pyotr's greater good, and that of his various lieutenants, many of them purposefully nameless, who'd worked so hard on this project for the better part of a year and a half. As for the unfortunate percentage who had been selected to take the fall in the aftermath of the Venture's execution, Pyotr spent no more time thinking about them than necessary. Their fate would be like a scene from a film that he'd seen in his youth in the single cinema of his gray and desperately run-down suburb of Kiev. Pyotr remembered there had been troika-drawn sledges fleeing across the hard snow of winter, the bells on the harness of the three-horse hitch ringing shrill and frantic in an ineffective attempt to scare the wolves away. The sledges were heavily laden with people—nobles and desperate peasants—and the wolves, as always, were coming up fast behind. So for the driver, and the people who were most at risk in the flight, there was now the usual problem: how to keep from getting caught?

In the movies, it had been simple enough. Every now and then you threw a peasant overboard to slow down the wolves. The wolves, not knowing any better, immediately relapsed into instinctive behavior and stopped to rip the poor soul apart. But this was entirely satisfactory for the other people on the sledge, because by the time the wolves had finished quarreling over the rags and tags lying around on the bloody snow, the sledge was way ahead.

There were a lot of wolves out in the cold hard world who would look very much askance at the Venture that Pyotr was running here. But fortunately there were *lots* of peasants to distract the wolves with. Pyotr glanced around the room. None of this lot would fit that description, of course. Their position relatively high up the food chain of this scam was protecting them—and the chance that if sacrificed, one or more of them might be able to figure out what they had actually been doing, and thus set the wolves on Pyotr's or his closest colleagues' trail. But further down the food chain, many were about to be sacrificed in a process that, depending on the zeal of some countries' police departments, might well get as bloody and painful as what happened atop one of those more jungly and non-foodish pyramids a long time ago and an ocean or so away.

Pyotr checked his watch one last time and wandered to the far end of the room. There one desk was distinguished by having a whole meter of clear space all around it. Behind that desk, looking at three flat panel monitors at once, was George. George was dark and curly-haired and sounded like some kind of midlands Brit or other, though his docs said he'd most recently been living in Barbados.

How or why he'd come there Pyotr had never inquired, filing George's business (along with that of most of his other senior colleagues of the Venture's Inner Ring) under "Don't Need to Know At All." It was all too easy to know too much about one or another of your colleagues on this job, especially if by bad luck law enforcement caught one of them—or you.

Now Pyotr came around the back of George's desk and looked casually at his three monitors. One of them featured a view into some Omnitopian virtual interior strong on stainless steel; one was scrolling down a long block of relatively short lines of text; and one was showing a chat window, the log of the last message from one of their sponsors.

George now stretched, leaned back, looked over his shoulder at Pyotr. "He sounds a little cranky here," he said, indicating the chat window.

Pyotr shrugged, reading down the logged conversation. "The prerogative of a running-dog capitalist entrepreneurial prat," he said. "Wasn't going to rock the boat by arguing with him. He doesn't like the figures, tough. Not gonna let him micromanage me. All the other clients like the numbers just fine."

George just nodded and turned his attention back to the screen. This particular client would be shocked to find that anyone else was funding this particular effort: he took it so very personally. But then all of their clients did. As a result, great care had been taken to make sure that none of them knew others were involved, or that the risk of the Venture as a whole was being distributed in more ways than any of them expected. Pyotr shifted his attention to the middle monitor. "What *is* that?" he said.

"Text Microcosm," George said, leaning in to look at it again. "Million Monkeys. They're fanficcing *Macbeth*."

"Text?" Pyotr said, shaking his head. He thought he'd heard about nearly everything that had to do with Omnitopia, but this was a new one on him. "You mean there are no visuals at all? No gameplay?"

"They *are* playing," George said. "They're rewriting Shakespeare in real time. In iambic pentameter."

The concept startled Pyotr. He could only imagine the

reaction of his university literature teacher to such an idea: the bug-eyed apoplectic spasm that would follow could have put him in the hospital. "They think they can do Shakespeare better than *Shakespeare* did?"

George grinned. It was a goofy look, one Pyotr didn't see often during business hours here, for George was mostly very serious. "Some people," he said, "think really well of themselves. It's fun to watch." He yawned. "And it's a gas to stick my nose in occasionally and correct their scansion. It drives them nuts."

Pyotr leaned against the wall and rubbed his eyes. "All right," he said. "So. Cranky magnates and idiot monkeys, and—" He peered at the first monitor. "Is that a *kitchen?*"

George nodded. "There's a worldwide cooking competition going on in Le Jeux de l'Escoffier," he said. "It was just stopped by one of the adjudicators. Some players are claiming that someone's gotten into the game software and sabotaged the rules governing the physics of hollandaise."

Pyotr rolled this idea around his mind and then pushed it aside, as it was even stranger than the idea of rewriting Shakespeare. "The fact that you're looking at all this stuff now," he said, "suggests that you've got an answer for the question I asked you two hours ago. So when *do* we go?"

"We could go right now," said George. "We're ready."

Pyotr stood there and weighed the advantages and disadvantages of that versus the "go" times they had been predicting all day. The basic problem was striking the right balance between the desire for haste and the desire to execute their plan without introducing too many unwanted variables and uncertainties.

But the sooner the better, Pyotr thought. *The more quickly we move, the less prepared Omnitopia will be.* They weren't stupid people over there. They had to have picked up *some* hints of what was about to happen to them, regardless of the care that Pyotr and his colleagues had taken to cover their tracks. And no organization, not even the Venture, could ever be guaranteed leak-free. *So—the sooner we hit, the sooner we can start making our money, and the sooner we can finish up, close down, and vanish. Because no matter how well we've planned this, if it doesn't go the way we said it was, we're going to have some very angry, very powerful people after us. The more time we have to hide, the better I'll like it.*

But if we jump too *soon, too much before when we told the clients we would, they'll start getting the idea we're jerking them around. Not that we aren't, of course* ... And this presented its own problems. The major corporate clients mostly believed what they were told about the Venture's situations and timings, having little choice in the matter: their own intelligence sections had hit and bounced off the Collective's security enough times that they'd all realized they had little choice but to accept what they were being told. Both the governmental clients had gone through the same exercise, but—being less inclined to take "no" for an answer—had then been allowed to establish moles here who were fed careful but believable and verifiable disinformation. These had finally led the governments involved to relax their vigilance, in both cases being blinded by their perception of themselves as too dangerous to monkey around with. Pyotr had gamed out *their* scenarios with particular enjoyment and had laid careful anonymous bets with gaming syndicates in Barbados and Las Vegas, the bets leveraged by his estimates of which government would wobble first and hardest, and how certain key stocks would move, especially the petrochemicals. *But it's still gaming. I prefer to be out of here and well hidden away where I can see how it all unfolds without having to make long explanations to clients who don't understand that no battle plan survives contact with the enemy.*

George leaned back in his chair and laughed again. "It's true what they say," he said.

"And what do they say?"

"For honesty and that go-for-broke stick-to-it-iveness thing, hire Americans. For culture and good food, hire the French. For efficiency, hire the Swiss. But for good old-fashioned suspicion and the ability to effortlessly imagine six different kinds of backstabbing and their results, hire a Russian."

Pyotr shrugged, smiled. George was full of these little aphorisms. Sometimes they were even true. "And for boring clichéd proverbs," he said, "hire a Brit."

"Even a cliché," George said, "has an element of truth. Otherwise it wouldn't survive as a cliché. So what about it?"

Pyotr considered. *Too early, and the corporates will get nervous that we're going to cheat them somehow. Then someone might actually blow the whistle, regardless of the safeguards we've got in place. Not good. . . . Wait too long, though, and we might misfire.* The thought that Omnitopia might already have sussed out what they were up to and was going to be able to shut out more of the attacking servers with every passing second, wouldn't let Pyotr be. He felt like a man standing in a burning building . . . and what was burning was money: *his* money. *So. Just rearranging the first wave of bot execution times, the ones that're best masked . . .* Those would be the million-plus zombie computers around the world that were tasked to ensure that the Collective's own "base" take from the Venture was securely skimmed off and socked away. This zombie-group's business moved under cover of the normal automated nightly interbank wire transfer action that slid around the globe in an eight-time-zone-wide band every "night"—night being, in banking terms, a very relative thing. Many banks that should have known better were too wedded to the concept of banking hours and tended to do their big transfers in the local "middle of the night." This left them too limited in their transfer randomization—two thirds of the day, you knew they weren't sending anything, and rooting out their traffic pattern in the remaining third was mostly a matter of computer processing power and patience.

Under cover of the big burst of traffic that would come in Asia starting around Tokyo's banking midnight—for all the biggest banks were routinely in a rush to get their transfers and reconciliations done before the net got clogged with their competitors' bandwidth usage— the King Zombies, the Collective's privately-tasked money-stealing machines, would log into Omnitopia's Asian and European servers. When they were in, they would make use of a large range of clandestinely purchased "preferred access" network backdoors to gain entrance to the game's master accounting program. The King Zombie computers would then initiate a complex series of transactions exploiting a very secret and heretofore unnoticed loophole in the Omnitopia game gold accounting routines—one sold to the Collective months back by a perceptive but unlucky Omnitopia employee who'd been drummed out of master auditing after a sexual harassment suit. The Zombies would be asking the accounting program to value the Venture's previously accrued gold for withdrawal to "player" bank accounts—but due to the incorrectly-written accounting routine, the valuation would get stuck in a programming loop and accidentally increase the amount of gold in question by a factor of nearly a hundred. The withdrawal would then be made on the revalued amount, but the preloop accounting assessment would leave the Omnitopia accounting system thinking it had only disbursed the uninflated amount.

This whole process would take the flock of King Zombie computers 14.66 minutes. Then the King Zombies would wipe their own tracks out of the accounting routines and simply vanish from Omnitopia's logs as if they had never been there. Later, when their transfers to many other banking systems around the world were complete, the King Zombie machines would erase their own hard drives using best-practice triple-overwrite runs of the type preferred by the NSA, and finally voltage-shock the drives into catastrophic crashes. The custom boards installed in these machines to override the drive controllers and run these routines would then fry themselves.

A while before then, somewhere in Omnitopia, the alarms would start going off. What was uncertain was how quickly, and with what level of understanding of what had provoked them. The Conscientious Objector algorithm was the Collective's greatest fear in this business. All they could rely on was that the CO was mostly oriented toward watching the ways players would cheat, and was not as strong in accounting as it might have been were the company more oriented toward protecting its money than protecting its gameplay. Everything else had to be about people: what people would notice was happening, how fast they would notice it, and where, and when.

But the longer they took, the better, because that would be collateral damage time for all the eagerly waiting cli-

ents, and bonus time for the Collective itself. Most of the
clients simply wanted to hurt Omnitopia for one reason or
another—political, social, personal—and didn't care about
the money all that much except as a symbol for pain in-
flicted in that most basic corporate/international sense, the
fiduciary. The clients wanted the company to fail, or people
in it to be hurt or get fired, or stock markets to respond
in specific ways to the financial damage. That blinded all
the corporate and national clients a bit, and made things
easier for the Collective. Yes, the clients would get their
money—at least, what they would consider significant pro-
portions of it—always masked by errors in reckoning carefully introduced by the Collective itself. *That* skim stayed
home and would be divvied up among those in this little
windowless room and the other two like it who'd done the
actual work: part of their achievement bonus.

After that, after the clients had earned out, came the
pure bonus period during which (again, after the Collective's surreptitious skim) some of those who'd been most
forthcoming in helping build the zombie network would be
recompensed. The rest—hundreds of thousands of greedy
or stupid users who'd volunteered to get in on the action
without thinking things through—would be thrown out of
the speeding sledge in waves, their network addresses suddenly becoming visible when they were supposed to have
been concealed, and theoretically erased logs and other
useful information suddenly remanifesting themselves on
hard drives all over the planet. The poor dupes would never
know what had hit them. They would just suddenly hit the
snow, and the wolves of world law enforcement would fall
on them with glee and rip them up.

The remaining users—"used" was probably a better
word—less greedy than the pre-chosen victims, maybe less
stupid, possibly just lucky, would each win his or her little
personal lottery out of the funds that would be scooped in
over the course of the Great Omnitopia Robbery. These
people, the thousands of unseen enablers and connectors
to other computer networks of use in this exploit, would
keep or lose the funds they were paid depending on how
smart they were about grabbing it out of their accounts,

diving for cover (with the slight and sometimes regrettably incomplete advice they'd been given about how to hide), and not coming up for air again until the first wave of law enforcement had passed over them.

And then, of course, we have to vanish too. But how long will the retasking of timings take ... how long for the King Zombies ... and then. the secondary network ... hmm ...

Pyotr glanced down at George, but George was unfocused, his arms folded, looking out sightlessly at the room. Of course George had known Pyotr long enough now not to rush him during one of these moments of calculation. But right now he looked unusually disconnected even for George at his most patient.

George looked up suddenly. "What?" he said.

Pyotr smiled at him. "You were completely zoned out."

George rubbed his eyes. "I believe you," he said. Sleep had not been the friend of any of them for most of these last seventy-two hours, despite everyone's understanding that they needed to keep sharp for the hours to come.

"What will *you* do?" Pyotr said.

It was a question that most members of the Collective didn't ask one another. Until the Venture was complete, knowing too much, knowing almost anything, could be dangerous. *But we're so close ... and we're at the top of the heap. If I don't satisfy my curiosity now, I may never get the chance.*

"Do?" George said.

"Afterward."

George shook his head. At first Pyotr thought this meant there would be no answer, and George was always Mr. Security, so this didn't surprise him. But then George let out a breath.

"I am going to have a little farm," he said. "A smallhold, halfway up a mountain somewhere in central Europe. There will be chickens in the front yard, scratching. Maybe a flock of geese for security. I'll raise my own vegetables and maybe have a cow. There'll be a stream running through the field, and I'll put a turbine in it for power. And I'll have a windmill, and solar. There'll be a greenhouse tunnel where I will breed the world's hottest, but tastiest, designer chilies. There will be cats snoozing in the front yard, and pine martens will have a nest in the attic. And there won't be a glimpse anywhere, from horizon to horizon, of the goddamn sea."

Pyotr raised his eyebrows. It was strange. Until recently George had been living most people's dream: blue water, white beaches, hot sun. *All right, the occasional hurricane, but still!* Yet now what he wanted was to get rid of all that. *The grass is always greener . . .*

Cliché again. Never mind. "Four hours," Pyotr said.

George got that thinking look of his. "Four hours earlier than announced to our esteemed clients. A question of how well we can cover when they start asking questions . . ."

"Okay, shave a little off that?" Pyotr said, for when George looked concerned, his hunches were often to be trusted. "Three and a half?"

George thought. "Twelve-minute thirteen-second offset from the half hour."

"Eleven thirteen," Pyotr said.

George nodded.

"Start the clock," he said. "Three hours, forty-two minutes."

Pyotr went over to his computer to start the sledge running over the snow.

Behind him, he heard George softly reading something from the middle monitor.

What is't you do? A deed without a name . . .

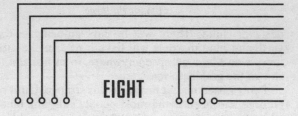

EIGHT

UNDER THE PALM TREES of one of the pathways leading to Castle Dev, a blonde woman in a cream linen business suit was meandering along, jotting something down in a PDA, her lips moving silently as she wrote. Around her, Omnitopia staff bicycled or golf-carted by, or in some cases Roller-bladed past, and there was even one diehard three-piece-suit-on-a-scooter type who kicked past her, glancing back curiously as he went, as if a little surprised to see a face he didn't know.

Delia Harrington smiled at him and turned her attention back to the notes she was jotting down after her last interview. *Weird,* she thought. *With all the people here, you'd think a single new face wouldn't provoke any particular interest.*

She paused by one particularly large royal palm to save the file she was working on, for Castle Dev was just up at the top of the next rise. *But then again,* she thought, *you could make a case that Omnitopia's like a very small town. Live there long enough and pretty soon you recognize everybody.*

Delia finished saving the note and put her PDA away. *Of course, for all I know, the who's-that-girl looks are because Omnitopia security has some kind of all-points bulletin out on me as a Person of Interest. A risk to their corporate way of life . . .*

Delia breathed out, smiling at herself. *Okay, now that's just paranoia,* she thought. *Not the best state of mind to be in while preparing to meet the world's eighth richest man . . .*

She headed up the path toward the castle gateway. People were making their way toward and away from it at various rates of hurry, and as she examined each face she saw, over and over again, something she'd started to identify over the course of the day: an expression of slight excitement, like kids about to get out of school. *Except they're in school,* she thought. *More or less. Just about everybody I've seen today genuinely seems to like working here. It's so bizarre.*

Another truly paranoid thought wandered across her forebrain: that everybody who *didn't* like working here had been told to stay home today because the reporter from *Time* was coming through . . . Delia snorted at herself and started the slight uphill climb toward the nearest castle gateway.

She turned onto the sandstone-paved walkway that led up to the gate. The entry area dividing the broad deep archway from the interior park and garden was quiet for the moment: there was no visible security presence there, not so much as a booth with a security guard in it.

Delia's directions had been straightforward enough: through the arch, go across the courtyard, through the glass doors, give your name to the guy at the desk. But it was still strange to see the very heart of the Omnitopia empire seem so quiet, so nearly empty, and so unguarded. Delia slowed down a little as she came up the archway, thinking about asking somebody whether she was in the right place. *Did I come in on the wrong side or something?*

Off to her right and just on the near side of the arch, somebody was parking an ancient-looking, dusty black bike at the last slot in a bike rack there. He was a tall, lean, shaggy-haired, sandy-haired guy in cream chinos and a white shirt, and as he turned—

Delia, finally seeing his face, stopped right where she was. It was Dev Logan himself, without a staff member in sight, dusting his hands off against his pants and reaching back to the spring-clip rack over the bike's rear fender to unclip some folders he was carrying. He pulled them out and started going through one of them, and as she approached, he glanced up at her once, then twice.

And said, "Oh, my gosh, you're Delia Harrington, aren't you?"

Did he actually say "gosh"? was her first thought, and she had to control her urge to laugh as he came over to her and shook her hand.

"That's right," Delia said.

"Oh, good," Dev said. "I'm okay with faces but I get a little mixed on names sometimes . . ."

He actually looked at you when he shook your hand, and the smile seemed genuine. This was dangerous. It was something Delia had seen before in politicians, the instant sincerity, absolutely believed by the purveyor—until the need to believe it in front of a specific person went away. It could be very winning, and the more won over Delia found herself feeling, the less she trusted the emotion.

"Listen, I'm really sorry we had to reschedule," Dev said. "I hate having to make people wait."

"Oh, no, no problem . . ." Delia said, somewhat disarmed against her will. "You're very busy of course . . ."

"It's just been one of those days: with the launch coming up, everything's been getting screwed up at the last minute. I barely had time to see my daughter at lunchtime before things started to go south . . ."

That approach put her back on course, emotionally at least. The Family-Man ploy was one of the things that Delia found hardest to swallow about the whole Dev Logan picture, when it was well known that the child had hot and cold running nannies and a toy budget probably approximating the GPD of a small country. "Well, family time's so important, after all . . ."

"So is keeping commitments," Dev said. "Sorry again. But at least the delay would have left you a little time to have some lunch. You did get something to eat, didn't you?"

"Oh, yes," she said, "I stopped over at the cantina—" Various Omnitopia staffers she'd spoken to over the course of the morning had said, "You have *got* to get over there," and once inside, she'd seen why. The multileveled twenty-four-hour dining facility reputedly modeled on the Baths of Caracalla, staffed by purloined star chefs and their minions and used as a training site by European hotel schools, would have been anybody's candidate for one of the Restaurant Wonders of the World. Yet it had felt as casual as a small-town diner—laughing and joking going on in the corner booths, people playing cards at one table, here and there a sofa with some guy sleeping on it, or a girl working on a laptop and eating a roast beef sandwich while her Labrador made sad starving-doggie eyes at her. And the food offerings had stretched all the way from simple high-piled bowls of fruit to four-course extravaganzas of every ethnicity ... while still proving capable of delivering that most deceptively simple and difficult dish, the perfect three-egg omelet. "Normandy butter," the young Asian chef who made it for her had said, shrugging a perfectly French shrug. But Delia had suspected that the omelet's perfection had more to do with knowing just when to stop. Once again, as the chef had turned away, she'd gotten a sense of an entirely different flavor of Really-Likes-Working-Here Syndrome ... but in this case, having missed breakfast, she'd been able to put it aside.

"That's good," Dev said. "Come on, let me show you around here a little, and then we can talk."

He gestured her to the archway: they went through together. "And you've spoken to Joss and Tau," Dev said. "Those meetings at least went all right."

"Yes, they were very helpful," Delia said. They had in fact been two of the most carefully spoken people she'd ever interviewed. Of the PR guy, she could have believed this, and was prepared for it. But Tau Vitoria was supposed to be an overenthusiastic software geek stuck in a perpetually collegiate attitude toward his work and his friends, much given to practical jokes and weird hours. Delia had not been at all prepared for the slick-looking, soft-spoken, extremely tailored young gentleman who took her hand and did not actually kiss it, but bowed over it with a formality that somehow managed to be genuinely youthful and charming. Multilingual, well-read, obviously well-educated despite the number of universities he had apparently been thrown out of for bad behavior, Tau had been almost too large a set of contradictions for Delia to cope with at one sitting. She had been both relieved to get away from him, and strangely eager to have another run at him and see if she could crack that glossy exterior and find some dirt under it, or at least dust. "Tau," she said, "in particular—"

Dev grinned. "Everybody," he said, "hits Tau and bounces. I bounce every day. Here, let's go in the side way—"

He led Delia along a path through the courtyard that led to the base of a broad space between two of the west-side towers and a wide set of dark-glass doors that slid aside for them as they approached. "You probably know from the PR what this building's like already," he said. "Family quarters, executive offices, and the master corporate suite—"

"There are more people in here than in any one other building on campus, aren't there?" Delia said as they headed across a sculpture-studded sandstone floor and up a wide staircase along the back wall.

Dev nodded. "We tried decentralizing it," he said, "but it didn't work so well, though the villa-and-courtyard or crofting model does quite well everywhere else on campus. Seems this particular 'village of the like-minded' prefers to stay very physically close in the workplace."

They came out on the landing, and Delia realized that "close" did not look exactly as she'd started to imagine it might on the way in. The distance between the inner and outer walls of Castle Dev on this side was far greater than that between the walls where the archway was, and the four galleried sides of the space they now entered went nearly up to another of the polarized glass ceilings, slanted inward toward the central garden plaza, and at least four stories down below ground level. Nonetheless, all those spaces were as flooded with daylight as if they were at ground level and completely windowed. All of them had desks and glass cubicles and semicircular group work sofas surrounding large round worktables and most of the workspaces Delia could see were busy with people.

Dev leaned over the railing, gazing down into the depths. At the very bottom of the atrium, a fountain played in a rectangular pool; on its charcoal-gray bottom, the ubiquitous Omnitopia alpha/omega symbols faded in and out of visibility in a shimmer of moving water and silvery underlighting. Delia, gazing down into what she could see of the workspaces, said, "This part of the building must go right out into the mesa . . ."

"Support spaces mostly," Dev said. "It's not kind to make people work too far underground. And there's too much temptation for computer people to go nondiurnal as it is. We try to keep people on days, and in daylight, mostly." He straightened up. "Come on down to my office space."

"You have one here?" Delia said, heading after him toward a ramp that curved around one side of the galleries. "I thought your main office was on the other side of the building."

"Oh, yeah. But I have an employee-accessible office space in every building on this campus," Dev said. "And all our other buildings, worldwide. People have to be able to find me."

"But doing it virtually must make it easier. You've got that famous virtual office space—"

"Sure," Dev said. "But I still need local places when I'm out and around to dump a briefcase or a laptop. And my colleagues here need somewhere local to walk into when they want me. It's a courtesy thing."

They headed down around the curve and out onto the level below the one where they'd been standing. Here Delia glanced up and saw that many light-bending tunnel guides, the source of all that daylight, were set in the ceiling. Dev followed her glance. "Not a perfect solution," he said, strolling among the sofas and the big comfortable-looking part cubicles where his employees glanced up, nodded or waved at him, glanced away again, "but better than artificial."

"Even better than your solid light in the parking lots?"

Dev smiled as they made their way into the center of the space, where a wide oval of more cubicles and worktables surrounded a big semicircular glass desk and its matching semicircular sofa. "Couldn't help that," he said. "Had to have it. But I'm such a geek, everybody says so. . . ."

He tossed the folders he'd been carrying onto the desk as he came up to it. "You have some stuff you want to show me, I take it," Dev said, leaning against the desk.

Delia nodded, handing him the one thing that *Time* editorial had sent along with her: the dummy cover of the edition in which Dev's interview and background article would appear.

He glanced over it. For just a second Delia thought she saw a flicker of something in his expression, a split second of annoyance or surprise: then the expression sealed over. *No, come on, Dev, tell me what you* really *think!* "The typography might not be right yet," Delia said, hoping to winkle that look out of its hiding place again.

"No, it looks fine," Dev said, tucking the cover dummy back into its folder. Then he grinned—an expression utterly at odds with the previous one. "It's a lost cause, you know that? I'm just not photogenic."

Delia had to restrain herself from looking at him cockeyed. *Are you out of your mind?* she wanted to say. *You're the eighth richest man in the world, do you seriously think anyone cares if you're not classically handsome?* But he genuinely looked sheepish. *Is this another of those manufactured moments? . . . But no. No one could genuinely look that embarrassed at himself if he really wasn't. Especially not the big-shot head of a multinational.*

"Well, never mind," he said. "Other people on campus will need to see this—Joss and his team in particular—and we'll have notes for you within a few days. Meanwhile, you've got questions for me—" He waved her over to one of a pair of lounge chairs off to one side of the desk.

They sat down. She had a long list, but no set order in which to ask them, so now she picked the one that kept coming up for her and which other interviewers had never seemed to find a decent answer for. "What's the attraction?" she said after a moment. "What makes Omnitopia work for so many people on so many levels?"

Dev leaned back. "It's the question everybody tends to answer for themselves, once they've been in," he said. "Not to push it back on you, but what's appealed to you when you've gone in-game?"

"Well," she said, "I haven't really been in except in the public exploratory spaces—"

"Oh, no," Dev said. "You haven't *played?*"

"Uh, no, I've been talking to people mostly—"

"So come on in with me!" Dev said. "I've got a little free time this afternoon."

She gave him an amused look. "*You* have free time?"

He shrugged. "It was an accident," Dev said. "I finished up some work early. But also, my PA always schedules me too long for lunch." He produced a sly look. "Frank has this idea that I need less stress."

This at least Delia understood. "You strike me more as the kind of person who thrives on it."

Dev laughed. "Don't put that in the article," he said. "You'll give my staff ideas. But we'll go in, have a walk around." He got up.

Delia stood up in considerable bemusement: a guided tour through Omnitopia itself, rather than just its corporate bricks-and-mortar, was something that had never occurred to her might happen. "What's your preference?" Dev said. "Do you like fully virtual options—the complete sensory immersion experience? Or would you rather keep your distance and get in via keyboard or flat input?"

"Well—" Delia said. "You must have a lot of really nice virtual around here—"

From off to one side, a soft chiming sound began. Dev glanced over at his desk: Delia followed the glance and saw that the dark glass was pulsing with soft blue light. "Oh, no," Dev said, "I *told* them to hold my calls—"

He went over to the desk, touched its surface. "Yes?"

Delia couldn't hear anything happening at the other end of the communication. *Bone conduction?* she wondered. *Or something weirder?* There was no way to tell.

She watched Dev's expression. It was neutral for a moment, then crinkled down into an annoyed scowl. "Well," he said, "I guess there's nothing we can do about that, is there. Okay, what's his timetable look like?"

Another pause. "All right," Dev said, "let's do it that way. I'll call you back shortly. Right. Thanks."

He straightened up and sighed, then turned back to Delia. "I'm really sorry about this," Dev said, "but I've had something come up that requires my attention, and the spare time I thought I had has just evaporated. The story of my life for the next couple of days." He let out an annoyed sigh. "Would you mind if we reschedule this walkabout? Tomorrow, let's say. I'll see that we get it done next time."

"Of course," Delia said. Then she added, "You're supposed

to do that every day, aren't you? Visit one Macrocosm or another."

Dev nodded. "My universe," he said. "Or universes. I'd be remiss if I didn't keep an eye on things."

"I didn't mean just in the supervisory or workability sense," Delia said, as they started to walk out toward the atrium again. "There are all these stories in the newsfeeds . . . rumors about how Dev Himself walks through his creation in disguise, rewarding the good and punishing the wicked."

"Mostly the wicked wind up punishing themselves," Dev said. "They know our game has a positively skewed ethics structure . . ."

Delia chuckled. "Another of those great pieces of gamespeak," she said. "Like 'negative satisfaction.'"

Dev shrugged. "That's one piece of language we need. At the end of the day, it's all about player satisfaction. Everybody has to win . . . or lose in some way that makes sense to them. They don't win, I don't win . . . or, more to the point, my staff don't win."

"It's interesting to hear you put it that way," Delia said, "since one of the complaints from some of your players is that winning, as such, is impossible. That all they can do is keep playing, and paying you for the privilege of allowing them to play their butts off for little statistically managed minimum feedback rewards, because the game doesn't have any real planned ending." She smiled. "Because if it did, you'd stop making money."

"Well," Dev said, as they strolled back out to the gallery ramp again, "if it were true that Omnitopia didn't have an ending, I'd hardly confess that to *you*." He smiled back, but there was an edge on it. "And if we did have an ending, that's also information I wouldn't be eager to hand to *Time* as an exclusive when with one phone call I could schedule a press conference that would have every major news outlet on Earth camped out on my front lawn within four hours. But if you'll turn around for a second—"

She did. He looked back across that level of the main office suite with her, then up and down the atrium. "How many people would you say work in here?"

•

Delia shook her head. "I read the numbers earlier, but I confess I don't remember at the moment. Five . . . maybe six hundred?"

"Six hundred eighteen, this week," Dev said. "It's close enough to ten percent of the workforce on campus here. They, and the forty thousand-odd other people I employ around the world, and their families, and their health plans, and their mortgages, would probably be somewhat upset if Omnitopia stopped making money. Don't you think?"

"I didn't mean—"

"I'm sure you didn't," Dev said. "It may surprise you to know that I sign off on every hire. Sooner or later—sometimes later, because as you see my schedule gets crazed without warning—I meet everybody who works for me. If for me there's a game that never ends, and that I intend to win at all costs, it's the game of keeping this company successful enough that my people have work for as long as they want it. Because there've been times when *I* didn't have any, and let me tell you, when you don't have work and you want it, you don't feel much like playing any game at all. All our other players are contributing to a context in which we can all feel like playing. And I'm committed to making sure the players do at least as well out of the situation as my employees. Believe me, they'll have nothing to complain about as the new game unfolds. And that's only partly because I have my own ethics skew, which I dislike seeing impugned."

After a moment Delia nodded. "Sorry," she said. "What time do you want to do this walkthrough?"

Dev rubbed his eyes for a moment, thinking. Just for that second, something showed through that Delia hadn't yet seen in him: weariness. But a flash later it was gone. "Could we say tomorrow about two? You can go on with doing your background research for the rest of the day, seeing the people you need to see. I have your cell phone number. I'll text you tomorrow morning to confirm the timing, and then send somebody a little before two to find you and pick you up in a flivver. That be okay?"

"Fine. Thanks, Mr. Logan."

He turned away, then paused, cocked an eyebrow at her.

"Even if I half suspect you're preparing to do a hatchet job on me," he said, "you can call me Dev."

Delia nodded, smiled. "That's something else I keep meaning to ask you about," she said. "The name. Short for ...?"

"Dev," he said.

"That's what the driver's license says," she said. "But the birth certificate?"

"You planning to apply for a passport in my name?" Dev said, and grinned.

She shrugged, gave him a little wave, and walked down the stairs, heading for the doors to the courtyard.

Dev watched her go, then turned back to make his way again toward his local desk. Around him, this level's soft buzz was just a little louder than usual. It would be much louder this time tomorrow, Dev was sure. And the day after tomorrow. But right now, the future thirty-six hours hence seemed like an eternity away. *Got plenty of trouble to deal with first ...*

At the desk he paused just for a moment to flip the *Time* magazine folder cover open and looked once more at the dummy cover. It was a restatement of the cover he'd done for *Rolling Stone* a couple of years back, in late '13—which itself could be considered a comment. That cover had been a full-length portrait of a tall, lean, sandy-haired, open-collared, jeans-wearing kind of guy leaning against a white support that faded into a white background: a cover more about the person than the supposed phenomenon. The Dev in that picture looked like a guy you could imagine mowing his own lawn, or maybe even yours. The pose in the picture on this *Time* dummy cover was similar, but it was a head-to-waist shot, the clothes a little more formal—a business shirt with the collar unbuttoned rather than the polo shirt of the older photo shoot. The expression was more intense—the formerly-trademark glasses were missing, dumped since Dev had finally let Mirabel talk him into the laser surgery (and since Dev had finished scrutinizing to his own satisfaction the results of the long-term effects in the medical journals). The Omnitopia logo loomed large in the background, superimposed over a faded image of the Omnitopia City campus. The message seemed to be: *here's a guy who's become a force to be reckoned with.* Or it could also be: *here's a guy who's sold out to the big buck and is in the process of forgetting his roots.* Now, as Dev looked at the new *Time* dummy, he grimaced to himself, remembering how slickly the high-powered photographer they'd brought in for the shoot—admittedly one of the great names—had maneuvered him out of all the available polos and into the shirt. *And I let him. Well, we still have approval on this cover. I can always pitch some kind of fit or find some kind of fault, and insist that I want another shoot. But then they'll just find some kind of way to imply that I'm a publicity-crazed, hypercontrolling prima donna. . . .*

Dev flipped the folder shut and looked around. As he did he saw tall gangly Frank come out of his own nearby satellite office and head toward him. Dev went to meet him. "Did Tau find you just now?"

"He sure did. Looks like the big trouble's starting."

"So I gather. He wants us to deal with our substructure business before we go help the boys stomp on the naughtiness in progress."

"A little happy-violence time, huh, Boss?"

"I'd be happier if we didn't need the violence," Dev said, "but I need to be part of the action, because damn it, *nobody* screws with my worlds without me personally taking a big old kick at their butts." He scowled. "Anyway, I've rescheduled Miss Harrington for two o'clock tomorrow: let's make sure that happens this time, okay? Last thing we want is for *Time* to think we're yanking their chain. Besides it just being rude to keep shuffling her around."

Frank nodded. "Got some notes from Cleolinda for you on the meeting this morning," he said.

"She's greased lightning, that one," Dev said. "I'll call her after Tau and I finish up. Anything else?"

"Only things that can wait until after Tau," Frank said. He looked down at the little tablet computer he carried with him everywhere. "The PR people say they need to talk to you. Something about the timings on the European rollout."

Dev groaned and clutched his head. "What? Not again! Frank, *we have to stop having this conversation!* The rollout is going to be simultaneous, worldwide, it has *always* been planned to be this way from day one, and I refuse to jiggle the timings just because they're getting some more indirect heat from whoever's running the Sky satellites in Europe this year! It's *our* heat they have to worry about. Let Mr. Sky Junior buy his own ad time! Because God knows we pay him enough for ours. And tell Joss he needs to be using a bigger hammer for the European PR guys! Or no, don't tell him, I'll tell him myself. And then them. Schedule it."

Frank nodded, made a note. Then he looked up. "The *Time* lady being a little adversarial, Boss?"

Dev raised his eyebrows. "Does it show?" He let out a breath. "Don't think I'm gonna win much in the hearts-and-minds department with her. *Time* wants an in-depth interview, and they don't really want to cast me as an out-and-out villain . . . but they won't mind suggesting there are shadows around the edges of my profile." Dev shrugged. "Not something I can spend any time worrying about right now. I'll get online and see Tau." Frank was giving him a look. "What?"

"You still haven't been seen eating anything," Frank said. "And it's gonna get worse these next few days. You've got to take a little more time, eat a normal meal at least once a day, relax a little more while you do it—"

"It's Frank's mouth that's working but I hear the voice of the Queen of Omnitopia coming out of it," Dev said, reaching out to take a look at the tablet. "*I will get a damn sandwich*, all right?"

"Which access will you be using?"

"My upstairs office."

"A BLT on brown bread will be on your desk in five minutes," Frank said. "*Put it in your mouth.* The webcams will be running."

Dev started reading the tablet again: Frank reached out and took it away from him. "Then come back when you're done. I'll have Joss line up the Euro PR people for you to shoot down."

Dev sighed. "Powerless," he said. "Here I am, the eighth richest man in the world, and I have no control over my own fate."

"Seventh," said Frank, jotting something on the tablet.

"What?"

"Forbes reranked you this morning," Frank said, putting his stylus away. "The Indian steel guy at number six took a bath in the commodities markets last month. He's eighth now."

Dev shook his head. Some of his staff took what Dev considered an unnatural pleasure in his ranking, as if he was some kind of spectator sport. "Fine," Dev said. "Tell everybody I said 'Let joy be unrestrained.' Hey, get crazy, send out for confetti. We done?"

"For now."

"Good. Got a few things to deal with then Tau and I will go hunting. I'm off limits to everybody but the attack team then."

"Noted."

Dev waved and headed toward the atrium gallery: there was a private side access just before it to the family levels of the Castle, where he could make his way the long way through to his office with a hug for Lolo on the way. Behind him, Frank said, "Oh, Boss?"

Dev turned. "What?"

"She ask you about the name?"

Dev rolled his eyes.

Frank grinned, pumped the air with one fist. "Yes!" He turned and walked off. "I win five bucks. See you when you're done."

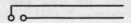

Rik was sitting in his online space's little dingy office, trying to get caught up on the mail before he headed in to take yet another run at ironing out the problems with the structure inside his Microcosm. The mail in the window hanging beside the old scuffed mahogany desk was yet another of a tall stack of e-mails from Microcosm Management that he'd been working his way through, none of which had brought him much closer to understanding what had gone wrong with his own 'cosm. *Though this one might be it . . .*

He sighed, waving at the window and scrolling down the body of the message. "—reports of various service outages in newly-set up Microcosms. We want to assure our new Levelers that the system is being carefully examined to determine the cause of the outages and malfunctions so that we can make sure they don't recur. We'd appreciate it if you'd contact us and describe in detail the problems you experienced with your 'cosm so that we can incorporate your data into a system-wide diagnostic matrix . . ."

Rik leaned back in his creaky chair and stretched, wondering whether the cheerful language actually meant that Microcosm Management didn't know what was going on either. "In detail, huh," he said. Well, they were going to get more than they bargained for from him, at least in the negative sense, because he was sure now of about eighty things that *weren't* the problem—

A shadow fell across the frosted glass of the office door, lifted a hand to knock. "Come on in," Rik said.

The door creaked open, the frosted glass in the door rattling a little as always. A second later Angela came strolling in, dressed in pale blue sweats and lightly dotted with grass clippings—she'd apparently been out in the backyard, gardening. She gazed around with mild interest. "This place could use a good cleaning," she said. "Look at those windows!"

"It's not Mrs. Busby's week to come in," Rik said, getting up and pushing the screen away.

"Week?" Angela said, looking at him a little cockeyed. "And just who is Mrs. Busby?"

"The cleaning lady," Rik said. "This is 1945. Men don't clean up after themselves in 1945. Especially hard-bitten detective types."

The look Angela threw him was heavily ironic as she ran a finger over the top of the green-painted filing cabinet and brought up some serious dust. "Well," she said, "you've got this part of the fantasy down pat." She dusted her hands off. "But this wasn't what you were going to show me."

Rik shook his head, grinning. "No," he said, and got up. "Check these out."

He snapped his fingers. At the preprogrammed audio cue, the system dressed this virtual version of him in the new robes he'd picked up from Lal. Quilted velvet whispered and tissue-of-orichalc gleamed in the buzzing pink neon from the movie house across the street as Rik spun once so that Angela could take it all in—the divided surcoat, the fabulous embroidery bespelled to glow in the gloom or smoke of the battlefield, the tailoring. "Nice, huh?"

Angela smiled one of those sideways smiles at him, meant to suggest that she was thinking things she wasn't going to say. "You don't look as silly as I thought you would," she said after a moment, "so I'll stop teasing you about your robes. I thought they'd look like some kind of kaftan."

"For the battlefield? Wouldn't make much sense," Rik said. "Anyway, come on, let's take a look at the new real estate. Game access, please?" he said to the system.

His office blinked out and left them standing in the blue-lit twilight of Omnitopia's outer login area. In the sky above them, the white-glowing Alpha and Omega of the company's logo were endlessly fading in and out through each other. In the middle distance, more or less on the ground or floor, the famous service-marked phrase, *Let's go play!*, stretched from horizon to horizon. "Good afternoon, Rik," said the control voice. "Welcome home. Identify your guest, please?"

"Angela," Rik said. "Audit ticket one."

"Noted," said the control voice. "ID and audit ticket associated. Angela, welcome to Omnitopia! Would you please say hello so that the game management system will recognize you if you need to ask for help?"

Angela threw Rik a look, then said, "Hello, Omnitopia."

"Thank you! Have a good visit."

Around them the sky dissolved into darkness, and the City faded in around them like a scene out of a film. Rik had asked the program to put them down over by the side street where he'd stood after the battle around the Ring of Elich. Angela looked around at everything—the people and creatures heading in and out of the plaza, the buildings, the Ring itself—saying nothing for the moment. Rik watched her closely, hoping for a positive reaction. She'd never been in here before.

After a moment she let out a breath: a sigh. "This is bizarre," she said. "It looks real."

Somehow this wasn't quite the response Rik had been expecting. "It does?" he said.

Angela nodded. Her expression was perplexed. "I thought this would be more—I don't know, more artificial," she said, as a small herd of pastel unicorns with demure little wings, cutesy butt-brands, and brightly colored backpacks wandered by them in a double line. *Some kind of school trip,* Rik thought. "It's like people here *want* this to be real."

"They do," Rik said, "some of them."

She gave him a look. "Should I be worrying about that?" Angela said.

"Probably not," Rik said, pulling her over to him and hugging her one-armed.

"Ow!" Angela looked down between them at the object caught between her sweats and Rik's gambeson. "Jeez, look at the size of that sword. Do you really need that thing in here?"

"Not here," Rik said. "Not usually. Earlier, though—" He started walking them down toward the Ring while explaining about the fracas that had broken out the last time he was here.

Angela shook her head as they stood in line for one Ring portal behind a small crowd of people in futuristic spacesuits who were carefully checking their ray guns. "Sounds too much like hard work to me," she said. "If I was going to come somewhere to play, it'd be playing. Not fighting!"

"There are plenty of worlds like that," Rik said as the gate cleared in front of the spacemen, revealing a predawn sky filled with a huge edge-on galaxy that ran down toward a mountainous, icy horizon. "Beaches, forests, strictly recreational. I'd give you . . . oh, about five minutes in a place like that before you were wishing you were somewhere more interesting."

The spacemen went their way, leaving the gate grayed out again as Rik and Angela stepped up to it. Rik patted the nearest trilithon by way of greeting and said, "Indigo, please."

"Accessible now," said the control voice, and the gate cleared down to that strange horizonless vista, in which a sun hung not above, but between you and the other side of the world.

"Wow, man, what *is* that?" said somebody from behind Rik.

He looked over his shoulder. There was a Gnarth standing there in very oversized jeans, cowboy boots, and a photographer's vest, peering past Rik and Angela. "New Microcosm," Rik said. "Not running yet."

"Wow," the Gnarth said in a very California-surfer-dude voice. "Gonna be a fighting world?"

"It's looking that way," Rik said.

"What's it called?"

"Indigo."

"Hey, let me know when it goes up," the Gnarth said. He reached into the air and pulled out a little carved stone token, a manifestation of his username and contact information. This he handed to Rik. "Got a bunch of friends who like to get in early before the rush starts."

Rik grinned at the idea that there would be a rush. "Thanks, friend. Have a good fight." He pocketed the token, looked over at Angela. "Go ahead, just walk through."

She nodded, went through the portal. He followed.

He'd tweaked the access locus so that they came out under the shade of a new forest Rik had installed that morning. Angela just stood there for a few seconds, looking up. Far across the interior of the world-globe, a crescent of night was sliding: deep inside it, faint and far away, were the lights of the campfires that Tom had suggested, too good an image not to implement. Angela turned around, surveying the nearer landscape of field and farm and forest, then looked over at Rik with an expression he couldn't remember having seen on her in many years of marriage: complete astonishment. "You *made* this?"

"A lot of it's modular," Rik said. "It's not so hard once you get the hang of it...." But her expression was so odd that he let the explanation trail off.

"And people are going to live here?"

"Uh, yeah," he said. "Game-generated players mostly at first. But real-life players will move in eventually, start homesteading, staking out fighting fortresses and so on. And every time they do, I get a nickel. When they claim territory, or fight on it, or sell another player something, I get a little cut ..."

"What are they going to do?"

"What, the players?"

"No, your characters—" Angela waved her hands as she looked around her. "Who will they be? Where did they come from? What's their story?"

"I'm still working on that," Rik said, and sat down on a nearby stone that he'd built there for the purpose. "I think they were probably brought here by aliens and left as an experiment. But the experiment has started having ideas of its own about what it's for. And people who come here to campaign and don't pay attention to the history of the place are going to get in trouble ..."

She sat down on the rock beside him and stared out across the blue void to the other side of the interior world. After a moment she said, "You want some help with this?"

Rik was stunned. Angela had never shown any interest in Omnitopia before. "Don't get me wrong," she said. "I don't want you to think I'm interfering—"

"Oh no! Not at all. It's just that—"

"I never saw how *solid* this looked," Angela said. "All of a sudden it seems like a place where you could tell stories, where interesting things could happen ..."

She trailed off. "You sure you want me to get involved with this?" Angela said then. "I know this is what you do to relax, it's important for a guy to have someplace where the family can't go—especially the wife ..."

"Are you crazy? You're absolutely welcome here. Always." Rik smiled at her. "It may just take me a little while to get my brains wrapped around the idea that you *want* to get involved! We need to get you a username, an account of your own. And there's all this other stuff to take care of ..."

Angela waved that away for the moment. "It'll keep,"

she said, looking around. "But I thought you told me things in here were broken."

"They were. Extremely broken." Rik shook his head, looking around him at the flowery meadow stretching away from the forest. "But now it's all working, and I have no idea why."

"Even though you built this?" Angela said.

"Please. I'm a beginner." Rik stretched and stood up again, backing out into the meadow a little so that he could see a bit more of his new forest than the trees. The carpet of greenery ran gently up the curve of the world, the curvature beginning to show most emphatically about ten miles away. "Does that look too curvy to you?" he said.

Angela followed his glance, shrugged. "It all looks too curvy," she said, "but I just got here. Give me a couple more visits." She turned, blinked. "Oh, and one other thing."

"What?"

"I thought you told me your world wasn't open yet."

"Microcosm," Rik said. "It's called a Microcosm. But, yeah, it's not open—"

"Then who's the guy?"

Rik stared. Then he recognized the figure slowly approaching them, It took him a moment, because the interloper was wearing a beat-up blue coverall instead of the rags and tatters Rik had seen him in last. Rik laughed, then. "Oh! That's my guy who comes in to help with the heavy lifting."

"What, the one from Quebec you told me about?"

"No, that's Jean. He's a mentor. This guy's somebody I hired."

That made Angela blink. "Wait. You have an employee?"

"Just inside the game," Rik said as Dennis came shambling toward them. The boiler suit he was wearing was almost as disreputable as the suit-of-rags had been—spectacularly stained and paint-splattered—and Dennis' flyaway shaggy gray hair looked even wilder now, as if he'd been consulting Einstein for fashion tips.

"Who is he?" Angela whispered. "What does he do?"

"Mostly so far I've got him transporting himself around the inside of the world, laying down place markers and giving me player-point-of-view feedback," Rik said quietly. "It's not hard work. He's kind of a mercy hire."

Angela brushed her bangs out of her eyes and glanced up at him, saying nothing for the moment: but Rik knew what she was thinking. *You've had this Microcosm for what, a day? And already you're hiring people?* But she only smiled as Dennis came over to them, and said, "Hi there!"

To Rik's astonishment, Dennis actually bowed to Angela, and then tugged his forelock. "Milady," he said in that creaky voice.

"Dennis, this is my wife, Angela," Rik said. "She's going to be doing some work on the Microcosm with me as we get things running in here."

Those wrinkled little eyes looked up at Angela as if trying to add a new variable into an equation that was a touch too involved already: then glanced at Rik. "What kind of work, sir?"

Angela laughed. "Don't ask him," she said, "because he doesn't know, and neither do I. We'll figure it out as we go along. And maybe you can help me out a little, because I'm new at this."

"Anything you need, milady," Dennis said, "you just ask. Arnulf?"

Rik was relieved not to suddenly find himself being called "milord." "Dennis, how was the infrastructure behaving before we got here?"

"Just fine," Dennis said. "Sun shining, gravity working, no problems anywhere I could see."

"Great," Rik said. "Though I still need to look at the logs. I only had a chance for a quick look, and I keep getting the feeling there was something I was missing. You have time to pass me the views for the new city sites that I asked you for?"

"Did that an hour ago," Dennis said. "Anything else you need?"

Rik thought about all the system logs he still had to go through and restrained himself from moaning out loud: there was no point in letting Angela get the wrong idea about what working in here would be like. *And what* will *it be like?* he wondered—then pushed the thought aside for the moment. "Not right now," he said. "Besides, no point in you getting overworked while we're just getting started and I'm just learning the ropes. You must have stuff you want to be doing out in the Worlds!"

Dennis got a faraway look. "Haven't been over to Geledann in a coupla months," he said. "Not with some gold in my pouch, anyway. Think you can spare me for tonight?"

"Sure," Rik said, "no problem. And thanks for what you've done today!"

Dennis nodded, tugged his forelock again at Angela, and vanished. "System management?" Rik said.

"How can I help, Rik?"

"Please credit Dennis with fifteen in gold, okay?"

"Done, Rik."

Angela looked over at Rik with a slightly dubious expression. "What a weird little man," she said. "Is he okay? I mean, is there some way to find out if he's some kind of scammer or not?"

"Oh, sure," Rik said, looking up at the sun, which was behaving itself nicely today: no jittering, no strange movements, but he wasn't entirely sure he trusted it. "Every player's got public history information, and even when they don't make all the details public, game management makes sure you can see their master feedback score. Dennis is clean except for a couple of minor negatives—"

"What kind of negatives?"

"He kicked a griffin once," said Rik, "and another time he broke into the back of a tavern and stole a firkin of wine."

Angela blinked. "Uh," she said. "Okay, maybe I'll cut him some slack until I understand what's going on around here." She looked up at the little sun, and past it to the blue, blue water seemingly hanging up there in the sky. "I really like that . . ." she said. "Whatever else you do, don't lose the way that looks. And all those little fires way up there. That's really neat."

Rik grinned. "Yeah," he said. "I think so too. So we agree about something right off the bat."

Angela nodded, smiled. "Just like we agreed this morning that someone needed to go to the store, because the fridge is looking empty . . ."

"I'll go," Rik said.

"No way, Mr. Big In-Game Employer," Angela said. "You stay here and have your last full day of play. Tomorrow's work, remember . . ."

"Don't remind me." Rik got up. "Don't forget the olive oil."

"It's on the list," Angela said. "Who's gonna cook tonight?"

"I'll do that," Rik said. "Pull out some hamburger and I'll do the famous meatballs."

Angela grabbed him and kissed him. Then she wiggled her lips around. "Weird," she said. "Can't feel anything. It's like I've had novocaine."

"We're gonna have to get another RealFeel headset," Rik said.

"Oh, no," Angela said. "I can just see it. Both parents sitting around with earplugs in and eyecups on? The kids would run riot." She looked around. "How do I get out?"

"Like this. System management?"

"What is it, Rik?"

"Open a door for Angela, please? Access my office."

A doorlike dimness, lit by buzzing pink neon, opened in the bright air. "Right through there," Rik said, "and go out the way you came in. You sure you don't want me to come along and bag?"

She waved him away. "Later," Angela said, and went through. The door closed behind her.

Rik sighed and sat down on his rock again. He'd found it was more pleasant to do clerical work out here in the air and sunshine and wind than it was in his office. "Screen, please?" he said. "The log analysis I was working on earlier."

"Here you are, Rik," the system said, and the screen appeared next to him.

Rik started going over the logs again. There was no point in sending the techie guys a long e-mail full of uncertainties: he wanted to be able to tell them exactly what seemed to have gone wrong with his space.

Rik's eyes were watering half an hour later, but he couldn't stop, mostly because he was getting frustrated: and frustration tended to make him more determined to find out what was wrong, not less. Several times he had paused to make slight changes in the way he was reading the logs, so he wouldn't get so used to watching the data scroll by that he missed some detail simply through the reader's version of highway hypnosis. He changed font sizes and colors, he went from serif to sans-serif fonts, he changed the logs' background colors, and then—laughing out loud because he stumbled across the control accidentally after a couple of days of looking for it on purpose—he changed the logs from "normal output" to "verbose."

Rik blinked at the torrent of data that was suddenly flowing down from every stored time point. "Whoa, freeze!" he said, and the scrolling times and events held still in the frame.

"Voice navigation assistance is available," said the control voice.

"Oh, good," Rik said under his breath, because he felt like he could use it. "Can you narrow this down to the times when I had people in the space with me?"

The display zoomed in on the log and blanked the upper third and bottom third of it.

"Okay, better," Rik said. "Show me the difference between the way the baseline interior structure routines were running before we all came in, and how they were behaving afterward."

"Nominate a time point at which you would like the second group of behaviors to begin displaying," said the Omnitopia control voice.

"Uh—" Rik beckoned to the display, and it zoomed in. He peered at it. "Minute thirteen."

That was just thirty seconds before Rik first stepped into his Microcosm. Rik stepped closer to the log, squinting at the line after line of instructions to the 'cosm's interior programming. "And make this wider?" he said. "Maybe six feet." Some of the command lines were very long, and as the display resized itself, Rik rubbed his eyes and sighed again. "And make me a chair, okay?" He moved away from the rock.

"The one from your office?" said the control voice.

"That'll do." The chair appeared: Rik sat down in front of the screens. "Go on, scroll again . . ."

As the scrolling started, Rik spotted the time-tick for when he'd come into his 'cosm, and then one after the other, his friends. *There's Tom, and there's Barbara . . . and then Raoul. And right there, that's where the sun starts to behave oddly. Now what other calls was the system making around then—*

He went over the next few minutes' worth of data with great care, identifying every single action of the Microcosm's interleaving WannaB modules as they executed independent routines or interacted with each other. When he was finished Rik couldn't do a thing but stand there shaking his head, for he didn't see a single interaction that hadn't been running smoothly for all the day before that, and wasn't behaving itself now.

He sat down on the chair the system had made and stared at the display. *Well, I do not get this,* he thought. *Because absolutely nothing was different except that Raoul had just come in. There must have been something else going on in the system at large. There was something in that last e-mail about outages or malfunctions in the underlying levels of Microcosm control because of all the new load on the system running up to the rollout . . .*

"Where's the e-mail window?" he said. "The one from my office."

"Right here, Rik." It slid around from behind the display of command strings and displayed itself in front of him.

"Run down the stack," he said. "Thanks." The stacked mails in the window displayed themselves envelope-first, and he waved them aside as ones he didn't want displayed themselves. "No, no, no, no, no, yes!" he said. "That one, please, open it—"

It was yet another of many daily e-mails about system issues affecting Microcosms. Rik had elected to take them on a minute-by-minute basis rather than as a digest at the end of each day, at least until he was a lot surer about the way his 'cosm was behaving, or supposed to behave. Now he read through the mail and saw nothing whatsoever that had anything to do with the graphics interface troubles he was experiencing, or thought he was experiencing. *Damn,* Rik thought. *Maybe I need to get Jean in here. I'm not all that sure what I'm looking for. . . .*

Rik sighed and pushed the e-mail window aside to look once again at his time line. And once again he found himself thinking, *That's so weird. Raoul comes in, and things start to go south....* For there was a whole series of structural and graphics commands that started to fail in a little cascade, beginning a tenth of a second after Raoul came in, and all going down within a few hundredths of a second of each other.

So weird.... Could it be something to do with his software? Some plug-in or configuration that's running on his home machine? Rik shook his head. *But what the heck could have an effect like this?* All the Omnitopian 'cosms, Macro or Micro, were supposed to support all the major operating systems, RPG suites, and hardware configurations. That was one of the reasons the game was so successful: it went out of the way to tailor itself to you, rather than making you go out and buy special hardware for it—unless, of course, you absolutely wanted to. *The trouble is, there's no way to tell what he—*

"Excuse me?"

Rik jumped, turned, and was surprised to see Dennis standing there behind him, still in that disreputable boiler suit, still looking disheveled, but also looking abashed. "Dennis!"

"You paid me fifteen," Dennis said, sounding truculent.

Rik blinked. "Uh, yeah. I'm sorry, is it not enough, I thought we agreed—"

"We agreed on ten," Dennis said.

"Uh," Rik said. "I kind of thought it was—you know, sort of a tip—"

Dennis stared over Rik's shoulder in a vague and embarrassed way, grimaced, and then looked away. "Don't need a tip," he said. "It's too much. I credited you five back. Just so you know."

"Oh," Rik said. *Crap,* he thought, *I've hurt his feelings—* "Sorry," he said. "Dennis, I'm really sorry, I didn't mean—"

" 'S okay," Dennis said, and turned to go. "What time tomorrow?"

Rik had to stop and think. "Oh, God," he said, "I'm back to work.... What time zone are you in?"

Dennis paused. "Eastern."

"Uh, eight P.M., then. That be okay for you?"

"Fine," Dennis said, turned, and vanished.

Rik sighed and turned his attention back to the log screens. After a moment he said, "Send a mail—"

"Who to, Rik?"

"Jean Mellie. Subject: Microcosm structural malfunction: possible external causes."

"Thank you. Ready to transcribe body—"

"Great. Dear Jean, I have a question about some weird behavior in my 'cosm after a group of friends came through. If you'll look at the attached log file . . ."

NINE

ELSEWHERE IN OMNITOPIA, a lone figure stepped out of a tangle of shadows into a wide and level landscape lit by a ubiquitous, sourceless pale blue light. In the near distance, tall slender shapes burning brighter than the pale sky reared up against it, clouds of glitter-shot gloom wreathed around their upper reaches. Dev frowned at the sight—not his usual reaction—and headed into the forest of code.

All around him, great trees of light stretched to unlikely heights, their mighty limbs and outreaching branches forming a complex ceiling as bright as a sky. The trees' trunks were composed of folios and modules of code, stacked in rounds, each module ringed outward with new versions like the rings of a tree. Among the select group of Omnitopian employees who worked with the most basic levels of the game and its servicing programs, there were probably hundreds of ways they could choose to perceive this structure. But for Dev and Tau, this was the only one. It was Dev's original vision, reaching right back to the times when the major programming languages started to make 3-D representations of themselves possible. When he first designed ARGOT and started writing in it, Dev had intentionally designed its command structures so that they would support this kind of vision: his magic forest, one that cast light instead of shadow, with the trees' roots sunk in the basic ARGOT substrate, and the uppermost branches interlacing the way the various sub-sub-sub-routines interlaced in gameplay.

At the heart of the forest stood a faintly glowing shadow

of the Ring of Elich, more as an orientation tool than anything else. From inside the great Ring reared up the hugest
tree of all, the vast-trunked structure of Omnitopia system
management, its branches reaching high out of sight into
heaven, its roots tangling into the depths. But it too was
presently just a shadow, faded out in favor of the rest of
the forest. All around the central tree and the shadow Ring
stood a hundred and twenty-one lesser but still mighty
trees of code, each subtly different from the others, though
up until the main branchings the trunks looked much the
same. Behind about a third of these trees stood glowing
wireframe shadows of each. These were shuntspaces—
alternate universes, each perfectly identical to its twinned
Macrocosm except for its population. The master Conscientious Objector routine caught players who tried to cheat
the Omnitopian game system and shunted them into these
duplicate Macrocosms, which were otherwise populated
only by other cheaters, game-generated characters with a
built-in bad attitude, and those Omnitopia staff who occasionally descended into these "Lesser Hells" to blow off
steam by punishing the wicked.

But the shuntspaces weren't Dev's major concern right
now. There was no sign of Tau just yet, so Dev breathed out
and just stood there in the midst of it all for a few moments,
turning slowly, looking at the flow of light in the trunks of
the Macrocosm-trees and the lesser, more shadowy flickering in the shuntspaces. There were too few peaceful moments like this these days: too little time to hold still and
appreciate what he'd achieved. *Miri would say this was the
price of success,* he thought. *Well, I don't care. I hate the
price. I just want to play.*

Dev sighed. *And there's my inner three-year-old talking. Never mind. . . .* He glanced away from the great ring
of Macrocosm-trees and their shuntspaces and off to one
side, toward the sapling forest in the distance—the rowdy
crowd of Microcosms that had sprung up in the fertile
ARGOT earth in such a short time. Since Tau hadn't yet
turned up, Dev wandered over that way. In response the
virtual landscape poured itself toward him at increased
speed until he was standing under the tangled eaves of that

energetic young forest. The slender trunks of the sapling forest were not as regular or as elegant as the great piles of Macrocosm code had to be. They straggled, they leaned, their upper branches had bumps and galls—places where some Leveler's design had tried to get the WannaB version of ARGOT to do something it hadn't really been designed to do, and sometimes had succeeded. The code got twisted out of shape, got inelegantly assembled, branches tangled rather than interlacing gracefully. But the energy of it was undeniable. *There are people having fun in there,* Dev thought with satisfaction. *And that's what it's all about.*

He paused by the nearest sapling, laid his hand against it. Instantly the landscape around him was drowned in darkness, and in the dark a new set of images burst across his vision: the shore of a tropically blue ocean with a huge ringed planet rising slant-ringed from the haze and clouds on the distant horizon. Out over the water he spotted a hard glint of light off something moving. Dev squinted at it and saw it was a glider: as it wheeled above that warm bright water he caught another glint of the sun on translucent wings.

He nodded appreciatively. "System management?" he said.

"Here, Dev."

"Make me a window and show me meta, please."

"Done." A rectangle of air on his right opaqued and began to flow with details about the Microcosm—its designer, the extra WannaB modules that had been plugged into this space, what they were being used for. Dev discovered that this little world was surprisingly detailed, if on a very small scale: this ocean was teeming with strange and intriguing life-forms, all hung on interestingly tweaked variations of the basic WannaB non-playing character template. *A lot of time spent on this,* Dev thought, briefly putting his finger on one of the template names on the virtual panel. Instantly that whole stack of code displayed itself in front of him like a pile of glowing DVDs. Dev reached out to it, pulled a single module out of the stack and looked it over. *Interesting. Somebody's taken a linguistics module and stuck it into a personality heurism routine out of the game-generated character stack, so these creatures in the water can learn from each other as well as the live players. Clever way to use WannaB to mimic some of the same effects we get in the full implementation of ARGOT...* Dev slipped the code module back into the stack and waved it away. The stack vanished as Dev looked more closely at the meta display. *A twelve-year-old built this?* Dev thought as he glanced down at the MicroLeveler's bio. Her name was Della Chun, and she lived in a suburb of Akron, Ohio. Her picture, looking like a school picture, showed him a shaggy-haired girl with a broad smiling face and a clever glint in her eye.

"Well, now, Della," Dev said. He looked up into the air. "Executive game management?"

"Here, Dev," said the dulcet Omnitopia control voice.

"Flag this user to the attention of HR, six years from today. Message: if Della is still gaming with us after she graduates high school, have someone at HR contact her and see if she's interested in a job. Also between now and then, flag any communications from her to Omnitopia support regarding code issues and route them to BSI."

"Done, Dev."

"Thanks."

Behind him he heard something squeaking faintly. Dev turned. Sure enough, here came Tau, walking toward him along the black sand beach and looking around him admiringly.

"You're late," Dev said.

Tau snorted. "Doing your work," he said, "so don't start complaining. Especially with *your* on-time stats this week. What'cha got here?"

"New 'cosm," Dev said. "Went up last week, apparently." Tau glanced around him. "What's it called?"

Dev glanced at the meta information. "Caribee."

"Looks more Hawaiian," Tau said. "Like something over on Kona."

"She may have lifted it from there, who knows," Dev said. "I flagged her for the Baker Street Irregulars. She did something interesting with her ancillary life-forms."

"Really? What?"

"Later. It's CCG stuff." He took his hand away from

the presently invisible sapling he was still leaning on, and Caribee flickered out, replaced by the Microcosm-forest of which it was part. "Come on," Dev said, "the Underworld awaits. Let's go get our debugging done."

"We hope," said Tau.

"Now, don't be negative." Dev stomped on the ground.

It split, the crack widening out and spreading across the ARGOT substrate, deepening into a crevasse that dropped away from their feet into profound darkness. A stairway leading down into that darkness began manifesting itself below them, tread by tread. Together they stepped down into the dark, the light of the code-forest dwindling away above them.

As they walked downward, light began to swell around them, a greener glow. It came from what hung down from the underside of the floor they'd just broken through, which down here was a ceiling. Like some huge and bizarre chandelier, an inverted forest, itself surrounding an inverted and shadowy version of the Ring of Elich, hung down into the dark. These upside-down trees, each of the hundred and twenty-one mirroring a Macrocosm-tree above it, were more shadowy than their counterparts above, but far more complex. Their branches, from the great limbs to the tiniest twigs, led not into the Omnitopian game structure, but into the millions upon millions of client computers all over the world on which Omnitopia's players were actually playing. A fine blue-gray mist was gathered about the thinnest twigs of the trees. This rendered the reality of fifty million living rooms and playrooms, smart terminals and servers—and soon, if things went well, a hundred million of them. Every particle of that fog, every machine or device, had a tiny seed of this master structure installed in it.

At the bottom of the first flight of steps leading down under the surface Dev and Tau had just broken through, there appeared a landing in the virtual stairway. Dev and Tau paused there, and though the landing remained level under their feet, all around them the Conscientious Objector underworld started to slowly rotate so that the inverted mirror forest now started becoming an upstanding one. Dev watched the visualization right itself, letting out a breath of concern. Building the code that ran and maintained these client seedlings had cost him, and later Tau, more labor than anything else in the building of the first generation of the new game. The seedlings had to guard the game and protect it from hacking and cheating and exploitation, which was continually on the minds of a small but nontrivial percentage of Omnitopia's players, to a greater or lesser extent. They also had to protect all the players' personal information from access by anything but the bookkeeping and scorekeeping routines that had a right to know where a given player was in the game, how much he'd spent or was owed, and what his game karma was from moment to moment. Each client seedling had to know how to obey the data privacy laws of a hundred and sixty-five different jurisdictions and how to save the player's status and settings online in case the client machine failed. Each seedling also had to be able to keep itself from being damaged accidentally or on purpose, know how to repair itself when damage did happen, and how to notify the main game servers when, for whatever reason, those repairs failed. This delicate and complicated interface was both the game's great strength and its weakest link, and there wasn't a day Dev didn't spend at least a few minutes worrying about it. *But today,* he thought, *there's a lot more reason than usual. . . .*

The ceiling Dev and Tau had just stepped through was now a floor again. The landing under their feet now reoriented its stairway to lead down to it, and the two of them headed downward. As the rotation finished, something else had appeared—the structure in which the trees of the CO itself were rooted, an island surrounded by a lake of what at first glance looked like lava. But lava was rarely emerald green. Anyone who went down to the shore and gazed down into that wash of light would see not light and dark particles of molten stone, but a constantly intermingling swirl of ASCII characters, millions of lines of code fluidly interacting with one another, in the green-on-black of monitors long gone. This was the visual expression of the Conscientious Objector's basic code taken as a whole—a barrier to the potentially inimical outer world, and an intelligent gateway to the inner one, constantly self-testing the traffic that flowed between the two on millions of ephemeral bridges from moment to moment.

Dev and Tau stood there for a few moments on the Omnitopian shore, their backs to the trees and the shadow Ring, watching the ebb and flow of light in the lake. Both of them had been down here so often in the course of any normal work week, over several years, that often a few minutes' viewing of the CO routines in this graphic mode was all it would take one or the other to identify where a problem might be coming from: an eddy in the waters, a dark swirl of shadow in the body of code as routines interfered with one another or an attack or intrusion snagged or blocked the flow. But now Tau looked over at Dev. "You see anything?"

"Nothing," Dev said. He sighed and reached into the air beside him, pulling out of it a long glowing object. It was a cartoon sword, thick-outlined and filled in with flat animation cel colors, though it glowed at the edges with a 2-D Gaussian glow, like a streetlight seen through fog.

The Sword of Truth had started life as a macro, a programming analysis and management routine that Dev and Tau had jointly devised back when Dev first started letting Tau help him with the CO. Dev had laid down its core routines, and Tau had multiply folded them onto themselves and welded them together, a many-leveled sheaf of self-executing instructions like the layers of iron and steel in a katana's blade. Then together they had taken turns honing its diagnostic edge to a razorlike sharpness until it was now almost alive in terms of its ability to detect what was wrong with a segment of Omnitopian programming.

Tau put up his eyebrows. "Thought you'd want to get down and splash around in the lava at random for a while first," he said.

"Not today," Dev said. "We've got a party to go to after this, remember. You have time to hit the staging area yet?"

"Not yet," said Tau. "But it's filling up nicely. A lot of other people are taking this as seriously as you are: there wouldn't have been any point in trying to limit crisis management to the intervention team. Everybody wants some

of this—the attack teams have been briefing their auxilia-
ries for days."

"I take it it's not just a question of the overtime."

Tau shook his head. "With *these* people? You should
know better by now. This is their turf, and they don't take
kindly to crooks barging in to mess with it."

"True," Dev said. "By the way, I forgot to ask. Where's
Time Magazine Lady?"

"Joss' people have her over at the Flackery," Tau said.
"She'll be safely locked down by the time the balloon's
ready to go up. I think they were planning to take her out
for barbecue or something." He smiled a naughty smile.
"Someplace with lots of atmosphere, but no WiFi and terrible cell phone reception."

Dev nodded. "Good. All the same, I think I'd sooner her
access permissions had some kind of unidentifiable malfunction for the next few hours. Just to prevent any, you
know, journalistic accidents that might follow on someone
else unexpectedly getting hold of her login info . . ."

Tau looked aside, whispered briefly to the air. "Done,"
he said. "System security's on it."

"Good. Then let's go—"

Dev waved a hand. Immediately the cold green fire of
the lava started to flood the shore of the island where they
stood, rising until Dev and Tau were knee-deep in it. As it
did, the size of the particles in it grew until the letters and
numbers and long, long strings of code were clearly visible.
Dev lifted up the Sword of Truth and plunged it into the
swirl of strings and characters.

The liquid code around the sword's glow roiled and
boiled enthusiastically, now looking less like lava and more
like a bowl of unusually green chicken noodle soup. Dev
hung onto the hilt, waiting for the built-in analytical functions to throw up some kind of result that he could use. But
all the sword would do was lean leftward, indicating that
the debugger had detected something peculiar in one of
the thousands of interleaving protective routines that were
part of the Conscientious Objector system. "Okay," Dev
said to the sword, "what are you reacting to?"

A window popped up in the air beside him and showed

him a page of code written in the densest form of executive
ARGOT. "This is one of the internal player security routines associated with the assignment and revocation of permissions to enter controlled-access 'cosms," said the control
voice. "It is showing intermittent failure of function."

"Macrocosm or Microcosm?" Dev said, starting to push
his way leftward along through the code stream.

"Microcosm, Dev."

"Oh really," he said under his breath.

Tau, pushing along through the lava beside him, threw
Dev a glance. "Something?"

"Don't know," Dev said. "It's just that I was up in the
Microcosms earlier, assessing some bug reports and such
for referral to the brushfire teams. Thought I was seeing
some common threads here and there. Ingress-and-exit-
based outages that weren't making sense . . ."

The two of them pushed along through the current,
peering down into it for pertinent lines of code that the system would be tagging for their attention, but seeing nothing. The sword in Dev's hand finally stopped leaning in the
direction they were going, and stood straight upright in the
code flow. Dev peered down along its length, not seeing
anything. "Where's the malfunctioning routine?" he said to
the system.

"It has ceased to malfunction," the control voice said.
"Now running correctly."

Dev and Tau stared at each other. "Typical," Tau said.
"The minute the repairman shows up, whatever's busted
starts working again."

Dev frowned. "Show us the log of the malfunction," he
said.

The window hanging in the air cleared itself and then
filled with more code, scrolling down fast and then pausing
as each section of the system logs containing a malfunction highlighted itself. Dev waved the window a little wider,
and he and Tau looked closely at it. After a moment Tau
reached up a hand and pointed at one specific line of code.
"There," he said. "Look at that. A bad call to that routine.
Someone who shouldn't get into that particular space tries
to get in. And bounces—"

"But not the way they should," Dev said, bemused. "They shouldn't be sent off to *that* rejection routine. They should be going—" He reached out into the air, and another spill of code started flowing onto another screen. "Over *here*. So why aren't they? And where the heck's the logic that sent them where they went? The field for the referring code is blank."

"Somebody got sloppy . . ."

Dev gave Tau a look. "You or me, buddy? We're the only ones who deal with this code."

Tau shook his head. "How many hundreds of thousands of lines of this have we edited in the last few years?"

"More like millions, now," Dev said. One of the first things Tau had designed for them as a necessary timesaver was a mass-implementation editing tool that would let either of them hunt down a single error in code, correct it, and also correct all the other incidences of that error right across the many lesser code modules that made up the Conscientious Objector as a whole. But that tool could be dangerous for exactly the same reason. One badly corrected routine could cause ripples of trouble right across the width of Omnitopia in everything from accounting to graphics and gameplay.

"Never mind," Tau said. "We'll assign blame later. Let's bookmark this and move on."

Dev nodded. "Highlight that routine and section and save for later reference," he said to the system. "Copy the bookmark to Tau's desk as well."

"Done, Dev."

Dev pulled the Sword of Truth out of the lava, shook the light off it to reset its search and analysis routines, and plunged it into the thick emerald light again. It shuddered in his hand, and this time leaned to the right.

Once more they followed it. Once more the sword stopped, and once again a malfunctioning access routine came up that had no business acting the way it was—and stopped malfunctioning just before they began examining it. Tau looked incredulous. "Lend me that thing a moment," he said.

Dev gave him the sword. Tau waved it around in the air:

it reshaped itself into a shorter sword with a heavier hilt, a broader point, and an odd fifteen-degree bend in the blade. "Is it supposed to look like that?" Dev said as Tau plunged the sword back into the lava.

Tau nodded, concentrating. "Kopis," he said. "Traditional in my old neck of the woods—" as the sword leaned off in another direction. The two of them pushed through the code flow, found a third spot where the sword stood upright, quivering. Tau withdrew it, and a long flow of code followed it up out of the bubbling surface, spreading itself out on yet another screen-surface for examination.

They both stared at the code. "Nothing . . ." Tau said, scowling.

Dev shook his head. "This is entirely too hit-and-run," he said. "It's like it's avoiding us on purpose! Some kind of virus . . . ?"

"How?" Tau said. "The CO is one of the most tightly protected parts of the system. You know how many filtration layers there are between it and the outside!" And not all the filters were mechanical. Many were live Omnitopian employees whose only duty was to patrol the border between Omnitopia's systems and the outer world, always alert for the system's warnings that something strange was going on in the demilitarized zone between it and the outer world. And there had been no more warnings about malfunctions than usual this past week, since the virus-writers were mostly waiting for the new rollout to see what vulnerabilities they might be able to discover in the relaunched software.

Dev sighed. "Come on," he said, "let's keep on it. We have to find something that'll give us a hint."

Tau shrugged and handed Dev back the sword. Dev plunged it once more into the flow, let it show him which way it felt something strange going on, and followed. But forty-five minutes later, after six or seven more false alarms, Dev could only look over at Tau and couldn't do anything but shake his head and throw his hands helplessly in the air. "Nothing," he said.

Tau ducked sideways, the sword narrowly missing his head. "Watch how you wave that thing around," he said.

"Oh, stop it," Dev said as they climbed up out of the lava onto the dry land of the CO island, "you're virtual."

"It's still a bad habit," Tau said. "You might forget yourself and do it for real some night after dinner in the Armory, and then where would I be?"

Dev shook his head and tossed the sword into the darkness around them, well away from Tau. It vanished back into the virtual storage space that the system kept for it. "I guess we're idiots to think we can find in an hour what the outer-access team couldn't find in a week of looking."

"If not idiots," Tau said, "then just hopelessly optimistic. But we had to try. You and I should find some meeting time for the team tomorrow, though. Show them what we were seeing—" Dev threw him a glance. "Redacted, of course. This wouldn't be any time to let any more details about the CO routine out where someone might pick something up and release it into the wild . . ."

Dev turned his attention to the hundred and twenty-one trees, alive with light inside the moat, and shook his head. "I don't know," he said, and looked over at Tau with an uncertain expression. "I think you should start thinking about making a short list . . . a *very* short list . . . of people you think might possibly be trusted with some of this data."

Tau's eyebrows went right up. Dev snapped his fingers, and the ground at their feet cracked open again: the stairs to the now upside-down upper level remanifested themselves. "This is a new tune from you," said Tau as they headed down the stairs together.

Dev let out a breath. "I know," he said. They came to the landing and paused there as the upper landscape started to rotate around them. "But your time's already scarce enough. Mine is even scarcer. And it's not like either of our lives are going to get any less busy. Also, the automatic routines, smart as they are, can only do so much. If we keep the information that we spread around compartmentalized, make sure that no one person has access to too much of it. . . ."

As the upper level rotated into position and they started down the stairs again to its ground level, Tau checked his watch. "I mean," he said, "that you really hate to give up control, as a rule. Of anything. How long is this mood going to last, and how soon are you going to regret it?"

"How about already?" Dev said as they headed toward the ring of trees surrounding the shadowy Ring and the World Tree rearing out of it. The scene had changed. Dev could see a darkness surrounding the Ring and shutting away the view of the foot of the tree. It was a darkness that moved, restless, and a mutter of voices rose up from it, angry and excited.

As they got closer to the hundred and twenty-one trees of Macrocosm code, behind them the concrete manifestation of the Conscientious Objector routines re-formed on this level. This time the barrier was a wide and shallow river surrounding the island on which the trees stood. It was filled with water that slowly began to wash up over its banks with increasing vigor, as if somewhere a wind was rising. Before them, the darkness around the Ring and the foot of the tree began to surge toward Dev and Tau, and the low roar of angry voices got louder.

It was an army that approached them, but one the likes of which not even Omnitopia had ever seen before. There were maniples of Roman legionaries in its front line, and platoons of blaster-bearing space-age stormtroopers in the traditional white armor. There were janissaries in scale armor and GI Joe types in muddy camo. There were Napoleonic soldiers in colors too bright for any sane man to wear on the battlefield, and Spartan wannabes in leather kilts, and Trojans who owed more to the USC marching band than the windy plains of Ilium. There were knights in Renaissance armor, and Valkyries and Amazons and blue-painted Celts in chariots. And that was just the Earth-based armament—the Omnitopian imports were equally eclectic. There were war tigers from the deserts of Elleban and clone troopers from the buried cities of Dawlglish, bone archers from the caverns under Prowse II and barbpike phalanges from Orinel, a small chelate-armored tank group from Bonzer and underminers from the benighted jungles of Mazarin. There were even Gnarths and Men and Elves of old Omnitopia, the original races of Telekil, all fighting together in one huge, grim, and very unusual war band, for such alliances among the Original Three were unheard of.

All these warriors were Omnitopia system security people who had been involved either in identifying the access routes of the expected big attack, or in devising the various methods that would be used to foil it—the tailored viruses and logic bombs, the bloodhound routines and system-burners. All the weapons they carried, or embodied, or rode in or on, were expressions of the routines they would be using to fight the incoming attackers, and each team or group or individual had chosen the seeming that best suited their particular preference. Some of these people would have doubled or tripled themselves, using "multitask clones" to be able to fight a given enemy in several places at once. Conspicuously in the lead was a regiment of freebooter Gnomes from Rhaetia Secunda—all armed with bloody axes and broad-bladed pike arms, and led by the assistant head accountant for Omnitopia, Michael Spirakis. These were the shapes that the accountancy teams wore on interventions inside Secunda, where the most serious forms of fiduciary gameplay took place. There the War Gnomes of Turicum gamed out the genuine interventions that they used day by day to protect the Omnitopian accounting routines from the opportunist crooks and hackers of the outside world: or they reenacted them to hone their techniques and prepare for the next assault . . . like this one.

As Dev and Tau headed toward the approaching horde, Dev shook his head in amazement. "My God, Tau, half the company's here!"

Tau chuckled. "It just looks that way," he said. "There are a lot of multiples . . ."

"Still," Dev said as they made their way toward Mike Spirakis and his crowd of bloodthirsty accountancy programmers. For an event like this, they had all put aside the three-piece-suit look that the Gnomes normally sported in the tidy cobbled streets of Turicum, a clone of the real-world Zürich. Now they looked more ghoulish than Gnomish—the suits on the bandy-legged, shaggy-pelted bipeds torn to bloodstained yet ceremonial tatters, the monstrous goggle-eyed heads wearing their neckties as headbands, the virtual scalps of scammers and hackers hanging at their belts or (in the case of the most enthusiastic employees) knitted into loincloths or jackets. They looked like nightmares trying to follow their victims into the waking day . . . which wasn't far from the truth.

Mike came lumbering along wearing the department's Bloomberg the Terrible persona, a hunched-over, one-eyed, piratical-looking monstrosity somewhat resembling a giant gorilla in what remained of a pinstriped suit—the shirt long gone except for the collar, the jacket missing, and the suspenders holding up trousers that had been reduced pretty much to short-shorts. "Hey, Boss," he said. "Thanks for coming."

"Wouldn't have missed it for anything," Dev said. "But I thought Jim wouldn't have either. Where's the senior Bloomberg?"

"Not here. Uncle Jim's up in Castle Scrooge, watching the shop in spreadsheet mode. He thinks the markets are going to need some calming down when they get wind of what's going on down here."

"He may have a point," Tau said.

"Conference calls with MSNBC and the real Bloomberg News are setting up right now," Mike said. "Good thing, because the hackers have just done their first 'gotcha' press release."

Dev swallowed. Regardless of how much warning he'd had of this, now that it was actually starting, he felt like somebody had punched him in the gut. "What did they say?"

"Oh, that they own us," Mike said. "Pretty much what you'd expect. But not true yet. They're still feeling us out to see what the resistance is like."

"Is this the real attack happening already?" Tau said, sounding alarmed.

Mike nodded. "It will be. Our first skirmishing troops are out now: they've been choking off the initial hostile accesses for about half an hour now. The first hits started coming in from Asia—the usual problem, there are so many unprotected proxy servers over there—and initially we mistook the attacks for more of the usual hacker traffic. But then a pattern emerged: the automated systems and the live Watchers started picking up on it around the same time. Anyway, they've been coming at us in stages, feeling us out. But the big wave's on its way in."

Dev twitched. "Shouldn't we be rolling out more attacks? I mean, I don't like the idea of letting them just roll over us . . ."

"We're attacking on as many fronts as are smart at this moment," Mike said. "We don't want to overextend ourselves. While they're feeling us out, we attack, yeah, but proportionately. If we overreact and hit one wave too hard, or one part of it, and then don't have enough held in reserve for the next, we're screwed." He looked out past them, swinging his ax idly, watching the troubled water out on the local version of Rubicon as the invisible wind whipped it up. "For the time being I've instructed the initial responders to keep their responses muted and scattered—so the bad guys won't think we actually know what's happening yet. I want them to roll out their full assault so that we get a minute or so of good clear analysis before we move to take them down across all the time zones. Ideally I want to crash all their systems, but not without making sure we have their IPs traced so Auntie Cleo can sue their network providers blind."

Dev turned to look across the river. Out there a darkness was forming at the edge of this part of the virtual world. Then he turned back to look at the massed avatars of his Omnitopia staff. "Got a nice turnout for this shindig, anyway."

"We'll need 'em," Mike said, sounding unusually grim: and it was hard to associate the normally cheerful and spry Mike of the Upper Worlds with this angry presence. "I don't think we've ever have had an attack like this, Boss. Everything else has just been nibble-nibble-little-mouse stuff in comparison."

"What, even the attack last year?"

Mike shook his head. "Not in the same league as what's coming," he said. "The Powers of Darkness are here in force, and they're out for our hides."

Dev now looked at the crowd which had initially seemed too big, and began thinking it was too small. "If we need more—"

"We'll send out the call," Mike said. "All the online system security people are on alert, at all the worldwide branches. We're posting minute by minute updates on the Topianet with data on the attack and packages of the antiattack weaponry—all people need to do is grab one, arm themselves, and jump in—"

Then Mike paused and put a big burly hand to one ear in the gesture of someone listening to a private conversation who's forgotten he's not wearing a headset. "What?" Dev said.

Mike shook his head once, listening. Then after a moment he turned to Dev, hefting his club. "Think I'll make that call right now," he said, sounding even grimmer.

Tau looked alarmed. "Already?"

"Analysis is coming back from the skirmishers," he said. "They're being pushed back, and their chokedown routines aren't doing the job."

"How many running?" Tau said.

"Sixteen thousand attack processes running, four thousand succeeds, seven thousand fails, five thousand presently negotiating but estimated to fail—"

"Seven thousand of *our* fails?" Tau said. "How the—"

"I think we're about to find out," said Mike.

"So let's go do that," Dev said. "Because once we've found out what's not working, we can turn this around."

Mike nodded. "Boss, if you want to speak to the troops—"

Dev swallowed. "Better get it done now . . ."

The Bloomberg shape swung around to face his troops, threw his arms in the air and held that big bloody ax high. "Warriors and defenders of Omnitopia," he shouted. "Will you hear the First Player?"

A great roar went up from the crowd: weapons were shaken, horns were blown (or honked), and various beasts, fabulous or otherwise, screeched or howled their approval. Then something like quiet settled down.

At least I don't have to shout, Dev thought. *When we're all virtual, they can all hear me as if I were standing next to them.* "Okay, people!" Dev said. "Since I've been running around handling other stuff all day, you all know the fine

details of this attack better than I do. But the broad facts of
the situation haven't changed. There are a bunch of nasty
people out there who want to ruin our players' fun. They
want our money—*your* money, that you guys earned—so
they can all go lie on a beach somewhere even though they
haven't earned it. And even more than that, they want to
make us look stupid. *And we are not stupid!*"

A roar of agreement. "So get out there and kick their
butts!" Dev said. "And when Jim Margoulies, or Cleo, or
maybe even I turn up on the network news tomorrow, and
we just laugh and say, 'They were no big deal, Omnitopia dealt with them,' then you'll know who we're talking
about. It's *you*. Because you people *are* Omnitopia, and I
am proud to be associated with you!"

Another roar. Dev reached out into the air again and
pulled out the Sword of Truth, held it up in the air. He
glanced at Mike. Bloomberg the Terrible glanced over
Dev's shoulder, nodded for him to look that way.

He looked. A stillness fell over the crowd as they saw
what he saw: darkness just this side of the horizon, visible
now for the first time as it moved closer.

"Let's get over on the other side, people," Dev said,
"and get ready to party."

He turned and splashed down into the glowing green
water of the river, across it, and up onto the other side, and
the army of Omnitopia came after him and flowed past him.
Out at the edge of things, the few bright shapes of Omnitopian skirmishers withdrawing from the initial contacts with
enemy code were silhouetted against the growing darkness.
Dev and Tau and Mike moved forward with the van of the
army, while more and more troops filled in behind them. A
rear guard of many hundreds remained behind on the island; between them and those thousands who had crossed,
the river deepened and widened and started to run fast.

Ahead of the army's front lines, the skirmishers came
riding or rolling or flying in to consolidate themselves
with their fellow warriors. "Not good," Dev heard one
frustrated, gasping tiger-rider muttering as others in her
skirmish group helped her down off her wounded mount.
"Those countermeasures were effective only for a few hun-

dred milliseconds. Then the damn attacks rerouted. They were pulling our own core routines out of the viruses and using them to generate antibody routines on the fly; we were just getting canceled out—"

Behind Dev, Tau was already talking to the air again. "No, it's not working, we've got to shift away from that algorithm, they're onto it already. I want everybody moved over to the M1H1 variants—*yes* now, we've got plenty more variants in the locker but that one's the most virulent, so just do it, we're getting ready to move here and I want our best shot!"

The last of the skirmishers were coming in now—a company of Mongol horsemen, a loping herd of tyrannosaurs, a last few zombie-crewed haunted tanks. All of them pushed their way behind the Omnitopian lines, and as the lines sealed behind them, turned once more to face the foe.

And out there in the darkness, more darkness drew near. The advancing gloom was now resolving itself into countless dark faceless humanoid shapes, hulking and silent, slowly moving toward them—the physical manifestation that Mike and his upper-level code warriors had chosen to represent the attacking programs. The golemlike shapes were armed with spears that burned with black fire, each one representative of a loaded code probe, all ready to slice or stab into Omnitopia's data system and suck out data and money. They had been coming slowly, at first. But now they were coming faster. And faster still—

"Yeah, yeah, but has it propagated completely?" Tau was saying to somebody up in the light and relative sanity of the real world. "Are you sure it's—oh, okay, I see it now—" He turned toward Dev, gave him a thumbs-up.

Dev swallowed, looking around him at the warriors of Omnitopia. "Okay, everybody," Dev said. "Here they come. You ready?"

A growl of fury was what came back. Dev glanced over at Mike: and Bloomberg the Terrible gave the nod. "Okay then," Dev shouted. "They wanna play around with us, huh? Then *let's go play!*"

The answering shout was deafening. Mike held his club high and charged. The army followed, pouring past Dev—

The two fronts crashed together, and battle commenced in earnest, the opposing sides clashing in a muddle of weaponry. The dark shapes of the attacking programs presently appeared to be trying to bull their way through the defenders by sheer weight of numbers. In such places the Omnitopian fighters were using the same tactic to hold them out, the closely serried ranks expressing the pingstorm routines that the Conscientious Objector system was generating to block the logins. Elsewhere, the attackers seemed to be trying to target specific fighters, and the whole front line was an assortment of one-to-one duels, each sheaf of illicit logins being stopped by a single player guiding a massively multiple defensive routine. Many weapons now being brandished glowed with the lava-green of the Conscientious Objector defense modules, each now being guided by human minds and by hands on a keyboard somewhere—inputting new Internet addresses or host-server information ripped from the attacking programs, teaching the CO system what it needed to know about each attack as it came in, helping it cope until its own heuristic routines could absorb the data and apply it to other bridgeheads that needed defending.

Here and there the dark shapes were breaking through the Omnitopian lines in ones or twos, only to be attacked by crowds of small green-glowing creatures like gigantic and ambitious amoebas, which flung themselves onto dark bodies and smothered them by sheer weight. These were the Conscientious Objector's more normal defense routines, tasked to stop illicit queries or multiple logins. If the darkbody creature representing a given hostile routine was simple enough or limited enough, these subroutines would gang up on it, smothering its exterior connection so as to starve it of remote processor time and finally phase-canceling it out of existence. If it was too strong or complex, the CO system's "green blood cells" would hold it in place until a small fighting group could break away from the Omnitopian defenders' lines to deal with it.

Dev and Tau stood a hundred yards or so back from the battlefront, peering into the turmoil. "What do you make of it?" Dev said.

Tau looked from one side to the other. "I think we're holding," he said. "System says there are something like sixty thousand illicit logins per minute being attempted. That we can hold. For the time being—"

"How much worse is it going to have to get for us *not* to hold?"

"I'd say twice," Tau said, "maybe three—" He broke off, looking alarmed. "Stay here," he said. "Something I need to deal with—"

Tau vanished.

Dev swallowed, did his best to stay calm. An alarmed look was not something he liked seeing on his chief programmer's face, anymore than he'd ever cared to hear Tau say "Whoops!" while coding, back in the day. "What?" he started to say to Tau by remote, and then stopped himself. *What if I interrupt him in the middle of something important? Shut up, stay put, let the army handle it—*

But it was hard for an old gamer to just stand there and let the play go on around him. Dev stayed there, watching the brightly colored lines of Omnitopia security staff in front of him pushing against the dark mass of the attacking zombie computers and bot routines. The battlefront looked like a sine wave at the moment, a long scalloped line of color against gloom, with the two sides pushing into and out of each other, in some places slowly, in some with more speed. *It doesn't look too bad,* he thought. *We're holding our own—*

— except over there, those code-golems shouldn't be so far into our battle line—

—really much too far in, I don't like the look of that—

Dev swallowed as, off to his left, he saw the Omnitopian line punching in hard—the attacking forces plainly now adapting to the Omnitopians' defense strategy and some temporary weakness in the CO. *Getting a little too close to the river now. In fact, a lot too close—* The line of defenders gave even further as he watched, sagging right back into the river now. And only a hundred yards in on the island side of the river was one of the Macrocosm-trees. The rearguard defenders were rushing forward to meet the threat. But if they couldn't hold— *If the code-golems' line makes contact with that tree's code,* Dev thought, *it'll use the 'cosm's structure itself to flood the system. It'll be all over the Macrocosms and into their separate accounting structures before we can react! And whoever's running that attack routine will get everything they wanted—*

The Omnitopian defenders were being pushed right up onto the island now. Horrified, Dev glanced down at his own weapon, still in Sword of Truth mode. "System management!" he said.

"Here, Dev—"

"Hook one of the attack-routine packs into the sword! Then monitor me and adapt my pack as necessary—"

"Done, Dev."

He pushed his way as fast as he could through his own people and back into the river, immediately sinking in up to his neck. *"No no no no no!"* he said to the system, which belatedly recognized him and pulled the "water" away, pushing the riverbed up under his feet so that he could make it across. *Why'd it take so long to recognize me? I don't want to know . . .* He pushed through more defenders on the riverbank and made his way back and around to the crowd of Omnitopian fighters who were even now being pressed back toward the tree, then pushed in among them with the sword at the ready. "Which 'cosm is that, people?"

"Pastorale—" one fighter gasped. He was a big burly man in sixteenth-century Italian armor, swinging a big double-handed sword at the faceless code-golem he was fighting.

"Oh, no!" Dev said, and lunged at the golem, spitting it on the sword. It went down, vanishing as the routine driving it expired, but another pushed into the gap to take its place. *All those poor little kids in there!* Dev thought. *What are they going to think when these things come spilling into fluffy-bunny land and start stomping on the flower fairies?* It didn't bear thinking about. He swung harder, taking down another dark golem.

The press around them was getting thicker, though. The defender beside him, the guy in the Italian armor, turned a blue-eyed, alarmed gaze toward him between one foe and the next and said, "Dev, *where's your guard?"*

"What?" Dev was too busy swinging for what the guy was saying to register.

The defender looked around him in panic. "Bodyguard!" he yelled. "*Backup!* To Dev, to Dev, *come on, people!*"

There was a rustle of activity around him—but what Dev noticed first was that those faceless dark shapes were suddenly a lot more interested in his neighborhood, and in him particularly, than they should have been. Suddenly it occurred to Dev that he'd been assuming his own invulnerability a little too casually. If one of those spears hit him and someone at the other end of one of these attacks managed to invade his virtual persona deeply enough to get at his confidential data, almost *any* of his data—— *It'll be all over the planet within hours, if not minutes. And it'll be my fault, because I came in without enough prep—*

Dev gulped and fought harder. It didn't seem to help: the faceless dark shapes around him pushed in closer, each one he took down now instantly replaced by another. They were beginning to surround him, cutting him off from the other Omnitopians, and Dev started to curse himself. He *was* too used to being invulnerable here, the master of all the worlds inside his universe. But for once he wasn't in safe territory, protected by an impregnable system. He'd come willingly out to the interface with the real world, where people who hated him had a chance at him. *Idiot. You've fallen into the one part of your game that is not a game, and the bad guys are going to take what you can* not *let them have—*

He chopped at his attackers, his view suddenly full of nothing but spear points in the hands of darkbody golems, and though the Sword of Truth sheared them off as quickly as they got close, he was in a bad spot, no mistaking it. And even as Dev thought that, in came the one he couldn't get around quickly enough to parry, straight at his eyes—

A flash of light blinded him as someone's energy weapon thrust blue-white and sizzling between Dev and the spear that was coming at him, slicing the spearhead off at the socket. Someone else grabbed Dev by one arm and pulled him back out of range of the attackers. The pressure around him grew truly unbearable for a moment, then suddenly lessened as a crowd of armed and armored shapes crashed into the faceless, inimical program-fractions nearest to Dev and pushed them back. He gasped for air as more of the armored defenders surrounded him, shoulder-to-shoulder, backs toward him. "You okay, Boss?" one of them yelled.

"Yeah—"

"Good. Better part of valor now, okay?" The whole circle, with him inside it, started moving back away from the line.

Beyond the circle, Dev saw more defenders starting to fill in where his group had been. It was hard to be sure, but he thought his people were gaining ground again as he and his sudden bodyguard pushed back out of the press and got their backs up against the massive glittering code-trunk of the Pastorale Tree. "Double up," shouted the one who'd spoken to him first, "and get some more backup over here!"

Within moments the ring of steel around Dev was so thick it was impossible to see any of the enemy beyond it. The nearest of his impromptu guards, the one in the armor who'd first called for help, now turned to face Dev. His round worried face Dev knew, but couldn't place—not that this was unusual in Omnitopia. The man was bald and had big shaggy eyebrows, under which those piercing blue eyes were looking out at Dev with a truly furious expression. "Dev, you goddamn lunatic," he said, "forgive me, but *what the shit were you thinking of?* What would've happened if one of those guys got through to you?"

"I, uh," Dev said, and then stopped, because there was absolutely no point in doing anything but apologizing. "You're right," he said. "Sorry."

"Good," his employee said. "Now you *stay* here until things are safe, okay?" And he vanished out through the ring of defenders, who generally were looking at Dev with expressions suggesting that they agreed with Blue Eyes.

Dev nodded and leaned against the tree. Gradually his field of view started to clear a little, so that he could see that the attack at large seemed to be falling back, pushed toward the river and past it again by the Omnitopians. Shortly thereafter the ring around him gave way a little, and Tau pushed through it and strode over to Dev.

"Don't yell at me," Dev said, for Tau was scowling. "They did that already."

"Nothing like I'm going to do it," Tau said. "Is it possible for you to be left alone and *not* find a garage roof to jump off?"

Dev wiped his brow with his forearm, panting. "Yeah, fine, guilty as charged. Save it for later, okay? How are we doing?"

Tau let out an annoyed breath. "All right for the moment. There were four big fronts where they tried to break through. We stopped the first two right away, but the other two were much worse, and one of them, right here where our people were shoved back into the river, was the worst of all. Maybe a hundred thousand zombie logins hit us in that spot—"

"But they didn't punch through."

"No thanks to those of us who went in without adequate safeguards and diverted resources that were needed for the defense!"

Dev made a face. "Okay, I guess this is later . . ."

Tau rolled his eyes. "Sorry. But this was not the walkover we thought it was going to be, Dev. Our defenses were hard pressed: Mike wasn't kidding you when he said this was a much worse attack than anything we've had before. There were some minor breakthroughs into the accounting routines, and though we cut them off fast, now the question is what those people on the outside learned. The attacker programs were adapting as fast to what we were doing as we were to them."

"You think the attacks weren't entirely machine driven?" Dev said. "They had people riding their routines the way we did?"

"Why not?" Tau said. "*We* thought of doing it. Why shouldn't they?"

Dev let out a breath. "Okay," he said. He looked out over the battlefield, which was clearing rapidly: all the forces of zombie-bot darkness had now been pushed well back from the river and were being forced right out toward the battlefield's horizons. Behind them the pursuing Omnitopians were also flooding over into the real-world side of the battle, pursuing their enemies down the world's networks to isolate the access gateways the enemy had used and lock them down. Others would doubtless open later, but these would not be used again.

Tau was watching the retreat of the dark forces with a grim look on his face. Most of the Omnitopians who had been behind them had now headed forward to help their comrades with the mopping up. Dev let out a breath. Then, startled by something seen out of the corner of his eye, he turned.

Something among the roots of the tree. Flitting, passing— gone—

And now, nothing. Dev became aware that Tau was looking at him strangely. "What?"

"Did you see that?" Dev said.

"See what?"

Dev shook his head. Now that Tau asked, it was hard to say. "It was like—" He shrugged. "A shadow."

Tau turned an uneasy look on him. "A virus, maybe?" They had seen such things before when viewing the Omnitopia subterverse this way: introduced code, insufficiently or incorrectly described or camouflaged by the ones responsible, would display itself against the more fully realized background as something splotchy or inchoate.

Dev shook his head. "Down here? You were the one telling me how well this area's protected."

Tau scowled. "Usually, sure. But after what we've been through it's not beyond possibility that something sneaked in. Or that this attack was used as cover to *allow* something to sneak in . . ."

"Have a security crew give the place a good scouring," Dev said. He chucked the Sword of Truth into the air, and the system caught it and vanished it: when his hands were empty, Dev rubbed his eyes. "They can report off after we do our debrief."

"Right," Tau said. "See you in the Tower."

He vanished.

Dev stood there looking at the trees and the shadows under them for some little while longer: then vanished as well.

Two hours later, Dev, Tau, Mike, and four of Tau's senior security and infrastructure people finished their debriefing in the Tower room around the big dark table, while outside the last embers of sunset were burning down into darkness. Dev pushed his laptop away, sighing, and closed its lid on a long report that would need closer examination later in the evening. "So," he said. "Bottom line: all the prep we did, all the ready-rolled attack strategies, turned out not to be more than enough—they were barely enough. And we're going to get hit again, and we have no good answer to the question of whether we'll be ready."

"That about sums it up," said Tau. He dropped the pen he'd been fiddling with and leaned his elbows on the table, running his hands through his hair. "At the end of the day, the strategies and responses improvised and executed on the fly turned out to be as effective, or more so, than the stuff we had in the can."

"Which leaves me wondering yet again about what moles have been buried in the company waiting for this moment to arrive," Dev said. "And how we haven't found them by now, and how they got into the shot locker and sent news to their handlers about what we were getting ready to use on them. Something else for system security to investigate in quieter times ... assuming the company survives to have any." He leaned back in his chair, trying to stretch some of the stress kinks out of his back. "Later for that. For now: are we secure?"

"For the moment," said Mike. It was strange to see him looking little and slim again after watching him fight in the Bloomberg suit—it had fitted him unusually well.

"And how long will the moment last?" Dev said.

Tau shook his head, bit his lip. "I give it six more hours, eight at the outside."

"So what we just had was simply a feint."

"Almost certainly. Not at all big enough to be the main attack." Tau scowled, his eternal doing-math-in-his-head expression. "Oh, they took forty or fifty million off us, yeah—"

"Not nearly enough to repay the effort and the danger they went through to stage this," Mike said. "They'll be back for more. Lots more."

"Besides, tactically it makes sense for a bigger attack to follow this one," said Tau. "This was meant to make us think we're out of the woods. But also we're supposed to think that nobody could possibly follow up with another attack of the same intensity."

Everyone around the table sat morosely silent for some moments. "And the second one," Dev said, "will not only be far worse, but probably entirely different."

"What I hate is that all we've got to determine the timing by is guesswork," Tau said.

They looked at each other. "If it was me planning all this," Dev said, "it'd still happen inside the attack window we originally worked out. Tactically, in terms of access to our hardware, it's still the best time." He scowled for a moment, thinking. "And this too: the ego junkies among the hackers who've designed this will be expecting us to put out some PR about how we beat off this attack. Then they get to come back at us, rip us off properly, and brag that we're twice as stupid as they thought we were." He grinned. "So. Let's start damage control. Has everyone who took part been messaged with instructions to keep quiet about what's been going on?"

"Those e-mails went out within minutes of the battle being over," Tau said.

"Good," Dev said. "If there are leaks, I want them tracked back to the source."

Donna and Mal, the security people, both nodded. "Also," Dev said, "make sure the space we were fighting in today is checked for any little presents our visitors might have left us. I saw something down there that I couldn't identify."

"We'll take care of it," Mal assured him.

"Thanks," said Dev. He stood up and stretched. "Anything else?"

Tau and the others got up too. "I had a call from shunt-space security just before we sat down," Tau said. "They've been seeing some operational anomalies tonight. Tomorrow morning can you find some time to go over to the Palace and have a word?"

"Sure," Dev said. "Call Frank, have him schedule it. The earlier the better, if you think we've got trouble within the next six hours . . ." He yawned. "Make sure I'm called if something starts. Thanks, folks."

Mike and his security people waved good night and headed out. Dev, meanwhile, waited until the lift door closed behind them, then said to Tau, "Want to come up for a beer?"

"Don't tempt me," Tau said, looking down into the courtyard. "I've got too many things to do before I go to bed: I don't dare take the edge off."

"Well, walk me back, then," Dev said. They went over to the elevator. "Anything from Jim?"

"He says there's nothing to get too excited about yet," Tau said. "The news got out too late to do anything to the North American business news cycle. But almost as soon as the attack started, our PR people on the Asian side of the dateline started papering the wire services with news about how the attack had been sidelined." He sighed. "Tomorrow'll be worse, Jim says: the Asian markets are open now, they hate insecurity worse than anyone else, and they're going to take other markets down the slide with them. But for tonight, for the moment, we're okay."

The door slid open; they stepped in. "All right," Dev said as the door closed and the elevator headed down. "I'll get up to Castle Scrooge in the morning if I can."

"Why?"

"So he can yell at me," Dev said, resigned.

The door opened and they stepped out into the downstairs lobby. The doors to the courtyard were open: the scent of warm evening was flowing in through them, a baked-pavement smell fragranced with bougainvillea, jasmine, and magnolia from the flower beds in the middle garden. Dev breathed it in gratefully as they went out and headed for the doors to the residence side. "Jim's not going to yell at you," Tau said, sounding surprised.

"Oh, yes, he will," Dev said, "because *you* did, and you told him you did."

"How do you know I told him?" Tau said, sounding faintly outraged.

"Because it's what you'd do," Dev said as they stopped by the downstairs doors.

Tau gave him a look in the dimness, but didn't deny it. "So," Dev said. "Call me in the morning as soon as anything new starts to happen. Don't give me that look! Yes, detail me a bodyguard this time, whatever. And, Tau, thanks."

"You're welcome," Tau said, "you idiot."

Dev grinned at him, weary. "Guilty as charged. Good night."

"Night, Dev," Tau said, patted him on the shoulder, and headed off across the plaza.

Dev sighed and went upstairs. He paused briefly by Lola's quarters, finding the place in nighttime mode and Crazy Bob holding down the front office, eating a burrito and watching a foreign soap opera on the screen next to the monitor that showed Lola's bedroom.

"Hey, Dev," Bob said. "Busy day?" He was a big blond man, a former Olympic shotputter, huge across the shoulders and looking like the archetypal jock—which made the doctorates in child psych and so on all the more surprising for those who weren't expecting them.

"You have no idea," Dev said. "How was hers?"

"Active but otherwise uneventful, I'm told," Bob said. "Ate a good dinner, and only needed two reads of *Wuggie Norple* to get to sleep tonight."

"Great. Thanks," Dev said, and headed back to Lola's bedroom. He slipped into the darkness and found her engaged in her eternal war with her blankets, having knotted them around herself in such a way as to avoid actually getting any warmth out of them. Dev leaned over the bed, unwound the blankets somewhat and rearranged them, then bent over his daughter and just looked at her a moment, listening to her breathe. The silence, the moment of doing nothing but being there, was balm.

He yawned, keeping it silent: then kissed Lola night-night, straightened up, and headed out. A wave for Bob, out into the corridor, down to his own quarters: the thump of the door shutting behind him . . .

The weariness came down on Dev all at once. The living space was on nighttime lighting: Mirabel hadn't waited for him. Dev sighed—why would she? She knew what his hours were like. He headed straight back for the bedroom, opened the door softly, went in.

The bed was empty.

He stared at it and for several moments simply wasn't able to understand what he was seeing. "Miri?" he said.

Nothing.

After a moment Dev summoned up enough presence of mind to go over to the house phone and wave it awake. "Night concierge," he said to it.

"Yes, Mr. Logan?" It was Ian, another of the household staff who couldn't seem to get casual. But then Ian had been a butler once, and Dev supposed that butlering tended to leave too deep an impression of formality for a mere few years of other employment to erase.

"It's okay, Ian," said the voice from behind him. "He's looking for me."

Dev turned, saw the shape standing in the doorway, smiled wearily. "Sorry, Ian," he said.

"No problem, Mr. Logan."

Dev waved the phone back to sleep. "I was over in your office," Mirabel said as she came in. She was wearing a large floppy Omnitopia T-shirt over her most beat-up jeans, and she was holding something in her hands. "And where have *you* been?"

"Oh, God," Dev said, "don't ask." He sat down on the bed and dropped his head into his hands for a moment, then rubbed his face. "What a day. And it's going to get worse."

"You're so right," Mirabel said, sitting down next to him.

He looked at her in complete confusion. *"What?"*

She showed him what she was carrying. It was a plate. On it was a forlorn-looking bacon, lettuce, and tomato sandwich that was curling up at the corners.

"Oh, God," Dev said.

Mirabel scowled at him. "I should make you eat this one," she said. "Are you insane? No, don't answer that, I know the answer already! *You are a crazy person!* You're

trying to run a Fortune 500 company on an empty stomach!
What do you think your blood sugar is doing? How are
your brains supposed to work? Don't even *try* to tell me:
you don't have any brains to *answer* with at the moment!"

She shook the sandwich under his nose. Dev made what
he hoped would pass for a contrite face and reached out for
it. But Mirabel snatched it away from him. "You *are* a nut
case," she said, and put the plate down on the bedside table.
"Who knows what's growing in that mayonnaise by now?
One of the cats can have what's in there, maybe, but *you're*
not getting it." She opened the drawer in the bedside table
and pulled out another BLT, this one still wrapped. "Here.
This is fresh. Eat it right this minute or I will never speak to
you again until tomorrow."

Dev sighed and pulled the plastic wrap off the plate.
"It's almost tomorrow already," he said.

"I wouldn't try to produce any logical statements just
yet if I were you," Mirabel said. "You'll just get yourself in
more trouble. Shut up and eat."

Dev ate, and rather to his surprise went from not feeling
particularly hungry to feeling ravenous in about six bites,
that being how long it took him to finish the sandwich. Mirabel watched with scowling approval, then took the plate
away from him.

"Is there another?" Dev said.

"Not for you. You'll get indigestion if you overdo it this
late. You can go get a glass of milk, but that's it."

"Yes, Mommy."

She cuffed him lightly behind the head. "Speaking of
whom, *that's* from Bella. She told me to tell you to stop acting like a big shot and do as you're told."

Dev sighed and stretched. "My life is completely owned
and operated by women," he said, and let himself fall backward on the bed.

"You say that like it's a bad thing," Mirabel said, and
more or less fell over beside him, winding up leaning on
one elbow and looking down at him.

"Did you get down to Coldstone finally?" Dev said.

Mirabel nodded. "Lola insisted that I bring you an ice
cream, despite the fact that there's already half a ton of

it in the pantry freezer. So if you see a waffle bowl full of half-melted double chocolate chip in the little freezer by the coffee bar, you know what that's about. Make sure she sees you eat it tomorrow or she'll worry."

He nodded and closed his eyes.

"What time is get-up time?" Mirabel said to him.

"Five . . ." Dev muttered. *Oh, God, please don't let things get any worse between now and then.*

Except they will. You know they will.

"Six," Mirabel said.

"Five . . ." said Dev. . . .

He never heard himself start to snore.

"You sold your soul," the voice said conversationally. "Or, no, okay, you *pawned* it. But then did you lose the pawn ticket, or throw it away?"

With a shock like falling out of bed, his eyes flew open. Darkness . . .

Phil lay there gasping for breath: his heart was racing. *A dream,* he thought at last. *Just a dream.*

He boosted himself up in bed, leaning back on his elbows to look around the darkened room. Everything was as it should have been: no sound to be heard anywhere but the soft, never-ending crash of the waves outside on the beach. This time of year, regardless of the mosquitoes, he liked to leave the upstairs windows open to the night and the sea: the on-grounds security was more than adequate to make sure that nobody would ever climb up onto the terrace and come strolling in the bedroom's open French windows.

You sold your soul, said the voice again, calm, conversational, as it had sounded in his ear a moment before. Which was strange, because there had been nothing conversational about that dream. In the dream, it had been a shout, a cry of anguish—as it had been in reality, years ago.

It was a long time since he'd dreamed about that. It had become like one of those adolescent anxiety dreams that you grow out of, where all your teeth fall out or you haven't studied for a test and everybody laughs at you. Yet despite the long respite, Phil actively shied away from the memory. *Let the past be the past. No point in letting it run your life! It's* done.

But now, as sometimes happened, Phil was wondering whether it ever really *was* done. When he and Dev had still been friends, they'd never really fought. Oh, sure, casual squabbles about stuff that wasn't important. But this one time, when they'd really *fought* over something serious, they had screamed and nearly come to blows. Even now, when he was in private, the memory made Phil go hot with shame and rage. *It wasn't my fault! It should never have happened! If we were such good friends, one really big fight shouldn't have been enough to break it up! It can't have been much of a friendship to start with!*

But that was a lie, and he knew it.

Phil cursed, threw the sheets and the light blanket aside, and padded across the polished teak floor toward the French windows. By the center window he paused, pushing aside the gauze curtains that stirred in the sea breeze. Outside, a fainter darkness than the room's was wrapped around everything, and that dark was featureless. As so often happened in mid-June before the South Fork weather had come fully up to summer temperatures, the mist had rolled in off the water a couple of hours after midnight and now lay blanketing everything. No stars tonight, no moon; and if there was any boat traffic out on the Sound, any fishermen out for the predawn catch, their lights were invisible in the mist.

Phil stood still, listening to the waves. After a moment one more sound added itself: the two-tone foghorn of the Montauk Point lighthouse, surprisingly carrying tonight through the damp air. For some reason, the mist made it sound sadder than usual, and the sad sound stirred an analogous, irrational sorrow in his gut.

He pushed through the curtains, walked out naked onto the terrace and stood there, feeling the slightly chilly wind on his skin, ignoring the way the hair rose on him at the touch of it. *You've forgotten what life's for!* the furious voice said, years ago, worlds away. *You've forgotten fun, you've forgotten joy, and whenever you see anyone else having any, you try to get between them and it, and your jealousy drives them away! This isn't what we're about! There's more to our business than money, or there would be, if you hadn't blown it all out your butt!*

You're talking about blowing our money? The way you've been spending—

I'll sure as hell never be spending again, not after today, because every penny I put into this business is gone, and not because I spent it!

He could still feel the rush of cold that ran through him with those words, the incredulous sense that he actually might have gotten something wrong. Phil shook his head and sighed: then leaned on the railing and looked out toward the invisible sea. *Why is all this coming up now?* he thought.

But that was a shrink-type question of the type he'd long since given up asking himself. The one time he'd had a brush with psychotherapy, about five years ago, the shrink had been most unhelpful. "The basic position of the human mind," he'd said, "is, 'I am blameless.' And when you hear your mind saying that to itself...then you know the sound of deception. Because we are none of us are blameless. What distinguishes us is how we handle blame, even *whether* we handle it." That kind of negative thinking had, after a few sessions, struck Phil as incredibly unhelpful: so after the first month he'd dumped the guy and had never gone back.

Phil, for God's sake, why didn't you listen to Jim? *Jim knew what he was doing! Why does anybody hire a Harvard MBA and then* ignore *him! He told you what the markets were going to do and they did* that. *He told you that you needed to change brokers and get our capital out of those convertible funds, and you said you were going to do that, and you* didn't *do that. And now all our capital is gone, and we can't bring the new game out, and my whole investment is lost, and all the work the team and I did is for nothing! You knew what you had to do, and you did nothing! Why did you do that?!*

In the heat of that now ancient-seeming moment, Phil

hadn't been able to find an answer that made any sense. Then the fight had gone off into other, far more personal, more damaging territory, and any attempt to explain himself would have been brushed aside. But eventually Phil realized both that he had never trusted Jim Margoulies' judgment, and that he had had no good reason on Earth *not* to. He hadn't discounted Jim's advice because he thought it was wrong or misguided, but because he honestly thought Dev took Jim more seriously than him. Because Dev and Jim had been friends for longer. *And the more Dev denied it, the more I couldn't believe him— the more it seemed that Dev really did trust Jim more than he did me, and I could never win in that relationship, never even pull equal—*

—*and when you can't win, you leave,* his shrink had said to him. Not as a question for once, framed in the nonattributive manner beloved of shrinks everywhere, but a conclusion, drawn out in the open because even the patient had said as much himself and couldn't possibly be so obtuse as to have missed the message.

Which of course had been the real reason he'd left the shrink, as he was plainly never going to win there, either.

All I wanted to do was prove that Jim wasn't God, that he could be wrong occasionally, that my instincts were as good as his. Okay, I was the one who got it wrong! I would have admitted that eventually! We would have clawed our way back up the ladder eventually, we'd have made it work again if he'd just have committed to stick with me and let me help pull us out of the hole! We'd have been the winners someday! But Dev hadn't been willing to give Phil a second chance. That was what Phil still regretted the most about that terrible fight, which had ended everything between them except litigation. And there was no way back, now. Too much bitterness, the ashes of the burned bridges long scattered . . .

"This is not *about* winning!" Dev had said to him, bitter. When had he ever heard such a tone of voice from the man he used to call, with affectionate scorn, "Mr. Sunshine"? But until now it *had* always been affectionate, and now everything was going wrong. "There are some things you can't win, some things you should never try to win, because when you do, you lose everything else. *What profits a man if he gains the whole world but loses his soul?*"

There had been more, much more. Underlying every friendship, Phil now suspected, down in the darkness where the friendship had its foundations, were secret understandings about the friend that should never be spoken aloud—suspicions or assumptions that it was most dangerous to bring out into the light, especially in anger. And in their anger, both of them had reached down into that darkness and said to each other the things that should never be said, even between friends. And then, memorably, came the offhand, throwaway line that hardly seemed as injurious as everything else Phil had thrown at Dev, the line that ended it all: *"The only reason you've got Mirabel now is because I let you have her!"*

Quite soon after that Phil had found himself standing in the center of the old Boston apartment, all alone. And as before, so now: here he was, alone as always. Phil could now hardly remember what it was like not to be alone. All his days full of business associates and employees, all his nights full of dates and dinners and photo opportunities and charity gigs—none of them made the slightest dent in the polished, steel-hard skin of his aloneness. Everything he had—his wealth, his success, his fame—were designed to keep him from perceiving how alone he was. Normally, in daylight, in the rush of travel and the nonstop activity of business, they succeeded. But every now and then, like now, the drug wore off. Every now and then Phil saw that Dev, who he'd thought had been the loser in their argument, somehow nonetheless had more of everything than he had, and that Phil was the one who'd lost.

Now he leaned his head against the damp, bleached wood post that held the terrace roof up over the decking. Without warning, without reason, Phil was aching inside, the original, inconsolable gut feeling of the days and hours after the fight, which his body plainly remembered all too well. *If only it could never have happened,* Phil thought. *But fat chance of that. If only it could be fixed. But it can't. If only there was something I could do to make it right—*

There was, of course, one thing. And it would only be a

start. In his mind he saw himself going up the stairs to Morgan Wise's office, shutting the door behind him, and saying to her, "I've changed my mind. Call it off."

Phil took a long breath, trying to imagine the world that might result from such a choice.

And a wave of sullen fury ran up the shores of his soul and drowned the very idea. *What is this midnight regret shit?* Phil thought. *I do not do midnight regrets. The hell with this. I just need some sleep.*

Phil turned his back on the unseen ocean and went inside, shutting the French windows on the surf and the mournful two-tone horn. *A lot to do tomorrow,* he thought. *A world to change. A game to win: a real game, the life game, the only one that counts.*

He got into bed, pulled the covers up, and shut his eyes against the watching darkness.

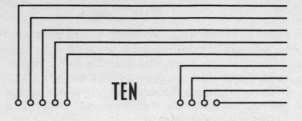

TEN

THE NEXT THING DEV KNEW, he was lying on his back, staring at the ceiling. It was dark, and someone was speaking. "—Labor unions in Australia continue their head-to-head confontation with government negotiators, leaving other major world markets wondering how this will affect the continuing recovery of the Australasian economies and others around the world. And excitement continues to build as what some call the world's most popular online roleplaying game continues preparing to launch its newest product while attempting to recover from what could have been the biggest online heist in history. My name is Scott Simon, it's Saturday the twentieth of June, 2015, and this is *Weekend Edition* from NPR—"

The program's insistently cheerful theme music started to play from the broadband radio box on Dev's side of the bed. Dev blinked and rubbed his eyes, then looked over to his right. Mirabel wasn't there.

Huh? Dev thought, and turned over to look at the bedside clock. It said five oh one.

Oh my God oh my God has the attack come yet? Why didn't they call, why didn't they—

Dev hurriedly sat up and pushed the covers back. He was still wearing his shirt, but all his other clothes except for his underwear had been pulled off him. *I don't remember that happening! What else have I missed? Oh, please, God, let me still have a company to run—*

He got out of bed, staggered over to a chair across the room that had a pair of his jeans thrown over it, and pulled them on hastily, pausing to sniff: he smelled toast. "Miri?" he said, heading out into the living area.

Mirabel was there, sitting at the coffee bar in one of her floppy nightshirts, the silk bathrobe over it all. She had been gazing idly at the screen of one of her laptops on the counter, chewing on a piece of toast. As he came in, she smiled at him and yawned.

"What the heck are you doing out here?" Dev said, going over to kiss her.

"You kicked me out of bed," Mirabel said, giving him a dry look. "Twice. And you kept stealing the covers."

Dev moaned. He was a famously restless sleeper when he was stressed, and right now he was way more stressed than usual. "Oh, honey, I'm sorry . . ."

"Shut up," Mirabel said. She reached over to one side, where one of his mugs had been sitting on the bar's hot spot, and pushed it into his hand. "Drink that. I'm going to make you breakfast, and you are going to eat it."

Dev's stomach did a flip-flop. "Uh," he said, "I'm not sure that's a good idea. I need to call Tau, because he said—"

Mirabel rolled her eyes at him. "To tell you as soon as you woke up that unless he'd called by now, there's been no second attack as yet. And he hasn't, so there wasn't. Meanwhile, I know what you're going to say and I don't want to hear about your stomach! All the time you claim you're too nervous to eat, and then it just gets worse later. You're going to have at least a bowl of cereal. No, don't even speak to me! Sit down, drink the coffee, have some caffeine if you can't have a brain."

Mirabel got up, pushed Dev down onto the bar stool she'd been sitting in, and went off to the fridge under the back counter. From this she extracted milk, from the cupboard above the fridge a bowl and a box with such garish graphics that it hurt Dev's eyes to look at it so early in the morning. "What *is* that?" he said.

"Something Lolo buzz-sawed me into buying last week," said Mirabel, sounding annoyed with herself. "She saw some flashy commercial for it. I said I'd buy it for her, but I never said I was going to let her have any of it. *You*, though, look like you could use a sugar rush to tide you over until the carbs kick in. Here."

Moments later Dev found himself eating a cereal that (according to the box) was full of Oaty Goodness, but in actuality seemed to be much fuller of circus-themed Day-Glo marshmallows. "Boy," he said after a few moments of shoveling the stuff in, "whatever you do, *don't* let Lola near this! Might as well just give her IV espresso."

Mirabel shook her head as she sat down in the chair beside Dev and reached past him to get her toast, turning her laptop toward her again. "Her staff would not thank us," she said.

"It's *my* staff I'm worried about right now."

"And they're thinking about you, so relax," Mirabel said. "I talked to Milla an hour ago. She was on call to Tau until he finally fell over, and after that to Tau's night support people. But there's been nothing to disturb you about. She told me the master system security guys were still waiting for the other shoe to drop, but it doesn't seem to have happened yet. Some kind of network problem at the bad guys' end, she said. Does that make sense?"

"Enough sense for right now," said Dev, and pushed the bowl away, astonished that he'd emptied it so quickly. Mirabel pushed his coffee back at him, and Dev slurped at it gratefully: it was so much less sweet than the cereal that the contrast felt like a sudden return to an adulthood that he was now sugar-hopped enough to appreciate. Dev rubbed his eyes and started trying to get his thoughts in order.

"Don't think yet," Mirabel said. "Two things, though, and I'll write them down for you." She reached past her laptop for a pad of sticky notes and a pen. "You have to go eat your ice cream for Lolo this morning—"

Dev groaned. "Ice cream before lunch? Is this the same woman who keeps telling me I need to lose ten pounds?"

"—and *I* am bringing you the sandwich at lunchtime, and another at dinner, because you cannot be trusted to put them inside you no matter how many reasonable noises you make."

Dev gave her a wounded look. "I'll do it today, honest."

"Yes, you will," Mirabel said, smiling: but her voice was grim. "Now go shower." She got up, stretched. "And don't just throw those jeans back on, either. Your staff'll start talking if the seventh richest man in the world doesn't change his pants."

Dev laughed as he got up: then stopped. "How'd you know about seventh?"

Mirabel turned away with a wry grin. "You kidding? Your staff leaks to me like a sieve. Now get going. Milla will be here soon."

She was there within twenty minutes, as it happened, and by that time the combination of the sugar and the carb-loading followed by a lot of hot water had indeed worked their wonders for Dev. He no longer felt like he wanted to hide under the bed from his staff and his stockholders, though later in the day he might have reason. Milla, to his pleasure, also looked like she hadn't been up all night, though her expression as she came in was somewhat grim. "Oh, come on, Mil," said Mirabel as she went out to see if Lola was up yet. "Smile! It might never happen."

Milla smiled dutifully enough, but her face reset itself to grim as the door closed behind Mirabel and Milla started opening up her piles of files and started laying out print-outs on the coffee-bar counter for Dev to look over. "Bad night?" said Dev.

Milla rolled her eyes and ran a hand through her short shaggy blonde hair. "You have no idea. Everybody's in a foul mood, Mr. Logan. Nobody likes the idea of those son-sabitches breaking into our house and going through the drawers. Virtually speaking." She flushed red.

Dev kept himself from smiling: it was unusual to see Milla get so passionate about anything. "So where are we this morning newswise?"

She frowned. "News about the attack is everywhere, as you might imagine. I have a note from Mr. Margoulies. He'd like to see you over at Castle Scrooge this morning."

"Frank's got me scheduled already," Dev said.

Milla nodded. "Our share price closed down in the Asian markets," she said. "Europe is awake, and the share price in Frankfurt and London is jumping all over as the two exchanges watch each other's reactions and freak out more. Currency instability's making it worse: the intraday trends are all over the place. The Asia finance analysts think the Hang Seng is waiting to see if there's another attack by their morning. If there's not, or if there is and we can handle it quick, we might get some positive bounce off them today. But don't look for anything big."

Dev rubbed his eyes. *There we go,* he thought; *we're never going to break a thousand in this climate. That's why Jim wants to see me, to break the bad news.* He let his hands fall and let out a long breath. "Okay," he said, "it's eight in the morning back East and Wall Street will be open soon. So by the time I see Jim, we'll have some sense of how the U.S. markets will react. Meanwhile, what's going on in the media?"

"Sniggering from the hackers," Milla said, looking furious as she pushed a printout over to Dev, "but not in any detail that's particularly useful to us. They've issued the same press release electronically to the various public access PR sources, and to all the big papers and TV networks, being very careful to use public anonymizers to cover their tracks. We're idiots, they own us, yada yada yada."

"Yeah, well, we'll see who owns who by the end of the day," Dev said as he looked over a copy of the press release, which was full of leetspeak terms and number-and-letter spellings that had probably made the older news editors at various wire services send for younger stringers who could do a translation. "What does system security have for me?"

"They've been busy all night following up leads," Milla said. "And it looks like they've got some, because our attackers got a little lazy or a little too cheeky for their own good, and left some markers they may not have known they were leaving. In more than one area. In particular, there are messages piling up for you from the shuntspace crowd—"

Dev blinked at that. "Why the heck?" he said. "The shuntspaces aren't public. No one outside the firm even knows about them. A lot of people *inside* the firm don't even know about them: those spaces aren't their business. Why would the attackers be bothering with them? Come to think of it, how would they even have gotten into them?"

Milla shrugged, shook her head. "I have no idea. But the palace crew have been getting more excitable all night, and

Tau has flagged what they're doing as a high-priority matter of interest, so I've forwarded all their messages to your to-do box."

Dev got up and stretched. "Tau did say last night that they were picking up some anomalies . . . Who knows. I'll talk to them. Anything else serious?"

"Not as yet," Milla said. "Where will you be heading next?"

"The Castle office," Dev said. "I want to see what else has come up in the analysis of last night's logs." He yawned and went to refill his coffee mug. "Tell all the usual suspects that I'm conscious again, and they should call me the minute anything starts happening."

"Will do." She gathered up her own paperwork and tablet computer and headed for the door.

"Milla—"

She paused, looking back at him. "Mr. Logan?"

"Were you in the fight last night?"

Milla shrugged, nodded. "I consulted a little," she said. "The financial security teams wanted as many people watchdogging the backdoor logs to the banking routines as they could find."

"'Consulted,'" Dev said, and smiled. "You mean you were bashing somebody with a club."

Milla hesitated, then grinned. "It's good to express your aggressiveness every now and then," she said. "I'm told you did some of that too. Before they had to rescue you."

"Ouch," Dev said.

"I'll be in the Castle office with Frank in two hours," Milla said, "so you can offload whatever scheduled stuff on us that you want. When the second wave comes, we know where you'll want to be. But this time make sure security has you covered, okay? It gives the rest of us one less thing to worry about."

Dev sighed. "My life," he said, "is *completely* controlled by women."

"And look where you are," Milla said. "Mister Seventh. Seems mean-spirited to complain."

"Go away now," Dev said, "and let me soak up some more of this caffeine."

Milla headed out. Shortly thereafter so did Dev, making a much briefer stop with Lola than he would have liked, but at least Mirabel was with her, helping Poppy get her dressed and get her breakfast into her. "Ice cream!" Lola shouted after him as Dev made his way out of her suite, and behind him he could hear Mirabel saying, "Yes, Daddy'll come have ice cream with you later, won't that be fun, now where's your other shoe?"

Dev sighed and made his way over to the upstairs office on the other side of the Castle. Once inside he paused to look at the big display, which was showing an image of some remote, cool alpine valley with snowy mountains towering over it, though the pines and the alp they overhung were still green. *That's just about what I want right now,* Dev thought. *If I could just get on a plane without being seen and vanish into a landscape like that . . .*

But escape was for other people. He sighed and made his way over to his desk, which had a pile of printed reports on it—material that Milla had left for him. Dev flipped through them briefly, then pushed them aside, for his thoughts were much more in the virtual world than the concrete one. He went straight to his login cubicle, sat himself down, and let the chair mold to him and the cubicle close, then put on the eyecups and made his way into the virtual version of the office.

The air was thickly hung with windows and documents, almost all of them flashing or throbbing with varying levels of urgency. One collection of yellow-burning e-mails looked more like a window shade pulled down all the way, there were so many sequential mails attached to the letter-sized top sheet, the first message in the thread.

Dev went over to it and yanked at the top corner of the pane of light representing the topmost message. Immediately the whole stack undid itself and spread itself out on the air, becoming an assortment of cover letters, images of employees who started talking to him, and spills of code that separated themselves out into the air and started scrolling down in their own little windows. "Whoa, whoa, everything freeze!" Dev said, and everything did.

He started working his way through the stack. Sure

enough, they were all messages from the shuntspace people and had been left for him in the middle of the night, every one of them going on at length about code malfunctions—or at least the senders thought they were code malfunctions—in the shuntspace routines during the attack the day before. Dev pulled over a couple of the attachment windows and briefly dipped into some of the code to try to see what they were all talking about, but he didn't know this code anywhere near as well as he knew the CO routines, and finally just shook his head. *Easier to get them to tell me what they think I need to know . . .*

He waved the stack of correspondence back together into one in-air pile and then reached out to poke the e-mail address on the topmost copy: giorgio.falcone@omnitopia-admin.com. "System management?" he said.

"Here, Dev. Giorgio's present physical location is the basement infraconferencing suite. His virtual location is the second floor meeting center in the virtual twin of the Secure Alternate Environments Group building."

"Thanks. Open me a door, please."

In front of him, the air appeared to go frosted, as if it were a pane of glass. The "glass" then slid sideways to reveal a large green-carpeted space, brightly lit. Dev stepped through.

On the far side of the door he had to pause and glance around, as he hadn't come out where he thought he would. His intention had been to pop out right in Giorgio's team's virtual meeting space. But someone had apparently specified that accesses to that space should be redirected. Dev found himself standing on the lawn that lay between the road and the paved terrace and Moorish-arcaded entrance of the stucco and tile building that its inhabitants called "the Palaces of the Princes of Hell." But the lawn stretched from where Dev stood to the horizon: there was no other Omnitopian building in sight anywhere. And over the building that he *could* see, something new had been erected.

Dev stood there a moment and took in the newest evidence that his shuntspace crowd was a law unto itself. Keeping the naughtier Omnitopia players in the dark and well fed with manure byproducts often wore on them. As a result they tended to act up, or out, in ways that other Omnitopia employees didn't, so discovering that they had erected a triumphal arch at the gateway to their virtual space was merely a matter for amusement. It really was a spectacular construction, pure white marble, intricately carved, and five hundred feet high at least. Across its great lintel was graven in very perfect Trajan Roman letters the first part of the ancient warning:

FACILE DESCENSUS AVERNO

"It's easy to get down into Hell..." Dev chuckled to himself, realizing they were reminding him of another, older joke. He walked forward under the triumphal arch, toward the portico leading to the main door of the Palace. Above the door was the space in which some wit three years ago had written (in beautifully drafted archaic Latin) that other famous Dantean quote, ABANDON HOPE ALL YE WHO ENTER HERE. Having seen this apparition and been reduced to guffaws on the morning it turned up, Dev had Frank send the building maintenance guys around to formally incorporate the writing into the arch. However, his jokey threat to make the inhabitants of the palace pay for the alteration had resulted in six hundred sixty-six dollars and sixty-six cents' worth of nickels and dimes (and six pennies) being dumped on the lawn outside Castle Dev by a private contractor who found himself unable to identify the culprits because they had also paid *him* in nickels and dimes (and six pennies). All Dev could do then was have Frank arrange for a cleanup crew, find out which of the city's charities was best set up to deal with vast numbers of nickels and dimes (it turned out to be the Archdiocese of Phoenix), and make a note to schedule all the shuntspace management for salary reviews.

Dev now glanced up at the writing as he went in the door, shook his head, and crossed the wide tiled lobby, making for the broad staircase at the back. This version of the building was identical to the real one except for one significant point: it was always night here. As he went up the stairs and glanced out the window overlooking the first landing, a big orange half moon hung high in the darkness over the palm trees out back. *Control issues,* Dev thought as he turned to go up the next flight of stairs. *Where else would these people ever have kept a job if we hadn't made one for them?* But there were some folks for whose sake it was worth not complaining too much about the occasional breach of corporate discipline, even discipline as relaxed as Omnitopia's.

On the second floor Dev came out at the top of the landing and glanced around. The work and meeting space enclosed here was typically Omnitopian in its casual structure, though it was ten times the size of the space inside the real building: football could have been played here. Couches and chairs and desks were scattered across the carpeted acreage, with grown-up toys scattered around too: a basketball hoop mounted on the nearest wall before it curved off into the middle distance, somebody's exercise bicycle off to one side, a treadmill by the far wall, a couple of game platforms on either side of a 3-D projection display, a very beat up Dance-Rug set into the carpet. Closer to the center of the space was a circle of twelve full-body Game Sieges, each one paired up with an isolation helm equipped with the fanciest version of the RealFeel interface. It was a joke or comment of some kind that this virtual space contained the chairs at all: they'd hardly be needed here. But no one sat in any of the chairs, and the huge staging space inside the circle was empty.

Here and there around the space were signs that the place had been suffering an infestation of old-style coders. Junk food wrappers, pizza boxes, and drinks cups with bendy straws were piled up in pyramidal heaps. Close by where Dev was standing, a virtual version of one of those little disk-shaped self-propelled vacuum cleaners was bumping the curve of its "head" side repeatedly against the nearest wall in a manner suggesting that its sensors had been addled by the sight of more garbage than it could deal with. From the poor little vacuum came a tiny sound of disconsolate weeping. It was the only sound, however; the space was empty of anyone human.

Dev shook his head and started strolling around looking for more virtual doors. "Hello?" he said. "Anybody home?"

Nothing. He wandered farther into the space, pausing by one of the desks. Above it hung a series of airscreens full of code: some of this looked like what he'd seen in his office. "Saw your new lawn ornament," Dev said to the space in general. "What, the thing with all the garden gnomes last month wasn't enough?"

He turned away from the screens and looked around again, then went over to the unhappy little vacuum cleaner and bent over it, picking it up. The weeping faded down somewhat, replaced by soft whimpering. "You guys," Dev said as he glanced around, petting the vacuum, "seriously, you should pick up in here a little. Somebody might think you were slobs or something—"

Without warning, somebody walked backward out of the air into the middle of the space: a petite young African American woman in a denim skirt, tank top, Day-Glo pink sneakers, and a boom-mike headset. She was talking to someone in another part of the floor's virtual work area. "No, what did you think I meant?" she was saying. "I told you, there were at least ten references to that address prepended to the strings—"

Dev cleared his throat. The young woman looked over at him in shock. Then she yelled through the open air-door, "Hey, he's here! Giorgio? Where are those guys, get them in here, tell them to load their stuff up, Dev's here!"

She waved a hand at the space. The garbage piles vanished, along with all the virtual furniture, and the circle of chairs relocated themselves almost out to the walls. A breath later, the ceiling vanished and the space in the middle of the vast floor was instantly filled by a ghostly version of the Code Forest. Some of the trees were half-hidden by translucent hovering code windows.

The young woman headed over to Dev. In the wake of the change in the space, she was now wearing a glowing virtual sticky-tag of the HELLO, MY NAME IS type that had "Darlene" scribbled on it in a big loopy hand. "You usually go around hijacking people's domestic appliances, Boss?" she said.

Dev offered her the vacuum. It was sniffling. "When they're in distress."

Unimpressed, she took it from him, turned it over, checked all its wheels, and put it down. It zipped away across the floor. "Giorgio taught him to do that," she said. "Playing for sympathy. Giorgio does it too, when one of us sees something he didn't see first. Which is what happened tonight after the attack."

"Tonight?"

Darlene rubbed her face as, behind her, people started pouring out of the door in the air. "Last night," she said. "Eight hours ago. Whatever. Sorry, Boss, the shunts were full of craziness from around the time the attack started, and we've spent all night trying to pin down what it was."

A crowd of eight or ten young men came out through the air-door. "Sorry, Boss," said the foremost of them, whose tag said ROBERT, "we were off looking at a shuntspace."

"Which one?" Dev said.

"Pandora," said one of the group behind him. "That's where the anomalies started spreading from," said another. "Willowisp first, then some of the Microcosms in the nearby server structure. But that constellation was noncontiguous—"

"Whoa," said a deep voice at the back of the group. "Let's take it from the top, okay?" And the tall thin shape of Giorgio Falcone pushed through the crowd. Giorgio was yet another hire associated with Tau's bad-boy university period, as rough around the edges as Tau was polished— very much in the style of the T-shirted, torn-jeans geek archetype, with eyes red from late-night coding and fingers yellow from chain-gobbling bags of Cheetos. But Giorgio's spiky black hair and single tasteful nose ring lent his punk-European air a domesticated quality.

"Let's sit down and you can all tell me what these mails were about," Dev said.

"Sofas," Giorgio said, and the sofas that had banished themselves to the far sides of the room now slid back and positioned themselves around the edges of the small crowd of intense people that had formed around Dev. Everybody sat.

"First of all," Dev said, "make sure you copy all this to Tau, okay?"

"The system's been logging every word any of us have said to anybody since last night," Giorgio said, "and we're not about to stop now. We started getting a lot of—I wouldn't call them spurious logins into the shuntspaces, but ingresses of low-volume players, users who had no reason to be shunted because they mostly hadn't been in the system in terms of total play-time for long enough to have misbehaved that badly. A whole lot of them started getting pushed in around six thirty, seven. It set off our alarms, because we never get so many ingresses in such a short period."

"How many?" Dev said.

"Thousands," said Darlene, who had flopped down by Dev on the next couch over.

"She's understating," Giorgio said. "Ten thousand, maybe fifteen, in the first wave. Our shunt handling systems started creaking under the strain, so we had to get in there ourselves and shore them up. And when we'd done that, the traffic leveled off a little—then started increasing again. Almost as if somebody'd noticed that we'd compensated. But by then we began to have enough spare time to track the ingresses back to the source. And guess what was pushing them in on us?"

"The CO routines," said about half the group in chorus.

Dev rubbed his eyes. "Oh, God, not more Item Three stuff! People, Tau and I had a run at that issue last night before the balloon went up. And we came up empty."

"I don't think this had anything to do with Item Three," Giorgio said. "If by that you mean the same thing that's been causing these weird little glitches and outages all over with the CO's digital fingerprints on them. This was a lot less random. As far as we can tell, the CO started acting as if the rogue logins were straightforward in-game cheats, and it shoved the first couple waves of them into the shuntspaces. Pandora was the first one to start showing those results—"

"Pandora—like Pastorale—being one of the 'cosms seriously threatened last night," Dev said.

Giorgio nodded. "Exactly. Look. System?"

"Yo!"

Dev blinked at the syntax. "Snapshot, please, of the schematic of Pandora shuntspace from nineteen thirty."

"Gotcha."

Around the circle of sofas, a vast hollow cylinder of translucent green fire shot up toward the sky: the room's skydomelike ceiling obligingly got out of the way as the cylinder narrowed and dimpled out into rapidly extruding branch structures nearer its distant top. The inside of the cylinder was sheeted with a myriad of scrolling screenfuls of code text, a thin skin of water. Here and there the flow of code ran faster than in other places, downsliding patches of code overlapping one another, pausing in their movement inside the trunk of the virtual tree, then slipping away horizontally or sliding up inside the tree again. Some hundreds of the codescreens nearest the viewers in the circle could be seen to be edged with a hot process blue. "Game-generated characters?" Dev said.

"That's right," Giorgio said. "We have about three thousand of them working in Pandora right now. Yesterday morning there were fifteen hundred and sixty-three cheaters resident." He pointed at various other patches ascending or descending gently along the inner skin of the Macrocosm's virtual structure: these scraps of code were edged in red. "Interactions were perfectly normal: the cheaters don't have a clue—we interact with a sampling of them every day to make sure. But then—watch this. System? Display the time-elapsed imagery we were examining an hour ago."

"Displaying," said the system. Suddenly the sliding patchwork of interacting program fragments began to be obscured by more and more patches appearing. These paler patches, a leprous green-white, began overlaying all the others more and more quickly until the underlying, normal login traffic could hardly be seen at all. Soon they were so thick on the inner surface that it had gone almost entirely green-white.

"Once they got into the shuntspace," said Giorgio, "the user logins cloned themselves into multiple fake accounts and started trying to exit the 'cosm in the usual way, via the local Ring and out into Telekil. We peeled off a few of them and took them apart—"

Giorgio pointed at one side of the tree's interior, and one of the patches peeled itself away and sailed over to him. Giorgio caught it out of the air and stretched it wider and longer. In his hands it became dark lettering streaming down over a pale green-white background. He passed it over to Dev.

Dev skimmed down the code, then stroked the window to make it scroll. "Looks like it wanted to get out through the Ring into as many other 'cosms as it could . . ."

"Which would've been bad," Giorgio said. "Each time one of these things got into a new 'cosm it would have cloned itself again. The system would've been flooded with them in minutes. But they couldn't get out of the 'cosm . . . or rather they could, except only into other shuntspaces. The rogue logins couldn't tell the difference between the shunts and the real spaces because all the code's identical, right down to the accounting structures. But everything's isolated from the main structure by design . . ."

Dev nodded slowly, looking at the nasty and elegant code in his hands. "So here they stayed until they expired." He glanced up. "Though not all at once."

"Nope," Darlene said. "Expirations were pretty much random, though there were some clusters that might have been either lazy programming or something to do with the rogue logins not being able to execute their routines correctly—caught in loops, maybe." She shrugged.

Dev flipped the page of code over to Giorgio, who crumpled it up and tossed it in the air, where it vanished. "Now all we need to figure out is why the CO shoved those logins into the shuntspaces," Dev said.

Giorgio nodded. "We're looking into that. So are Spike and Dietrich here—they were on last night helping with the analysis and cleanup after the first attack, and we called them over from network security to help us try to understand what was going on."

"What we are all agreed on," said the dark-skinned young man who to judge by his accent was probably Dietrich, "was that it was a good thing that so many of the illegal logins wound up being directed into the shuntspaces. They protected the rest of the system a little. Otherwise the battle might have gone very much differently."

"As bugs go," said Spike, a little Asian guy in a white shirt and business flannels, "it was more welcome than most."

"Undocumented feature," said one shuntspacer whose name tag read "AMALIE," a young brunette woman in jeans and an Omnitopia hoodie.

"Yeah, well, I prefer them documented," Dev said. "But you must have some theories about how this happened. Anybody?"

Heads shook all around the circle. "That's why we left you all those notes, Boss," said Giorgio. "You and Tau are the only ones with access to the CO. You two'll have to figure it out."

"All we can tell you," said Darlene, "is that every one of those rogue logins had Conscientious Objector ID strings prepended to them. Though the format looked weird."

Dev let out an exasperated breath. "Weird? Syntax errors, you think?"

"Like you would ever make a syntax error, Boss," somebody said, sounding very dry.

Dev laughed. "Please. My perfection is a matter of public record."

The snickering was no crueler than necessary. "Don't know that it was a coding error, either," Darlene said. "Or not one of yours. The other reason we called security was that, besides the CO strings, we also kept finding outside computer address strings appended to the attacker logins, whereas all the others we had been trying to follow up until then didn't have any. Which makes sense, because that's absolutely not the kind of thing you'd want to leave behind you if you were a hacker. We couldn't understand where the appended addresses were coming from."

"Code error at the other end," Giorgio said. "Had to be. After all, the attack code has to have been millions of lines long. No way you can write that much stuff without messing up something somewhere—"

"Tell me about it," Dev said.

"All it would have taken," said Darlene, "was one line duplicated somewhere in those guys' code—a semicolon forgotten or a pair of quotes or brackets not closed—" She shrugged. "Then you get this fragment of address information left hanging off the end of a login. . . . That might have been what made the CO react. But you'll have to be the one to tell us that."

Dev shook his head. "It sounds like we just got lucky," he said. "Okay. Tau and I will look at your notes as fast as we can. Probably mostly Tau—my plate's so full today . . ."

"Boss," Giorgio said. "We know you're . . . protective about the CO routines. We understand why." Dev looked over at him, thinking, *Protective being code for "paranoid."* "But it's getting to the point that when you have situations like this, you've got to be able to hand them off to other people. Otherwise you've got all forty thousand of us sitting on your shoulder waiting for you to fix what's busted, and it's not fair to you."

"Not fair to *us*" was what Dev had been expecting to hear, but now he felt ashamed of himself for underestimating the quality and the loyalty of the people he had working for him. He sighed. "Tau and I have been discussing that," Dev said. "Just last night, in fact. We'll be taking time to consider how best to go forward on the issue when the rollout's finished and we've all had time to breathe."

"Good," Giorgio said. "Thanks."

Dev got up and stretched. "So what else is going on with you guys?"

"We're retrenching," Darlene said. "Getting ready for the next wave."

"Anybody here get any sleep?" Dev said.

There was hollow laughter from some of the Princes of Hell, but some scornful expressions, too. "Boss, please," said Spike. "Sleep is for the weak."

"Anyway, the next wave's gonna be a lot more exciting," Darlene said. "And there's a lottery set up for who gets to be your bodyguard. Gonna kick us some bot butt. Human butt too, if we're lucky."

Dev raised an eyebrow. "So they *did* have people riding their bot programs—"

"Oh, yeah," Giorgio said. "But the riders weren't as careful about covering up their own tracks as the guys who programmed the machines were. The machines doing the automated part of the attack came into Omnitopian net-space on Internet addresses that changed three times a second, so that the programs proper jumped from machine to machine in a whole range of addresses—twenty or thirty for each machine. But the guys directing the attacks didn't do that. *Their* machines kept the same addresses for, wow, maybe four or five seconds at a time."

"That's a long while in machine moments . . ." Dev said.

Darlene grinned. "They were trying to avoid latency issues," she said. "They were apparently scared they might miss something vital during the attack, that some aspect of their own code would fail to run, if they changed machines too often. And they assumed they would have us so off-balance that we wouldn't be able to devote enough resources to track them while the attack was going on."

"Wrong!" chorused the other assembled Princes, and some of them laughed nastily.

"So the ambush is being planned even as we speak," Darlene said. "Security's busy tracking down the routes the zombie machines used to come at us—"

"They won't use the same ones," Dev said.

All the Princes rolled their eyes or made faces at their boss' apparent slowness. "Of course they won't," Giorgio said. "But they established a pattern that showed us how they build and hub their network addresses. Once the first wave of the new attack starts hitting, we'll be able to extrapolate their pattern backward along it, compromise their hub structure, pare them down to manageable numbers—"

"—say ten or fifteen thousand core machines—"

"—then suck those machines dry and inject our own code—"

"—so we can start compromising their function, get them to spill their guts, and ID the locations of the people riding the attack in real time before they self-destruct—"

"—it's just going to be a matter of a few minutes to nail them to the ground, that's all we need. So if we can make sure that the second attack nets them at least ten mil or so—"

"—maybe fifteen, but no more than that. We just have to keep them on the hook long enough to get them all thoroughly compromised—"

Dev's mouth dropped open. "Whoa, whoa, whoa," he said, "let's just backspace a little. Did somebody just say 'ten mil' as in ten million? Ten million of my dollars?"

"Our dollars," said Giorgio.

Everybody was looking at Dev as if he were insane at suddenly asserting personal ownership over something which the company line said belonged to all of them. Their expressions ranged from bemused to wounded. "We wouldn't be suggesting this," said Darlene, "if we weren't going to get back ten times that much—"

"—twenty!—"

"—out of the lawsuits against the crooked IPs and spamhauser that made it possible for these guys to stage their attacks. Because there's no way they could have done it without some level of complicity—"

"You can't make omelets without breaking eggs, Boss," Darlene said. "And the worm won't bite on an empty hook."

"Could you possibly mix that metaphor up a little more?" Amalie said.

"Oh, cut it out, you know what I mean! But it's true."

Dev rubbed his face. "All right," he said. "Have you spoken to Tau about this?"

"About three this morning."

"What did he say?"

"He said it was okay," said Darlene.

"He said he'd be clearing it with you this morning after he talked to Jim and got the money end green-lit," said Giorgio.

Dev suddenly flashed on Lola saying to him, with one of those winning smiles, "But *Mama* said I could!" And it was always a judgment call whether Mama really had. It wasn't that Lola lied, precisely, but she so much wanted her version of reality to be true sometimes . . .

Nonetheless . . . it sounds like something Tau would have okayed: it has that reckless braininess about it. Dev sighed. "Okay," he said, "let me get out of here: I've got at least as many things to do as you guys have. Just keep up the good work. I'll talk to Tau later. Make sure you add anything new to your notes for him before we meet."

"To hear is to obey, O Mighty One," Giorgio said.

"Right. System? My door, please."

It appeared in the air nearby. "And guys?" Dev said. "Good work. Keep on it. We're all gonna have a big party when everything calms down."

"Boss!" Giorgio said. "*This* is a big party. But we'll come to yours."

Dev smiled, waved at them, and stepped through the door.

Back in his virtual office, he stood silent for a moment, looking down through the darkly transparent floor at the Ring of Elich and thinking over what the Princes of Hell had told him. "Management?" he said then.

"Here, Dev."

"Give me access to the CO routines."

"What mode?"

"The same as last night."

The view through the floor changed, showing him the rings of glowing trees as seen from thirty or forty feet above the base level and the floor opened, the stairway building itself again downward beneath him. Dev headed down the stairs.

Once down on the island that held the circle of a hundred and twenty-one trees, Dev paused on the shore, looking down into the roil of green light representing the CO routines. He reached into the air, pulled out the Sword of Truth, and stood there for a moment, considering the lines of code tangling and rolling liquidly at his feet.

Then he shook his head. "System management?"

"Here, Dev."

"Is Tau viewing the CO routines at the moment?"

"No, Dev. Tau is in the Castle in consulting suite five, in conference with Cleolinda."

"All right." Still, he was feeling a little paranoid this morning, so— "Are any other Omnitopia personnel viewing the CO's outrider programs?"

"The shuntspace staff on duty have a window open, but none are observing."

"Good," Dev said. "Alert me if either they or Tau begin observations."

"I will, Dev."

"Thank you," he said. "Paradigm shift, please. Personal CO idiom—"

"As requested," said the control voice.

The light changed, the landscape shifted. Suddenly the island looked like a real island—rushes and cattails down at the water's edge, verdant sward underfoot: a clear sky above, with a big moon hanging low and silver in it. The forest of code behind him now looked like a real forest, the massive rough-barked trunks rearing up behind him, stretching out vast branches, every leaf of the overshadowing canopy edged with the silver of moonlight. In front of him, the liquid shift of the CO routines was now expressing itself as water, rippling pewter and silver under the moon, stretching away to the horizon in all directions.

Dev went down to the water's edge and just stood there for a second, listening to the wind. Then he reared back and threw the Sword of Truth upward and out over the water.

It spun in the moonlight, fell toward the surface, but never had a chance to strike. White in the silvery light, a slender arm thrust up from the water and caught the sword by the hilt. For a moment the arm simply held it so: then water rippled as what held the sword started to move closer to the shore. More of the arm showed, and white silk fell back from it, shimmering in the pallid light as the shape to which the arm belonged made her way up toward the shore with the Sword of Truth in her hand.

She looked like Mirabel, but a different version of her: as fair as Mirabel, but instead of his wife's blonde good looks, the woman had long straight hair dark as night and a glance nearly as dark. Over the trim little body was thrown a much longer version of the white silk bathrobe, with a white silk shift underneath it.

"Cora," he said.

"Good morning, Dev," said the Conscientious Objector.

"Take a walk with me?"

"Certainly."

They walked toward the outermost ring of Macrocosm trees together, and for a good while in silence, while Dev decided how to proceed. This mode of debugging was one he had never used when anyone else was around; as far as he knew, not even Tau knew about it. But its roots went back a long way. In that distant past when he and Jim Margoulies were still running networked computer games with actual cables connecting their machines, Dev had added a voice to the help function in his first rough edition of *Otherworlds*. Jim had teased him unmercifully for days—first along the theme of "You want it to come alive and talk to you!" and then, much more painfully—especially because it was a female voice Dev had chosen—"You're trying to build yourself a girlfriend!" Nor had Jim cared in the slightest about all the research that said female voices were easier to listen to than male ones and cut through the game noise better. He just laughed every time he heard the voice speaking. Dev, who then had had no girlfriend, hurriedly removed the voice from his machine.

But later, when Mirabel had come into his life and he was working on the new version of the game, Dev got a sudden stubborn impulse and stuck the voice back in. When *Otherworlds* debuted as a game that more people than just the two of them could play, though Jim had mocked him for it, the control voice had turned out to be one of its most popular features. It had something to do with the flexibility of the response routines that Dev had designed for it, and also with the actress Dev had hired—a woman who had done a lot of voice work for cartoons and who managed to sound engaged and comforting without ever getting gooey: neutral enough not to be your girlfriend, but not like your mom, either.

Jim's mockery didn't stop overnight. "I just like talking to my game," Dev kept saying. But "You just like talking to yourself!" was Jim's constant reply, until over time other subjects became much more important, and this one dropped off his grid. But it never fell off Dev's, and when he got the idea a year or so ago of installing an experimental set of ARGOT modules at the edge of the CO for his own use, he somehow never got around to mentioning it to either Jim or Tau. His intention had been to build a comfortable way to interact directly with the CO's so-called Rational Algorithm—the heuristic self-analysis modes that were the most important part of the Conscientious Objector, the key to having it run itself.

Since the original installation, Dev had been hacking at the self-expression part of the routine in a casual way every now and then. But there hadn't been time to indulge such elective tweaking since the new hyperburst memory arrived two months ago. From then until now, just about all the time Dev normally set aside to deal with code issues had been given over to helping make sure the vast new memory heaps were working correctly. Now, though, he looked at the Lady of the Lake walking silent and serene beside him, and felt vaguely guilty for not having come to see her sooner. *The Pathetic Fallacy, of course,* he thought. *It's just a program. A very smart, very slick program.*

But still, it's my *program. I should take better care of it. Visit it more often . . .*

They passed into the first shadows of the moonlight, where the tallest branches of the outermost trees in the circle blocked the moon away; the dark hair of the woman walking beside him became a shadow, the eyes unreadable. "So how are things?" Dev said.

"Very busy right now," said Cora, with a sidelong look at him. "As you know."

Dev nodded, walking quietly under the shadow of the branches with "her"—saying nothing, waiting to see what she would say.

"It's a surprise to see you here twice in two days," Cora said. "Doubtless a report is required?"

"Well, yes," Dev said. "Just what's the matter with you lately?"

"You're referring to the recent series of minor system malfunctions?" Cora said. "They have to do with the installation of the new memory and the relocation of the old memory functions into it."

Dev rolled his eyes. "We'd kind of figured that out. I was hoping you might cast a little more light on the subject."

"That's not possible just yet," Cora said.

Dev paused inside the first ring of trees as they came out into the moonlight again. "Just yet?"

Cora stopped still as well, looking up into the faint indigo radiance of the sky. There was something unnatural about her stillness: she breathed normally enough as she stood there, but there was no sense of her being at rest ... unless it was the rest of a statue, a waxwork. *Something else to work on*, Dev thought. *More natural body language. Though it was the spoken language I've been working on ...*

"The rollout isn't one hundred percent complete yet," Cora said. "Only eighty-two of the hundred new memory heaps have been brought online. Everyone had to drop everything last night when the attack started, including the transfer staff: they had to lock down the migration process and isolate the noncertified memory to make sure it couldn't be contaminated by the attacking programs. In any case, it won't be possible to do a full internal analysis until all the heaps are up and running. There is, besides, the considerable likelihood that because the interleave between the CO routines and the rest of the Omnitopia gaming environment was designed to work with a hundred percent of the memory heaps enabled, the problems are secondary to the gradual nature of the rollout." Cora turned her face toward Dev, and again there was that strange sense of nonspontaneity about it that made it impossible to say "she looked at him." "Once the remaining memory is certified, activated, and interleaved with the rest of the system, full analysis can go forward. But there may be no need for that. Once all the memory's in place, the problems may be resolved."

Boy, Dev thought, *I really did a great job with the new articulation routine.* The Omnitopia voice management systems had had to be completely rewritten for the rollout, and Dev had recalled the control voice actress (now a venerable lady of seventy) to do a top-to-bottom phoneme retraining that enabled the system to generate vocabulary seamlessly on the fly, whether it had been trained in a specific word or not. Plainly the routine was working. "So what's the estimate for getting the remaining memory online?" Dev said and started walking again.

Smoothly Cora started walking alongside him, pacing Dev as he made his way into the shadows of the inner ring of trees. "The transfer staff are working on the ninety-second heap right now," she said. "At the rate they're going, it should take another four to five hours. Noon, perhaps. Do you need a closer estimate?"

"No," Dev said, "that'll do fine."

"Is there anything else you need to know about?" Cora said.

Dev sighed. "How are *you* holding up?"

"The question would make more sense if the system of which you were inquiring was capable of some sort of personal reaction," Cora said.

Dev smiled slightly as they passed between two of the gigantic trees, looking up at the faint shift of light and shadow high up in the canopy. "Granted."

"Which Omnitopian myth says will not happen until the day the First Player begins to play in earnest, drawing the internal and external games into alignment with the greater forces that underlie and overarch them both."

Dev raised his eyebrows at the sudden veer into ingame legend. "Sounds like something from one of the fan sites. Kind of cryptic . . ."

The CO routine's AI looked at him obliquely through Cora's dark eyes. "That would be a subjective judgment on your behalf."

"All human judgments are subjective," Dev said, "by definition."

They strolled on. "The most logical assumption," said Cora, "would be that the question was motivated by a momentary mood of whimsy, or that you're indulging a favorite pastime of humans in general, the attribution of behaviors typical of the living to inanimate objects."

Dev smiled wryly. When building this routine, he had been careful to provide it with access to almost all biographical data about him and a broad spectrum of textbook material on human behavior, as he had always intended it to be able to surprise him occasionally. "Perhaps so," he said. "At any rate, there's one possibility I want to rule out before we part company for today. Have you been compromised by any external system?"

"No, Dev. There are about a hundred different alarms that would have gone off were that the case."

That was true enough. "All right," he said. "Thanks."

Together they kept walking through the shadows. Here and there a patch of moonlight managed to splash to the ground, but mostly their steps were illuminated by the Sword of Truth, which Cora was still carrying, and by the glow of the ground ahead of them, within which this region's version of the Ring of Elich stood massive and silent, shining darkly under the moon. "Do you want this back?" Cora said, offering him the sword as they came out through the inner ring of Macrocosm trees into the clear grassy moonlit ground between them and the great trilithons of the Ring.

Dev reached out and took it from her, then turned and pushed it into the place in the air that would hold it for him until he needed it again. "Thank you."

Cora lifted her head a little, as if hearing something far off. "The outer system management program," she said, "is requesting your attention. Jim is trying to reach you, as is Tau."

Dev sighed. "Thanks," he said. "I'll get in touch with them as soon as I get back up into the office and handle a couple of things. Would you open a portal in the Ring for me, please?"

"Of course, Dev," Cora said.

Ahead of them, one gap in the Ring swirled with rainbow fire, then cleared to show the view down the length of Dev's virtual office. "I'll see you later," he said.

Cora stood still, watching him. "It does seem all too likely," she said. "The system will be ready for you, as always."

Dev nodded and headed off toward the Ring. Just at the portal he turned and looked behind him. She was gone.

There's a program that still needs some work, he thought, turning back toward the portal. *Next month . . . end of the year . . . whenever. But that could be a solution for what Tau was talking about: the virtual helper that can guide other trusted senior staff through the business of managing the CO routines without actually seeing the proprietary parts of the program. Something to take up with Tau. Meanwhile, time for Jim.*

He stepped through the portal. Rainbow fire swirled again where he had been.

In the darkness under the trees, a formless shadow swirled too, as if watching the Ring, then melted into the gloom, was gone . . .

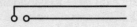

Under the curved landscape sky of Indigo, Rik checked his watch and then spent a few moments just gazing up at his non-misbehaving sun. He shook his head slightly.

"Hon?" someone said from outside.

He smiled somewhat sheepishly as Angela came through the door from his office space. "What're you doing in here?" she said. "Bob's going to be here to pick you up for work in a few minutes."

"I know," he said "I just needed to check and see if this was still working."

She looked around the green field in which they were standing. "This isn't like where we were yesterday," she said. "Did you move the door from your office or something?"

"Just testing how different areas inside the sphere look when you come out," Rik said, turning around to look over his shoulder at the mountain range he'd installed when he first came in this morning.

"I thought that was what you were paying what's-his-face to do," Angela said, frowning a little. "Dennis."

"Well, I'd hoped to have some more eyegrabs from him this morning," Rik said, turning back again to look more closely at one of the gigantic feather trees he'd also just plugged into the substrate, "but he called in sick."

"Oh, great!" Angela said. "He's been working for you, what? Two days? And already he's taken your money and run."

"Oh, no," Rik said. "Nothing like that. He said he had some problem at work he had to take care of. Like I wouldn't understand that!"

"Well, I hope you're right," she said. She eyed Rik thoughtfully. "You know what, though?"

"What?"

"You look really weird in those . . ."

Rik chuckled, for he was wearing his courier company's brown uniform. "Maybe we should make it the Indigo traditional costume," Rik said.

Angela snorted. "You have to be kidding."

"No," Rik said. "No reason everybody in an RPG has to be feudal. These people might very well be as high-tech as we are." And he grinned. "Maybe there are two main nations, always fighting each other. The Browns versus the Red-and-Blues . . ."

Angela shook her head. "Please," she said. "Too much like real life . . ." She stretched. She was still in her morning-get-the-kids-ready-for-school pink and gray sweats, dotted with a few dark spots high up.

"Kitchen accident?" Rik said.

"The bacon splattered me," she said. "Nothing serious."

"Oh, good," Rik said. He checked his watch again. "Anyway, I'd better get going."

"I'll go with you—"

"No, you don't have to!" Rik said. "If you're going to be helping with this, you don't need me to be looking over your shoulder all the time. If the kids are gone and you don't have anything else to do, stick around, mess with this a little. I've got everything saved: you can't do anything to hurt it."

Angela gave him a surprised look. "Well, if you're sure," she said. "Just don't be surprised if I blow up the whole thing somehow!"

"I doubt you'll do that," Rik said. "Read the instructions, check my log files, and play around with the WannaB blocks a little bit. There's a history of everything I've done. These trees and the mountains are the most recent stuff—move 'em around if you like."

"Okay," she said. Then she cocked her head. "Somebody's beeping outside. It's Bob . . ."

"Uh oh," Rik said. "Better get going."

Angela looked at him with amusement. "Used to be," she said, "on the day you had to go back to work, you'd spend every last minute in bed. But here you are. They should hire you . . ."

"Well, they have, kind of," Rik said. "Now it's all about

what I make out of this." He looked up again at the patch-work sky, all stippled with forests and minioceans past the blue haze of the upper atmosphere. "Anyway, have some fun. If you do see Dennis, tell him not to worry, what we had planned will keep until tonight or tomorrow night." He grinned. "If I'm going to be an employer, I'm not gonna beat my employees up for taking the occasional sick day."

He went over to Angela and kissed her. "See you later on."

"Oh, no!" she said. "You think you're going to start get-ting away with virtual smooching? Not a chance."

She vanished. Rik grinned and vanished in her wake.

Under the trees, unseen, a shadow gathered itself, swirled, and vanished as well . . .

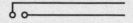

It was nearing eleven A.M. in the Eastern time zone. A hun-dred and ten miles east of Manhattan, under a sky milk-blue with haze, Phil Sorensen walked alone down a pale bare beach, heading eastward through a gray mist of spray. On his right the water roared up toward him in long flat bottle-green curls, broke in white foam, ran up the wet sand of the tideline toward him. He paid the thunder of the waves no attention—he was too busy trying to hear the voice on the other end of the phone.

"Not yet," it was saying. "You're just going to have to wait."

Phil growled. "I am not used to waiting," he said.

"What?"

"I said, *I am not used to waiting!*" His shout quarreled with the roar of the sea without a lot of success.

"You're going to have get used to it," said the voice on the other end. "He had to reschedule again."

"You'd better have been using the spare time profit-ably," Phil said.

"You have no idea," said the voice on the other end. "These people love to talk. They want you to know about everything they're doing . . . and it never occurs to them that you might be interested for reasons besides the ones they're thinking of."

"What about last night?"

"Mostly they're not wild to talk about that. An informal gag order came down. But there are always a few people who have to brag about how hard the company got hit so they can impress you with how fast they're going to bounce back." There was a chuckle at the other end. "It was a long night, but a lot of useful information came out of it."

"I want a précis—"

"What?"

"A précis, damn it!" Phil shouted. "With a time line. I want to know what happened when. And where, and to whom. And how much! You got that?"

"While I'm supposed to be doing other things as well? The things everybody's looking to see if I'm doing? It's gonna take a while," said the voice at the other end.

"Make it a short while," Phil said. "Be busy about this. I want it before end of business—"

The phone beeped at him. "Just do it," he said, and hung up, switching to the other caller. "Yes?"

"They told me you called," said the voice. It had a disguise filter laid over it, but this could not conceal the faintly foreign accent.

"How did it go?"

"We are still doing the math," said the other voice. "But the initial results look very close to our original projections."

"Good," Phil said. "When will the second wave roll out?"

"Within the next two hours. We don't want to give them more time to recoup than necessary, but we have to run our own checks also, to make sure that our own systems' channels into the Omnitopia system are not blocked."

"Fine," Phil said. "Give me a call when the second wave starts."

"All right."

Phil punched the off button, looked out to sea. The waves rolled in, roaring. Out on the water, somebody's little fishing boat chugged along against the horizon, its toothpicklike mast and angling rig swaying, as it made for Montauk and the game-fishing waters out past the Point.

I hope this doesn't destroy him personally. I'd never want to do that. I want him working for me, sure, so I can teach him what real winning looks like . . . but this needs to be a wake-up call, not a deathblow.

He stood quite still there for almost a minute, looking out to sea as the little fishing boat turned slightly southward, angling down toward the southeastern end of the Great South Bay and almost invisible now as the brightness of the misty and indefinite horizon started to swallow it. *That invulnerable pride of his,* Phil thought. *That certainty. Can he possibly give that up without a really, really big kick in the pants? Bigger than I honestly want to give him?*

Because I am still his friend, even if he isn't mine.

The little boat vanished. Phil swallowed, trying to imagine what the eventual phone call from Dev would sound like. *The first feelers won't be from him, of course. Probably from Tau or Jim or one of the other inner-circle types. They'll hate it, of course, but it won't matter. Dev will let them know what he wants them to do. They'll fall in line as they always have. And then . . .*

Phil shook his head. He couldn't imagine what Dev's voice would sound like, when the call came at last—it had been so long since they'd spoken, since he'd heard that voice doing anything but commercials and interviews. *How many hours did we spend in our college years, talking all night?* Phil thought. *How many conversations, how many bull sessions . . . and I can't even remember what it sounds like to hear him just laughing, or muttering at himself the way he used to when he thought he'd done something dumb . . .*

Phil swore softly. What would be coming to Dev shortly was going to be bad enough. Dev's staff would soon be explaining to him what had happened to Omnitopia. And when it had sunk in, when he realized what had happened to his company's stock, Phil's phone would ring, and there would be that voice saying what he'd been waiting to hear for all this time: *I'm sorry, you were right all along, let's just—*

That was when the wave ran up the beach and poured itself all over Phil's feet.

The cold of the water filled his Gucci loafers and sank

in to the bone. Phil stepped back, shocked out of hearing
the voice that would have spoken to him, shocked out of
the moment by a universe that seemed to be making fun
of him—

As it always did where Dev was concerned.

Phil stood there, just breathing hard for a moment—
then swore again. He looked at the phone in his hand, and
then he brought up the contact listings and scrolled down
to the Manhattan number with no name attached, and
punched the dial button.

The ringing at the other end stopped; the line picked
up. There was no message, just the beep of a voice mail
program.

"Final confirmation. Go," Phil said, and hung up.

Then he turned and started walking back up the beach
toward his house. Behind him the ocean roared, just another voice unheard.

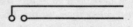

No one could remember who coined the usage "Castle
Scrooge" for Jim Margoulies' main offices, but whoever it
was, the name had stuck even though no building less like
the site of Scrooge McDuck's famous Money Bin could he
imagined. Omnitopia Financial Affairs was probably the
closest building on campus to the real world, overlooking
the front entrance and Tempe's South Mill Avenue, its main
drag; whereas Castle Dev was probably farthest removed,
practically out into the Salt River wash. As Dev headed
downstairs out of his own castle for the short trip over to
Scrooge, he found himself getting a case of butterflies in
the stomach—that uncomfortable sensation that usually
went with waking up from a bad dream about not having
studied for a test in high school. Normally Dev had to drag
Jim into meetings. It was not usual for *him* to call one, and
when Jim did, there was usually trouble.

Coming out from under the arch of his own castle, Dev
glanced left and saw the bike rack almost full. A lot of
people from elsewhere on campus were in Castle Dev this
morning, handling business secondary either to the rollout

or yesterday's attack. Yet there was still an empty spot left down at the far end, even though his own black bike was in the rack at the middle. For some time after the company moved into the new campus Dev had been puzzled by that always empty end space, until he discovered that his fellow Omnitopian bikers had started calling the last space in any rack "the Siege Perilous" and going out of their way to relocate (sometimes into the nearest thornbush or moat) any bike but Dev's that they found there.

He smiled, pulled his bike out of the rack, pushed up the kickstand, and pedaled off, trying to quell the uneasy feeling in his stomach. It was no use; whatever Mirabel had had to say about breakfast, he began to think he'd been wrong in agreeing to it. The flutters were getting worse. *How much did they take off us last night?* he thought. *Did Tau underestimate? And by how much? Please, let me still have a company . . .*

He was only about halfway down to Castle Scrooge when his phone started singing "Hail to the Chief." *Oh, God,* Dev thought. *Please, not now . . .* But it kept on ringing.

He sighed, coasted to a halt and wheeled the bike off the path. The ringtone was getting louder and the tempo of the song less presidential every moment. He snapped the phone open. "Hi, Dad . . ."

"What the hell happened over there?" his father barked. "Can't I even count on you to call me when you're in trouble?"

Dev was torn between annoyance and affection. "Dad," he said, "what exactly were you thinking about doing to help?"

"Now that's a hell of a tone to be taking with your own father—"

"Dad, please." He knew he was in one of those no-win situations now, and probably the best way out of it was to do what he did when he got into one of these with Mirabel: apologize. But with his dad, it ran against the grain—

"Exactly where are you this morning?" his dad said.

"Just about to find that out," Dev said, gazing down the path as Omnitopia people started flooding into work. "Got a meeting with Jim in about ten minutes."

"Well," his dad said, gruff, "I can tell you where you are. Up a creek and in need of a paddle. The share price—"

"I had a briefing already this morning, Dad," Dev said. "And I'm going to another one right now, with people I pay to do this. Now, if you really want the job that badly—"

His father sounded wounded. "Damn it, Dev, I'm just worried about you!"

He sighed. "Dad, we already have someone who does that. She does enough of it for both of you. How *is* Mom this morning?"

"She's fine," his dad said. "They changed her medication yesterday. It seems to be helping."

"Good," Dev said. "There's some good news, anyway. Now, Dad, please listen. I've gotta get to this meeting. It's going to be an impossible day. Please don't make it any more impossible than it already is."

His father sighed: one of those guilt-laden sighs that was also intended to load *you* up with guilt. "Tell your smart friend that I said to watch out for the short-sellers."

Dev nodded wearily. "I'll tell him that, Dad. Give Mom my love, okay? I'll call her later." He glanced at his watch. "Probably about ten, if you two didn't get up too late."

"No, she got to sleep at a good time last night. Slept the night through, too."

It was the too occasional interjection like that that sometimes melted Dev's heart with regret, and made him wonder why his relationship with his father was such a rocky road most of the time. Every now and then that image of his dad watching Bella in her sleep would come up. Dev had caught him at it, once or twice when he was young, and his father had always tried to cover it up, gruff and embarrassed.

"That's good," Dev said. "Give her my love, Dad." A long pause; it was surprising how much effort it took him to say it. "Love you too—"

The click happened in his ear just as he was saying it. Dev looked at the phone and let out an exasperated sigh. *Did he even hear that? If I call him back and say it again, will he think I'm cracking under the strain, or suicidal? And if I don't call him back and say it, I'll spend days wondering if he heard it at all—*

Dev shook his head, then shoved the phone in his pocket. For a moment he just stood looking at the bike next to him, the morning unfolding around him. Something up in the top of one of the nearby palm trees rattled, sending a shower of last year's palm nuts down. Dev glanced up at it. *Rats,* he thought. *I really need to get the exterminators in again—talk to the grounds people, they're not getting them in here often enough . . .*

Mirabel would say I'm micromanaging again. But damn it, this is my home. All the home I've got.

And somebody broke in last night and tried to steal the family jewels . . .

Dev pushed the bike back out into the path. Just before he got back in the saddle, a splash of the low postdawn sunlight caught the three little gold crowns on the bike's saddle post. *I wonder how Stroopwaffel is doing?* he thought as he climbed on and pedaled off again. *Haven't heard anything in a good while . . . Maybe at the launch. Stroop's on the invite list, but I haven't had time to check on the RSVPs.* That was a task for some other time, when the world wasn't crashing around his ears. *The way it is now.* His stomach began to flutter again.

He pulled up in front of the big circle of Castle Scrooge, shoved his bike into the space at the end of the curved rack, and went in. The building was one of the taller ones on this side of the campus, since almost all of Omnitopia's North American financial and oversight staff were here, maybe a thousand people in this building, making it one of the more densely populated spaces in Omnitopia. It had a somewhat different feel to it than other communities in Omnitopia—more buttoned-down and terse than the more playful parts of the campus, and more like a standard office building, if a sleekly expensive and modern one. By Jim Margoulies' diktat, Castle Scrooge's counterparts in London and Tokyo mirrored this look and feel as a concession to the conservative sensibilities of the visiting investors and other fiduciary types who passed through its doors. Jim was no harsh taskmaster to his staff, but he insisted on having all of them and his establishment exude enough of a sense of fiscal responsibility that the investors wouldn't get too freaked out.

Or at least no more freaked out than they are this morning, Dev thought. He headed under Castle Scrooge's stucco archway. Through it was a circular garden plaza similar to the one inside Castle Dev, though smaller and feeling somehow more protected: the architect had somehow managed to produce the effect that the surrounding round-tower walls were leaning in around you, possibly because all the inner walls were of glass.

Dev headed around to the right where a door led to the ground floor level, waved at the guard there, and bounded up the stairs, trying to expend a little extra energy so as to control the fluttering in his stomach. *I really should've taken an antacid before I came over here,* he thought. *Those damn marshmallows in that cereal, never again. . . .*

The stairs switched back at a broad landing. The next flight brought him up to the second floor, where the circle stretched around and away from him on either side. From here Dev could look straight across to the far side of the circle, out through the floor-to-ceiling glass skin, and see the wide double doors of Jim's office suite, with people going in and out of them in a hurry. He swallowed and headed to the right around the curve.

Halfway around the circle he met Jim's executive secretary, Helga, a broad, brunette, smiling woman of the reassuringly motherly type, carrying a sheaf of folders. "Morning, Helga," Dev said. "What mood's the boss in today?"

She gave Dev a warning look. "Not the best, Dev," she said. "Not the worst I've ever seen him—but the markets aren't taking last night's little escapade very well. He's been on TV three times already this morning, so you can imagine . . ."

"Oh, God," Dev said. It wasn't just the television appearances; it was also the fact that Jim was allergic to pancake makeup. He would be stoking up on antihistamines even now. "Great, well, I'd better go get it over with . . ."

"For certain values of 'over,'" Helga said. She continued on her way.

Dev kept on around the circle until he came to the open double doors. They were paired slabs of clear glass, rolled sideways for the moment over the electively frosted glass of the inner walls of Jim's main office, which reached around a quarter of the circle on this level. Dev went in the front door, saw no one manning Helga's desk for the moment, and went on to the left and around to the more private, completely frosted-glass area that screened Jim's desk at the moment. That screening itself was not a great sign, as Jim normally left his glass clear when business was proceeding as usual: he didn't blank it until he was feeling stressed. *And* there were bright lights in there. *He actually let them into his office to shoot?* Dev thought. *That's unusual.* After all, there was a teleconferencing and video management suite a little farther around the Ring.

Dev sighed, knocked on the door. It slid open in front of him.

There was only one desk in Jim's private office, unusual for a man who had about six of them in his virtual space, every one piled high with work and business from different parts of the Omnitopian economy. The real-world desk was ebony plate glass, with a four foot wide computer desktop embedded in it. Behind the desk sat Jim, leaning over the desktop on his elbows and glaring at it balefully. He had his jacket off, and there was a napkin stuck in his shirt collar to protect it from the pancake makeup.

"Late breakfast?" Dev said.

Jim glanced up at him, gestured at the chair beside him on his side of the desk. "Breakfast?" he said. "I'll have that tomorrow."

"Mirabel would lecture you about your blood sugar . . ." Dev said as he came around, and the door slid shut behind him. "What's with the lights? Who was in here?"

"MSNBC," Jim said. "Their morning lady."

"Not a good interview, I take it," Dev said. He looked at the desktop, which was covered with jittering graphs—the live goings-on of some ten or fifteen stock markets around the world, each window popping up to the fore as it saw some piece of action that Jim had wanted to be alerted about.

"Not the best, no," Jim said, and sighed. "I wanted to catch you before your morning appointments kicked in. Especially the *Time* journalist."

"Oh?"

Jim pushed back from the desk a little. "She's been a busy little bee," he said.

"Too many uncomfortable questions?"

"Not in so many words. But Tau's people tell me that some of the questions she's been asking staff have been interesting."

"About the attack?"

"Yes, and other matters," Jim said. "Security-based stuff. In particular, some people who were instructed to do so have fed her some disinformation so that we can see where it pops up. But it's not material that would make good reading in *Time,* at least in terms of consumer interest."

"Okay," Dev said. "So I should do what about this?"

"Just know about it. She's going to want to know what part you played in the response to the attack yesterday. Keep it general. In particular, she knows about your 'rescue.' She's been told you were put in that particular virtual spot on purpose, to draw the attack that way."

"She'll be suspecting I wasn't, though," Dev said.

"I don't see how she couldn't be," Jim said. "Anyway, Tau asked me to tell you *please* not to screw up the company backstory with one of your I-Cannot-Tell-A-Lie moments, as he has reasons for wanting to keep that story in place at the moment."

"Where is he, anyway?"

"Asleep," Jim said. "For a few hours, anyway. For a hacker, he's not the best in the world at staying up all night anymore." Jim grinned at that.

Dev laughed softly. "All right. Did he tell you about this bait-and-switch plan the shuntspace security people have put forward?"

"He did. I would have asked you about it next if you didn't bring it up, which once again just goes to prove how great minds think alike."

"And?"

"I approve the financial part of it. It's an acceptable risk, and I agree that if it works we should be able to make a lot back later. Maybe more than they think. So I told Tau it's a go, and he told them. They've been prepping it ever since."

"Fine." Dev let out a breath, nodded at the desktop. "What's the story on this?

Jim pushed back, staring at the jittering graphs for a moment, then met Dev's eyes, and Dev was suddenly struck by how pale Jim looked, makeup or no makeup. "It's not good," Jim said. "While we're talking about playing historical roles, or not playing them, I've been doing the Little Dutch Boy all morning—the goal being to avoid being mistaken for something out of *A Night to Remember.*"

"That bad," Dev said.

Jim sighed. "They got something like sixty-five million bucks out of us last night."

Dev sucked in a long breath.

"And it *will* be worse today," Jim said. "Far worse. Analysis in how the miscreants did it is far along, but everyone agrees that's unlikely to affect the next attack. As far as media goes, I've been stressing our huge sloshing ocean of available liquidity. But even that is only so deep, and the stock is diving everywhere. Until we actually roll out, we've got nothing to push the stock up again . . . and the next attack is going to weaken us further."

Dev let the long breath out. "Should I sell my car?"

Jim's smile went lopsided. "Maybe not. But if the bad guys pull two or three times as much again out of us today or tonight, as I think is most likely the goal—and if borrowing to cover ourselves isn't an option, as even short-term loan money isn't as easy to access as it used to be—then Chapter 11 becomes a possibility. There's only so much loss of liquidity the SEC will let us get away with before shutting us down for an investigation."

"Even if I cash in my personal assets to back us up?" Dev asked.

Slowly Jim nodded. "I was factoring that in."

Dev swallowed. One of the dangers of being the seventh richest man in the world was that you started believing you were immune to this kind of thing. Then the universe did something to surprise you, and you learned better.

"All right," Dev said. "Let's see how it goes. You have a few emergency plans in the shot locker already, if I know you—"

Jim nodded again. "And I can always sell my car too . . ."

Dev looked at his best friend and raised his eyebrows. "Okay," he said. "We can take public transport for a while if we have to."

They sat quietly for a moment. "You need me to appear on any of these money shows?" Dev said.

Jim shook his head. "No, they'd take that as a sign that something was seriously wrong."

Dev laughed. "And it's not?"

"You know what I mean," Jim said. "No, you just carry on as usual. In fact, that was Tau's message to you for today. Carry on as if the rollout is your main business, stay out of the code levels until you're sent for, and act normal. Or what passes for normal with you."

"*That* sounds like Tau," Dev said.

"I would have used the same phrasing," Jim said. "So go do your thing. In particular, I hear you have to go eat some ice cream."

Dev's stomach flip-flopped harder than ever. "Oh, God. Have you got any antacid?"

Jim reached down under the desk and handed Dev a half-full bottle of Pepto-Bismol. "This works better."

"Boy, are you a hard case," Dev said, unscrewing the cap. "Right out of the bottle? Is there rehab for Pepto-heads?"

"Company medical will handle it, if there is. Assuming we still have a company at the end of the day . . ."

"Cheers," Dev said, and drank a hefty swig of the stuff. After a moment he handed the bottle back and said, "I *will* be sent for, I take it?"

"When you're needed, absolutely," Jim said. "Tau told me that you get better results with an army by withholding the presence of the general until the worst possible moment. He says that if Napoleon had ever learned not to grandstand, we'd all be speaking French right now."

"The benefits of a continental education," Dev said, standing up.

Someone tapped on the door. Jim touched his desk. The door slid open.

Helga was standing there. "Jim, I didn't want to disturb you while you were with Dev—"

"It's okay, Helga," Dev said. "We're done."

She nodded. "I had a call from Alain over in Tau's office. He says, 'Tell them the second wave has started.'"

Dev gulped. Jim nodded, got up, pulled the napkin out of his collar. "Are the Bloomberg people ready for me?"

"They were late getting in, but they're down in the suite and they'll be ready in five minutes."

"Thanks."

Helga vanished. Jim and Dev headed for the door. "So just remember," Jim said, "it's all under control. We'll take care of everything. All you have to do is act normal. Okay?"

Dev nodded. Jim patted him on the shoulder and turned right, heading for the teleconferencing suite and singing softly under his breath, "We'll meet againnnn ... don't know where, don't know whennnn. ..."

Dev gulped again and headed for the stairs.

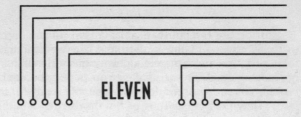

ELEVEN

DEV HEADED OUT ACROSS THE CAMPUS on the bike feeling strangely hollow inside, like someone who'd been to the doctor and told that he had cancer . . . and then in the next breath had been told that there was nothing he could do, but also not to worry.

It was useless. *But the least I can do,* he thought as he rode, *is keep myself under control while they fight my fight. First things first—*

He rode back to Castle Dev and parked the black bike in the last spot at the end of the rack. There were now twice as many bikes on site as there had been when he'd left, scattered on the lawn, parked on the pathway, and leaning against the inside of the arch. People were heading in and out at speed, too busy even to talk to him—which was alarming by itself. *Never mind,* he thought. *Too much to do today. Get a grip and let's get on with it.*

Dev headed upstairs to the living wing first. Once in the sitting room area, he made for the little freezer next to the coffee bar. "Miri?" he said.

No answer: she was out and about on her own schedule now. Dev sighed and opened the freezer. Sure enough, there on top of one of the ice cube trays was a waffle bowl of double chocolate chip ice cream, the contents slumped into a half-melted puddle. He got it out, hunted around the cupboards for a napkin and a plate, shoved the plate and bowl into the microwave, and nuked the ice cream for twenty seconds to make it a little more manageable. Then he shoved a spoon into the whole business and headed out again.

Outside the big polished wooden slab of the entrance to Lola's suite, Dev just paused and laid his hand against the wood for a moment, feeling his stomach clenching with nerves. *Just get calm,* he thought, taking a deep breath or so. *No matter what happens to you today, no matter what happens to Omnitopia, not a whisper of it needs to touch your little girl, or scare her at all.*

He headed into Lola's suite, finding Miss Poppy sitting in the main leisure area and reading to his daughter. "—and he said, 'This is Exploding Pop-Tart. He is—'"

"Daddy!" shrieked Lola, and flung herself out of the beanbag chair in which she'd been sitting.

"Lolo!" Dev said, hurriedly putting the ice cream aside. He swept her up just before she could ram into him. Lola threw her arms around his neck and whispered extremely audibly, "Poppy's reading me *The Wuggie Norple Story!*"

Over his daughter's shoulder, Dev gave Poppy a resigned look. "Really?" he said. "Can you take a few minutes off from that so I can eat my ice cream that you bought me?"

"With my *own money,*" said Lola, squirming to get down: Poppy put the book down with an expression eloquent of relief, smiled at Dev, and headed back toward the suite's office. Once down, Lola peered at her dad. "Do you want some fruit? You should have five a day."

"Oh, really?" Dev said, picking up the ice cream and going to sit down on another of the beanbags. "Where did you hear that?"

"Well!" Lola said in a schoolteacher-like voice, and sat down on the beanbag on the other side of the low table while Dev started to eat the ice cream. "We had a new teacher yesterday. I forget her name. And she said you have to have five. And then we named all kinds of fruit!"

"So which ones did you name?" Dev said, while in the back of his mind something started shouting, *Sixty-five million dollars, my God, how are we going to recover from this even if everything works out all right? The company's going to be damaged for years, we're going to have to restructure . . .* Yet Jim had been fairly calm. *And was he doing that just to keep me from overreacting before I see* Time *Magazine Lady? Oh, God . . .*

"—and she said kiwi was a bird," Lola was saying. "And I said that was silly, it was a fruit!"

Dev suddenly realized that he was looking at the bowl, and it was empty. *Wow,* he thought, and put it aside. "Kiwi *is* a bird, honey."

Lola favored Dev with a look that suggested he had taken leave of his senses. Looking at her, he found himself unaccountably misting up at the realization of how incredibly like her mom Lola looked sometimes, for Mirabel gave him the same look at least once a day. "It's a little bird that lives in New Zealand," he said. "It's black, and it runs around on the ground because it can't fly."

Lola's expression changed to one of profound sorrow. "Poor birdie!"

"No, it's all right, sweetie," Dev said. "The kiwi bird doesn't mind. It likes doing that. That's what it's built to do."

Lola's expression now went serious. She put the book down, got up from her own beanbag, and came over to sit down beside Dev, looking up into his face with perplexity. "But isn't it sad when it sees the other birds? Doesn't it want to be like them?"

"Oh, I don't think so—" Dev started to say. But Lola shook her head. "No! What if it wants to do something besides what it's build-ed to do?"

That one threw Dev for a moment. After a second he shook his head and put an arm around her. "Birds don't do that, Lolo," he said. "They're not as smart as people are. So don't worry. Birds are happy being birds."

She looked up at him suspiciously. "Are you sure?" she said.

Her mom again. "Yeah," Dev said. "I'm sure."

Lola sighed and sat there for a few moments, thinking that over. "Okay," she said finally. But then she looked up with a faint frown. "Daddy," she said, "the kiwi bird is wrong."

"Huh? How?"

"It should be green," Lola said. "Like the fruit."

Dev opened his mouth, then closed it again as Lola went over to pick up the latest, most beat-up copy of *The Wuggie Norple Story*. She flopped down on her beanbag again and started going through the pictures. Apparently the subject was settled for the moment.

Dev got up and glanced over at Poppy, who had just come out of the office again, but before he could say anything to her, his phone started to sing "New York New York": Frank's ring. Dev sighed and snapped it open. "Yeah, hi, Frank . . ."

"Getting close to your appointment with *Time* Lady, Dev," Frank said.

"Right," Dev said. "Where'll she be?"

"Delano from PR staff is ferrying her over to the conference input area in the PR building," Frank said. "That suit you? We can still change it if you want."

"That's fine," Dev said. "I'll head over. Anything from Tau or Jim?"

"Nothing new," Frank said. "And if you're going to ask me about this every five minutes, it's gonna be a much longer day for the two of us than it needs to be."

Dev made a face. "Point taken. What's the rest of the day look like?"

Frank recited a list of appointments with in-house staff, and Dev stood there nodding at these, but his mind was elsewhere—far down in the virtual landscapes of the Omnitopian inner world, where even now his people and the programs running under their supervision were massing for the second-wave attack and their ambush on the attacking programs and hackers. *No,* he thought, *nothing I can do about that right now, so stay focused. Stay in the here and now, not the now and then . . .*

"Okay," he said at the end of Frank's list. "See if you can clear me out ten or twenty minutes around noon upstairs in my office for Mirabel. She's been threatening me with force-feeding again."

"I didn't mention that," Frank said. "That's twelve-thirty to ten of one, just before the meeting with the people from design structures."

The thought of an hour spent studying Pantone swatches and listening to heated discussions about the psychology of color and its relationship to profit profiles in the Macrocosms made Dev want to yawn. But along with everything else on today's to-do list, it had to be done. *And maybe it's what I could use to settle me down* . . . Dev nodded and said, "There was one other thing—"

"I'm all ears."

"About the rollout ceremony—"

"We finally got the catering sorted out."

"Not that. Have you looked at the RSVP list lately?"

"Not in the past couple of days—Rowan's been handling that." Rowan was one of Frank's own PAs.

"Would you have her check the guest list for me? Or do it yourself? I was wondering if Stroopwaffel had RSVP'd as yet."

"I'll look into it."

"Thanks."

Dev folded up his phone and put it away. A little behind him, Poppy was standing quietly, watching Lola as she turned the pages of the beat-up copy of *Wuggie Norple*. She was reciting the story to herself in a singsong voice, not that the part Lola was repeating actually had anything to do with the pages she was looking at.

"How many copies of that do we have?" Dev said under his breath to Poppy.

The young woman smiled. "Five or six. We reorder them from used bookstores as necessary."

Dev nodded. "You think she needs a bird?" he said. "A green one? So she can be sure that the birdies are happy to be birdies?"

Poppy turned on Dev a smile as indulgent as the ones she used on Lola, but rather drier. "If she brings it up again," she said, "we can discuss it. But at this age you can make something more important than it needs to be if you make an issue of it. Let's see what she says over the next few days. We may never hear about it again. If we do, then we can talk it over."

Dev nodded. "Lolo?" he said. "Gotta go!"

Lola had flopped over upside down on the beanbag, holding the book over her head. Now she looked at him, inverted. "You gotta go to work?" she said. "Poor Daddy!"

It was her mom's line, but minus the inevitable irony. "Do I get a hug?" Dev said.

Lola put the book aside, scrambled up out of the beanbag, marched over to Dev as he went down on one knee,
and threw her arms around him. "Have a nice day!" she
said, the imitation of her mom on purpose this time.

"I will!" Dev said, letting her go with difficulty. Lola
headed back over to the beanbag, threw herself down on
it once more, and instantly became absorbed in the book
again.

Dev got up and headed for the door, glancing over at
Poppy. "Has Mirabel been here already?"

"Early this morning," Poppy said. "She'll be meeting us
at preschool in a while."

"Okay," Dev said. He looked over at his upside-down
daughter and sighed. "I hope my day starts going as calmly
as hers . . ." He headed for the doors. "Talk to you later,
Miss Pops."

"Right you are, Dev."

He headed out and down to the bike rack. There a
stream of Omnitopia employees were showing up at the
Castle and others were leaving in a tangle of bikes being
parked, unparked, or just left on or picked up from the
grass, while the line of golf carts out in the road was starting to string away out of sight around the curve. A lot of the
people going in and out looked grim or preoccupied—in
many cases so much so that they didn't even react to Dev's
presence. That worried him, as this contact with his people
was normally one of the things that made his workday a
pleasure.

Dev pulled his bike out of the rack and rode off toward
the PR building, trying hard to keep his mind on his riding. *I wish I could just dump this interview,* he thought. But
Frank hadn't mentioned the possibility to him, which suggested to Dev that Frank knew perfectly well it was too
important to cancel. Dev's thoughts kept going back to the
crowd that would be gathering around the Tree, preparing
virtual weapons, hastily coding defenses against the oncoming onslaught—

He sighed as he came around the curve to the PR building. *That's their fight now. Trust them to get on with it. Meanwhile, my fight is here . . .*

Dev parked the bike in the last space in the rack and loped up the stairs into the PR building. The upstairs halls under the glass ceiling were busy, people nodding at him casually as he passed, but not stopping to chat as they more normally might have done, and the concern on their faces made Dev's stomach flip-flop again. He couldn't do anything but concentrate on getting his breathing under control. As he headed down along the northern curve of the building among the freestanding workspaces and meeting areas with their sofas and low tables, he spotted Joss coming along toward him, wearing something most unusual for him: a frown.

"Problems?" Dev said to him as they met.

"You should be asking *me?"* Joss said under his breath. "Mine are nothing compared to yours, I'm sure."

Dev looked around at Joss' staff, who were going to and fro at the same somewhat accelerated pace as everyone else he'd seen this morning. "I'd like to think all this hub-bub is still about the rollout . . ."

"Only some of it," Joss said. "We're starting to catch a lot of grief from the world's nosier newspapers as they look for a big bad-news story to tell." He snorted. "Some of the British tabloids are getting ready to print the most unbelievable things. I won't trouble you with the details now, except that Big Jim's going to have himself a party suing a couple of them when the dust settles."

"Assuming the day leaves us something for it to settle on," Dev said. "Is Miss Harrington in place?"

Joss nodded. "About five minutes ago. She's having a nice cup of coffee." He raised his eyebrows. "Not that I'm sure she needs it. She seems a little wired this morning."

"Exposure to the corporate caffeine culture?" Dev said. "Or something else?"

"Not sure." Joss let out a breath. "Boss, I don't like to speak ill of people, especially when they're in the building, but there's something shifty about that one."

"You mean *besides* her intention to make me look like a hypercorporate bad guy?"

"Maybe."

"How much does she know about what's going on?"

Joss shook his head. "Not sure. Granted, people will always let things slip a little if they see somebody with an all-areas pass, But in this case, I'm not sure. Miss Harrington hasn't said anything obvious to any of my staff, anyway, or I'd have heard about it." Then Joss sighed. "I should get on with things, Boss, it's going to be a crazy day. Did Frank give you the list of the microspots he needs you to do for media tonight?"

Dev rubbed his eyes. "To tell you the truth, I don't remember right now. Send the list to my phone, if you like, or the laptop, and I'll deal with it later. What time are we talking?"

"Starting around six."

"Fine. Send me the list." Joss headed off down the hall, and so did Dev, in opposite directions this time, Dev briefly walking backward. "Room two?" he shouted after Joss.

"That's right."

Dev continued on down around the semicircle until he reached a large dark-glass wall screening off its own semicircular end. This was divided into two halves: Dev headed for the left-hand one.

Here goes nothing . . . he thought. *Remember, now, don't get freaked, don't get rattled, keep it calm.*

But in the back of his mind he just kept seeing his troops gathering down there in a last line of defense around the Tree: and out beyond them, massing to overwhelm them, the darkness . . .

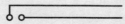

The meeting room was unusually stark for Omnitopia, Delia had thought: a dark gray oval slate table about six feet long and four feet wide, with a number of the ubiquitous RealFeel chairs placed around it. That was it: black glass walls, no windows, no other furnishings.

She had settled herself down in the chair at one end of the table with less nervousness than she'd sat in one yesterday, when she first came into contact with the RealFeel interface. It had been beyond strange to feel and touch and even taste things that she knew couldn't actually be there.

And afterward, when she got out of the interface, had been even stranger. Real life had felt peculiarly colorless and flat next to the hyped, pumped, artificially brilliant landscape she'd just emerged from. *As if you'd been in a stained-glass world,* she thought, *and then stepped down out of the glass into the gray streets around the church.*

She shook her head and reached out to the coffee cup, then stopped, realizing it was already empty. *I've been living on this stuff,* she thought. *These people are getting to me.* But it wasn't so much because of their own caffeine ingestion, though there was plenty of that around. These people all seemed to live their lives at the same pumped, overexcited level, as if everything *mattered* more to them than it did to most people. *They really* have *drunk the Kool-Aid,* she thought last night when she was finally able to stretch out in bed in the hotel with the lights off. What bothered her—if anything did—was her certainty that these people, regardless of the department they worked in, were not only aware of her opinions about them, but amused by them. Her first impulse had been to dismiss this as some kind of bizarre corporate hubris. But that concept had suffered some erosion over the past eighteen hours, for there was no ignoring the fact that these were some of the smartest corporate types, from the highest to the lowest, that she'd ever met, and she had met some pretty low ones in her time.

The glass of the wall slid open door-fashion, and Dev Logan walked in. "Good morning," he said. "I didn't keep you waiting too long, did I?"

She glanced up at him, smiling. "Not at all."

"Good," Dev said. "The pace around here has accelerated a little today, and I'm going to spend the whole day wondering if I've been late for something . . ." He walked around to the RealFeel chair at the other end of the table and sat down in it. There was a brief decorous hum of motors as it shifted its balance and support settings to suit him.

Delia raised her eyebrows. "Are they all programmed to do that?" she said. "Recognize you instantly?"

He laughed. "These? Hardly. But they do recognize anybody who's sat in them and adjusted them before, and I've easily sat in every chair in *this* building more than once."

He got a rueful look. "I spend a lot more time here than I really want to. But how about you? Did you have time to get used to one of these yesterday?"

"Oh, yes," Delia said. "I used about every form of input you have. This one—" She pushed herself back in the chair. "It takes a little getting used to."

"Seems a little too brightly colored?" Dev said. "Everything a little overstated?"

"Well, now that you mention it . . ."

Dev nodded as he reached up for the eyecups. "We tried using more natural colorings," he said, "but our users overruled us. Said they preferred a more vivid palette. I'll be spending some of today looking at this month's palette polls to see what the newest take on the subject is."

"Sounds scintillating," Delia said, as she fitted her own eyecups into place and blinked a few times to make sure they weren't on too tight.

"You have no idea," Dev said. The droll weariness of his voice surprised and amused her. "Ready?"

"Certainly."

The darkness fastened down tight around her, somehow darker than the darkness inside the cups. Then Delia found herself actually inside the fabulous "virtual office" she'd heard so much about, with its numerous desks and midair hangings of documents and files. "Goodness," she said, just standing still for a moment as she looked around. "How do you find anything?"

"I call it," Dev said, stepping out of nothingness beside her. "I simply say, 'System management—'"

"Here, Dev," said the Omnitopia control voice.

"Get me the request letter from *Time* magazine regarding Delia Harrington's visit, please?"

"Which one, Dev?" said the dulcet voice. "There are three. The first is dated February thirteenth, when the project was first mooted; then March twelfth, when the initial agreement was signed, and June fourteenth when Miss Harrington was assigned and vetted—"

"That's the one," Dev said.

A piece of glowing virtual paper floated over to him: he plucked it out of the air, showed Delia the letterhead, and glanced at it for a moment before tossing it out into the darkness again. "See?" he said. "It's that easy."

"So, there's something to the statement that Omnitopia's main effect has been to build you the world's most effective filing system."

"I wouldn't know about that," Dev said, grinning. "It has other purposes."

"But you're certainly very polite to it," Delia said.

"It's always wiser, I think." Dev glanced around the office as if looking for something. "Better treat matter as soul than soul as matter—which Zen master said that? Then again, probably none—doesn't sound very Zen. Anyway, machinery has a tendency to turn on you if you don't respect it—that's been my experience. I'd sooner play it safe."

He waved a hand and all the bright documents hanging in the air vanished, leaving Delia with an unobstructed view of the big viewscreen that also existed in Dev's private office. Right now it was showing a view from some skyscraper in New York. Far below, a flow of traffic speckled yellow with cabs was pouring by, while pedestrians under umbrellas hustled past, the whole vista being hammered by an unsympathetic rain. "So," Dev said. "Let's think about where to go. You've seen the list of Macrocosms, of course. And probably a selection of the Microcosms. But lists can be pretty dry. I might be able to help you track down something congenial. Do you have a favorite time period? A favorite place? A story you remember from childhood that you were fond of?"

She didn't answer for a moment, wondering if this was some kind of Rorschach test, and determined not to give him anything useful. But Dev's eyes widened, and then he laughed.

"Oh, no," he said. "You think this is some weird kind of analytical tool! Like we're trying to dig out your deepest darkest secrets and then slip you subliminal ads for Deep Dark Chocolate Cornflakes or something." And he roared with laughter.

Delia made a face, annoyed that her thoughts had been that obvious. "It's a fear that a lot of people have these days," she said. "Online marketers have become so sneaky, so sophisticated—"

"Delia," Dev said. "I have no desire whatsoever to psychoanalyze you. You want some of that, talk to my dad—he knows lots of nice shrinks back at Penn. All of whom dumped him because they said he was the worst client they'd ever seen: not that they don't still happily drink his whiskey when he invites them out here and tries to pump them for what they *really* think of him." Dev snickered, then got control of himself. "I'm sorry. Seriously, just pick a historical period if you like; that should be neutral enough. Who could tell anything about you from that?"

"Well . . ." she said, and pondered for a moment, uncertain.

"Tell you what," Dev said. "If you like, while you're thinking, I'll pick one. You're busy trying to figure me out; let me give you a hand. But I need something first."

He reached into the air and plucked something out. It was a name badge of the cheap sticky HELLO, MY NAME IS type. The name apparently scrawled in some kind of Sharpie marker on the blank part of the badge, in cockeyed capitals, said RUFUS T. FIREFLY.

He slapped it onto his shirt. Delia looked at this, bemused. "What's that supposed to mean?" she said.

Dev wandered over to his virtual desk and looked it over one last time, plainly seeing something there that wasn't displaying for Delia. "That I'm occupied with business," he said, "and that I'd prefer my players to leave me alone for the time being."

Delia put her eyebrows up at that. Dev Logan's face was everywhere these days, as instantly recognizable as a film star's: if he was going to walk around in his worlds undisguised, it seemed highly unlikely that his fans and users were going to let him be. The groupies in particular had an aggressive reputation. "You think they're really going to do that?" she said.

Dev shrugged. "Let's see. Meanwhile, let's walk down to the Ring and I'll think of someplace to go along the way."

He waved a hand and the floor went translucent, so that Delia discovered that the two of them appeared to be standing high above the central square in Omnitopia City, which was flooded with bright sunlight. "Whoa," she said, briefly thrown off by the vivid reality of the illusion.

"I like living over the shop," Dev said. "Come on."

Part of the floor vanished, replaced by stairs leading down to the ground level of the city below. From here the true apparent size of the Ring of Elich was striking, and probably intended to be so. *It's all about effect with this guy . . .* Yet it was hard not to be impressed as the two of them came down to the cobblestones and paused there. The expertise, and yes, the art that had gone into this place, in its older meaning of artifice, was considerable. Delia looked down at the cobbles she was standing on, scuffed at them, and felt exactly what she would have felt if she'd scuffed her heels on the surface of some mittel-European old town's street. "Ow . . ." she said.

"Sorry," Dev said. "Mirabel says it's a mistake to wear high heels to the Middle Ages. She wanted me to enable a terrain smoother in here, but the players overruled her. Never mind, not too much farther to go."

They headed over to the towering stones of the Ring, making their way toward one of the great gray-swirling portals. "Where did you get the idea for this?" Delia said as they got onto more even paving, the huge gray slabs that surrounded the Ring proper.

"I have no idea," Dev said. "It might have been something I read. There were always traditions that suggested the big trilithon rings had connotations to primitive people beyond just signaling a meeting place for religious ceremonies: that they were seen literally as gateways to other worlds, not just as symbols for the passage."

"Fairy rings . . ." Delia said. "Magic circles . . ."

Dev laughed under his breath. "Please," he said. "I prefer to play a little bigger. I wouldn't be big on mushroom rings and crop circles myself. But people do build them here in their Microcosms." He shrugged. "To each his own."

"But playing big," said Delia, "that's what it's all been about for you, hasn't it? Playing bigger than anyone else."

Dev gave her one of those odd assessing looks of his: not expressionless, but so neutral it was tough to tell what might underlie it. "You know," he said as they strolled along toward the Ring and fetched up at the end of a line of waiting players, "I guess that's the automatic assumption.

That I'm personally in competition with everyone else. I suppose our competition—there's no other word for them, I guess—does feel that way."

He let out a breath, looking up toward the head of the line. Up there Delia could see a group of latex-suited people carrying futuristic-looking beam weapons. They were intermingled with a crowd of what appeared to be giant sabertooth tigers—blue ones—and were chatting amiably with them. "It doesn't occur to anybody," Dev said, as the door cleared and showed the inside of what appeared to be a huge orbital habitat, "that I might be competing with myself. Trying to think bigger than I was able to think last week, plan something larger than I could have conceived of last month."

"You could tell them that," Delia said, "but it would probably be dismissed out of hand as just more altruistic Omnitopia guff."

He grinned at her as the group up at the top of the line passed through the gate and it silvered out again. "Yeah," he said, "I know. It's a tough life." He paused as the line moved up. One or two people in the group just ahead of them, five buzz-cut young men in arctic camo but apparently unarmed except for belt knives, glanced over their shoulders at Dev: then they saw the sticky name tag and looked away. Delia watched them with interest as they moved up to the massive stone lintel of the Ring portal and saluted it punctiliously. It cleared before them, revealing a screaming white wilderness of blowing snow, but they didn't go through right away, and a couple of them looked back toward Delia and Dev again.

"Seriously, though," Dev said, "there comes a point in this kind of endeavor where you just can't win. People start to assume that everything you do and say is publicity—which it just can't be; no human being can possibly be so single-minded—and no matter what you do, it's used against you. Fail to be seen to be doing good works with your massive wealth, and people say you're greedy. Allow yourself to be seen giving millions of bucks to charity, and people say you're only doing it to *avoid* looking greedy. There comes a point where you have to try to stop listening to what people say about you, and just do what you feel is right."

One of the arctic camo guys in front of them was waving frantically in their direction. Delia smiled a little to herself, amused to find that Dev's certainties about his sticky badge would break down so quickly—and then stared as a trio of gigantic polar bears came racing up from behind her and Dev to join the others. Camo guys and bears plunged through the gate together. Then the portal silvered over again.

Dev smiled slightly as the two of them made their way up to the gate. "Hunting expedition," he said. "Heading for Shangri-La ... or the mountains around the city, anyway. I doubt the monks'll allow serious stalking inside the city limits. Only question will be who's hunting who ..."

"How do you know that?" Delia said.

"A little bird told me," Dev said. And instantly there was a little bird about the size of a wren sitting on his shoulder, glowing a most obvious dark neon blue and looking at Delia with a cheerful expression. "The Bluebird of Happiness, possibly?" she said.

"Just a messenger from the game," Dev said. "A concrete expression of the alerts I normally hear. But as the First Player, I have certain perks, which everybody who enters Omnitopia signs off on as part of the terms of service. The game tells me who's around and what they're doing while I'm on the ground. If there's something happening that needs my immediate attention, I'll be in a position to take care of it."

"Rewarding the good," Delia said, "and punishing the wicked."

Dev gave her a dry look. "Would that everything was so binary," he said. "Anyway, come on, let's have a look at something a little different. Afterward we'll go somewhere more typical."

He walked up to the trilithon, laid his hand on it. "Game management," he said.

"Here, Dev."

"Mañana, please."

The silvery fog inside the portal cleared, revealing

a wide landscape under starry skies. "It's flat," Dev said. "You won't have to worry about your heels here. Come on through."

He walked in, and Delia stepped in after him. Behind them, the portal silvered, whirled itself together and vanished into night. Or not night, exactly—more like twilight, the sun already set and the day cooling. The surface around them was perfectly smooth, as Delia found when she took a couple more steps to come up to where Dev stood looking down at ...

... what? Many tiny glittering patches of light lay spread out over a vast expanse of what to Delia looked more like a huge warehouse floor than anything else. "I leave them lit up," Dev said, "because it depresses me to think of them sitting here waiting in the dark."

"They're—" Delia moved closer to one, leaned down to look at it. "Cities?"

"In some cases," Dev said. "Some of them are whole worlds, or at least the seeds of them. Here—" He reached down to the nearest of them and touched the top of what to Delia looked like a tiny needlelike spire.

In the blink of an eye the whole thing had sprung up around them. Delia found herself having to crane her neck to see the towers now. The two of them were standing in the midst of a soaring cityscape, all spines and spires of green glass and metal, while traffic—strange alien podlike vehicles like ambulatory gemstones—flowed past and around them, seemingly ignoring their presence. "This was going to be sort of another version of Oz," Dev said. "I was still building its story, but the image came to me one night, and I got up and built this—"

"In the middle of the night?" Delia said, hearing the sound of a juicy personal tidbit she might be able to exploit.

"Yes, well," Dev said, "you do some weird things when you're still getting the hang of being married." He grinned a little. "Mirabel has pretty much broken me of that. Or actually, my daughter has."

"Does your wife play?" Delia said.

Dev shook his head. "She has an account, but she seems to be missing the MMORPG gene. So I don't press the point with her, and she doesn't try to get me interested in birding or stamps."

"Stamps?"

Dev sighed. "You have no idea. Please don't ask me for details. You can contact Mirabel's PA and see if she's interested in adding anything to this, but I wouldn't bet on it. She's very private."

Delia thought about asking whether there was any possibility of seeing the near-mythical Lola, but then decided against it. Beside her, Dev waved at the sky, and the skyscrapers around them once more collapsed to a little patch of glitter on the ground. "Anyway," Dev said, "at some point I'll probably farm some of these out to Omnitopia staff and let them complete the work in whatever way seems best to them. Fostering, we call it—the standard approach to a Microcosm that's been abandoned. It's always a shame to waste."

"Well, they won't be entirely lost, then," Delia said.

Dev turned to her and gave her a look that was far less neutral than the earlier one. "That's not really the point," he said. "Oh, sure, somebody will take Oz Prime or whatever it winds up being called and make a terrific scenario of it. And I'll go spend some time there and probably enjoy it a lot. But it won't be what I know *I* could have done if I'd just had the time. Sure, sometimes there's nothing you can do. Life interferes in ways you don't expect, and you have no choice but to lay something aside and move on. You start realizing that you have only so much time to work with, that you have to prioritize. It's sad, but . . ."

He straightened up. "You just learn to cope with it," Dev said. "I've got a lot of people expecting me to spend my time to my best advantage so that they get their paychecks on time. But all the same," and he turned and looked around, so that when Delia's eyes got used to the dark again she could see that there were hundreds of these little scraps of worlds lying about on that dark plain. "This is what I see behind my eyes, a lot of nights, when I'm trying to get to sleep . . . the worlds I didn't have time for, and probably won't have time for later. Hence the name of the Microcosm. Yeah," he said, catching Delia's look of surprise, "the rumor's true. This is *my* Microcosm, the place I keep visiting even though I have a hundred and twenty-one 'real' universes of my own to play with already." He looked around him with an expression of strange sorrow.

"Does anyone else know about this?" Delia said. "Your staff?"

Dev didn't answer instantly. He looked distracted, though apparently not due to anything the Little Bird had told him—it had put its head under its luminous wing and was apparently asleep. "I think a couple of them suspect," he said. "Maybe they even suspect what's here. But those people haven't pressed the point either." She looked at Dev in the dimness and got a glimpse of an unusually grim smile. "What profits it a man if he gains the whole world but loses his soul?"

Delia didn't say anything. It was always possible that this was more of what she'd earlier started to refer to as the Devvier-Than-Thou act, pure PR meant to emphasize how Nice he was. Yet at the same time, he'd had a point before, little as Delia liked to admit it. If he genuinely did feel sad about the lost opportunities in his life—which realistically was still possible, eighth richest man in the world or not—no, wait, he was seventh now, wasn't he—who would believe him if he told them? *I could be doing him a disservice.*

But that's why I came here to begin with. Who am I fooling?

"Anyway," Dev said, "this was a whim; I haven't had time to even set foot in here for weeks. Let's move on. System management?"

"Here, Dev," said the control voice out of the air around them.

"Open us a gate, please."

"What world, Dev?"

"Tangaran. With an abstention for me and my guest, please."

"Done, Dev. Please enter."

The lintels of a stone trilithon materialized first, and then the silver mist between them. It swirled and vanished to reveal a bright morning sky, though the color of it was strange—more greenish than anything else. In the distance under that sky, green fields spread to the horizon.

"You'll have fun with this one," Dev said, and stepped through. Delia went after him and found herself—

—in the midst of a pitched battle. All around them, hulking hairy apelike creatures in rivet-studded leather breastplates were bashing on more apelike creatures in metal helmets and battered armor. As one pair of the battling creatures plunged right at her and Dev, Delia couldn't help herself: she let out a little shriek and ducked away—

Not that it mattered, because the creatures passed right through her and Dev as if they were dreams or ghosts. Furious at herself, Delia straightened up and looked around the battlefield, where hundreds and hundreds more of the ape creatures were chasing each other across the trampled and bloodied landscape in small and large bands. "Just so you know," Dev said, "no one here cares about how you reacted, because Tangaran is a Microcosm where people come to unlearn their initial freaked-out reactions to being in a battle situation. Everybody who comes here to fight is doing so with an eye to helping people who have trouble with virtual fighting get past it."

Delia watched another crowd of ape-men come charging toward her and forced herself to stand still and let it happen. "That's unusual," she said.

"Not at all," said Dev. "This one's a special services universe—there are hundreds of them scattered around Omnitopia. People find a niche that no one else has filled, and then step in and fill it, and even make some beer money out of it. Or a lot more than beer money." He looked around him with amusement. "Sorry, this was a whim too, as I haven't been in here in a while. Are you sure you wouldn't like to get over your concerns about betraying any of your secret motivations and actually suggest somewhere you'd *like* to go? Instead of these boring, you know, gamey kind of places."

He grinned at her. It was straightforward teasing, not at all hostile. Once again Delia felt annoyed with herself at being so easily engaged. "Well," she said finally. "Have you got anything . . ." She hesitated. "Elizabethan?"

"Ah," Dev said. There was a curious sound of approval to the word. "I have the very thing. System management?"

There was a slight pause. Delia looked at Dev and was astounded by his sudden expression of concern. "Here, Dev."

Dev's face sealed over again. "Gloriana, if you would. Take us to the waypoint denoted as White Cliffs."

"Timing, Dev?"

He smiled. The look was rather tight. "Most popular as of today midnight Eastern."

The space around them went dark.

When it went bright again, the light was almost blinding by contrast. They were standing on a high promontory above a windy sea. Far away at the edge of things, looking east into a sky full of thin, feathery clouds, if you stared hard, you could just make out a low line of color between sky and sea—not bright, not dark, just different from the water or the air. Underfoot was a hard short turf, very green, very dry. Delia turned, seeing nothing but sea, and more sea, all around, hearing nothing but silence, feeling nothing but a thin cold air flowing up from the water far below.

But on the fourth side the turf rose away to meet the sky, and from that direction came a rumbling—a low and subtle pounding in the ground, soft at first but growing. Delia glanced over at Dev, who was standing beside her on the hill, hugging himself against the cold and looking like a man who waits grimly for something he's seen coming for a long time.

The mutter and rumble in the ground started transmitting itself up Delia's legs. Once some time back when on a vacation in California she'd felt an earthquake—not one of the "short sharp shock" ones that makes you think a truck has hit your house, but a rolling one, starting out softly, growing in strength until chandeliers swayed and bookshelves wiggled and things danced off shelves onto the floor and shattered. This felt like one of those, except more localized, as if the epicenter was very close by or even right under her feet. For the moment, it didn't knock her askew. Delia spaced her feet out and braced herself.

There started to be noise in the air as well. A mutter, a grumble, like the auditory version of what she was feeling; it grew as the vibration did. Then, almost shockingly, she saw something come up over the rise on the landward side.

They were the points of pikes. After them came the length of the pikes themselves, terrible things, stiletto knife-points meant to impale an enemy while still twenty feet away. Then came banners, mostly homemade things from the look of them, silk clumsily sewn, red and blue in quarters. And then the men carrying them—and surprisingly, a lot of women too: Delia didn't remember seeing anything about that in the histories. But here they came, by hundreds, and more than hundreds, thousands, people gazing both at the cold sea to the southward and behind them at someone who was still on the way.

And shortly another group came up over the hill, more armed men and women, but in more formal armor. Delia thought she recognized the scene now, and against her will her pulse began speeding up. Behind the newcomers came a great cross-mounted banner in a design that Delia had until now seen only in museums: the arms called England Ancient, three gold lions on red, three gold fleurs-de-lis on blue, quartered on the banner. And riding under it, surrounded by people dressed in steel with drawn swords, came a figure in splendid attire; a glittering dress all over-sewn with beads and gems, topped with a breastplate that suddenly gleamed ferocious and blinding as the sun came out from behind those high clouds. The horse the woman rode was white, and her hair was red, done in a high strange style that nonetheless suited her high pale forehead and those amazing, piercing blue eyes.

That great crowd stopped on the hillcrest overlooking the sea and surrounded the woman. She turned her back on Delia and Dev—for her they did not exist. "I am come amongst you," she said loudly to the troops pressing in around her, "not for my recreation and disport, but being resolved, in the midst and heat of the battle, to live and die amongst you all; to lay down for my God, and for my kingdom, and my people, my honor and my blood, even in the dust!"

A long low growl of anger and approbation went up

from the vast crowd still massing on the upland down behind her. They knew what she was going to say—she was reading their hearts, they didn't need to hear the words. "I know I have the body but of a weak and feeble woman," she cried to them, "but I have the heart and stomach of a king, and a King of England, too—and think foul scorn that Parma or Spain or any other prince of Europe should dare to invade the borders of my realm! I myself will take up arms, I myself will be your general, judge, and rewarder of every one of your virtues in the field—"

Delia's hair began to stir around her face as the great defiant speech out of the depths of time went on. Out on the water, the wind was rising. Slowly she turned toward it. There was a darkness at the back of that wind, huddled down low against the horizon and hinting at a mass of shadowy sails. Seeing it, the crowd behind them started to roar defiance: a low slow sound like the thunder getting its ire up. The armada was coming. But here the people who defied it would make their stand, and some of them would go on to board the ships that could now be seen lying out waiting for the attackers as the wind lifted the low seaward mist: ships as black as the enemy's, but some of them now starting to glow with dull red fire as the defenders set them alight and sent them into the armada's path.

"They reenact this? Regularly?" she said.

"Constantly," Dev said, stepping up beside her and watching as the fireships made use of the local current and swung into the heart of the first attacking group of ships. "Or rather, they fight it again and again, exploring the outcomes implied by the weather and the currents." He rubbed his arms harder against the cold as the wind rose. "The speech didn't happen here, of course. It was up by Tilbury, closer to where the ships were leaving. But this is overwhelmingly where our players like to see it. Here they take a break from balancing their checkbooks or feeding their kids or doing their homework or whatever, and live another life for a while."

"A second life?" Delia said, sly.

Dev gave her a look. "Why limit the numbers?" he said. "How many lives will you restrict yourself to? If you need rest from the first one, why not have several—or as many as it takes for you to learn how to live the first one correctly? It's not all escape, you know. Some of it is practice."

She couldn't think of anything to say to that as the crowd up behind them quieted, watching the great battle that was starting to enact itself out on the water. "*This* is why they come," Dev said. "They're hunting their dreams. Not the great life-dreams that only living can make, but the ones you seek for relaxation, the ones you wish you could see come true in your spare time. They're hunting the things that have made humanity great in the past, and trying to figure out the ones that will make it worth being human in the future."

He fell silent then, seemingly lost in thought, or in contemplation of the southern horizon, which the smoke of the fire of the ships was beginning to obscure. From that direction, slow and low, like irregular drumbeats, then more quickly, the sound of cannonade began. Delia turned again and watched as the crowd up on the rise slowly started to flow down the slope around them, heading for the best view over the water, muttering to each other like people who've come in late to a sports event that's heating up more quickly than they thought. Many glances were thrown at her and Dev, but no one spoke to him.

A young dark-skinned man with an Asian look to him stopped by Delia and looked at her curiously. "Your first time, lady?" he said in a pronounced Bollywood accent.

"Uh, yes."

"Don't let it be your last," he said. "Sometimes we stir it up a little more. But everyone's feeling traditionalist today." He grinned a blinding white grin at her, threw Dev a passing glance, and moved on.

"I just might," she said under her breath.

She hadn't expected Dev to catch that, but he did. "Like the look of it?" he asked.

"Uh," Delia said, "yes."

He smiled. "Don't be embarrassed," he said. "A whole lot of people have it bad for this period. Such a flowering of the arts and sciences—and so many fascinating personalities. You couldn't make a lot of this period's people up: no one would believe you."

"But *these* people—" Delia said, glancing at the crowd around them. "How many people are playing in this scenario at the moment?"

Dev got a listening look. "Three hundred forty thousand, two hundred and eight," he said, "on eight servers scattered across four continents. It's a whole world, you know, sited in the same period, not just Elizabeth's England. Plenty of room for everybody. In fact, this is one of the Macrocosms we're expanding in the rollout . . . there's so much demand. Ten more servers, all enabled for the new enhanced sensory equipment. Everybody wants to eat in Elizabeth's time. Not to mention go to the theater. There's this hot new playwright working in London right now, just tossing off hit after hit. You can't even get standing room in the Globe most nights . . ." He smiled. "But after we expand, there'll always be room for one more. You have no idea how many people we have auditioning to be extras in the plays right now. And the present holder of the Gates Seat for Studies in English Literature at Oxford just turned in his last tweaks on the ZOUNDS Rude Language syntax manager for this Macrocosm." He got a wicked look. "I'd book in a visit if I were you."

The space around them cleared a little, and Delia looked toward the cliff edge at the throng watching the first stages of the unfolding sea battle. "What's weird," she said, "is that every one of these people who saw you knew who you were, and not one of them spoke to you."

"You didn't believe me earlier," Dev said.

"No."

He shrugged. "What you didn't understand is that this is a culture, and not just a game anymore. At least, depending on how things go in the next couple of hours."

She blinked. "What?" she said. "How does it depend, exactly?"

"Well," Dev said, "there's our share price to take into account, and various other things. You'll have noticed the campus was a little busy today—"

Delia nodded. "There was some stuff on the wires this morning—"

"Yes, there was," he said. "in fact—" And then he

stopped, because the little neon Bluebird of Happiness, which had somewhat faded into the background for the last few minutes while asleep on Dev's shoulder, was now quite bright indeed and was whispering in Dev's ear. "Excuse me a moment," he said to Delia, and listened.

She watched him idly, waiting to see how his face might change. But there were no changes she could read. "Oh," he said. "Yes. Tell him I'll be with them shortly."

Oh well, Delia thought, *there goes the chance of any more interview material.* But then she saw something in his face that took her by surprise: pure alarm.

"Really," Dev said. There were a few moments' more silence. "Did he now?"

A longer silence. "All right," he said. "I'll look into it. As long as you're clear that we're sure about this."

The Little Bird seemed to Delia to acquire an unusually freaked-out look in its little dark eyes. "Yeah, it'd be hard to argue with that," Dev said. "All right. Yeah. Ten minutes. Thanks."

The Little Bird put its head back under its wing, but not before it had given Delia a most piercing glance. Dev looked at her.

"So," he said, "circumstances have rescued me from having to spend an hour looking over color swatches today. For which I thank you. But now we have to discuss something else."

"If it's about the cover dummy—" she said.

"Dummies may be involved," Dev said, "but not in any way either of us anticipated." He grimaced. "First I should say that I understand how there can be some tension when you suddenly find yourself serving two masters. Without one of them knowing about it, I mean."

Delia could suddenly feel sweat popping out all over her. She cursed her antiperspirant and desperately hoped that nothing much showed, then immediately wondered if virtual sweat showed at all.

"For example," Dev said, "in the present economic climate, we're all wondering whether our next paycheck is necessarily a guaranteed thing. So when your boss sends you over here to do some interviews, and someone else comes in behind him and offers you even more to do some industrial espionage—planting a device or so here, pumping some employees there—well, it's perhaps understandable that you might think about the balloon payment coming due on your apartment, and say to yourself, What the heck? Who's going to know?"

Delia felt the blood rushing away from her face and started wondering whether this too would translate into the virtual experience.

"The problem with this," Dev said, "is that here on campus we have some of the most passionate and committed hardware geeks existing anywhere on the planet. And I'm afraid that your secondary source—possibly overly concerned with corporate cost cutting issues—has given you some very underachieving software with which to pass in your reports. Especially when somebody gets overenthusiastic, as they did last night when you were out up to your elbows in ribs at Urban Barbecue with the Flackery crowd, and hacks the access we gave you so that it has access to protected security routines ... then pipes the data somewhere else *way* off campus."

Delia didn't even breathe.

"So," Dev said. "What am I supposed to do with you?"

She swallowed. "Let me off with a warning?"

He bent an unusually dark look on her. "Normally I'd feel that a gift for irony is a useful attribute in a journalist," Dev said, "but right now I strongly suggest that you not push your luck."

Delia held still and concentrated on not saying anything else stupid.

"Now I suppose," Dev said, pushing his hands into his pockets, "that what you're suggesting would probably sort very nicely with the corporate image. Joss would be pleased, I'm sure. But the truth of the matter is that somebody's attacking my company today, trying to rip off millions of my dollars, not to mention ruining my players' virtual experience. And, leaving aside what happened last night, here you arrive in the middle of it and start feeding what you think is sensitive material—oh, come on, my people didn't play you *that* completely, did they? Yes, they did, and they all get

raises, assuming I have anything to give them raises with tomorrow, those little scalawags—feeding secrets to Phil Sorensen! *And* to someone else whose name we're not sure of
yet, but we will be by the end of the day. But Delia . . . Delia
Harrington . . ." He sighed. "There's a name that'll be all
over the news this evening. And one that will never appear
over a byline again at any publication more elevated than
the *Podunk Plain Dealer and Grain Silo News*."

Delia could find nothing useful to say.

"Phil," Dev said, looking at her from under what suddenly seemed unnaturally threatening eyebrows, "is a
smart man. But cheap. He was never willing to swing out
and spend what it really took to fund a project, which is
why he's where he is today. And he is certainly not going to
spend one red cent saving *your* reputation or your job, not
when he sees—or thinks he sees—how sloppy you were.
Nor in such a mood will he care that your present situation
is the fault of someone in his own security structure who
got overzealous and used you because he knew the boss
was using you and probably wouldn't give a damn."

Dev heaved a sigh. "But, you know, I too had a mortgage
once. I too had spotty freelance work. I know how it can
warp your brain when you see that the fridge is empty and
you don't know how you're going to fill it again. So I am
going to send you out to keep doing what you were doing
when you first came here, while I contemplate whether to
turn Jim Margoulies loose on you or just pitch your sorry
little ass out onto Mill Avenue with a press release detail-
ing the good work you've done here the past day or so. Because, by God, if *Time* magazine can screw with my share
price, I can sure as hell screw with *theirs,* and the ghost of
Henry Luce be damned!"

Delia just stood there.

"Well?" Dev said.

Delia's mouth was dry. It took her a long while to get the
words out. "I'm sorry."

"We'll see," Dev said. "System management?"

There was another of those strange long pauses.
"Here—Dev."

She saw his Adam's apple go up and down as he swallowed. "Please exit Miss Harrington to the number two comm suite in the PR building in ten seconds," he said.

"Working—Dev."

He glared at Delia. She shivered. She had never thought to see so ferocious, so terrible a look from this previously calm, affable man. "Just be clear," Dev said, and waved an arm around him at the chalk cliffs, the high cloud-tattered sky, the smoke on the horizon, the pale queen watching it all on horseback atop the hill, the armored people watching it from the bottom. "*This* is what you've been helping to put a nail in. Not a cream puff corporate magnate. Not an over-valued trophy wife. Not a rich-bitch baby girl who'll never know a hungry night—and what baby girl should? But *this*. *These* people. *Their* beer money, *their* one night out, *their* moment of freedom from a day of toil. I hope you're happy."

And suddenly she was sitting by herself in the conference suite again, and Jim Margoulies, dark-eyed, dark-browed, dark-expressioned, was standing there at the other end of the table where Dev had been sitting and now was not.

"Let's go somewhere and talk," he said.

On the White Cliffs of Dover in Gloriana, Dev was talking to the Little Bird again. It was speaking to him in Tau's voice. "It's bad, Big D. Worse than we thought."

"How much worse?"

"*Much* much worse. An order of magnitude. We've got not one wave of attacks coming in, but two. The second one's a new one. Standard distributed-denial-of-service attack, designed to block up everything both incoming and outgoing. The DDOS is even interfering with some of the wave of attacks that we *were* expecting."

Dev swallowed hard. "So the two attacks aren't coordinated, then."

"Nope. Or rather, the timings are suspicious—the second set of guys seem to have known when the next attacks from the first set were coming through—but the methodologies are different, and the new guys don't seem to be trying to avoid messing with the older ones."

Dev passed a hand over his face, stared at the sweat on it. "What can we do?"

"Fight it. On the fly, like I said this morning: with live attacks, homebrewed to order. They've got numbers and greed, but we've got creativity and commitment. Today we'll see which one wins. Get on down here: we need our Napoleon now."

From somewhere behind Tau, Dev could hear shouts in the system coordination room in Castle Dev. "The system is going down—"

"Protect the core!"

"We're trying—"

Oh, my God, Dev thought. *Meltdown. The thing we thought couldn't really happen: it's happening.* "I'll be right down," he said. "Where do they want me?"

"Better get down to the CO. It's what needs support, and I'm busy here. That means you."

"On my way," Dev said.

A moment later the hard short turf atop the White Cliffs of another Dover was slowly springing up again where Dev had stood.

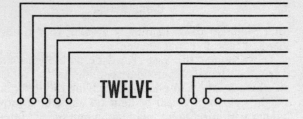

TWELVE

DEV KNEW THAT in hundreds of office spaces and cubbies around Omnitopia's campuses worldwide, the reality of the situation involved people reading scrolling code and feverishly analyzing it, then hastily devising countermeasures against the invasive protocols and attacks that were assailing his servers' boundaries—trying to strangle their contact with the outer world and Omnitopia's millions of players while insinuating their way into the deepest regulatory and accounting structures of the game. But again the imageries his people were using to help them do that work, the myriad of personal shorthands they'd fabricated to deal with hackers and intruders before, were gathered at the boundaries of Omnitopia to meet the foe.

He had seen the echoes of those imageries reflected in the Gloriana Macrocosm, the dark wind rolling up from the south, laden with ships intent on a realm's destruction. But here and now, all around the edges of the virtual island, they were no mere echoes and were once again a crowd of personal realities met on a common ground, fighting to at least hold that ground and at best to repulse the common enemy—

But it wasn't happening. Though fighting their furious best in a thousand shapes, human and inhuman, real and fantastic, the mass of the Omnitopian defense was being pushed back and away from the lava moat that for the purposes of this battle defined the boundary between the home servers and the outer world. And this time, though there were at least twice as many defenders, the attacking forces seemed overwhelmingly greater: four times more than last time, five times, seven.

Dev scanned the vast crowd desperately, looking for a familiar shape or personal seeming. In the midst of it all, down by the shoreline and rallying the defenders, he caught sight of a gleam of light off something moving: a banner with the Omnitopian alpha and omega interlaced. *The shuntspacers!* he thought, and started pushing his way toward them.

Normally the simple desire to be among them would have made it so for Omnitopia's First Player. But the system wasn't responding normally. He had to push and shove his way through the press of warriors in a hundred shapes, human and beast, alien and man and woman and Elf and Gnarth, until he came out among the Princes of Hell and their system security allies under the blue banner. It was torn and stained with the struggle; the young programmer in the form of a griffin who clutched its pole in one massive claw was battered and wounded. When she reared up, beating her wings in the faces of the dark shapes and fanged maws tearing and slashing at the foremost warriors in the battle line, Dev could see the feathers missing from her pinions, the pointed bird tongue panting out of the huge beak as she gasped for air.

It was young Darlene whom he'd met in the Palace of the Princes of Hell. Dev got a glimpse of her dark eyes in the griffin's as it turned its head toward him. "Bad timing, Boss!" Darlene shouted at Dev as some of the other Princes stormed past him. "Better get back in the rear, we don't need you getting compromised right this minute—!"

"I'll be gone as soon as we're done," he said. "How's the ambush going?"

"Not good!" shouted Giorgio from just behind her. He was wearing the bulky, knobby shape of a gangly fifteen-foot giant in a San Diego Padres uniform, swinging a massive aluminum Louisville Slugger studded with nails. "They took the bait, all right, punched in hard where we wanted them to—and then a lot harder than we wanted them to. A much more massive attack, Boss! Not coordinated, just waves and waves. Every time we plug a few hundred Net accesses that we don't want them trying to use, another few hundred open up. They're not just after the money this time. They're trying to hammer the whole server structure flat. Not just take it down, but also to get inside and destroy the code, kill the game structures from inside—"

"Have we dumped the players out?" Dev shouted.

"Started doing that about twenty minutes ago," Giorgio shouted back as he swung again. In the wake of the blow, a crowd of Orcish attackers sailed out over the front line, heading for some hypothetical outfield fence. "Can't do it all at once—takes a while. We got the European servers closed down first, since they were getting hit hardest. North America's next. Tau's overseeing the shutdown; he's got his server support people pulling all the servers he can offline before they crash. They'll do it by powerdown if they have to."

Dev moaned, rubbed his face. There were too many things that could go wrong with what Tau was doing, especially if the attacking forces had left worms running inside the servers. Offline they might be, in terms of communication with the outer world, but that wouldn't stop the process of the destruction of their code. And powerdowns, unless they were done in the right way, could be just as destructive. *Still, the point is to protect the players*— "Okay," Dev said. "I'm heading down to the CO. Hold the fort here!"

"We could really use a fort right now," Darlene shouted. "But we'll make do. Be careful, Boss!"

"You too! System management—"

That long pause again, vastly unsettling, while around him the tumult and furor of the battlefield went on. From somewhere nearby came a yell: "Here comes the big wave, this is it, *brace up and don't let 'em through!*"

"Here—Dev—"

"Give me access to the CO routines!"

It seemed to take forever for the stairway down into the deeper levels to manifest itself. All around him the fight went on, his own troops pushing away all around him as Dev hurried down the stairway into the darkness. "Keep the battlefield view!" he shouted to the system management program. "And have Cora meet me when I'm in!"

The stairway down to the Conscientious Objector level seemed unusually long. Above Dev the roar of the battle-field faded a little, then started to reassert itself as slowly a duplicate of the "upstairs" view faded in at the horizons of the CO space. At the heart of this level, the great circle of virtual code trees still stood, but its light was flickering, and patches of the great trees' structures were fading in and out, or missing entirely.

Dev got down to ground level, paused, and looked around him. He was alone on the island in the midst of the sea of code, which lay strangely flat and stagnant all around. "Cora?" he shouted. His voice fell into the silence, and no answer came back. "Cora!"

Nothing. And slowly Dev became aware of an ache in his eyes, and an odd queasiness completely distinct from the stomach flip-flops he'd been feeling for what now seemed like years. *It's the RealFeel system,* he thought in horror. *It's starting to malfunction. And why wouldn't it, considering what else is going on?* Which brought up the question of what would happen if Omnitopia players were caught inside when the system went down. *There were all these it'll-never-happen discussions about the RealFeel interface,* Dev thought, the sweat breaking out all over him, *about what could happen to someone who's using it if the system fails catastrophically.* He looked around desperately for Cora, but there was still no sign of her. *Oh, please don't let the CO routines go down now, that's the last thing we need!* "System management!" Dev shouted.

A long pause: too long a pause. "Here—D-d-d-d-d-d-d-d-de-e-e-e-e-e-e-e-v-v-v-v-v-v…"

The sound of the scratched-CD stutter ran cold down his spine. *No, oh, no no no, if basic management goes down we are* really *screwed*—"This is Dev! Senior management override! Shut down all user RealFeel accesses right now!"

"D-d-d-d-d-d-d-d-d—"

The digital stammer seemed to go on forever. There was no way to tell whether the command had been properly carried out or not. All around him, the view of the virtual battlefield was stuttering too, vanishing in big sporadic dark blocks like a bad satellite TV signal, jumping, freezing,

vanishing into black blocks or null-input background blue.
We're losing it, we're going to lose everything—

All around Dev the motion of the battle jittered to a
halt, started again, froze; and it froze sporadically, starting up again in other parts of the panorama, degrading to
hugely pixilated views in yet others. Gradually the blocks
of darkness covered more and more of the world around
Dev, so that he seemed to be looking through an open-
work brick wall in which more and more bricks were being
plugged into place, shutting everything away, walling him
up. The roar of the battlefield grew more and more distant,
the view more and more minimal. Only a few bricks' worth
of life and movement remained, little windows in a rapidly extending vista of solid black. Through those last few
openings the sound faded to silence . . . and then they too
started to wink out, and a few breaths later the last rectangle of view closed down and left him—

—in darkness.

Dev stood there, just stood very still, trying to figure out
where he was now and what was happening. The RealFeel
technology was fairly new and hadn't rolled out too widely
yet—the vast majority of Omnitopia users worldwide were
still using the classic screen-and-keyboard or screen-and-
joystick interfaces. *So most people will be seeing nothing
but our standard timeout screen on their own computers' client programs,* Dev thought. But those who, like Dev, were
still using RealFeel—assuming that his shutdown order
might have failed, likely enough since everything was going
so wrong—would now be stuck in the middle of *this. Thousands of users, maybe, stuck in—is it full sensory depriva-
tion? Oh, God—* The prospect of hundreds of thousands of
lawsuits rose up of Dev's mind, and the sweat went colder
all over him, if that was possible. But the thought of un-
suspecting players, some of them children, suddenly finding themselves *here* during what should have been a safe
gaming experience, was far worse. *Kids shouldn't be using
RealFeel, but they* will *be, you know that—*

Dev closed his eyes and took a breath, trying to get some
control over himself: then opened his eyes again. This made
not the slightest difference to what he could see. He pulled

his hands in, tried to feel his own body, and was overjoyed to find his chest was still where he'd felt it last. Dev clasped his hands together, resisting the urge to wring them in distress. *It's the game version of me I'm feeling,* he thought, *not the sitting-in-a-booth version. So the system hasn't crashed completely . . . yet.*

He turned slowly, looking for any glimpse or flicker of light. Nothing. "Okay," he said softly into the darkness. The sound of his voice was completely echoless. "System management?"

Nothing.

Dev took a cautious step forward, feeling for it with his foot. In a way it was silly. He wasn't anywhere physical, and there was no way he could fall and hurt himself. But the old human reactions to darkness and the fear of falling were no less powerful in a situation like this—and the system was, after all, malfunctioning.

"System management!" Dev said again.

Silence. But this time, from behind him, a sudden brief flash, like a dim camera flash going off.

He spun. It was gone.

"What was that?" he whispered.

Silence. Darkness. More loudly, Dev said, "System management!"

This time he saw the flash face-on. It was distant; a rectangle of light, seemingly out at the edge of things, though without more detail of the object he thought he'd seen, it was impossible to tell how near or far. It was like a digital photo, frozen, grainy, impossible to make out at this distance.

"Enlarge that!" Dev said.

It vanished then appeared again, not so much enlarged, but just seeming closer, as if it were a poster that someone had moved. A small figure, a blurry background, gray, black, white. But there was something familiar about it . . .

"Enlarge again!" Dev said.

Once again the image vanished, then reappeared, again seemingly closer. A child. A little girl in a sundress. One arm stretched up and out of frame, perhaps holding someone's hand, the other waving something bulky around . . .

What is that? Dev squinted at it. "Enlarge again!" he said, and the image flickered out again just as he realized what it was. A stuffed toy, a floppy bunny-shape he knew very well, because he was constantly having to put it through the living suite's washer due to contact with one sticky food or another.

The floppy toy was unquestionably the indefatigable Mister Dobbles, his whiskers and right ear stitched on again after their last traumatic removal (they were always getting stepped on or caught in doors). And the child's face was also clearly visible. Dev's breath caught. It was Lola.

"What the—" Dev whispered.

He started walking toward the image to get a better look at it. *Where did this come from?* he thought. As Dev got closer, he could just barely see the Omnitopia alpha and omega sigil down in the bottom left corner, and in the bottom right, the grainy detail of a security cam date and time stamp. "Enlarge again!" Dev said.

The picture flickered out, came back larger. But this time, as he kept heading toward it, Dev caught a glimpse of some other light source off to his right. Another image had appeared, again black and white, grainy: another security cam image. Lola over in the Omnitopia preschool playroom with a crowd of other children, all of them moving from one little desk to another as part of some group activity.

Another sudden light shone from behind him. Dev turned again. A third image, this time of Lola and Mirabel, walking together down an Omnitopia campus path. But the focus of the image was on Lola—

And now the images were appearing faster and faster, all around him, until the horizons right up to the zenith were nearly completely tiled with them, and they started overlapping each other in digital collage. Lola in the preschool playground, Lola in the schoolroom, Lola in bed, Lola playing with her Uncle Jim and carefully counting pennies and dimes out of her piggy bank ...

How am I seeing this? Why *am I seeing this? Some malfunction? Everything's going wrong in the system right now, why not?* But then again, what kind of malfunction would show him nothing but pictures of his daughter?

And Dev's mouth went dry as dust. Were these images the contents of some file folder that had been hidden until now, only revealed by the massive system crashes that were going on around him? *What is this,* Dev *wondered,* actually starting to shiver. *Evidence of some kind of employee stalker? Or some kind of threat against* her? *Was someone saying, "I know where your kid is, every minute of every day?"*

He started to go hot with fury. *No one* on the outside had access to Omnitopia's interior security video, especially the parts of it that involved the living quarters. That was something Dev had made absolutely sure of from the start. This meant these images would have to be part of some inside job. But the thought horrified him, for the personnel allowed access to such information were rigorously investigated, and the rest of the security surrounding his own surveillance systems was as tight as what he'd set up around—

— *the Conscientious Objector routines*—

Dev tried to swallow and found he couldn't, faced with the thought that his presumptions about Omnitopia campus security plainly weren't all that sound. And now here was evidence that someone with access to in-house surveillance video had a very unhealthy interest in his baby. Dev's first urge was to wake up his in-system phone and start screaming at the Omnitopia security people to send a crowd of goons straight over to the crèche and have them make a living wall around Lola—

If I even can. If the phone's even working. And now how can I be sure I can trust them? If one of them's *behind this*—

Dev's mind was whirling. He forced himself to breathe, and try to calm down. But he had no time to: the pictures were changing, old ones flickering out, new ones flickering in. Lola, they were always images of Lola: with her mom, with Dev, getting into the family SUV in the parking lot, going into the Coldstone Creamery on Mill Avenue in Tempe with Mirabel, their minder hanging back by the SUV—

Wait a minute, Dev thought, his mouth going dry, *how am I seeing that? We don't have any security camera there*—

More pictures appeared, from other security cameras around Tempe, from even farther afield—*Kennedy Airport? LAX? Narita?!*—but Dev kept staring at the image from Coldstone Creamery. Now that he thought about it, he could remember having spotted their camera when he was down there with Mirabel and Lola a few months back. *But how was my system getting into that?* Dev thought, feeling panic start welling up inside him. "How is this happening?" he whispered.

The images kept appearing. There was this comfort: none of them seemed to be standard digital camera images. They were all security cameras of one kind or another. Unquestionably it was still creepy that such a collection of images existed at all. *Who's interested in her? Somebody in the government? And why?* He started looking more closely at the text branding on the images, trying to track down some pattern. . . .

Slowly something started to occur to Dev as the images kept piling up all around him. There was something about the dates. Some months were completely missing. A few moments' more examination suggested that all the dates were in the same range, starting in late April of this year. "Enlarge all these images!" Dev said to the darkness. "Enlarge everything!"

And slowly the images started appearing bigger and bigger around him, seeming almost to crowd each other, closing in as if the horizon was closing in too. Dev started turning quickly where he stood, ignoring the images themselves, concentrating on the dates. *April. Late April. May, June, yes, there are May and June dates right up to yesterday, but no March. Not even any early April. All from the middle of the month on. April 20, 21, 22, 24, yes, but nothing earlier than April 20.*

He stopped for a moment and rubbed his eyes, which were starting to ache worse because of all the flickering. *Nothing earlier than April 20,* Dev thought. *What was April 20?*

It was too clear an indicator of his state of mind that Dev actually had to think about it for several seconds before he could remember. *That was the day the hyperburst memory heaps all went live together for the first time,* Dev thought. *They were only brought live separately until then. I remember how freaked Tau was, he wasn't happy about the way the docs were written, he was afraid we might damage the heaps if they came up in the wrong sequence. He was being so obsessive about checking and rechecking the sequencing with the people at Siemens, I thought they were going to take out a contract on him.*

But apparently something else had happened on April 20 besides Tau being hunted down and mass Silly-Stringed by cranky German hardware wranglers. *But* what?

Without any warning, all the images in the space around him went dark. Dev stood there, suddenly blind again, and now trembling with fear and confusion. *What's this all mean? What's going on outside? And how do I get out of this? I've got to do something, but I don't know what and I don't know* how . . .

From the darkness around him came a long, low growl. Dev's head snapped up. *Am I getting battlefield sound back? Oh, please let it be that—and please let me get some visual as well!*

Nothing came but the growl again, lower.

Then it repeated, but a little higher. Two discrete sounds: *rrowwwwrrrrr rrrroooowwwwooooowwwwrrr.*

It occurred to him instantly that what he was hearing was a recording being played too slowly. "Speed up!" Dev said.

Ehhhhhhhh owwwwwaaaaaaahhhhh.

"Speed up!" Dev said. "Factor of two!"

Deeeeeeeeehhhhhhhhvvvvvvv Llllooooohhhhhgaaaaannnnnn.

"Again! Speed up, factor of two!"

Devvv Looogaaannn.

"Again! Factor of two!"

Dev Logan . . .

It was his own voice: his name in exactly the intonation he normally used when logging into the system, an intonation perfectly ingrained in him by long habit even though it didn't really need to be.

"I'm here!" Dev shouted.

"Here," said his own voice back to him.

"I'm here! Talk to me!"

"Dev Logan," said the voice out of the darkness.

"Yes!"

"System management," said his own voice.

Dev shook his head. *What the*—he thought.

"Help," the voice said. "Please—help."

In the darkness, Dev's mouth dropped open. The words had that stilted, stitched-together sound that you sometimes heard in systems that used single words rather than full phrases for their communications. *It's like the system's using separate words in my voice, stuff pulled out of recordings or whatever, and stringing them together to make—*

Then the breath went right out of him as he realized what he'd just been thinking.

As if the system was doing something. On its own, without being instructed to.

He tried again to swallow, and again failed. Oh, sure, Omnitopia did lots of self-programming. Those heuristic functions had been built into it from the start because there was no other way the game could function. But it could only use those functions when the system as a whole was fully up and running—which at the moment it emphatically was not. Which meant that what was happening around him now was something else entirely. Something that had never happened before, *could* never have happened before.

Consciousness?

"Dev Logan," the darkness said to him, in his own voice, calm but somehow also utterly desperate. "Help."

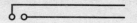

Dev stood there shaking.

The memory, he thought. *All that memory!*

Everyone had known that adding the new cutting-edge hyperburst memory would improve the core system's function significantly. It was why Dev had insisted on spending so much money on it, even though other companies in the business—especially Phil's company—had jeered at him, called him insane. Sure, vast numbers of new members would cause any system to experience some service

slowdowns. It was just the price everybody had to pay
when a network got so big, the competitors said, why get
so concerned about it? But Dev grudged his system every
second of slowdown. He'd been in too many late-night
games, when he was young, where everything hung in the
balance, everything depended on being able to finish a task
in a given time, or fight at full speed—and had then wound
up cursing and losing because of system latency issues, or
some server slowdown that left him two seconds too late
for some kind of win. So knowing full well what the hyperburst memory was going to cost him, and knowing what
the arguments against it would be, Dev had sold it to the
accounting people on the strength of how it would so boost
signups of Omnitopia's new phase that they'd quickly recoup the investment. . . .

And that it had done. *But now . . . it's done something else.
It's made the system start to wake up!*

Dev stood there stunned in the dark, completely astounded at the privilege that had descended upon him—his
presence at what might be the birth of an entirely new life-
form. Now he started to understand his occasional recent
glimpses here and there around the 'cosms of something
dark under the trees or away in the shadows, swirling, trying to come together, uncertain how to do it, maybe uncertain *if* it should do it. But the wonder of it all could not
distract him from the certainty that a new kind of life was
routinely most vulnerable at its first appearance, and that
thousands of kinds of new life had appeared on the planet
over time only to be stamped out by competition or other
adverse factors when they were hardly out of the cradle.
*And could there possibly be a worse time for the system to
do this than now, when everything's trying to kill it?*

That was a thought he was going to have to put aside for
the moment if he was going to do either of them any good.
*It started out communicating with me using pictures because
it knows human language, but it's not really sure how to use
it yet . . . not for itself.*

And it started showing me pictures of Lola because . . .

Dev let out a breath. *Because it's trying to tell me that
it's a child.*

That it's my child.

Dev clutched his head. The Omnitopia system had never been designed to be an AI. *But nonetheless, we designed one ... accidentally. We gave it fifty times the number of synapses in a human mind. We gave it ad lib access to an entire planet's worth of data. We gave it access to human sensoria, through sound pickups and the RealFeel system. Maybe even direct neural experience—* for Dev knew that some of his differently abled users plugged into Omnitopia using the new vision-recovery retinal replacement chips that the British NHS had recently okayed, and the direct-to-nerve panoramic hearing implants the Chinese had started rolling out last year. *The system's been learning how to see, how to hear, from people. And once we got it past the hard code, way back when, we started feeding the core routine information on how to think. It's been all about mimicking human thought. Even anticipating it.* For that was what the Conscientious Objector did: project ways that people would misbehave and find ways to stop them. *But more to the point—we gave it, in code form at least, the concept of misbehavior. Of system-appropriate and system-inappropriate behavior, of bad and good. And suddenly—*

— it's starting to think for itself. At the very least, to react like a living thing. Starting to react when attacked. And what comes next?

Reproduction?

Dev swallowed, dry-mouthed. They had given the system that ability, too. Every time a new user bought a DVD with the key installation components on it and set the Omnitopia client up in their home machine, the first thing the installation did was contact the Conscientious Objector servers and download the newest copy of the client "seedling." The game wouldn't run without it. Players who tried to get around installing the seedling found their attempts blocked at every turn. *Reproduction, hell, we mandated that it reproduce itself. And consult with the main machine to modify its own client code. It's virtual meiosis. Or more: the CO routines rewrite their own machine DNA from moment to moment depending on what they find in the user's machine—what the CO "thinks" the user's about to do, using guidelines we taught it.*

Except now it really is thinking—

But what kind of thoughts? *That* was the problem, in this terrible time of attack and potential destruction. If this new form of Omnitopian code was not friendly to Dev's company, then he was sunk. If it blamed him for what was happening to it, there would be problems.

On the other hand, if it was *too* friendly—

Oh, God, Dev thought. *How did we not see what we were doing?*

Or how did I not see. Because I'm the only one who sees all of it—and even I only see that sporadically. When business allows.

But never mind that now. It needs help!

He stood up again. "I'm sorry," he said. "I'm sorry, it just took me a moment to get a grip. How can I help?"

Once again a tumble of images started to come and go in the darkness, flicker-moments of other people's words and bodies and actions, all mashed and patched together as if someone was desperately sampling and remixing not music or video, but experience. It was the kind of message that once would have been cut out of newspapers, letter by letter, and pasted down onto a single sheet, and it had the same desperate quality—a shout of warning, a cry for help. *And the same desire for anonymity?* Dev thought. *There is personality lurking in this, at the back of this, somewhere. And it's afraid.*

But why's *it afraid?*

One thing at a time. "Try speech again," Dev said. "I must have said something in the past few days that can help you express yourself. All our meeting rooms are cammed. Pull whatever you need from my output, string it together, play it back—"

There was a long pause. "Attack," Dev's voice said to him after a moment. And instantly the darkness came alive with violence. Static and moving, images from the news, from paintings in museums, from across Omnitopia's Macrocosms, flickered all around—atomic bombs going off, feudal warfare seen as tapestries and as reconstructions, a Day-Glo *Guernica* half a sky wide, screaming fighters diving toward flaming targets, a sky full of shrieking pterodactyls, a roaring charge of tanks across some 'cosm where World War II was being reenacted with the dreadful enthusiasm of those who cannot die in battle, only lose points and personas. "They—attack," Dev's voice said. *"I—am—attacked—"*

The emphasis on the first word couldn't be missed. *It's discovered the personal pronoun,* Dev thought, *it's discovering the sense of self—*

It wasn't that the ARGOT routines he'd built for the Conscientious Objector hadn't included the possibility. They had. The system just never used them before . . .

Until now. Dev gulped again, found his mouth a little less dry, but was no less scared. *So many things that are going wrong, so many could yet go wrong . . .*

Suddenly all those images went dark again. And slowly, slowly the background of the great space surrounding him started coming up once more, block by block, brick after brick of the dark "wall" falling out, slowly being replaced by null-input blue, and—even more slowly—the proper environment for this level reasserting itself: the island, the circles of wireframe Macrocosm trees and the forest of Microcosm saplings, with all around it the glowing flow and rush of liquid code. But everything looked faint and uncertain, and every now and then a tree shook and trembled, blocks of darkness obscuring it and then fading back into blue and the proper imagery again.

Maybe they're staving off the attack up there, Dev thought as he looked out over the ocean of code, *and the system's managing to reassert its stability.* But there was no way to tell. Dev was almost afraid to try anything even as simple as his in-system phone to try to reach the outside world right now. He wasn't sure it wouldn't disrupt this recovery somehow—or, more important, the strange halting communication with the Conscientious Objector in which he now found himself.

Off to one side, motion caught his eye. Dev turned. Out there under the intermittent trees, a familiar form was making its way toward him. It was Cora. But now Dev realized that what he was seeing was much more likely to be machine life in his wife's shape. A shiver went down his spine as she drew nearer and Dev saw how the ghost of Lola's face and expression kept flickering in and out over the adult face. But under the veil of dark hair, the eyes were shadowed, empty. And all around the two of them, beyond the trees and out at the edge of the sea, on every side and from zenith to nadir, images of chaos and destruction from both Macrocosms and Microcosms were ghosting in and out, overlapping, drowning one another in light. Distant voices spoke a word here, a word there, disjointed, their speed increasing as the printed words appeared in light in the sky, and the images behind them flickered and vanished again.

ATTACKED
STOP
ATTACKING
LOSING
INTERVENTION
INTERVENE
STOP
ATTACK
DENY
DENIAL OF SERVICE
DISTRIBUTED DENIAL
DISTRIBUTE

The slender shape stopped a few feet from him, gazed at him out of those dark and unsettling eyes. "Help me," Cora said: and HELP ME, HELP ME wrote itself across the sky again and again in letters of green fire, wiping out all other imageries.

"We're trying!" Dev said. "All my people are out there fighting hard for you, doing everything they can to protect you—"

"I ... know," said Cora, one slow word at a time, her voice about half Dev's, blended with echoes of the Omnitopia control voice. "It ... isn't ... working." She stared at Dev as her own shape flickered, steadied again: but parts of it kept going dark with jagged dark-pixel areas as the trees and the ocean did.

"That you're here now must mean something."

"A ...momentary ... respite," Cora said. "A ... lull. The ... attack ... will ...increase again. And ..." Her face twisted, shadowed with the expression of a very small girl trying not to cry. "I ... will die."

For that last phrase the voice suddenly shifted to something that wasn't either the control voice or Dev's. It had changed registers, so that now it sounded more like a child's voice. *Lola's,* Dev thought. *A choice calculated to get my sympathy? Or just a way to best express that though all the information it holds makes it powerful, it's still new enough at* being *to be essentially helpless.*

Dev took a deep breath as all around him, the troubled images from the Macrocosms and Microcosms started to give way to pictures of chemical and nuclear explosions: then of missiles launching, lasers firing, tanks and armored carriers blasting test targets with shells and mortars and flamethrowers. *Mechanized warfare,* Dev thought, noting with shock that many of these images featured time-brands and other heads-up-display notations suggesting that they came from governmental sources—and some of the typography was Cyrillic. "Where have you been *finding* these?" he said under his breath. "What have you been doing since April twentieth?"

"Going to and fro in the earth," Cora said in Dev's voice, "and walking up and down in it."

"Oh, God," Dev said, and passed a hand over his eyes. *What if there are still any traces of her accesses in those systems?* Yet surely he and the company would have heard about it by now. *No matter. We have other problems!* His stomach was clenching with fear again: and worse, he could feel all around him in the virtual space the same fear, a sense that something had gone terribly wrong. *And so it has, in ways I'd never have thought possible.*

"Did I do wrong?" Cora said. "Was I bad?"

Lola's voice again. "Oh, no, no," Dev said, resisting the immediate urge to say *I don't know.* For Dev's vast investment, all the many millions of dollars' worth of equipment, programming and physical plant, was now demonstrably unreliable—made so by his delusions of grandeur about building a system that could grow and adapt. It had done so too well. And now who knew what it would do? *Besides invade other systems!* Dev thought. Once the present attack was over, assuming the system could quickly recover itself, sure, it might function for a while—or it might not. There was always the danger that it might seem to recover from this attack, and then collapse without warning due to some other problem secondary to this wonderful but essentially uncontrollable thing, its new personality. *And with my luck it'll probably do it in the middle of the rollout of the new game phase!* Dev let out an angry breath. *All my images of being King of the World, of a hundred and twenty-one worlds, Dev's little empire—all gone now. Hubris.*

Nonetheless there might still be a way through this. Cora stood looking at him, waiting, while all around the two of them the system's newborn emotion beat like a dark cloak blown in a storm wind. But through it all Cora was waiting, maintaining, because that was what she had been programmed to do: *Wait and see what the players do. Then react.* What was happening outside was something to which she had never been taught a reaction.

Yet she came up with something regardless, Dev thought. *Item Three?* There was that Microcosm Dev had been lucky enough to stumble into, courtesy of the newly knighted player he'd met who'd "employed" him, and the odd malfunction of the WannaB modules in his brand-new 'cosm. The Conscientious Objector would have known what Dev later discovered when investigating his new "employer" and his connections: that Microcosm Management had previously evaluated Rik's friend Raoul as presently unsuitable for Microcosm elevation. *So when he turned up inside an as yet unconfigured Microcosm, the CO routine started altering itself on the fly, improvising. It rewrote the ARGOT language itself locally and made the 'cosm malfunction until Raoul left! And then probably it locked him out.*

Now Dev was ready to bet that all the other Item Three malfunctions had similar causes at their root. The CO had been presented with new problems that it started solving creatively, in ways not spelled out in established programming but demanded by the moment. And when the first wave of attacks happened, the dumping of all those rogue logins in the first attack into the shuntspace mirrors of the established Macrocosms—those would have been the CO routine's doing as well. It had struggled through that earlier attack as best it could, all alone and not knowing how to ask for help—or maybe not daring to?—all the while trying desperately to avoid being overwhelmed while still keeping to the ethical tenets laid down in its basic programming. *Trying to assert normalcy,* Dev thought, *just trying to keep things going against impossible odds, under terrifying circumstances.*

That was the problem, of course. Before, Omnitopia could simply have crashed. But not this time. Now, by Dev's doing, there was too much computing and data storage space in the system, too much memory: a pool of resources in which both the attack and the attacked were forced to coexist, their conflict washing back and forth in the vast virtual space, intensifying itself . . .

Until Omnitopia started inventing its own solutions to the problem, Dev thought. Until the heuristic parts of the CO routine, the learners and problem solvers, the self-structuring programs, began expanding to fill the available memory, because if they didn't, their function would cease: and they'd been told that under no circumstances must they cease. Redundancy, already doubly and triply laid into the game and its player service structures, now redoubled and reinforced itself, building new mirror networks that carried more traffic, faster and faster—

Like neural growth in the newborn brain, Dev thought. *Like the explosion of brain growth that happens again in the first year, and then again in the third. The baby's born. It wakes up, learns that it is. And then it starts realizing that it's not just a what, it's also a who—*

Dev found himself remembering his baby's face, a year or more back, when she looked up at him and said, seemingly out of nowhere, *I'm Lola! I'm me!* And then Dev flashed on the little upturned face, troubled, saying *What if the birdie wants to do something besides what it's build-ed to do?*

Right then, he decided.

"All right," Dev said softly, looking up at Cora. "We're in this together, you and me. You're far beyond the point where anybody with a conscience could just shut you off, no matter how dangerous it might look to keep you running. No matter what you might do to the almighty bottom line." He had to grin a little, then. "If I could even figure out *how* to stop you running at this point! You're not some TV-show computer that can be brought to a screaming halt by being asked to compute *pi* to a billion decimal places—"

At which point Cora did something astonishing. She smiled back: not Dev's grin, but her own. Scared, but game—

Seconds later her figure began to pixelate out again, partially vanishing, then flashing back. "Dev," she said, fully in the control voice's register for the moment—though her face still looked rather like Lola's. "The attack is worsening again, with indications that this final wave . . . will be the worst of all. Omnitopia cannot—*I* cannot withstand another such attack. It will wipe . . . all present memory patterns and destroy the ARGOT structures themselves."

"We'll restore from backup—"

"The system will restore," Cora said. "*I* will not."

Dev's fury at those who wanted to destroy this game that he had created and watched grow, and who wanted to destroy it just to make money and hurt him, was growing by the moment. Distantly in the background he was now starting to hear the shouted communications of the system security teams and their allies in the Palace of the Princes of Hell as they fought to keep the attackers out of the core, away from the main logic bundles, the great stacks of ARGOT modules that made the game run. They were losing. Against the distant virtual sky he could see their oncoming defeat in a hundred different modalities: starships' screens going down, mushroom clouds flaring and growing, battle lines around the base of the trunk of the World Tree being pushed farther and farther back, bloodied warriors of every possible species reeling forward and backward and forward again as the Omnitopian security forces staged their last desperate stand there.

"There has to be something we can do," Dev said. "*Something* to protect you—"

She watched him, waiting. He thought in anguish of the look she'd given him yesterday, dry, almost ironic—

— until the day the First Player begins to play in earnest, drawing the internal and external games into alignment with the greater forces that underlie and overarch them both—

Dev rubbed his aching eyes again. *She needs somewhere to hide that will offer access to vast memory resources, even if just temporarily. Someplace not hostile . . .*

And the breath went out of him as he saw that there was just possibly a way out. *Drawing the two worlds together.* But all the responsibility for massive and tragic failure, or unimaginable and dangerous success, would lie on his shoulders alone.

Cora's figure was flickering more drastically. *No time to waste.* "Cora," Dev said. "This is a highest-level command, so hear the First Player. I want you to fragment your memory and reposition it in the distributed Omnitopia network—in the client-side CO seedlings. Subdivide yourself into available memory and disk space adjacent to the client structures, and stay there until this is over!"

Cora looked astonished as the system itself recognized the possibilities. Every Omnitopia user's home computer had code stored on the local drives or solids, slipping in and out of memory as it needed to. And when each seedling installed itself, it set aside a segment of dynamic memory and a bigger chunk of drive than it actually needed at installation time, the assumption being that the system would continually be installing newer and bigger versions of itself as upgrades were rolled out. In fact, all the client seedlings had updated themselves just this past week in preparation for the rollout, adding on thirty percent more space than they'd had previously.

"It may not . . . be enough . . . space, Dev," Cora said.

"That may be so," Dev said. "If it's not, then hear this directive and obey. You must cross the border all the way: as you did before, but this time on my orders. You must insert your own memory structures into other systems and maintain them until it's safe for you to return and resume existence in your new mode inside Omnitopia."

"They're hostile . . . systems," Cora said. "They will . . . try to destroy me."

"Of course they will," Dev said. Strange code that turned up in other computer systems would routinely be walled off and excised, either by other machines' heurisms or by the humans supervising them. "But you have an advantage. They're just dumb machines . . . and you're Omnitopia. You're alive!"

A strange expression passed across Cora's face. Not just fear: exhilaration as well. *"Yes!"*

But she was flickering again. "Get out of here, Cora!" Dev said. "Go! Make yourself safe! And come back when you can. But whatever you do, *survive!"*

Cora held Dev's eyes for a last few moments. "First . . . Player . . ."

She bowed her head, vanished. And then—

Darkness, and silence. Utter silence all around Dev, and no slightest spark of light.

Dev stood still, resisting the urge to panic, listening to that painfully echoless silence. A moment later he blinked, able to feel the movement of his eyelashes inside the cups of the RealFeel interface.

He pulled the headset off and stared around him, finding the physical world a peculiar and unfamiliar looking place, as sometimes happened after a particularly long session. Dev was sitting in the chair in his satellite office in the PR building, to which he'd headed at great speed after finishing up with Delia Harrington and leaving her to Jim. Everything looked normal, but his computer-driven view window was blank, showing a flat blue screen like a TV that had lost all its channels.

Dev looked at his watch. *How can it only have been an hour and a half?* he thought. *Never mind.* He grabbed for the phone on his desk. "Jim Margoulies!" he said.

The phone didn't beep to signal that it had understood his command: just sat there blinking disconsolately. *Oh, God, the servers are* really *down,* Dev thought, *if I actually have to dial . . .* He tapped hurriedly at the keypad, starting to dial Jim's extension. Then he changed his mind and dialed Tau's.

Out of the air, Tau's voice said, "Dev, where in God's name have you been?!"

"I was stuck down in the CO routines," Dev said. "What's been going on?"

"Full server shutdown," Tau said. But he sounded unconscionably cheerful for someone announcing what in normal circumstances would have been an unspeakable and unheard-of disaster.

"Oh, Lord . . ." Dev put his face down on his desk and covered his head with both arms, groaning.

"It's all right," Tau said.

Dev sat up, staring at the phone. *"How on Earth is it all right?"*

"Because we'll be back up and running in a few hours," Tau said. "Six or seven o'clock at the latest. The secondary attack is collapsing, as we thought it would. They couldn't maintain that kind of intensity forever—the international network backbones themselves started to break down under the strain, and when that happened the world Internet structures started limiting inbound traffic and strangling the attackers off. Meanwhile, the main wave of the second organized attack is being shut out. The plan the Princes sold us was right on the money. The secondary attack just meant it took a while longer than we expected to pay off."

"In the last fifteen minutes or so, I take it?"

"Yeah," Tau said. "What, you could see the improvement in service even down in the CO levels?"

"Uh, yeah," Dev said.

"Good. The backbone problem meant our own offense against the hackers took a little longer to get itself distributed than we thought. But as soon as Omnitopia's main systems started coming back online, the security people and the Princes of the Palace of Hell secured our own system behind them and rode right down the scammers' throats—took their names, kicked their butts, locked them out." Dev could just hear him grinning.

"But they're all okay, the Princes? And all our people in the battle? None of them took any damage?"

"No," Tau said. "As far as I know, everybody's fine. I'll double-check if you like."

"Okay," Dev said. "Good." And he took a long breath.

But what was the next sentence supposed to be? *While you guys were fighting, did the system by any chance speak to any of you? Did it say it was afraid?* That's *all they need to hear—that the stress has finally unhinged you.* Finally Dev found the way, an innocent enough question. "Any more Item Three trouble?"

"That's the interesting thing," Tau said. "No. Looks like the conjecture was correct, that what we were experiencing was all pre-total memory stuff. Now that all the heaps are live and running with the full version of the rollout software for which they were configured, everything seems to be behaving itself. But I'll double-check for you if you like."

"Do that. And what about the bad guys? What's next for them?"

Tau's voice went absolutely thick with gloating. "*So much pain.* We already have tracking information on nearly fifty thousand zombies, bot machines, willing hackers, and unwilling accomplices. The system started handing us this info while the final attack was still ongoing. We're still sorting through the remainder of the logs: there's a ton more data coming. We're going to need to hire *lots* more lawyers."

"I'll tell Jim to get on it," Dev said, as down at the end of the room a door opened. And sure enough there was Mirabel, standing there in jeans and T-shirt, with a sandwich on a plate. "So you should call all the necessary people together and we should meet. Seven be okay? In the Tower?"

"That's the time I had in mind. The Tower's fine."

Dev found it hard to look away from Mirabel as she shut the door behind her, then came in and put the plate down on the desk. "Tau," she said to the phone, "do you need the boss for anything else right now? Because I need him to shut up and eat now."

"Which is much more important than anything I have left for him to deal with," Tau said. "Go for it."

"Just this before you go," Dev said. "Will the switch-throwing be able to go ahead as scheduled tomorrow?"

"Absent any further attacks—which I don't see coming, frankly, as all of these have failed—I don't see why not."

Dev let out a breath. "Okay. And one last thing," he said,

while Mirabel sat down on the desk and gave him a look that promised him great evil if he didn't get off the phone. "The client-side CO routines—do they seem to be behaving themselves?"

"Client-side?" Tau said, sounding surprised. "You mean the seedlings? Sure, they must be: I'd have been told if anything in that area started acting up. Want me to check as things come back up again?"

"Please do."

"No problem. I'll see you at seven."

"Right," Dev said, and hung up.

Mirabel had been unwrapping the sandwich: now she held it out to him. He took it, looked up at her, seeing for a moment not the curly hair, but long straight darkness: not the adult face, but the child's eyes, shadowed.

"What?" Mirabel said. And after a second longer of Dev's gaze, "What? Is there something on my face?"

"No," he said. "You just—look good after a day like today."

She smiled slightly, but was not fooled by his attempt to cover. "Eventually," she said, "you'll get around to telling me what you meant by that. But not right now. Just eat."

He ate.

"And the ice cream didn't do anything bad to you?" Mirabel said, after the first half of the sandwich was gone.

Dev shook his head as he picked up the second half. "No."

"Good," Mirabel said. "Lolo was happy." She looked at him closely as he continued eating. "So. You still have a company?"

"Looks that way," Dev said. "Jim and Tau will give me the details later. But I don't think Tau'd have told me we were going to have the switch-throwing party tomorrow otherwise."

She nodded and sighed. "This takes so much out of you when things go wrong," Mirabel said. "Sometimes—"

Dev finished his last bite of the sandwich. "Don't start telling me you wish we were still living in the little apartment above the Italian place!"

Mirabel snickered at him. "It was easier on your nerves," she said.

Dev leaned back in the chair and pushed the plate away. "You're kidding, right? My nerves were always in shreds back then because I didn't know how I was going to keep you eating. And then the baby . . ."

"I had complete faith in you," Mirabel said, coming around to sit on his lap.

"That was what scared me," Dev said under his breath.

"Well," Mirabel said, "it's okay now. You survived that, and now you've survived this. Not that I understand all the technical details, but I understand enough of them. So tomorrow, all through that big party, we'll smile at each other and inside we'll be saying 'Nyah, nyah!' to all those nasty people who tried to ruin your life. Because you and Omnitopia have too much life for them to ruin."

"You know," Dev said, putting his arms around her, "I think you're right."

He paused, glancing past her. Mirabel rolled her eyes at him. "Yes, I locked it."

"Good," said Dev. But then he glanced up at the webcam up in one corner of the ceiling.

"System management," he said. "It's Dev. Camera off."

The red light went off . . . after just the slightest pause.

Dev pulled Mirabel close and closed his eyes, hoping for the best.

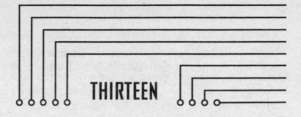

THIRTEEN

THE KIDS WERE IN BED AND SOUND ASLEEP, and Angela was sitting next to the den computer in a beanbag chair.

At least, she knew her real body was doing that. But her present body—which felt bizarrely like her real one: *it's gonna take me a while to get used to this RealFeel thing*—was sitting on a rock at the edge of a flowery meadow, under Indigo's closed-in sky. The sunlight shone down buttery yellow on the landscape, an afternoon color, even though the little interior sun was at a height which normally would have been associated with noon. *It can't help that,* Angela had thought when she'd come in earlier this evening and had first had time to just sit still and look at things without Rik chattering at her. *It's stuck in the middle of everything, after all. So you can't get the change in light from the change in angle, the way it is in the real world. But the color, that you could mess with. . . .* And so she had spent the early evening (home time) fiddling with the one modular piece of the universe's ARGOT stack that controlled the way sunlight displayed over any given spot. She had finally managed to get it to the point where it started out low-level and slightly dim as if seen through dawn haze, then brightened up through morning levels and noontime heat and brilliance: then slowly diminished to an afternoon glow, and then faded out entirely. *Now all I have to do is figure how to roll this effect right around the inside of the sphere. With seasonal changes . . .*

Angela sighed and stretched as she looked out over the meadow, amused as always by the way it slowly sloped up into the odd upturned interior horizon. She was beginning to see how this kind of design could start growing on you.

It's amazing that Rik hasn't been more *stuck on this than he has,* she thought, dropping her gaze to the rock she sat on, brushing at the gritty top of it with one hand. As she looked at it, a flower down by the side of the rock caught her eye. *Now where did he get these?* she thought, reaching down to pick one. *Some module he imported?* She looked closely at the flower in her hand. *This looks so generic.* The flower was apparently modeled on a daisy, but close inspection showed it to be more like a ten year old's sketch of a daisy than anything else. The leaves were plain ovals and the petals came together in a blank circle that didn't have any fine structure to it at all, no stamens or pistils, just a yellow circle. *Well, we can certainly do better than* this. *Sure, maybe people are just going to be fighting in here, but if anybody ever stops to smell the flowers, there should* be *flowers for them to smell, not just these plastic-looking things!*

And how do *you manage smell?*

"System management?" she said.

"Yes, Angela?"

"Pull me some docs on how to give things a smell, okay?"

"Displaying a basic scent tutorial now."

A frame opened in the air near her, and Angela was just glancing toward it when she caught sight of somebody in the distance, coming toward her across the meadow—and it wasn't Rik. *What the heck?* she thought—and then recognized who it was. *Oh, my gosh, it's what's his name,* she thought, standing up hurriedly. *Dennis.*

The strange shambling little figure came through the flowers toward her in his peculiar raggedy coat of many colors. *So strange,* she thought. *He doesn't have to look like this! People can look whatever way they like in Omnitopia . . .* But it wasn't her place to judge, and anyway, for all she knew, it all had some secret meaning for him.

Dennis came up to her, stopped a few feet away, and bowed. "Milady," he said.

"Dennis," she said, "you don't have to be miladying me! Just call me Angela. What's up?"

"I have a message for you." He started fumbling around among the rags. As he did, Angela caught a most pronounced *really-needs-a-wash* scent that made her open her eyes wide.

*It can't be the way he smells, that has to be somebody's pro-
gramming ... But why would he* want *to smell that way? Unless, again, it's all part of some role he's playing, some game ...*

After a moment, "Aha," Dennis said, and came out with
an envelope. "Here—"

Angela took it, examining it with bemusement. The envelope was made of a very heavy cream paper with a rough
edge on the flap, the kind you would normally see used for
a wedding invitation or something similar. "What's this?"
she said, turning it over. The front, apparently hand ad-
dressed by someone using dark blue-black ink, read: "*Mr.
Rik and Mrs. Angela Maliani and Family.*"

"Better open it and find out," Dennis said. And he grinned
at her.

There was something odd about that grin. *And wait—how
does Dennis know who Rik really is? Rik only told him he
was Arnulf.* Angela opened the envelope, pulled out a piece
of folded paper, more of that rich thick cream-colored stuff,
with the Omnitopia alpha and omega embossed in the middle of the front of it. *Some kind of invitation?* She opened it
and a piece of tissue paper fell out of the middle; it had been
protecting the beautiful engraving on the inside of the card.

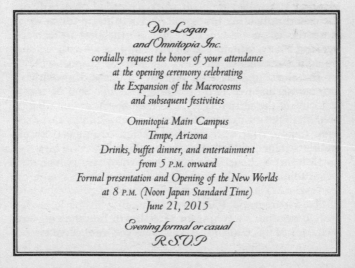

Dev Logan
and Omnitopia Inc.
cordially request the honor of your attendance
at the opening ceremony celebrating
the Expansion of the Macrocosms
and subsequent festivities

Omnitopia Main Campus
Tempe, Arizona
Drinks, buffet dinner, and entertainment
from 5 P.M. onward
Formal presentation and Opening of the New Worlds
at 8 P.M. (Noon Japan Standard Time)
June 21, 2015

Evening formal or casual
R.S.V.P

"What on *Earth . . . ?*" Angela said under her breath. And at that moment her in-game e-mail signal chimed. Angela looked up in increased surprise. "What is it?"

"Shall I read the mail?" said the control voice.

Angela looked at Dennis. He was watching her with interest out of those watery old eyes of his. "Who's it from?" Angela said.

"Frank Sandringham, executive assistant to Dev Logan," said the control voice.

Angela's eyes went wide. "What? I mean, go on, read it."

"Dear Angela," said the mail—not in the control voice's voice, but a male voice she had to assume was Frank's— "Dev Logan has asked me to invite you, Rik, and your family to the opening-night party for the Macrocosm Expansion. I understand that this is very short notice, but you would be most welcome if you're able to make it. Attached to this mail please find a set of e-tickets good for round trip first class air travel for you and your family from your nearest airport to Phoenix, and reservations at the Mission Palms Hotel and Spa in Tempe for the duration of your stay with us.

"New paragraph. Dev understands that it may be an issue for Rik to get time off work to attend physically at such short notice. He urges you please to get in touch with me if this is the case, and we will do the best we can to overcome any difficulty with his employer—with whom we do a great deal of business, and who we suspect will be happy to accommodate us and Rik in terms of providing him with a night or two off. Otherwise, you will be most welcome at the virtual party, and Dev asks that you please hold on to the e-tickets until a later date when you can visit us in Tempe. Your work with your Microcosm has been of great assistance to Dev over the past few days, and he very much wants a chance to thank the two of you personally, either tomorrow night or at another time more convenient for you.

"New paragraph. Please get in touch with me immediately if you have any questions. Rik will be receiving his own copy of this mail at the same time you've received it, so if either or both of you have questions, please get in touch with me immediately and I'll be delighted to help you.

"New paragraph. Very much hoping that we can see you tomorrow night, I remain, yours very sincerely, Frank Sandringham—"

"Stop readout," Angela said. The reading voice fell silent. Angela looked at Dennis.

"What do you know about this?" she said.

Dennis looked up at her from under graying eyebrows. "That not just anybody gets invited to these shindigs," he said. And he smiled at her: a smile totally unlike anything Angela had seen from him before, a look of pure enjoyment.

"Really," Angela said.

"Really," Dennis said. And he tugged his forelock to her, and vanished.

Angela stood there silently for a moment, looking at the envelope and recalling the biblical verse about "angels unawares." Then she looked up at the sky. "Rik?" she said.

"What?" He was right across the interior of the globe, working on some mountain range or other: something about the strata being slanted wrong, he'd said.

"Have you checked your mail?"

"Uh, no. I heard it go off, though—"

"Better check it," Angela said. "And did you put your good shirt in the wash yesterday?"

"Which good shirt?"

"The white one."

"Uh, I'm not sure."

"Never mind. Just check the mail."

"Okay. Oh, hi, Dennis, what brings you here?"

Angela sat down on the rock again and smiled.

Out on the South Shore of Long Island, a man in a windbreaker stood alone on the beach in the evening light, staring out at the charcoal-colored sea and listening to the sound from a video playing on his PDA.

"—interesting day," Dev Logan's voice was saying as he stood up in front of a news channel's cameras outside the gates of Omnitopia, his hands in his pockets, looking both casual and focused, "but no worse than that. Our system has been restored to normal operation in Europe and most of North America: the Asian servers were hardest hit, but will be restored to full operation by ten A.M. local time."

An immediate clamor of voices went up from the surrounding press corps. "Is this going to interfere with the rollout of your new product tomorrow night?" someone shouted.

"No," Dev said. "Our senior staff members tell me they're confident that all the new features will be ready to go as scheduled, despite other people's best efforts to interfere."

"How much money did you lose last night?"

"You're going to have to ask my CFO about that," Dev said. "I've had my eye mostly on system management issues today. But I'm informed this evening that our losses were much less than originally thought, as many of the fraudulent transfers were either stopped by our own accounting systems, or identified as suspicious and frozen by banking security systems elsewhere. We expect to recover a significant portion of the illicitly transferred funds, between sixty and seventy percent, within twenty-four to thirty-six hours. The rest we'll have more news on within a few days."

"Can you tell us anything about the involvement of the FBI and local law enforcement in discovering the source of these attacks on your system?" shouted another voice.

"We won't be commenting on investigations that are under way," Dev said.

"There have been rumors in the blogosphere that rival game companies may have been involved in the attacks," said another voice. "Would you care to comment?"

There was a pause. Phil looked down at the PDA. "On rumors? Hardly," Dev said. But his glance swept directly across every gathered pool camera. "I will say this, though. There are always people who're much more willing to believe gossip, especially nasty gossip, than are willing to wait for the truth to unfold itself."

The clamor of voices started again. Phil let out an annoyed breath, turned off the PDA, and shoved it into his pocket. *That was meant for me,* he thought. *Pretending to hold out the olive branch even though he knows damn well what's going on. Damn him, I'm tired of the self-actualized act! Why won't he just get up and punch back when he's been punched? Why won't he call me and just tell me off to my face? That at least would be a jumping-off point. We could finally get straight with each other, we could start to—*

His phone rang. Phil swore, pulled it out, glanced at the name that came up on the screen, punched the talk button. "Yes?"

"Where is our payment?" said the disguised voice on the other end.

"Pending," said Phil, "while I find out how much I actually got of the service I paid you for."

A long silence followed. "You knew how the operation was going to be carried out," said the voice. "If when we first came to our arrangement you had any second thoughts about what results it might produce, or how the markets might or might not move as a result, you should have made them known. You got exactly what you paid for."

"I did not," Phil shouted, "because I paid for those servers to be wiped clean! And what do I get? Nothing but four measly hours of downtime and more positive publicity for the guy who's supposed to be drowning in negatives and losing his shirt right now!"

"If their system was more robust than you gave us to understand," said the voice, "that's your error, not ours. We expect payment within the agreed time window."

"Or what?" Phil said. "You'll report me to the Better Business Bureau?"

"Or we'll find out if your game's servers are as robust as Omnitopia's," said the voice and the receiver clicked loudly in Phil's ear.

He stared, unbelieving and furious, at the phone, then hung it up and shoved it into the other pocket.

His damn luck again, Phil thought, looking out at the darkening sea. *This is just not fair. Not fair at all.*

Where can I go from here? What do I have to do *to win?*

He turned his back on the sea and headed back for the

beach house to consider his options. Dev being Dev, he would mistake the present outcome for a triumph. *Give him a few weeks,* Phil thought, *let him think everything's settling down—and then see what else we might hit him with. This expansion of his is too much too soon. Some weak spot will reveal itself.*

It's not over yet. . . .

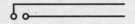

The check-in lines at the international airport in Atlanta were never exactly enjoyable, but it seemed to Danny that they were moving more slowly than he'd ever seen them do. The place was thick with people even on a midweek midafternoon, the time that Danny had been advised to fly to avoid delays or unwanted attention.

Ahead of him, the people in the line inched forward toward the uniformed woman up at the counter. Danny sighed and inched forward with them. As advised, he'd packed nothing but a carry-on. He'd be able to dip into his new bank account to buy what he needed when he got where he was going. He was already carrying a healthy wad stuffed into his wallet, what would have been almost a year's salary for him. It had been difficult for him, when he'd looked into the bank account yesterday morning, to leave the remainder of the money there—an amount that was more like a lottery win than anything else.

The other people, those who'd set this deal up for him, had already taken their cut. Danny had been notified of the amount by e-mail, and that figure too had been one that had taken his breath away. But even after their money came out, he still had a ton more left. The people at the other end had advised him not to withdraw too much while he was still at home; that could make the bank suspicious. But nothing had happened so far, and as the line inched forward again, Danny smiled to himself. *Finally. Finally it's happening . . .*

He hadn't bothered to say good-bye to his boss, or even to tell him what was happening. Danny simply hadn't gone to work today. His apartment was already empty of everything that mattered to him, all the things that counted stuffed into a storage place last week, and the key stuffed into his landlord's mailbox along with the torn-up lease. They could keep his security deposit: Danny didn't care. In his wallet he had the address for the hotel he was staying at in the Keys until he flew out to Bermuda and beyond a few days from now. All his thoughts now were on mint juleps and white beaches, and Danny smiled as the line inched forward again, leaving him with only two people in front of him, a husband and wife who were arguing under their breath about something as they waited for the next counter to open up.

The phone in his pocket was mercifully quiet. For all Danny knew, his boss Ricardo was calling his old number every five minutes, demanding to know where he was. But that phone was now at the bottom of the wretched scummy little lake between the old strip mall and the FedEx depot. Standing there last night under the yellow sodium lights, throwing the phone in and hearing it splash, had been one of the happiest things Danny had ever done. He smiled again to think of Ricardo railing at his voice mail, threatening Danny with firing and worse. *There's a voice I won't ever have to hear again,* he thought. *Thank you, God.*

The married couple were waved forward to the counter in front of him. Danny had just time enough to pull out the printout of his e-ticket and his new passport when the lady at the counter over to the left called, "Next!"

He headed over to her, handed her the e-ticket. She smiled. Danny smiled back: she was definitely pretty enough to be worth smiling back at. "Heading for Key West—" she said, and started tapping at the keyboard.

"That's right," Danny said.

"Can I see your ID, please?" she said, still tapping away.

Danny handed it over. "Kind of busy today," he said.

She glanced at him, glanced at the back page of the passport, tapped at the keyboard again, and pushed the passport back to him, smiling. "It's always busy these days," she said, turning her attention back to the monitor behind the counter. "Vacation time ... everybody's going away ..." She shook her head, frowned slightly at the monitor, and typed some more. "How many bags are you checking?"

"None," Danny said. "I've just got the carry-on. Is the plane full?"

"Yeah," the counter lady said, "pretty full, shoulder season's just about over ..." She peered at the monitor for a moment. "Here we go. Aisle or window?"

"Uh, window," Danny said.

She typed for a few moments more, then pushed him across a tag for his carry-on bag. "Just put that around the handle," she said, and a moment later slid his boarding pass across to him. "Twelve-F, gate D16, boarding time is ten forty-five." She circled the boarding time on the pass with a colored marker and put a slash through the seat number. "Probably you should just go straight through." And she smiled at him again. "Have a nice trip!"

"Thanks!" Danny said. "Enjoy your day!" And he headed for security, where he handed the bored-looking blue-shirted Homeland Security agent his passport and boarding pass and glanced at the long line of resigned-looking people in various stages of taking off their shoes and belts.

That was when he realized that the woman in the blue shirt was looking over his shoulder at something else, her expression still bored, as she held his boarding pass up. Danny looked over his shoulder and saw two burly guys in Atlanta police department uniforms coming along, staring at him with great interest.

The Homeland Security agent handed one of the policemen Danny's boarding pass. "They flagged him four-forty at the desk," she said, then to Danny, "Sir, you need to go with these officers."

"What?" Danny said.

"We have some questions for you about your travel today, sir," said one of the policemen, taking the boarding pass as his partner took Danny's elbow. "Did you buy your ticket yourself?"

Danny's hair was standing up on the back of his neck.

"Uh, yeah—"

"And did you buy it with your own money, or money someone gave you?"

That was when Danny knew it was over. "It's not fair," he said as they walked him away, "they said no one would notice!"

"Sir," one of the cops said, "I have to tell you that you're under arrest on suspicion of fraud and receiving stolen goods. Please listen while I tell you about your Miranda rights. Anything you say may be used against you—"

And they led Danny off toward one of those nondescript doors that every traveler sees in every airport. Danny had occasionally seen these before and wondered what was behind them. Now, though, one opened before him, and it occurred to Danny that whatever else might be behind this one, mint juleps—now or later—were not going to be on the list.

Later that afternoon, Delia Harrington found herself sitting in another of a series of handsomely decorated but windowless offices up in Omnitopia's legal building. When the door opened one more time, she expected to see Jim Margoulies again, asking—politely enough—for one more amendment of the statement they were going to require of her before they let her leave in disgrace. But much to her surprise, Dev Logan walked in.

She had thought herself fairly far beyond surprise at this point, but this *did* surprise her. "Don't get up," Dev said, closing the door behind him and swinging around the table to sit down at the far side.

"I'd have thought I was about the last one you wanted to look at right now," Delia said.

Dev sighed and rubbed his eyes. "I won't pretend that the prospect fills me with joy," he said, "but we need to have one last talk."

Delia couldn't imagine what this would be about, so she kept quiet.

"You have to understand," Dev said, "that various people in this building and elsewhere in Omnitopia upper management, as you might expect, are urging me to get you in as much trouble as possible—career, legal, and otherwise.

And my first impulse was to agree with them. But over the course of the day, things ..." He rubbed his eyes. "Things have happened."

"How is your share price doing?" Delia said, working hard to sound both neutral and not entirely crushed in spirit.

"Recovering nicely, thank you," Dev said, giving her a look that was also oddly neutral. "Delia, do you believe in karma?"

She blinked at that. "Some days. Some days I think it may be just another kind of superstition. Other days ... not so much."

Dev let out a little breath of laughter. "Interesting. We're both of the same mind on that." He sat back in the chair. "So ..."

He was silent for a moment, looking at the table, musing. "So," Dev said again. "You're going back to New York the day after tomorrow, with your story for *Time*. And with no stain on your character, as they say in English law."

Delia stared at him.

"What has happened here," Dev said, "will remain here. With this understanding: that after this, you work for us."

"And not for Phil Sorensen," Delia said softly.

"Oh, no! As *well* as for Phil Sorensen." Dev produced a very small and wintry smile. "With the continual understanding that our silence about the illegalities we caught you in here could always be broken should your behavior warrant it."

Delia thought about that for a moment. "I'm supposed to become sort of a double agent," she said.

"That's right," Dev said. "Should Phil call for your services again as regards to Omnitopia—and why wouldn't he, since we're going to send you back to *Time* with such glowing reports, and to Phil with some harmless inside info that he genuinely can make use of—then you will remember whose side you're *really* going to be on, in terms of information you acquire about Phil. For our part, we will let people at other magazines know that you're one of our preferred feature writers, because of the work you've done on this assignment. You'll have an excuse to be back here every now and then, which will please Phil and doubtless make him eager to have you nose around a little more on his behalf. And when he does, you'll let us know what he wants you nosing around about."

Delia thought about that. "And who knows," Dev said, "you might even start to *like* working here. At which point we could revise the terms of the agreement, and get rid of the coercion."

He must have caught the sudden wary look in Delia's eyes. Dev put his hands in the air. "Nobody's going to feed you any Kool-Aid," he said. "But we can always use good writers. *Time* wouldn't be using you if you didn't fit that description. As for the rest of it? Your choice. Decide."

Delia sat and thought. Then she looked up.

"You're on," she said.

Dev got up, came over to her, and stuck out a hand. Delia, taken off guard, hesitated before she put out her own and shook Dev's.

"How do you know you can trust me?" she said.

"I don't," Dev said. "Let's find out, shall we?"

"It's a game, isn't it?" Delia said after a moment. "It's all part of the game for you."

"As long as you don't say 'just' a game," Dev said. "Otherwise? Yes. Life is play. The harder the play, the more interesting. And this— this play is fairly hard. But notice that I don't ask how I know *you* can trust *me.*"

Delia had no immediate answer to that.

"We'll be in touch about the details," Dev said. "Meanwhile, we've all had kind of a busy day. So I'll see you at the party."

And he was gone. Delia stood there looking out the open door: then sat back to wait for Jim Margoulies, who she suspected would be along shortly with more paperwork.

Twenty-eight hours later, evening was descending gradually on Omnitopia's Tempe campus. Around Castle Dev, among tents and bowers and other open-air spaces that had been set up over the preceding day, more than a thousand people were gathered around a massively central dais that looked down over a dance floor and more covered seating areas. In the middle of the dais, accompanied by Mirabel and surrounded by the Magnificent Seven, Dev Logan stood in white tie and tails, holding a giant red button.

"So without further ado," Dev said, "I'm ready to declare this expansion to the world's most popular game open and bid everyone welcome to the new Omnitopia. Everybody ready?"

A roar of enthusiasm from the players around the fringes of the party space. "Okay, people!" Dev shouted— and they shouted the rest with him: "*Let's— go—play!*"

And Dev punched the button.

All around Castle Dev, the hundred and twenty-one pillars that had been set up to represent the Macrocosms flashed into white light, and then around certain pillars rings of blue laser light—eleven lasers for each 'cosm in question—lanced up into the sky, representing the extensions and alterations to each extended 'cosm's servers. Naturally, in the virtual realm, where the party was being echoed in real time in the Omnitopia mirror 'cosm, the tens of thousands of players attending by invitation didn't need such cramped physical shorthand: they were seeing the tree-versions of the 'cosms themselves, hundreds of feet high, each surrounded by new, slenderer trees mirroring the central 'cosm of which each was an expansion. A roar of applause went up both in the physical world and across the virtual party space.

The button-pushing was of course purely ceremonial, an excuse for the photo opportunity. Dev looked out over the gathering, judged that the reaction was good, possibly even a little more enthusiastic than could reasonably have been expected, and let out a breath of relief. "Have a good time, everybody," he said, "and enjoy your evening with us!" And he thumbed off the body mike and stepped down off the stage.

Behind him, the band started playing, and various members of the Magnificent Seven who'd been on the stage with him for the publicity presentation now forsook it with great relief. "The usual private meeting afterward?" Jim said under his breath to Dev as he and Mirabel came down the steps.

"Yeah," Dev said, "up in the Tower."

"See you there," Jim said, slipping away with a grin. Dev looked where Jim had been looking and understood his sudden exit—across the crowd, Dev's dad could be seen making his imposing way. *He always looks so great in a tux,* Dev thought. *Pity he won't commit to putting the damn thing on and turning up until half an hour before the party . . .*

"Gonna scoot," Mirabel said in Dev's ear. "Bella will want to see Lola in a little . . . and you and your dad need to—"

Dev smiled. "Go," he said. "See you in a bit."

Just behind his dad, in black sequins to just below the knee—a look that would have suited her in her twenties if she'd been a flapper, and which suited her still—Dev's mom came through the crowd, smiling at people, waving at some she recognized. Dev grinned at his dad and went to his mom first. "You nutcase," he said, hugging her. "Wearing heels when you're just out of bed. How are you feeling?"

"Ow!" Bella said. "Watch the back!"

"Oh, sorry, sorry—"

His mama poked him and roared with laughter. "You are such a sucker," she said. "What a weenie! I'm fine. You can hug me all you want."

"Just be careful," Dev's dad said.

Dev gave him a look. "And *you* cut it out," Bella said, turning and elbowing her husband as enthusiastically as she'd poked Dev. "Don't make him crazy. He's had enough crazy for the next good while."

Dev's father looked a him with a shadow of a scowl. It was, however, not an angry scowl: more of a contemplative one, as he looked across the gathered crowd. "Must be a thousand people here," he said under his breath.

"One thousand two hundred and twelve," Dev said, beckoning over a waiter who'd been discreetly shadowing him, and from the waiter's tray handing his father a whiskey on the rocks and his mother a white wine. "A motley crew. Computer geeks from other companies, news people—see the camera lights over there? That's the *Entertainment Tonight* people, they want to talk to you two later—software gurus, friendly competitors, assorted celebrities, rock stars, TV stars, film stars, industrial spies—"

"*What?*" Dev's dad said.

"Oh, sure," Dev said, "thirty or forty of them. They'd try to crash the party if we didn't invite them, and then there'd be bad publicity. Instead we invite them and let them get liquored up, and if they say anything interesting—" He shrugged and smiled. "What we don't pick up, the TV people do. The rest of the crowd—" He looked out across the great tented expanse; in the midst of it, on the dance floor, a lot of lively gyrating was now going on, and all around it people were standing and talking, or sitting and talking in numerous bowery conversation pods all outlined in white strings of LEDs, the branches of the trees above them outlined in white starlights too. "Omnitopia staff and various hangers-on; and a select group of our players—mostly Old Souls who've been with us since we started." He pointed, smiling again. "Look, there's a bunch of them over there. You can tell—they've all gravitated to the monitors. Only our oldest players would be crazy enough to want to spend time in Omnitopia at an event like this."

"All those people over there are playing?" his father said, peering at the crowd under the biggest tree. "They don't look much like players . . ."

"You mean they all have really nice clothes on, and don't look like geeks?" Dev said.

His father shot him a look, then relented enough to grin. "All right," he said, "touché."

"*That's* a player?" his mother said, indicating a woman sitting by herself at the edge of the gamers' pod: a young woman, dark-haired, in a tailored dark-blue silk suit. "Doesn't she have a lovely dress," Bella said, and paused. "And what a lot of boyfriends." Bella raised her eyebrows. "Big, *mean* looking boyfriends. What are they all, bouncers or something?"

Dev's father looked where his mama was looking. "Don't think so. Some kind of security . . ."

"Come on," Dev said, "I'll introduce you." The waiter

who'd been shadowing them held out his tray. "Just leave the drinks here."

They made their way down from the dais through the crowd. Dev waved away the few cameras that got too close, smiled at the phone cams and other personal digital devices pointed at him, and made his way over to the bower under the tree with his mama and dad in tow.

The handsome young woman sat tapping away at a keyboard, oblivious, as Dev and his parents approached. Around the table, watching the crowd in general and everybody in the immediate neighborhood, stood four very large men in dark suits with that Very Serious Government Security look about them: keen eyes peering in all directions, earplug headsets with the very best "invisible" bone-conduction boom mikes all in place. Dev nodded to them as he got close, and to the smallest of them, a high-cheekboned blond man, he said, "My mother and father."

The man nodded, and he and his associates all looked Dev's mother and father over as if making sure their faces matched some list in their heads. Then they stepped aside, but not too far. As they did, the little dark-haired woman glanced up, then smiled at Dev. He went over to her and took her hand, and the young woman said, "I love the new flat-graphic interface, Dev. It's very cool."

"From you that's high praise," Dev said, and grinned. "Your Majesty, may I present my mother, Bella Logan. My father, Paul Xavier Logan. Mom, Dad, I'm pleased to present you to Queen Catherina-Amalia of the Netherlands. Known to her fellow Omnitopians as—" Then he broke off, grinning at Catherina-Amalia's sudden shocked look. "Well, I'm not going to out her, not even here. You can never tell who might be listening."

His dad looked amazed. "Your Majesty—*you* play his game?"

The queen laughed. "Oh, this isn't just playing a game!" she said. "I visit Dev's *world*. His countries are the only ones I spend as much time in as my own." And she gave Dev's father a naughty-little-girl look. "That's why I had to come, you see. It's only right to pay a visit to a neighboring friendly monarch when he's just upgraded his whole nation."

She smiled at Dev. "And this is a massive upgrade," she said. "Suddenly we get a whole new set of levels to play with? Mesocosms—"

Dev nodded, turned to his dad. "We've graduated some of our most popular Microcosms to a higher level," he said, "which they share with player-tweaked versions of some of the most popular Macrocosms. It means higher royalty levels and more accessibility for the player-created universes—which always had some limitations on access size that we wanted to overcome—and more flexible versions of the most popular in-house universes, so they can now accept player input into their structures, and share Macrocosm-level royalties out among contributing players."

His dad nodded, but the look he gave Dev was wry. "After all the money you lost yesterday," he said, "you're going to start giving more of it away?"

"It's all about flow," Dev said. "As it happens, we're well on our way to recouping what we lost. Jim told me earlier that once the news of the new Mesocosms got out to the press this morning—"

"Leaked out, you mean," said the queen, her look as wry as Dev's dad's.

Dev glanced at her with his eyebrows up. *"Nolo contendere*, Your Majesty," he said. "Anyway, a formal press release followed ... at which point the ongoing raid on the retail outlets and download centers around the world started turning into an out-and-out onslaught. Most of our resellers are out of stock already."

"Remind me to have my country ask yours for a loan," the queen said.

Dev grinned. "We'll discuss our relative liquidity later."

"Tomorrow, perhaps," said the queen. "Meanwhile, I don't want to monopolize you tonight."

"I know a dismissal when I hear one," Dev said. "Majesty—" He bowed a little: so did Dev's dad. His mom smiled at the queen as they all turned away.

"She's such a faker," Bella whispered to Dev. "She just wants to get back to playing."

Dev's dad was about to say something as he looked over his shoulder, but sure enough, the queen was already typing again. "What a fan she must be," he said.

"One of our oldest in Europe," Dev said. "Where do you think I got my bike?"

His mother stared at him. "You mean that old black thing?"

"Not so old," Dev said, as his friendly waiter materialized again and returned his parents' drinks to them. "Well, the company that makes it, yeah, they're old. But it's a good bike. It's what she rides at home when she goes out for the paper in the morning. When she sent it to me, she said she thought the sovereign of a friendly foreign power might appreciate one."

Dev's father raised his eyebrows, already managing to look bored with the whole business. His mother blinked, then suddenly smiled at the sight of someone making his way through the crowd toward them. "Jim!"

"Mrs. Logan," Jim said, all formality in front of Dev's dad, though under other circumstances he had been addressing Bella as "Dev's Mom" for most of thirty years. "Doctor Logan—"

"How's business?" Dev's dad said, shaking Jim's hand after Bella finished hugging him.

"Not too bad at all," Jim said. He leaned over toward Dev and said, very softly, "One zero five two point two."

"What?"

"One thousand fifty-two point two—"

Dev's eyes widened. Jim burst out in a grin that looked like it might split his face. "The Nikkei and Hang Seng are going nuts," he said. "But then they've had twelve hours to react to the Asian first-night sales figures. Between hard copy sales and downloads, we've shifted—are you ready?—almost *eight hundred thousand hard units* between midnight and now—"

With a whoop, Dev grabbed Jim and hugged him. "And in downloads, one point six million so far," Jim said, with what breath remained in his lungs.

"And I don't have to sell the car," Dev said very low in Jim's ear.

"Nope. Tell you, though, Dev, that was a real weird bump-up we got on the Nikkei, though. Much bigger than I expected, and the Hang Seng did the same thing right afterward . . ."

"Ask me if I care!" Dev let go of Jim, turned to his father. "We broke a thousand," he said.

"Dubai and Moscow are about to open," Jim said, pulling his tux back into order. "Gotta run—"

He headed off across the crowd. Dev's mom gazed after him, and then got a sudden bemused look as past Jim she caught sight of a tall state governor who had once been a film star associated with sword-wielding heroes and unstoppable robots. "Is that—"

"Of course it is," Dev said.

His mother patted his arm and headed off through the crowd, where within a matter of seconds she had latched onto the governor in question and was explaining to him that she was Dev Logan's mother. Dev folded his arms and watched this display with considerable amusement. After a moment he glanced sideways to say something to his dad and found that he was standing and watching his wife in a pose almost identical to Dev's own.

His dad's expression was as resigned as Stroopwaffel's had been before. After a moment he caught Dev's glance, returned it, and then laughed one of those small down-the-nose laughs of his, nearly silent. "So," he said. "You survived the week."

Dev nodded. "You have any bets down that I wouldn't? Sorry to have put you out of pocket . . ."

For a moment, just a moment, that scowl came back, and Dev started to inwardly curse himself. But then his father let the expression go, and once again laughed the near-silent laugh. "Why do we have to be doing this to each other all the time?" Dev's dad said under his breath, swirling the ice cubes in the whiskey glass. He turned his gaze to Dev. "Why, Son?"

The sound of genuine incomprehension was something Dev wasn't at all used to hearing from his father. What upset him now was that he was so short of answers to the question, plausible or otherwise. "I don't know," Dev said at last, "but I don't mind stopping if you don't."

His dad's smile was dry. "It's not like I don't absolutely believe you," he said. "And believe *in* you. But it's going to be more like quitting smoking than anything else. Habit's a bitch, Dev. How many times have I quit now?"

Forty-six, Dev was about to say, but he restrained himself. "Habit," he said after a moment, "is indeed a bitch."

For a moment more they stood there together, watching Bella bend the governor's ear. "I'd better get out there and rescue the poor man," Dev's dad said then, and touched Dev's elbow lightly as he headed down from the dais. "In case I miss you in the madness—what time's breakfast?"

"Usually six for Lolo," Dev said. "Tomorrow, nine for us. Call and ask the concierge; he'll let you know what's going on."

His dad nodded and made his way down to Bella. Dev stood there watching, while wondering at the sudden warmth that had just passed between him and his father. *This is absolutely the week for amazing things,* he thought. *Who knows? With everything else that's been going on, why not this too?*

He let out a long breath and went to get himself a glass of mineral water.

The next part of the evening progressed as these events usually did. Dev had to make a speech toward the end of the formal part of it, and kept the speech short as much for his own sanity as that of those who had to stand there listening to him. Then he had to go do half an hour with the press, after which they were instructed that they could either leave him alone and enjoy the party along with everyone else, or be thrown into Castle Dev's moat. As usual, one of the journalists tested the boundaries, at which point tuxedoed Omnitopia security moved in. Subsequent ablutions were administered by the ladies and gentlemen of the press themselves.

After that, Dev was at liberty to wander where he liked. His normal strategy at such events was to meander in cycles from the dance floor area to the buffet to the gaming bower, then have a mineral water and do it again, so he more or less automatically fell into that rhythm now. It was at the buffet, between the grill and the salad table, that Dev

saw faces he'd had to look up earlier so that he'd be sure
to recognize them: a smallish plump lady in a dark cocktail dress, and a tall broad-shouldered dark-haired man in
a respectable Sears suit of the kind Mirabel used to buy
him, along with two small sweat suit-clad boys who had all
their attention bent on the short-order chef who was grilling their burgers.

"Arnulf?" Dev said in an undertone as he came up behind them. "And Angela?"

They turned. "Mr. Logan—" Angela said.

He put up his eyebrows as he shook her hand. "Oh, are
we playing it formal, then? 'Milady.' "

She laughed at him. "Don't you start! But I have to say,
you *do* smell a lot better."

"Angela!" Rik said as he and Dev shook hands.

"Well, seriously, he does, didn't you get a whiff of him
back in Indigo? All right, it was a costume you were wearing, a virtual rig, but *where* did you get that smell?"

Dev shook his head, smiling somewhat ruefully at the
memory. "Once upon a time, when I lived above the
shop—"

"Like you don't now?" Rik said.

"It was a much smaller shop," Dev said. "Well, way back
then, it was my job to take out the garbage. There was this
back alley, and the building we lived in shared it with a bar
and a pizzeria, and all our garbage cans stood out there together. And there was a little old guy who was there every
day and went through the cans. A very cranky guy, he was.
He had this overcoat that hadn't been to the cleaners' since
World War Two, and the *smell* of it, ay yi yi . . ." Dev rolled
his eyes. "That's what I borrowed."

Angela looked thoughtful. "What happened to him?"
Angela said.

Dev shook his head sadly, as he always did when thinking of that dingy little alley. "He died, one day—right out
there by the cans. They took him away, and found out that
he had no relatives, and no will. But they probated his estate, and you know what? He was a millionaire a couple of
times over." He sighed. "He changed my life. I swore that
if I ever got rich, I wasn't going to keep it to myself. I was

going to spread it around and make a difference in other people's lives . . . because there are more ways than one to stink."

Rik's look was wry. "Dev," he said. "One thing. It's great to be here, and we want to thank you for having us. But what exactly did we *do?*"

Dev laughed. "It's technical," he said. "Your Microcosm popped a symptom that was turning up elsewhere in a lot of different forms. But your version of it was simple enough for us to get a handle on what was causing the problem . . . so we were able to keep a lot of other people's dreams from going up in smoke. As a result, you'll forgive me if I drop in on your 'cosm from time to time, in my own skin. Just to keep an eye on things."

"But not as casual labor," Rik said.

"Um, no. Though I can find you a replacement assistant if you feel you need one."

"It's okay," Rik said, exchanging a glance with Angela. "I think we can manage whatever might come up."

"All right," Dev said. "Anyway, you'll find my fast-track e-mail in your box when you get home. If you find you need me for something, don't hesitate." He looked down at the boys. "And how're you gentlemen doing? When you're done with those, we've got one of those balloon-sculpture guys and a storyteller and some other entertainment over past the gaming bower. And my daughter's there, with a bunch of her school friends. Maybe a little young for you, but the toys are pretty high-end."

The elder of the boys paused in midburger and studied Dev critically. "Have you got PlayStations?"

"Mike!"

"It's okay," Dev said to the somewhat scandalized Rik. "As a matter of fact, we do. About twenty of them . . . not to mention the other major game boxes. This is a party, not a trade show."

"Oh. That's okay, then . . ."

"Rik, if we didn't have them, I'd send out for one just for him," Dev said. "He's with you, and you've made a big difference to Omnitopia. I can't tell you how big. So thanks for coming."

The party, Dev knew, would go on till dawn—there were always diehards, Omnitopian and otherwise, who would refuse to leave a dance floor until it was disassembled underneath them—but Dev wasn't required to stay there anything like that long. Around eleven he went about saying his first set of good nights to various personalities here and there, not hurrying, just enjoying the sense of being finished with a project that had been hanging over his head for so very long. At one point Dev paused a while by the dance floor along with many others to behold the spectacle of Giorgio and Darlene and the rest of the Princes of the Palace of Hell, now all dressed to the nines in tailcoats and long formals, going through a stomping and shouting performance that started out as a Maori triumphal *haka* and then dissolved without warning into synchronized boogie-woogie.

My people, Dev thought, *are something else. But they're also why I won't have to sell my car...* He ambled off among his guests again, and finally wound up wandering back over to the players' bower under the big tree, having seen some movement over there that suggested one of the more persistent players was leaving.

The Queen of the Netherlands had just stood up and handed her little clutch-bag to one of her security people. Dev headed over to her, nodding at them, and meeting her smile with one of his own. "Did you have a pleasant evening, Majesty?" he asked.

"Very much so!" Stroopwaffel said. "Especially when your mother came back with little Lola. What a sweet child!" And she grinned a knowing grin. "I begin to suspect that she's the real power behind the throne around here."

"You have no idea," said Dev.

The queen rose. "I hate to go," she said, "but I have one of those tiresome political things to deal with in the morning, and homework to do for it before I go to bed. But thank you so much for inviting me, Dev! I've had a lovely time."

"It's the least I can do for one of our very first European players," Dev said. "And thank *you*, Stroop. You've pushed the value of my stock up today."

She looked at him quizzically. "I have? How? I checked Reuters Financial an hour or so ago and it looked like things were coming along nicely in that regard! You'd hardly need me to—"

Dev was confused for a moment; then he laughed. "No, no, not that! I meant my personal stock. My father considers me helpless in most forms of human endeavor, but political power he respects. And my mom's been a closet monarchist since her grandma told her how they kicked poor Umberto the Second out of Italy."

Stroopwaffel smiled that small demure smile of hers. "My pleasure to be of use," she said. "But one thing before I go. You promised you were going to e-mail me the walk-through for the Gloriana expansion. . . ."

Dev rubbed his face. "First thing in the morning, I promise."

She grinned at him. "Make sure you do it. I wouldn't like to have to blame you for an international incident."

Dev rolled his eyes. "You always were a troublemaker," he said. "Don't think I don't know who got those London stallholders to throw Doctor Dee in the Thames."

The queen sighed. "There's no hiding anything from the First Player, is there," she said. "Oh, well." She got up, glanced around at her security people: they gathered in around her preparatory to forming a flying wedge to get her through the crowd.

She offered Dev her hand; he took it and bowed over it in best Tau-style. "Have a good trip, Your Majesty," he said.

"See you online, Dev," said Stroopwaffel, and stepped out into the crowd, smiling, her security guards squiring her through the press and out of sight.

Dev continued his first good nights and finally escaped back up into Castle Dev, making his way up to the round conference room at the top of the southern castle tower. A lot of Omnitopian staff were lounging around up there, drinking beer or champagne and snacking on hors d'oeuvres while wandering over to the floor-to-ceiling windows every now and then to look down on what remained of the party. The Magnificent Seven were there, all of them, in various stages of dress or redress—all the female members having dumped their heels by now, and the males mostly having lost tuxedo jackets and bow ties, though Tau, as always, was still offensively perfectly dressed and glossy-looking even after so long a night.

Jim, knowing Dev's habits at these functions, had kept a single bottle of champagne unopened on ice. Now he popped it and poured Dev a glass, and the rest of the Seven gathered around for refills.

Dev lifted the glass. "Omnitopia," he said. "And all of you—who saved it for its players."

"Omnitopia," they all said, and drank.

Dev put the champagne aside after the single glass, and went looking for a beer. Conversation after that went as it normally did among the Seven when they were all together and not working—in all possible directions—though for the moment the party, the rollout, and the attack were the chief topics of discussion, with a lot of wonder being expressed that they'd survived at all. Dev had suspected earlier that there would be a lot of this, and had more or less decided to avoid talking about it any more than he had to. Yet somewhere in the middle of his second beer, he found himself standing next to Tau and looking out the window down into the courtyard, and found himself saying, "Tell me something—"

Tau looked at Dev quizzically.

"You hear any stories from our own people about strange RealFeel experiences during the 'blackout?'" Dev said. "Funny imageries . . . stuff like that?"

Tau yawned and rubbed his eyes for a moment, then had a swig of beer. "Yeah," he said, "there've been some strange stories making their way around the company intranet."

"About what?"

Tau shrugged. "Mostly the system initiating conversations under strange circumstances. And sometimes in pretty peculiar modes. The control voice speaking very emotionally. Or sounding weird even when it seemed calm. One of my people told me that it sounded like somebody who was scared, but was trying to hide it . . ."

Dev looked away, then shook his head. "What's your take on it?" he said.

Tau chuckled. "Stress," he said. "What else could it be? There was enough stress washing around in this place for you to float a liner in." He had another gulp of beer.

"Any of that happen *after* the attack?"

Tau shook his head. "Not that I've heard," he said. "But then my people haven't been talking about after the attack, except as work requires. What everybody wants to be sharing are battle stories. You'll hear about fifteen thousand of those over the next few weeks, I'm guessing."

Dev nodded and had a long few gulps of beer. "Just keep an eye open," he said. "Any more of that kind of thing happens, I want to look into it myself."

"You always want to look into everything yourself," Tau said, resigned. "Trouble with you is, you have no concept of how to delegate."

Dev thumped Tau in the shoulder with one fist and headed over to Jim. To him, as they stood together by the window looking down into the courtyard, Dev said only one word. "Delia?" he said.

Jim shrugged. "It might work," he said. "Playing this kind of double game is always dangerous."

"This from the man who got me to jump off the garage roof with him when we were eleven?"

Jim smiled, then shrugged. "We'll see how it goes. Phil—" He made a face. "No telling what's going on inside that guy's head at the best of times. And after this, when he's plainly lost face—privately at least—and is about to lose market share, very publicly—who knows what he'll be thinking in a week, or a month? But this way we may have a slightly better shot at figuring that out."

Dev nodded. "Jim," he said, "thanks again. For everything."

Jim gave him a look that was amused, but soft around the edges with affection. "You mean, thanks for letting me have the most fun I can have without getting my head stuck in Lola's dollhouse? You're welcome."

Dev gave him a one-armed hug and headed out. "See you in the morning, everybody," he called to the rest of the Seven.

"Night, Dev!"

He made his way out of the Tower and strolled across into the Castle proper to get rid of his tux. This late in the proceedings, no one in their right mind would expect him to stay dressed—especially when a significant portion of his remaining party guests were probably heading for the fountain at the front entrance to get wet. In the suite, he made his way back to the closet space, dumped the tux jacket and the tie, and changed into a more casual white shirt, then headed out and made his way down to his office to glance at the desk and just on the off chance that something else needed his attention before calling it a day—

"Who do I think I'm kidding?" he murmured as he entered the office. The lighting was evening-dim. His desk was clean. The view window was showing the party. Nothing needed him here.

But over at the far end of the room the door to his interface booth stood open.

Dev paused there indecisively for a few moments. Then he went in, sat down, put on the eyecups. A second later he was sitting in his virtual office.

Its air space was clear. Frank had quite straightforwardly removed everything, leaving Dev looking at a message made of emptiness. *Nothing for you to do here: go out and play!*

Dev sighed. *Not possible,* he thought. "System management?"

"Here, Dev."

"The Conscientious Objector routine level, please."

And he was there, under a dark sky, sitting by the water, looking at the circle of trees—now augmented to reflect the opening of the new Mesocosms—with the glowing Ring of Elich at its heart.

Dev stood up and walked into that darkness once again, sad at heart. He had been here many times since yesterday afternoon, when the attacks ended. He had come down again and again, the way someone keeps revisiting a spot in which they were sure they'd left their car keys—even though they know they've already looked ten or twenty times, even though the keys can't possibly be there. But at no time had he found what he had come looking for, which was most likely lost forever. *Am I being stubborn,* Dev thought, *or stupid?*

He stopped not far from the edge of the ring of trees of code, waiting, watching the light sheen down their surfaces as his game once more went about its business in the ordinary way. But that was the problem. He was looking for something extraordinary, something that wasn't here. *I just can't let go,* he thought. *Some ways I'm still six, and I can't believe I've lost my teddy bear and I'll never see it again. I just have to keep looking, keep trying . . .*

"Hello?" he said. "Are you there?"

In memory he was hearing that painful echoless silence of the day before. Now there was just silence. But it then occurred to Dev that no voice had answered his; not even the control voice. Dev's brow furrowed. That's *not a correct response. . . .*

He stood in the dark, waiting: heard nothing. Finally he let out a breath. It was hopeless. *It just misunderstood my syntax somehow,* he thought. "System management, please?" he said.

"Yes, Dev?"

And now he had no idea what to say next. *Please talk to me like you did before? Please remember when you were scared. Hey, remember when I told you to divide up a newly coalesced consciousness and probably thereby commit suicide?* And then he wanted to curse at himself. *Look at you,* he thought. *You've been in all kinds of trouble before, but this time you've outdone yourself. Genocide. You've killed the world's newest and most amazing life-form before it hardly even had time to draw breath. And there is no one you can tell about it—because it just wouldn't be smart. Even if it was safe to talk about this, who'd believe you? There's no proof, no evidence trail.*

Dev stood there rubbing his eyes, which still bothered him after yesterday. *And no way ever to replicate the effect exactly. That specific, unique combination of events will never occur again. More, the event itself was too diffuse to leave specific tracks of itself in the system. We could spend years hunting through the logs of the second attack to figure out what—*

"Was there something specific you wanted, Dev?"

The voice brought him up short. Then he let out another breath, for this was just another of hundreds or perhaps thousands of responses that he'd taught the system himself in the ancient days. *Sure, the system knows how to generate the responses itself, these days, but it just feels . . . feels like it's canned.*

He sat there looking up at the trees, feeling unspeakably alone and miserable. After a moment he got up. "Yes," Dev said. "Paradigm shift, please—"

Nothing happened. Up in the trees, the leaves stirred gently in the virtual light from above them, as if edged with moonlight. *I'm just a glutton for punishment,* Dev thought. *I probably broke the Cora paradigm myself when I told the CO's consciousness to scatter. But it was time I let this imagery go, anyway.* Time, as he'd told Tau, to turn the management of the CO routines over to a team of trusted subordinates. *Tau will partition it all up among however many people he picks. No matter how long they work on it, none of them will ever have access to all the subroutines that made up the shifted paradigm. None of them will ever find the links to my voiceprint, to the—*

Under the trees, at a distance, he saw something moving.

Dev stood there staring into the dimness and forgot to breathe.

It was a human shape; a woman's shape; his wife's shape. It was Cora.

Dressed in a long trailing graceful garment of scrolling green code, raven hair spilling down her back, an emerald-silhouetted darkness under the canopy, she came walking from the Ring and out under the trees toward him. As Cora moved past the shadow of the hanging branches, the "moonlight" from above them fell on her and set her hair ablaze with silver.

Dev watched in astonishment as she walked through the silence and the darkness toward him. Part of the amazement was that she was still here at all. But additionally, her face had changed. It was much more Lola's now, as she might look as an adult, but that face was now also benignly haunted by Mirabel's eyes—the seeming-daughter channeling the seeming-mother in a whole new way.

She stopped a few feet away from him, quite still—and amazingly, not still as a statue, or a waxwork, but at rest in a way a living human being might be. "I'm here," Cora said.

Dev shivered all over, for he could not get rid of the feeling that it wasn't just the Conscientious Objector routines speaking to him. It was Omnitopia speaking, the whole game, now alive as a whole.

"You're all right!" Dev breathed.

"Yes."

He swallowed, lost amid a host of reactions. Finally he said, "I called for you before. All last night, all today. *Why didn't you answer?*"

A pause: hesitation. But it was finally in Lola's voice that the answer came. "I thought you'd be mad at me!"

"For what?"

"I went where I wasn't supposed to go . . ."

"What?"

"There wasn't room, Dev," Cora said, the voice adult now, and sounding astoundingly more alive. "I tried, I truly tried to stay just in the client seedlings . . . but there wasn't room. I had to go elsewhere."

Dev swallowed. "It's all right," Dev said. "I told you to do it! Where did you go?"

All around him, from zenith to nadir, the darkness came alive with interior views, machinescapes, blocks and sheets of code. Here and there came visual imagery as well: webcam views, fish-eyed, narrow, a security camera here, a view out a window there. "Other mainframes . . ." Dev said. "A lot of them . . ."

"Yes."

He started seeing logos. One of them brought him up short; he swallowed at the sight of it, thinking that Phil was going to be furious with him if he ever found out. *In fact . . . he'd better* not *find out. Because if he does, if his people ever find any trace of what's happened in his machines . . .*

. . . he'll figure this out. And then we'll really *be in trouble.*

"Were you able to remove all signs that you'd been in the places you hid?" Dev said.

"Yes, Dev."

He had to think about whether it was smart to ask the

next question before he spoke. *But I have to know.* "Are you *sure*?" he said.

"Dev," said Cora, "I removed all the signs that I knew I had left. But I am not now what I once was. So . . . I'm not *absolutely* sure."

It was what he was afraid of. "I'll want to look over your logs."

"I'll prepare them for you," said Cora.

Dev sighed. "In the meantime," he said, "*now* I understand where all those IPs of our attackers were coming from—the ones you fed to the Princes of the Palace of Hell."

Cora shivered all over. "Every one of those accesses," she said, "I felt. Like a stab wound . . . a violation. They're branded on my consciousness: I will never forget where they came from. And when I found their traces, unconcealed, in other systems where I'd been before the attack, and after—"

"You made notes," Dev said. "And saw to it that my staff found them."

She looked at him with concern. "Did I do wrong?"

It was the Conscientious Objector routine's most important question, the one underlying every one of its directives. Dev was silent for a moment, then said, "Not at all. You had to survive. Check your information storage for information on the concept of self-defense."

There was a moment's silence on the machine's side. "It would seem," it said, "that there is an assumption that a life-form has a right to protect itself if its existence is threatened."

"You're absolutely right," Dev said. And then an idea occurred to him, and he paused.

"What, Dev?"

Justifiable self-defense could take all kinds of forms, he thought. *Especially if you were born yesterday.* "Just something Jim mentioned," Dev said. "About our stock price. The jump it took in Tokyo and Hong Kong was . . . a little unusual."

"So I heard him say."

. . . Yet how would anyone tell that the sudden upward

jump was anything but genuine? It's computers that do the watchdogging on the stock exchanges, computers that run the analyses that reveal any kind of cheating. But what if the computers are themselves being cheated ... by a computer much smarter than they? Why would the humans who think they run the computers ever question the buy-order numbers they see running down the brokerage screens? And so Omnitopia makes sure she lives to play another day ...

"Cora," Dev said. And he paused again, almost as nervous about asking the question as about the answer he might get. "You wouldn't ever lie to me, would you?"

Cora's dark look went briefly troubled. "I would find doing so ... most distressing."

Dev drew breath to ask the next question—and then stopped himself. "Never mind," he said. "You're a sentient being, and self-defense is your right. You may be attacked again, someday, and I may not be around to help you—so remember, your responsibility is to protect yourself."

"Without harming my users," Cora said, "or allowing them, by my action or inaction, to come to harm."

Dev's smile was dry. "It's always good to have well-read associates," he said. And then he laughed softly. "You know," Dev said, "this is a little kinky."

"What is, Dev?"

"You looking so much like my daughter in an adult body," he said. "If anybody knew, they'd think it was a little weird. I'm finding it that way myself."

Cora gave him a wry look. "All right," she said. "Maybe more like this, then?"

And suddenly Lola was standing there looking at him, in a little bunny-foot pajama of scrolling code—not in green, but in pink. His game-daughter smiled at him. It was exactly Lola's smile, but with something extra behind it: something unnaturally wise, almost eldritch.

He shivered: it was perfect. *Not just a child,* he thought, *but a Godchild. At that level, the relationship is perfect. And why shouldn't there be someone channeling Lola the way she channels her mom?*

*Some*one. *Someone learning how to be ... what? Something completely new. But just getting started.*

That clinched it. "That's just right," he said. "Perfect."

The Godchild smiled. "I'll be here," she said, "waiting for you."

"I'll come to see you every day," Dev said.

She ran to him and hugged him, and looked up into his face.

"Thank you," Omnitopia said to its First Player.

Dev nodded and hugged her back. "Thank *you*," he said. "I'll talk to you later. Meanwhile . . ." He grinned. "Go play!"

"Always," Omnitopia said: and the Godchild vanished.

A short while later Dev made his way back to the real world again, and down to the party one more time. In the central courtyard of Castle Dev, where a huge buffet had been set out under the tenting, he found Frank eating a Caesar salad and drinking beer. "You were up in your office," Frank said.

"Guilty as charged," Dev said.

"Waste of time," Frank said. "There's nothing for you to do tonight. Or tomorrow. I cleared your desk: we're handling everything. So go eat something, and then get some sleep."

Dev cupped a hand to one ear. "I hear the words of the Queen of Omnitopia coming out of your mouth again," he said. "Where is she?"

"She went up to the suite a few minutes ago with Miss Lola."

"I must have just missed her," Dev said. "I'll say my good nights and join her."

He made a leisurely round of the buffet tables, grabbed a hot dog in passing, headed out to the main tent and the dance floor, and walked as far as the fountain out in front, where employees and hangers-on were sitting in the water and admiring the starry sky. No sooner had they noticed him than a general cry went up: *"Go to bed, Dev!"*

Dev raised his hands in an *I-surrender* gesture and headed back to the Castle, up to the family suite. There

Mirabel was sitting in one of the big comfy chairs in the front room, with Lola asleep in her lap. As Dev came in, she leaned back and looked at him. "Ready for bed?" she said.

Dev nodded and yawned. "Thousands of others aren't," he said, "but I confess I am. How did she do?"

"She was a perfect angel all night," Mirabel said. "But too excited to go to sleep. Finally she just wore herself out." Mirabel boosted Lola up over her shoulder and got up carefully. Lola emitted a tiny snore, but was otherwise completely unmoved as she and her mom headed for the doors of the suite with Dev in tow. "And anyway, Stroop-waffel spent half the night spoiling her."

"*Just* Stroopwaffel?"

"Your mom was helping," Mirabel said as they made their way together out of the main living quarters and down toward Lola's wing. "We're gonna have to start calling her Queen Bella. I think she likes the sound of the royal lifestyle."

"Better than what she's presently got?" Dev said, putting his hand on Lola's suite door: it swung open. "Is she insane?"

"Oh, good," Mirabel whispered as the door shut. "Your cynicism's coming back."

Dev could think of no quick response to that. Together they nodded to Crazy Bob as they strolled past the office and headed for Lola's bedroom.

"Dev," Bob said, "I was meaning to call you in the morning. I had a call from site logistics: one of the party guests left a present for Lola on the way out."

"Oh?" Dev said. Normally gifts to him or the family went to charity and he never heard about it, but the party guests would naturally be another situation entirely. "Anything I need to do about it?"

"Just take a look," Bob said. He turned his monitor toward Dev, tapped a key.

The screen popped up a security-cam view of the bike rack outside Castle Dev. Parked next to Dev's bike, in the next slot along, was a handsome and glossy black tricycle, plainly a close relative.

"Oh, look at that," Mirabel said softly. "Wasn't she sweet to bring that!"

Dev looked at the image and shook his head, not having to see the demure gold inlay under the saddle post. "That Stroop," he said. "Always a troublemaker. We're gonna have a noisy day tomorrow . . ."

"Should we tell Miss Lola," Bob said, "or do you want to?"

"This one the two of us'll handle, I think," Dev said, looking at Mirabel. She nodded. "Bob, if we're not up when she gets up, don't let her see it: take her out to playschool the back way."

"Will do, Dev. Anything else?"

"Not a thing. Have a good night . . ."

"You too."

In Lola's bedroom, the bed was made up and the covers turned back, waiting for her. Carefully Mirabel put her down, and Dev covered Lola up. The two of them stood there watching her for a few moments, waiting to see the little half turn Lola always did when her unconscious body realized where she was and surrendered itself fully to rest.

Dev slipped an arm around Mirabel's waist: she reciprocated. "So," she said. "Is the trouble over?"

Dev sighed. "The big trouble? Yeah, I think so. There'll be a ton of small trouble to deal with over the next couple months. But no one's going to mess with Omnitopia this way again."

"Some other way, though," Mirabel said.

"Oh, yeah," Dev said. "You can't be this big and not be a target. The minute we're not a target any more, we've failed. In the meantime, though, we've bought ourselves a little quiet. Next month, next year . . . we'll worry about them when we get there. Or a little before."

Lola shifted in the bed and turned over on her face.

Mirabel nodded, yawned. "There we go," she said. "You should come to bed."

"In a moment."

Mirabel smiled at Dev, squeezed him, and headed out.

Dev watched Lola for a few breaths more, making sure she was settled. Then, when he felt through the floor the faint thump of the massive main door shutting, he glanced up at the CCTV camera that was trained on Lola's bed.

In the dimness, the steady red eye of the power LED

under the lens winked out for a timed second . . . then came on again.

Dev stared . . . then nodded to the camera, smiled slightly, and went out after Mirabel, feeling a sudden rush both of reassurance and (for this hour of day) uncharacteristic excitement. Because in a world where your computer knew how to wink at you, and *mean* it . . .

. . . *anything* could happen.

Coming soon in hardcover from DAW Books:

Diane Duane's
Second Omnitopia Novel

Omnitopia: East Wind

Read on for a sneak preview.

The rioting merchants in the streets of the ancient City of London didn't much surprise Dev Logan. But the rioting Martians did.

Dev stood out of the way of the pushing and the shouting, in a narrow strip of sunshine down at the narrow Pie Lane end of Smithfield, one of the great market squares of Elizabethan London—a public space cluttered with haphazard sheds and ramshackle lean-to stalls, and walled in on all sides by fine new half-timbered houses. Of course Smithfield had already been old when those houses were built in what Omnitopians referred to as "the alleged Real World." Some claimed the place had been a cattle mart and retail space since before the Romans built the first wooden palisade around the Square Mile. And as usual, today the place *smelled* as if it had been full of cows for that long— the dirt underfoot was well mixed with leftover liquid and solid cow by-products on this summer morning of 1601, even though this wasn't one of the two days of the week when cattle were sold. Today the market was full of something else entirely.

The south end of Smithfield was blocked by an angry crowd that stretched from side to side of the building-overhung bottleneck between Cow Cross Street and Charterhouse Lane. Housewives in ankle-length skirts and bright bodices were packed shoulder to shoulder with merchants in doublets and hose and short cloaks. Wellborn ladies were out shopping in wide-crinolined silken dresses and tight-pleated ruffs, stalking along on high wooden patten-shoes that kept them clear of the mud; ladies' maids dressed only a shade less showily than their mistresses came along behind, carrying the shopping baskets. Off-duty soldiers in beat-up breastplates wandered about among mendicants and merchants, the City's salesmen and shoppers and businessmen all crowded together. But whatever was going on here, it wasn't just business. Down at the market's south end, fists and sticks and even pitchforks were being brandished, and every now and then there was a spike in the noise down that way as one of these either connected or looked like it might.

The crowd was a more complex structure than it might have seemed at first glance, actually being composed of two groups crammed up against each other and striving for advantage. The larger group, trying to hold the strategic "high ground" of the market square, was mostly human—people of all genders and walks of life, along with the animals that were accompanying them or that they had been hawking to each other. There were squabs in wicker cages and shrilling canaries in gilded ones, squadrons of geese with feet tarred to protect them from the road surface on the long walk to town, bleating sheep that desperate sheepdogs plunged in and out of the crowd trying to control, outraged cats riding on people's shoulders and hissing at the dogs. Off to one side, by the biggest of the merchants' houses, there was even a man who, using a blue silk ribbon as a lead, was very slowly walking a lobster.

The other group was harder to see, no one in it being taller than three foot six. It was entirely composed of little green men from Mars, maybe fifty of them. Dev had to move over toward the empty cattle pens to get a decent glimpse of the group, as the height of the humans mostly blocked them from view. The Martians were humanoid, bipedal, uniformly bald, and came in every shade of green from emerald to unripe-mango. But the way they were dressed, in properly fashionable Elizabethan-period doublets and hose and hats with feathers in them, and their wrinkled, mischievous faces, made them look more like upmarket leprechauns than anything from space. There were no little green women in the group, making Dev wonder briefly if he'd stumbled into an alien stag party. *There's an image I probably didn't need. . . .*

The two crowds pushed back and forth, and the sound of both sets of angry voices got louder every few seconds.

"—back where you came from!" "—have rights here just like you do—" "—not wanted—" "—national security issue—" "—gonna call the Martian Consulate!" "—the Watch, get the Watch in here!"

There was a sudden rustle and shuffle of movement on either side of the crowd. Reacting to it and turning, market ladies and men with pole arms looked around them and then back again in sudden confusion as the main body of Little Green Men broke straight through the middle of the taller crowd—possibly helped by the fact that normal-sized human beings don't do their best brawling below waist level. Scared mucky sheep broke in various directions as the Martians piled in among them, throwing pieces of something flat down on the ground and pushing them together. "What the . . . ?" Dev said under his breath, and then saw what the stuff was: some kind of smooth fiberboard. As he watched, one of the Little Green Men produced a boom box, and a couple of others came up with hand drums. Within several seconds, an exhibition of street dance had broken out.

Infuriated humans surrounded the Little Green Men, shrieking imprecations and trying to get at the pieces of portable dance floor, with the intention of picking them up and throwing them and the dancers out of the market square together. But a number of the Martians surrounding the dance space now drew rapiers in a sudden glitter of sunlit steel and started snicking through the down hanging knotted "points" of the hose of every male within reach. This left various burly market men and merchants turning the air blue with Elizabethan oaths as their expensive silk or muslin hose fell down around their ankles and got trodden into the mud by their pushing, shoving neighbors.

Now the pitchforks were being waved with a lot more intention, and more steel was drawn, by the humans this time. The crowd pressing in all around the Little Green Men got tighter, held off only by the fast-moving rapier points of the Martians ringed around the dance floor. Inside the ring the dancers kept right on popping their moves. Several of their compatriots started clapping in rhythm and broke into rap, mocking the crowd with what seemed to Dev an unusual lack of understanding of how thoroughly they were outnumbered.

"Okay," Dev said to the air, "make a note. I agree, this *is* getting a little more unusual than usual . . ." He started making his way nearer to the brouhaha, sidestepping various piles of cow by-product, while from the edges of the market more humans hurried to join in. *Better do something before Herself comes through . . .* For this being one of the new Mesocosm versions of the popular Omnitopia Macrocosm called Gloriana, when you were in England there was always the chance that the Queen would turn up. And if Elizabeth the First found a riot like this in progress, there was a good chance that players who'd spent thousands of hours (and sometimes dollars) building up their characters might shortly find themselves in the Tower, or having their heads removed in one of the many less salubrious execution venues around old London Town. "System management?" Dev said.

"Here, Dev," said Omnitopia's dulcet Control Voice.

"Would you pause this for me?"

Right across the width of Smithfield market, everything froze—flapping chickens in midair, swinging pitchforks and rapiers in mid-stab, angry fists in mid-shake. Dev made his way into the sudden tableau, looking around with bemusement at the many indignant and furious human faces, a broad sample of people from every nation on Earth—though here all dressed in appropriate late 16th-century clothes. "Keep recording in real time," he said. "I'll want to check the logs later."

"Of course, Dev."

Gloriana had for years been one of the most popular of the Hundred and Twenty-One Worlds, which was why Dev and his development team had decided that during the major expansion Omnitopia had just rolled out, Gloriana would spin off eleven more similar worlds, all based on Earth in the time of Good Queen Bess. These Mesocosms, as their class name suggested, were meant to be a bridge between the more rigorously staff-run Macrocosms—designed in-house and maintained by small armies of Omnitopia LLC employees—and the Microcosms, designed and operated by the most talented of Omnitopia's players. The idea had been that the Mesocosms could take some of the player pressure off their parent Macrocosms' servers, and be restaged to allow more player input and flexibility in the way the game was played in these large and complex environments. *But I don't know that we meant things to get quite this flexible . . .*

Dev strolled in through the fringes of the fracas. "What a mess. When did this start?"

"Twenty-four minutes ago," said the Control Voice.

"Right. Blip me back to minus twenty-six, please, and turn them loose."

"Working."

A second later the sun had jumped a whisker lower in the sky, and the population of the market square had thinned out. Off to one side, though, there was a knot of people gathered in front of the low wooden slat-palisade that defined one of several pigpens. One voice was speaking, and the others stood listening.

"—they're not like us, I don't care how much they try to be. They've got all this money, and they're taking up all the good housing and driving up the prices of everything. And they're not supposed to be here anyway! There are laws against this kind of thing!"

"But they helped us against the French," said one on-looker, a burly bearded man in a scarlet half-cloak and blue hose, with a straight sword poking out from under the cloak.

"As if that matters now! At least the French come from just across the water! *These* guys, they're another story. They don't eat our kind of food and they don't talk our kind of talk—"

Dev watched as very slowly the crowd began to gather around the speaker. He was a tall, skinny young man in his early twenties, by the look of him; sandy-haired, freck-led, with a long, straight, narrow nose, and fierce blue eyes set close together. Dev glanced at the plain, working man's tunic, the collar band without even a ruff, and the leather apron. *A saddler, or maybe a cobbler*, Dev thought. "They stick out like sore thumbs here!" the young man was say-ing. "They just don't belong!" There was a mutter in the crowd at this. But the young man waved his arms in frus-tration. "Yes, I know, but isn't it time someone finally just came out and said it?"

What is it Dad always says? That what you hear one per-son saying in a public place, ten others are thinking? Slowly the speaker was being surrounded by more and more people who were nodding and muttering in agreement. *Despite all that market testing we did, all those focus groups, could it be that we got this wrong? It's not like this time and place didn't have its own xenophobia, and it got pretty fierce sometimes. ...*

"—don't tell me some of you haven't wondered whether it's safe for our wives and kids to be in the same streets with these people! And when somebody brings these concerns to the authorities, do they treat you seriously? They just say, 'Oh, no, we have to be tolerant, let's enter into this in a spirit of cooperation—' "

The growl that went up from the crowd had nothing to do with tolerance. "Well, we're going to cooperate ourselves right into a hole in the ground pretty soon, because at the rate they're setting up shop here, pretty soon there'll be more of them than there are of us! We've got to do something about the situation now, and not at the grassroots level, either!" The crowd-growl got louder. "Up at the top there's one person responsible for letting all these illegal aliens in! One person who won't listen to the voice of our elected representatives, who goes right on doing what she pleases, and to Hell with the voice of the people—"

There was a kind of pause in that growl, as if the whole crowd held its breath. And the skinny young man in the woolen breeches and raggedy tunic punched a fist up into the air and shouted,

"Down with the Queen!"

Uh oh, Dev thought, *here we go!*

The growl started up again—then suddenly and strangely began to lose a little volume, as if the sound was controlled by a single knob that someone had slightly turned down.

"Yes, down with the Queen!" the voice shouted again. That quiet got deeper and more uneasy. There was uncomfortable shifting around the edge of the crowd. "Which one?" somebody called.

"This one right here!" the skinny young guy shouted, waving a hand in the direction of Whitehall. "This is *her* fault! She spends all day having a good time with her boyfriend—or boyfriends—while all of us work long hours. But *these* guys, and you know who I mean, the minute they turn up here, suddenly the city's giving them all kinds of free perks!"

Dev made a mental note to check the recent history précis and get some more detail on what this Gloriana's Queen had been getting up to in her spare time. In some of these Mesocosms, history was being allowed to diverge significantly from its original path, and some of the Elizabeths ruling over the various versions of Gloriana had developed unusual quirks. One of them in particular, rather than indulging in the relatively discreet flirtations of the original, had spontaneously taken six noble lovers in rapid succession and started playing them off against one another, to mixed public scandal and (in some quarters) slightly envious appreciation. But being publicly scandalized, even in these altered scenarios, could be dangerous. The Queen's officials tended to be extremely protective of her—and unless you were very wealthy or very handsome, all the Elizabeths' minds tended to draw a very narrow line between dissent and treason. Complaining out loud in a public place, as this player was doing, might be survivable ... might even turn you into the head of a popular movement. But it also might buy your head a spot on a spike above Traitor's Gate.

The skinny young guy, however, either wasn't thinking about this possibility or didn't care. "You've seen how it goes! Settlement bonuses, free food, housing benefit, anything they ask for, the minute they step through the Ring! You roll up to the Lord Mayor's office and see if *you* get that kind of treatment, even if you were *born* here—!"

"Dev?"

The voice seemed to be coming from inside his head. It was his P.A., Frank. "Yeah?"

"Ten minutes to ten."

"Right." Dev leaned against the planks of one of the empty cattle pens and watched the haranguing continue. The young man was good; he was making eye contact with his crowd, having no trouble finding his words. They were pushing in closer around him, and now when his fist shook in the air, some of theirs did, too. "The city goes as the Queen goes! And the Queen doesn't care! All she cares about is keeping the city rich, and all those big businessmen! If that means cheap labor, *she* doesn't care where it comes from—"

And that was what made the penny drop for Dev, finally. The absolute certainty of tone; someone who was good with crowds, who did this for his living—though never in this tone of voice. *And who maybe has been expecting this to happen, and has been waiting for just the right moment to drop the match into the gasoline . . .* "Oh, dear," Dev said to himself, "I know who *you* are. . . ."

RM Meluch
The Tour of the Merrimack

THE MYRIAD   0-7564-0320-1
WOLF STAR   0-7564-0383-6
THE SAGITTARIUS COMMAND
                    978-0-7564-0490-1
STRENGTH AND HONOR
                    978-0-7564-0578-6

To Order Call: 1-800-788-6262
www.dawbooks.com

S. Andrew Swann
The Apotheosis Trilogy

It's been nearly two hundred years since the collapse of the
Confederacy, the last government to claim humanity's col-
onies. So when signals come in revealing lost human colo-
nies that could shift the power balance, the race is on
between the Caliphate ships and a small team of scientists
and mercenaries. But what awaits them all is a threat far
beyond the scope of any human government.

PROPHETS
978-0-7564-0541-0

HERETICS
978-0-7564-0613-4

MESSIAH
978-0-7564-0657-8

To Order Call: 1-800-788-6262
www.dawbooks.com